A Gentleman's Honor

A Pride and Prejudice Variation

Melanie Rachel

Contents

	Copyright	V
	A Note from the Author	VI
1.	Chapter One	1
2.	Chapter Two	17
3.	Chapter Three	48
4.	Chapter Four	65
5.	Chapter Five	80
6.	Chapter Six	94
7.	Chapter Seven	121
8.	Chapter Eight	140
9.	Chapter Nine	169
10.	Chapter Ten	195
11.	Chapter Eleven	214
12.	Chapter Twelve	233

13.	Chapter Thirteen	252
14.	Chapter Fourteen	272
15.	Chapter Fifteen	290
16.	Chapter Sixteen	307
17.	Chapter Seventeen	322
18.	Chapter Eighteen	343
Acknowledgments		374
About The Author		376
Other Books by the Author		377

Copyright © 2021 by Melanie Rachel

All rights reserved.

No part of this publication may be reproduced, distributed, or transmitted in any form or by any means, including photocopying, recording, or other electronic or mechanical methods, without the prior written permission of the publisher, except as permitted by U.S. copyright law.

The story, all names, characters, and incidents portrayed in this production are fictitious. No identification with actual persons (living or deceased), places, buildings, and products is intended or should be inferred.

Book Cover by Midnight Muse Designs

A Gentleman's Honor begins with one major change to *Pride and Prejudice*—Mr. Collins does not arrive for his visit, having passed away of illness just before the story begins. Otherwise, the story follows canon until Elizabeth and Darcy finish their dance in Chapter 18:

> "I would by no means suspend any pleasure of yours," he coldly replied. She said no more, and they went down the other dance and parted in silence; and on each side dissatisfied, though not to an equal degree, for in Darcy's breast there was a tolerably powerful feeling towards her, which soon procured her pardon, and directed all his anger against another.

This is where *A Gentleman's Honor* picks up the tale. After this exchange, Mr. Darcy leaves the ballroom—and Elizabeth rather impulsively follows him into the hallway to press him for more details. In doing so, she inadvertently involves herself in the chain of events that comprise this story.

A GENTLEMAN'S HONOR

Copyright © 2022 by Melanie Rachel

All rights reserved.

No portion of this book may be reproduced in any form without written permission from the publisher or author, except as permitted by U.S. copyright law.

MELANIE RACHEL

This is a work of fiction. Any resemblance to actual events or persons, living or dead, is entirely coincidental.

Chapter One

Fitzwilliam Darcy stared down into the upturned face of Miss Elizabeth Bennet. Her fine dark eyes flashed with anger, and she had risen to the balls of her feet in an indignant fury. His heart did a strange, tender whirl in his chest when he realized that she was attempting to look him in the eye. He swallowed. It was damned unfair that she could not be his, although at this moment it was certain that Miss Elizabeth did not return the sentiment.

He glanced down the hall to the ballroom to be certain they were alone before addressing her.

"My history with Mr. Wickham is private, madam," he said flatly. "I do not see what right you have to know it. Even were you entitled to the knowledge, no gentleman would reveal such things to a lady."

She paused at that, but her expression remained skeptical. Her eyebrows pinched together as her heels returned to the floor. After a moment's hesitation, she said, "He claims you denied him a living that was left to him in your father's will."

Darcy glanced down the hall. There were a few people milling about the doorway back to the ballroom, but at least for the moment, they had a bit of privacy. What could it matter? She must already believe him a scoundrel. At least she would know the truth. It would give him some comfort, to know that he had at least made an attempt to protect her from Wickham's lies. He met her gaze as her eyes searched for an answer in his.

"May I inquire how many times you have met Mr. Wickham in company, for him to be so explicit?" he asked. Despite the affront, he was genuinely curious.

He saw the moment she admitted Wickham's impropriety to herself and was gratified.

"Not often at all, sir," she told him plainly.

She had not backed away from him or lost her composure, though her expression was . . . uncertain. He was reminded that for all her wit and intelligence, she had seen little of the world beyond her home.

It was painful, to recall how he and George Wickham had once been friends. *You have so much, Darcy,* Wickham had said. *You have a hard heart indeed if you will not share a little of it with your friends.* Darcy had helped Wickham many, many times, but it had never been enough.

"I did deny him the *second* time we spoke of it," he told Elizabeth quietly. "The first time we spoke, Mr. Wickham resigned any claim to assistance in the church, should he ever find himself eligible to receive it, and accepted three thousand pounds in lieu of the living." He heard a small gasp from Miss Elizabeth.

It was always this way. Wickham's good looks were all the proof required of his integrity. Indeed, Darcy himself had been George Wickham's friend until he learned how despicable the man truly was. Darcy's own father had brushed his concerns about Wickham's debauchery aside. "It would not harm you to engage in a few frivolities as George has done," he had said sternly. "You are a young man, but once you take on the management of the estate, you will not enjoy such freedoms."

Unlike his father, Miss Elizabeth seemed inclined to accept that she might have been mistaken. That was encouraging. Usually, people had to experience Wickham's treachery personally before they believed the truth.

"This was in addition to the one-thousand-pound legacy left to him outright by my father," Darcy added. "When Mr. Wickham had spent it all, he returned to demand the living he had willingly and legally relinquished and for which he had been compensated. I hope you will pardon me for refusing such a petition," he said gruffly.

Her cheeks pinked, giving him yet another vision to haunt him in his sleep.

"Will you tell me more of his habits, sir?" she asked. "If Mr. Wickham has been bold enough to slander you to me in such a way, if his habits are so extravagant, I must wonder whether this is the extent of his transgressions." Miss Elizabeth was embarrassed, but she was no wilting flower—he admired that.

The music down the hall started up again, which meant that the supper dance would soon follow.

Bingley had asked to meet in the library before supper, and Darcy knew it was important that his friend not be absent for long. Darcy could not comprehend what could be so urgent as to pull Bingley away from his own ball, but Darcy was loyal to the few friends he had.

As he gazed at Miss Elizabeth, it occurred to him that Bingley must wish to discuss proposing to Miss Jane Bennet, her elder sister. Bingley had thus far maintained all propriety with his attentions—but as Sir William's proclamation earlier that evening revealed, only just. If

Bingley did not remove himself from Netherfield for a time, he would surely find himself obliged to make an offer of marriage.

Darcy had no objections to Jane Bennet. She seemed a kind young woman, not unintelligent, with a sweet sort of fair-haired beauty. Her family, though—Miss Elizabeth excepted—would be a terrible embarrassment, and the sincerity of Miss Bennet's feelings for Bingley was difficult to determine. Bingley really ought to take time to seriously consider whether the lady was truly in love with him, for the consequences of such an alliance would make his life more complicated. Perhaps his trip to London would help him decide what to do before returning to Hertfordshire.

Darcy knew he was overdue in the library. He decided he would offer his advice and then return to the ballroom. Or perhaps he would just go to bed. This night had turned into a disaster. That Miss Elizabeth would defend Wickham and that he himself would lay open his private business to her!

He was expected elsewhere, but before he could take his leave, he was again distracted by Miss Elizabeth's countenance, which gradually transformed from skepticism to bemusement.

He could watch her face forever and it would never become tedious. What was it she had said? "People themselves alter so much that there is something new to be observed in them for ever." She was the proof of her own argument, and he almost allowed himself a fond smile. But he could not. Bingley had called for him and was perhaps even now waiting in the library. "Good evening, madam." Darcy turned away before he realized he had not answered her query.

Well. That had been rude. But it could not be helped now. He strode down the hall and, in an agitation of spirits, tossed the doors to the library wide open before stepping through.

He was startled to detect the soft whisper of slippers on the floor behind him. A trace of jasmine tickled his nose. Judging by that tantalizing scent, the owner of those slippers had stepped inside and to his right, out of the doorway. Without changing his position, he opened his mouth to protest. He had said everything he was inclined to reveal to Miss Elizabeth Bennet, far more than he ought. He would allow her to have her say and then insist she return to the ballroom at once. He would not have his honor questioned, especially not by the indolent Mr. Bennet.

Before he could turn and utter a single syllable, however, another woman entirely was in his arms, the force of her assault knocking him back two full steps, almost back out into the hall.

"What in the blazes?" he exclaimed. Bingley arrived a moment later to push them farther into the room and shut the doors behind them.

Darcy expected Bingley to peel his unmarried harridan of a sister off his person and take her away. He did not.

"Darcy," Bingley hissed, "have you lost your senses, man? There are a hundred people down the hall." He grabbed a quilt draped over the settee and wrapped it around his sister. Darcy had not seen the covering in this room before. *That was convenient.*

"I should never have believed this of you," Bingley said, incredulous.

"He has just now asked to marry me, Charles," Miss Bingley said softly, tightening the quilt around her as though her dress had been damaged. If it had, it was not by him. Still, Darcy had to admit that she sounded convincing. "We are engaged. I did not think there would be any harm."

Bingley must know his sister was prevaricating. Darcy shook his head. "That is not true. I have only just arrived, and I was responding to *your* summons, Bingley, not your sister's."

Charles Bingley looked him in the eye. "I never asked you to meet me here, Darcy. I was searching for my sister." Bingley stepped up to Darcy, who was a good four inches taller. "Shall we make the announcement at supper?"

Darcy met his friend's gaze and felt as though he were about to cast up his accounts. For he saw there what he had seen before. Deceit. Avarice. Ambition. His eyes almost teared up before he regained control. He had been so certain about Bingley's friendship. The betrayal hurt. It hurt as badly as though Bingley had run him through. Darcy felt his shoulders droop, and he lifted a tired hand to rub the back of his head.

Had there been more than a single candle lit, the Bingleys might already have noticed Miss Elizabeth who, Darcy believed, was now standing behind them only a few feet away. She might bear witness for him, but Darcy refused to call attention to her or involve her in this sordid business.

He might have succeeded in keeping her out of it entirely had she not cleared her throat. His initial instinct was irritation—*can the woman not remain silent even for her own good?*

"Mr. Bingley," she said as she stepped forward into the weak light of the candle, quiet but determined, "Mr. Darcy is not at fault. He would hardly have allowed me to accompany him to a liaison."

No, then.

Bingley rounded on her, the perfect image of concern and shock. "Was he to meet *you* here as well, Miss Elizabeth?" he asked. "I am ashamed that the man I counted as a friend has been revealed as a seducer of women. You should return to the ballroom."

Darcy's hands had formed into fists. He was ready to strike Bingley for that insult. He swallowed and uncurled his fingers. That was precisely what Bingley would like—to force a scene and draw a crowd. He would not play the man's game.

Miss Bingley began to weep, though she produced more noise than tears. "He asked me to marry him," she claimed peevishly, then hiccoughed, "but he said nothing about a mistress."

He watched Miss Elizabeth blink several times, surprise and offense writ clearly upon her features, and admired how quickly she rallied. "I came, Mr. Bingley, to determine why Mr. Darcy felt it necessary to warn me against a man of our mutual acquaintance," she declared coolly. "This means that I witnessed the entire scene. Mr. Darcy made Miss Bingley no offer. Indeed, he had not been in the room long enough to do anything of the sort."

She had vindicated him without identifying their mutual acquaintance. Not for the first time, Darcy appreciated both her delicacy and her intelligence. He was further relieved that he had not taken Bingley completely into his confidence where Wickham was concerned.

"I found the charge shocking, to say the least, and desired some privacy to discuss it," she continued. "However, Mr. Bingley, I must point out that both doors were open until you closed them."

"Miss Elizabeth," Darcy said, a little alarmed to hear how hoarse he had become. He was unlikely to see her again and could not leave her in any doubt about Wickham's intentions. Nor would he wish to leave her without saying the same about Bingley. "He is a liar." It would serve for both men.

She turned at the sound of his words, met his gaze, and gave him a small nod. She understood; she was clever. His lips did tug upwards at that, but it was too great an effort to keep them there.

"I apologize, sir, for having disbelieved you at first. I did not fully comprehend your situation." Her gaze slid to the side, to the Bingleys, then returned to his. "I believe I have a better understanding now."

Despite Darcy's misgivings about her involvement, he was grateful to have Miss Elizabeth take his side. He was, however, too miserable to do more than respond to her contrite words with a bow. She dipped a quick curtsy as he opened the door for her, and his eyes followed for a moment as she made her way down the hall to return to the ballroom. Miss Elizabeth's expression had been both gentle and compassionate, and he tucked the memory away. His heart yearned for hers even though he knew she did not wish for his. It was no matter. Her family, her low connections. He could never make her an offer.

He shut the door again and turned to face his hosts. After Miss Elizabeth's departure, the room was silent except for Miss Bingley's insincere weeping.

"Well, Darcy?" Bingley asked, evidently undeterred. "What do you intend to do?"

"I suppose, Bingley," Darcy responded grimly, "the real question is what *you* intend to do."

"We will arrange your marriage to my sister," Bingley replied, as though it was the only possible outcome.

Darcy shook his head. He had danced this dance before.

"And if I decline?"

Bingley played the outraged brother. "You will meet me. Surely you do not want that sort of scandal, but as Caroline's brother, I could do no less."

Darcy sighed and pinched the bridge of his nose. "Bingley, it is illegal to duel, and I have made no secret of the fact that I will not break the law. We are both aware that this is the only reason you feel safe issuing such a challenge. Even should such an improbable thing come to pass, I am both a better shot and a better swordsman, and I should have my cousin, Colonel Fitzwilliam, as my second. You would stand no chance."

Bingley appeared poised to argue, and Darcy felt his fatigue deepen.

"Furthermore," he continued, not allowing Bingley to interrupt, "your family's acceptance in the ton is largely dependent upon a connection to my own. You should now consider that connection severed."

He heard Miss Bingley's horrified gasp and pressed on. "At no time and under no circumstances will I marry against my will." He fought the tightness in his chest. "I have made this clear to you more than once, but it seems you were not listening. Had you ever really known me, you would understand that in this I am unmovable." *Had you ever truly been my friend.*

"We shall see," Bingley replied, but Darcy could hear the first fissure in the younger man's assurance. "We will canvas the subject again in the morning."

"No, Mr. Bingley," Darcy said slowly. "We will not." He could not look at Miss Bingley, but he addressed her. "Miss Bingley, you should consider yourself fortunate. Had you been successful in this scheme, you would have been throwing yourself into the power of a man who now despises you." He paused. "My family has a small estate in Scotland." He allowed the words to work their power.

"Scotland?" Miss Bingley asked timidly.

"In the north, near Cape Wrath," he informed her. "They raise sheep."

"You would never . . ." she breathed. She sounded terrified, the tremor in her voice quite pronounced.

Darcy released a heavy sigh. He lifted an eyebrow at Bingley. "Your brother is a betting man," he told her as he looked directly at his false friend. "Ask him to explain the odds."

He made his way back into the hall and took the stairs to his chamber. He was tired, but it appeared he would not sleep tonight.

Slipworth was startled when he entered—Darcy knew he was not expected for several hours yet.

"We are off again," he told his valet.

Slipworth's expression did not alter. A midnight departure was rare for Darcy, but not unprecedented. It was, however, the first time anyone had succeeded in herding him into a room with a woman who was unchaperoned. Thankfully, Miss Elizabeth's stubbornness had kept him from ever being alone with Miss Bingley.

"Shall I call for the carriage, sir?" Slipworth asked.

Darcy briefly considered bidding Miss Elizabeth a formal farewell, but he could not remain, and the ballroom was still crowded. For the same reason, he could not speak with Mr. Bennet before departing.

"No, you will take the carriage to London in the morning. I wish you to deliver a note to Longbourn. Help me change, then pack and get some sleep, if you can." Darcy dashed off a brief note for Mr. Bennet. Slipworth helped him change out of his evening attire, draping his jacket carefully over the back of a chair before assisting him with his riding clothes. Darcy left noiselessly through the back of the house, avoiding the ball, and swung up into the saddle. He would ride directly home to London. There was a full moon, and the morning was near enough that he would not need to bother with an inn.

As Darcy guided his horse down the sweep at the front of the house, he stopped to take a final look at Netherfield. The windows of the ballroom were aglow with candlelight. Framed in one was the young woman he could not banish from his thoughts. He could not discern her features, but her dark curls and delicate gown were clearly visible as were the gloved fingers of one hand that rested lightly on the glass. She lifted that hand in a half-wave, and he wished he could see her eyes one last time.

Darcy tipped his hat before he leaned forward and urged his horse into a gallop.

Lydia's undisguised yawns grated on Elizabeth's nerves. Miss Bingley was staring at her with such venom that the hair on the back of her neck stood up, but she would not be cowed. Mr. Bingley had his back to her but was conversing with Jane in a warm, modulated tone, low enough that she could not hear. What was he telling her?

When they arrived home, her mother and sisters streamed up the stairs to bed. Elizabeth watched them go and turned to her father.

"Papa," she said quietly, laying a hand on his arm. "Might I speak with you?"

He began to demur, but when his eyes met hers, he simply nodded and waved her into his study. "Now," he said gaily, closing the door behind them, "what mysterious event has occurred that you cannot wait to inform me until tomorrow?" His brown eyes twinkled. "Are you to confess a secret engagement?"

Elizabeth nearly rolled her eyes. "What I have to say involves Mr. Darcy," she informed him pertly. "Do you still believe I am engaged in a clandestine romance?"

Her father chuckled. "Would you have preferred to be matched to poor Mr. Collins? Your mother probably had plans for one of you in that quarter."

Mr. Collins, the heir presumptive to Longbourn, had passed of a sudden illness a few months before Mr. Bingley arrived at Netherfield. The search for the next heir was still ongoing.

"Are you suddenly so interested in making a match for me, Papa?" Elizabeth asked, impatient with his levity when she had such a serious matter weighing on her.

"I am not," he promised her. "But watching you and your sister Jane this evening, I know it will not be long before some worthy gentlemen carry you both away. And then what shall I do?" He gazed at her fondly. "Now, to this business of yours, Lizzy. What have you to tell me?"

Elizabeth sat on her usual chair and clasped her hands in her lap. The events of the ball were so entirely beyond her previous experience that she hardly knew where to begin. She had been angry with Mr. Darcy, provoking him with taunts about his taciturn disposition and his mistreatment of others. He had been justly offended when she mentioned Mr. Wickham, but he had remained a gentleman. She could not say she had behaved as a lady. Her cheeks warmed at the memory.

She had followed Mr. Darcy from the ballroom. Never had she done anything so entirely improper, but he had raised her ire to such an extent that she had not realized where she was until they were quarreling in the hall. Yet that was not the end. She had refused to allow him to quit the field of battle without answering her question. She could not blame herself for that—it had been an entirely reasonable inquiry. Still, to have stalked into the library after him!

It was only that she had been so *very* angry at his rudeness in walking away without even declining her request for information. She had been determined to finish their conversation no matter Mr. Darcy's sentiments on the matter, and she had been justly served by landing herself in the center of a scandal.

Her father cleared his throat. "Lizzy?" he inquired. "Are you well? You are not usually one to have trouble forming your thoughts."

She related the story in full and watched Papa's expression transform from idle curiosity to deep concern. "I was entirely mistaken about Mr. Darcy," she concluded, embarrassed. "As a consequence, I have also been very wrong about Mr. Wickham." She lifted her shoulders slightly and let them fall. "And I must say that Mr. Bingley's behavior is appalling. I would never have thought it possible." Even Miss Bingley's actions had shocked her, though she had never believed the woman to be of sterling character.

"Do not berate yourself, Lizzy," Papa said drily as he reached for a cigar. He cut the end, lit it, and sat back in his chair. "Mr. Darcy was clearly taken unawares, and he has known Mr. Bingley longer than we have."

"There was a man watching Mr. Bingley in the ballroom, after. I believe he was anticipating an announcement of some sort," Elizabeth mused. How many people had been involved in trapping Mr. Darcy into a marriage he did not desire? What a blow it must have been—she had not been able to see Mr. Darcy's face when Mr. Bingley accused him, but the way his shoulders had suddenly sagged when he discovered his friend's duplicity would stay with her always.

Papa puffed his cigar, and she waved the smoke away as she considered his words. Mr. Bingley had been at Netherfield for two months. Jane felt she knew Mr. Bingley, but it was not really a great deal of time. Even when Jane had been ill at Netherfield, she had not been able to spend much time in his company. Elizabeth had spent a good deal more time with Mr. Darcy, come to that. "We do not know Mr. Darcy any better, but in light of what you have said, I suspect this is not the first time he has been imposed upon."

"Indeed," Elizabeth replied, startled back to the conversation. "I believe you are correct." It would explain a great deal of Mr. Darcy's aloof behavior, in fact. He was protecting himself. What a fool she had been.

"I am afraid you must restrain your temper much better in future, my dear," Papa said seriously. "Had Mr. Darcy not behaved as a gentleman, your reputation might now be at risk."

"I shall, Papa." Elizabeth hoped either Mr. Bingley's interest in Jane or his concern for Miss Bingley's reputation would prevent him from spreading any rumors about her. She could not expect that his honor would compel it.

"Mr. Darcy was intemperate in his insult, of course," Papa continued. "However, as you say, he did ask you to dance tonight before all of this nonsense occurred. Surely that must alleviate the sting somewhat."

Elizabeth did not add that she had previously turned Mr. Darcy away twice before. She had not believed those offers sincere until he had asked her to dance again at Mr. Bingley's ball. "Not only that," she confessed, "I accepted Mr. Wickham's lies because my vanity was injured and the lieutenant tells a pretty story." She sighed. "I am quite ashamed of myself."

Her father stared off into the dark. "It is as much my responsibility as yours," he said. "I should have better acquainted myself with all the gentlemen in question before allowing them to visit Longbourn and dally with my daughters."

"Mr. Darcy," she replied archly, "has never visited Longbourn, and I believe I can safely say he would not stoop to dally with any of your daughters."

"Ah, I suppose all the talk of him in our sitting room fooled me into believing that he had," Papa said wryly.

Elizabeth sighed softly. She had always prided herself on her discernment, and yet she felt entirely mistaken in all three men. Perhaps it was only that she had known the people of Meryton long enough to understand them. Perhaps she was not such an excellent judge of new characters after all. She said as much to her father.

"Untrue," he replied. "You possess great insight for one so young. I have seen it." He gazed at her thoughtfully. "Perhaps all you lack is patience. First impressions are nearly always incomplete."

They sat in silence for a minute or two. "Will you tell Jane?" Elizabeth asked. "Mr. Bingley had no compunction in slandering me when I stood in the way of his plan. I fear for her."

Papa released a breath and a cloud of smoke at the same time. "If his primary reason for being here was to ensnare Mr. Darcy for his sister, I should think they will shortly decamp to London. There can be no call to . . ."

"Papa," Elizabeth said warningly. "If you will not, I must. Sir William might as well—he mentioned the expectations of our neighbors tonight. Everyone already believes Mr. Bingley will propose." She paused, then said quietly, "Jane cannot be left ignorant. I did interfere with their plans. The Bingleys might seek to punish me through her."

"Would they go so far, Lizzy?" Papa asked dubiously, raising one eyebrow.

"Given what I witnessed tonight," Elizabeth said stoutly, recalling Mr. Bingley's denial and Miss Bingley's accusations, "I must say they would."

Her father drew on the cigar and exhaled the smoke away from her, towards the window. He nodded. "Very well. I will speak with Jane, and if Mr. Bingley shows his face at Longbourn, I shall speak with him as well."

Elizabeth sighed, relieved. "Thank you, Papa." She waited expectantly.

"Yes, yes," Papa said brusquely. "And I shall include Mr. Wickham in my censure. Better to have it all done at once so the duration of the storm will be lessened, if not its strength. Go to bed now, child, and leave me to my thoughts."

Chapter Two

As he brushed past his butler Mr. Pratt, Darcy was already making a dozen decisions. A disheveled footman handed him a lit candle as he passed. Darcy took it and locked himself inside his study. He touched the flame to a few more candles and crouched to start a fire, unwilling to keep any servants awake to do it for him. As soon as he was able to warm his fingers, he picked up a pen. The note Slipworth would deliver to Longbourn was merely a polite leave-taking and a promise for a longer letter he hoped Mr. Bennet would do him the honor of reading. He had not been master enough of himself, at the time, to do more.

The long ride had allowed Darcy to compose his thoughts. Now he was able to write a detailed narrative of the events that had occurred during the ball, expounding upon Miss Elizabeth's innocence in the entire affair and his gratitude for her assistance. Though he did not mention Georgiana, he added what he had said to Miss Elizabeth about Wickham and offered further information about his former friend's other proclivities. Mr. Bennet had five daughters. He ought to be warned. Finally, Darcy offered to produce the document Wickham had signed as evidence of his claim should Mr. Bennet require it and included the direction for Darcy House. He sanded the letter and, when it was dry, folded, sealed, and addressed it.

Then he bent to write several more notes, including a call for assistance to Fitz and a request to attend Aunt Matlock before her visiting hours that morning. By the time he sealed the last missive, it was light enough to send for a rider.

Having completed what he could for the moment, Darcy rang for a tray. He returned to his chair and settled back into the cool leather. Miss Elizabeth had wanted to talk about Wickham. To defend the man. It had been a disappointment.

Darcy had believed Miss Elizabeth thought well of him, even if they were not friends, precisely. He certainly admired her. Yet upon reflection, he admitted that he had fought valiantly to conceal his growing esteem. He could hardly blame her for missing his approbation when he could not afford to display it.

Notwithstanding her evident dislike, she had given him a fair hearing, and, in the end, had said she believed him. His respect for her only increased, despite her initial championing of Wickham.

Everyone believed George Wickham at first—Miss Elizabeth was not unique in that. Even his sister Georgiana, whom he had warned against the man—even *she* had chosen to recall only her father's preference for his godson and allowed herself to be taken in by Wickham's lies. She knew now that her handsome suitor had been romancing her fortune rather than her heart, but she was not yet recovered from her disappointment. A disappointment she might have been spared if she had listened!

Darcy knew he was partly to blame for Georgiana's current unease—his sister was at an age where she wished for a measure of independence, and he had taken it away. His disapproval had deeply unsettled her. She jumped if he moved too quickly, her temper flared unexpectedly, and more than once she had left the room abruptly with tears in her eyes. He loved his sister more than reason, but her plans to elope with the very man he had cautioned her about had wounded him deeply. Evidently, he was not hiding that as well as he ought.

Aunt Matlock had finally suggested he take some time away, for both his own sake and that of his sister. He knew his aunt hoped that some time with a friend would clear his mind and help him to move past the bitterness that was beginning to take root in his heart. But Bingley had proven disappointing in that respect. Since the death of his father, Darcy somehow had been unable to find friends who had not eventually wanted something from him—a handout, support for a political endeavor, an investment, or his agreement to marry a female relation.

Masterman had come to him four years ago, mentioning a cousin barely seventeen, who had been seduced by a married neighbor and required a husband.

"I hate to ask, Darcy, but my uncle insisted," Masterman said contritely. "She is his favorite, you see, despite all this, and he wishes her to marry a gentleman. She was raised to be the mistress of an estate and could be of use to you, as we all know you have no plans to wed. You are your own man, so would not need permission . . ." Masterman could not look Darcy in the eye. He cleared his throat uncomfortably before adding, "He would send her to you with a rather spectacular dowry, and you know he has connections in the Lords that your uncle would appreciate."

Darcy had been shocked into silence at the request, and Masterman had taken himself off when it became clear he would receive no response to the entreaty. At the time, Darcy had been overwhelmed with the care of Pemberley, losing first his father and then old Mr. Wickham, the estate's excellent steward. He had not even known which bothered him more—the assumption that he did not wish to ever marry, or the attempt to sell him a bride. He had heard of such things, of course, but never had he expected to be approached in such a way himself.

Fawkner had been far blunter a few years later, when Darcy had made a brief trip to London. He had suggested that Darcy, being in need of an heir, might wish to make a bargain with his mother's new husband, an earl whose sixth daughter was unmarried and with child. The girl came with a large dowry and excellent connections. Darcy, having gained a bit more strength and understanding since Masterman's petition, had Fawkner escorted from the house.

Even Howard, who had a fortune that equaled or surpassed Darcy's, had tried to press him into marrying his *enceinte* sister last March. The fortune was substantial, the family—until now—entirely respectable. Darcy had sympathy, but no intention of granting Howard's request. When he had declined, Howard had all but given him the cut direct.

Now Bingley had joined the growing list of men Darcy could no longer call friends. He snarled at the memory of it and poured himself a drink. *I will marry where I choose, and my heir will be of Darcy blood*. It was unfathomable that anyone should be angered by either declaration, particularly when he had the charge of his young sister. His wife must be someone Georgiana could emulate. If he could ever find such a woman. Ignoring his heart's protest that he already had, Darcy downed the alcohol, loosened his cravat, and reclined on the settee. His chamber would have to be prepared for him, but until then, he could at least rest without fear of waking up shackled to some fortune-hunting harpy.

He was instead awakened by a flood. He sat up, sputtering. "What . . . Fitz?"

"Good morning, cousin." Colonel Richard Fitzwilliam stood a few feet away, placing a now-empty glass upon a tray. "I appreciate your willingness to join me, as it is your letter that has my father's house in uproar."

"Uproar?" Darcy repeated dully, his head still full of cobwebs. He sat up and noted that Fitz was not in uniform.

"If you were only going to sleep," Fitz said, a touch of annoyance in his tone, "and in your study, no less, you might have waited until a more reasonable time to send your missives. Mother was expecting you before calling hours. Fine way to spend my leave, being sent away without breakfast to track you down." He stared down at Darcy. "I have called for something to eat."

Darcy pulled out his watch. Half-past ten. He had been asleep for five hours. "Dash it all . . ."

"Spare me the dramatics, Darcy," Fitz said, and drew a chair up to the settee. "Just tell me what is happening. Why are you back? You were not to return until the week before Christmas."

Darcy glanced at the door, but of course Fitz had closed it upon entering. Despite his gregarious nature, his cousin was discreet when required. Darcy took a deep breath and ran his hands through his hair.

"Oh, bloody hell," Fitz exclaimed derisively before Darcy could speak a word. "Not Bingley too?"

Darcy closed his eyes and nodded. "Miss Bingley."

Fitz's eyes narrowed. "*Miss* Bingley or *Mr.* Bingley?"

"Both," Darcy replied, the sick feeling returning. "He sent me a message through a footman that he needed to see me in the library. It was during the ball . . ." He glanced up to see whether Fitz remembered that there had been a ball. His cousin held up one hand.

"You sent Georgiana a letter about the preparations. Mother related it to me in excruciating detail." He grimaced before saying sarcastically, "By the by, thank you for that."

Darcy tried to stretch his muscles—sleeping on the settee had been a terrible idea. "I was trying to entertain Georgiana. She always asks me for those sorts of descriptions." At least, she *had*. It had been a painfully dull letter to write, but he had hoped his sister would like it. "Did she even read it, or did she just hand it to my aunt?"

Fitz shrugged. "How would I know?" He sat back. "What happened at the ball, cousin?"

"Bingley sent . . ." Darcy began again, but Fitz sighed heavily. Darcy moved directly to the point. "As the host, I knew Bingley could not be away long. He was interested in a woman from a neighboring estate. I thought he was going to ask me whether he ought to propose, so I went right away. I meant to advise him that he should think before he offered. Lovely girl, but a terrible family, no fortune, no sign of any particular regard."

Fitz's face was drawn up into a half-scowl. "The important bits alone, please."

Darcy knew Fitz would never ask about the details of Bingley's love life. He was not certain how he himself had become entangled in it, come to that. "I stepped into the library as he requested, and Miss Bingley threw herself at me."

Fitz nodded. "Not surprised, really, though to make the attempt during her own ball was rather brazen. How did she do it?"

A snorting laugh escaped from Darcy before he could stop it. "No, Fitz. She *literally* threw herself at me. Nearly knocked me over."

Fitz looked at him incredulously for a moment before breaking into laughter. Darcy chuckled along with him, feeling some of the tension in his shoulders ease. Fitz rose and poured them both a glass of port.

"I had thought her to possess more self-restraint than to become a flying bird of paradise," he said, handing a glass to Darcy. "But then, she *is* unusually fond of feathers."

Darcy snorted. "I too had supposed her to possess a *modicum* more subtlety," he admitted. "But the part that really cuts is that Bingley knew. Came in on cue, played the outraged brother, threatened a duel. I played right into his hands." He ought to be accustomed to the pain of betrayal, but each time it wounded him anew. He set the glass aside. Fitz might be accustomed to port at all hours, but it was too early for him.

"So the pretty boy thought to challenge you?" Fitz asked. Judging by the grin on his face, he was highly amused. "I presume he has not seen you fence. Or shoot, for that matter."

Distracted from his darker thoughts, Darcy waved a hand. "He knows I would never consent to a duel. He used that knowledge to puff himself up without fear of any real consequence." He set his glass down without drinking.

"*You* might not consent to meet him," Fitz said ominously, "but *I* would not be averse."

Darcy shook his head. "It is all right. Bingley is not worth the trouble." Intellectually, he knew this, but this depression of spirits would not disappear because he wished it. "At least Bingley has shown his colors. He is not a patient man and it will cost him dearly with someone. But it need not be me."

Fitz sat, took a deep drink, and set the glass on the table next to him. His lips were pressed together in a straight line, and for once, he appeared penitent. "I *am* sorry, Darce. When I met him at the club last year, he was cheerful and good-natured. I encouraged your acquaintance with the man, and he turned out no different than the rest."

Darcy shook his head. "It is not your fault. We had, I thought, a steady sort of friendship, but I should have known. Nobody is that amiable all the time." He watched Fitz finish his port in three gulps and reach for the second glass. "It is not natural."

"How did you leave it?" Fitz asked quietly. "Were you planning to have Mother launch a campaign?"

"Indeed. You may be a colonel, but your mother ought to have been a general," Darcy replied, his spirits not entirely restored but certainly improving.

Fitz just nodded slowly.

"I would have her make it known to her set that I have dissolved all ties with the Bingleys," Darcy said. "They should be invited nowhere on my behalf. I need it done quickly, as I do not know when the Bingleys will journey to town nor the story they will tell when they arrive."

Fitz nodded and sipped at his port. "Now tell me the interesting part. How did you extricate yourself?"

"I threatened Miss Bingley with the sheep farm." Darcy grinned, and Fitz raised his eyebrows.

"Your great-uncle's little estate in Scotland?"

"Precisely. She was suitably horrified. I shall have no more trouble from her." *But her brother* . . . Darcy paused to think about Miss Elizabeth. Truly, things might have gone a good deal worse had she not supported his story. Bingley might have been more insistent without another witness in the room. He might not have persisted in calling Darcy out, but he would have done what he could to draw a crowd. Darcy would have refused to be caught in any case, but it might have become uncomfortable. Miss Elizabeth was too well thought of in Meryton for Bingley to spin such a tale—most of the local gentry would have questioned Bingley's story if it conflicted with hers.

No doubt Miss Elizabeth would claim she had come to his rescue. The corners of Darcy's mouth turned up. He supposed she had.

She had been exquisite. No dramatics, no hysteria, just the simple facts. *Mr. Darcy is not at fault. I witnessed the entire scene. Mr. Darcy made Miss Bingley no offer. Mr. Bingley, I must point out that both doors were open until you closed them.*

She and Fitz both possessed a sharp wit and a protective nature. He had seen it in Miss Elizabeth's determination to tend to her sister when she was ill at Netherfield, when she had held her own against Miss Bingley and Mrs. Hurst without trampling upon good manners, even when she had upbraided him about Wickham. He suspected Miss Elizabeth and Fitz would get on well.

Darcy knew it took courage to stand up to him. He was probably the wealthiest man Miss Elizabeth had ever met, yet she had defended a lieutenant in the local militia who could offer her nothing. Darcy recalled that he had even stupidly pronounced himself to possess a resentful character one night when she had stayed at Netherfield. She had every reason to be wary of him. No, courage was something Miss Elizabeth Bennet had in abundance.

Fitz shuffled his feet and stood. He lifted the decanter and tipped it slightly towards Darcy, who shook his head.

When Miss Elizabeth learned she had been in error about Wickham, she accepted her culpability and made amends. She had boldly revealed her presence in the library to speak in his defense mere moments after he had slighted her a second time and she had done it when she did not even like him. Even though her sister had hopes in regard to Bingley. Even though it might do Miss Elizabeth's own reputation harm. She acted—always, as far as he knew—not in her own interests or for her own comfort, but to do what was right.

He could trust a woman like that.

"What has you smiling after all this?" Fitz asked impatiently.

But her family. Darcy gazed at his boots. *Her lack of fortune and connections.* Miss Elizabeth was a dream from another life. One where he did not have so many responsibilities or carry the burden of his parents' expectations.

"Nothing," he said.

Elizabeth had been unable to sleep well after her discussion with her father, and after several hours, gave up trying. She changed into a walking dress and slipped downstairs. The house was quiet. Even Papa would be unlikely to rise before noon.

Mrs. Hill nodded at her as she entered the breakfast room.

"Good morning, Mrs. Hill," Elizabeth said, attempting to sound cheerful.

Mrs. Hill returned the greeting.

"How is your daughter?" Elizabeth asked. "Has there been any word?"

Unlike many housekeepers, Mrs. Hill had been married, then widowed, before she entered service.

"I had word not an hour ago that her labors have begun, Miss Elizabeth," Mrs. Hill informed her, the lines around her eyes giving away her anxiety.

Elizabeth gasped happily and clasped her hands together. "Then what are you still doing *here*?"

Mrs. Hill glanced around nervously. "I should not like to be missed when Mrs. Bennet rises."

"Oh, no one else will rise for hours yet," Elizabeth said. "We did not leave Netherfield until nearly four o'clock. And you know Papa gave you leave to attend Annabelle. Please do not wait on us. I shall tell Papa where you have gone, and Mama that I insisted you go." She was willing to bear Mama's complaints about her high-handedness for such a cause.

"Bless your good heart," Mrs. Hill said, unshed tears welling in her eyes. The housekeeper straightened, ran her hands along her skirt, and hurried out.

Elizabeth strolled out to the hall, where she tied on her bonnet and slipped on her pelisse before stepping out of doors. The cold morning air on her face revived her, and she headed towards the little wilderness on one side of the gardens. All she needed was a brief respite to think through everything that had happened—it was difficult to reconcile her impression of Mr. Darcy as a proud, haughty sort of man with the beleaguered, even vulnerable man she had conversed with . . . was it only this morning?

Honorable too, she admitted. Mr. Darcy had been angry when she mentioned Mr. Wickham, but he had not given way to his emotions. He had answered her questions—well, most of them. And in the library, he had not called on her to save him. Had she remained silent, she was sure he never would have. Finally, he had ensured she was removed from the situation as soon as he was able. He might have insulted her first by calling her "tolerable" and refusing to ask for her hand at the assembly, but she had more than repaid him for that slight by twice rejecting what she now suspected had been genuine invitations to dance. And her behavior last night! She could hardly bear to recall it.

Elizabeth cast her thoughts back to the first time she had met Mr. Darcy. Mama's exhortations about poor Mr. Collins's demise being

Jane's good fortune had been loud and lengthy. Papa had more than once tried to explain that they must first complete an exhaustive search for blood relations to replace Mr. Collins, and that Jane was not in line to inherit, even were no Bennet men to be located. Unfortunately, Papa had not accompanied them to the assembly that night, and Mama would not be gainsaid. Instead, she had happily crowed to all her friends that Jane's first-born son would be the heir of Longbourn. Certainly, her mother's vulgar glee must be one reason Mr. Darcy viewed them all with such contempt.

There—I have done it again. Elizabeth stood still and took a deep breath. She had been wrong about Mr. Darcy many times over—and here was another example. If Mama's uninformed insistence had mortified *her*, she could not blame *him* for being shocked by such behavior. She huffed, frustrated with her own blindness, and decided that she had a great deal to think about—which required a rather longer walk than a stroll near the house.

By the time Elizabeth stopped analyzing all her previous interactions with Mr. Darcy and decided he might *not* have been watching her with disdain all these weeks, she was nearly at Netherfield's boundary. She could see the great house from the top of the next rise if she wished—but she did not. Elizabeth had not meant to walk so far. Vowing not to allow herself to become so distracted in future, she turned back towards home.

She took a few steps but stopped to sneeze. She removed her handkerchief to dab at her nose. Truly, it would serve her right if she caught a cold. As she folded her handkerchief and tucked it away, there was a clomping of hooves on her right.

Two men on horseback emerged from a wider side path. They were dressed as gentlemen, and as she did not recognize them, she suspected they were friends of the Bingleys and had attended the ball. The men appeared startled by her presence but made no effort to remove themselves, and Elizabeth's sense of foreboding increased. They were between her and the path back to Longbourn. *Foolish*, she chided herself. *Foolish, foolish girl.* Mrs. Hill would be gone all day. Why had she told no one else that she was leaving the house?

"Can you believe our luck, my friend?"

The man who had spoken had very light hair and pale blue eyes. She glanced at the other man who also had light hair, though his was more like the color of honey. His eyes were darker, too, a less remarkable brown.

The first man spoke again. "We were just on our way to your home to call on your father, Miss Elizabeth."

He was lying. It could not be more than eight o'clock. No one paid calls at this hour. And how did he know her name?

The second man said nothing, but he swung a leg over his horse and dismounted. There was a small thump as his boots met the ground. Why? They were not acquainted. Elizabeth bent her knees slightly, preparing to flee into the woods where the horses would have a difficult time following. These men would be faster and stronger. She would have to be more cunning.

"I am afraid we have not been introduced, sirs. Why do you not call on my father later in the day?" she asked, taking a slow step back. "I am sure he should be pleased to receive you, although it is not quite the done thing to visit immediately following a ball."

"Yes," said the blue-eyed man, watching her from atop his mount.

Elizabeth shivered as though a pail of cold water had been poured down her back. It took a great deal to frighten her, but she would have to be very dim indeed not to be frightened now. These men had no intention of making a polite call at Longbourn.

He spoke slowly as the other man approached her. "I admit we thought we should have to come another day to Longbourn, but we will be departing the area shortly." He paused. Her attention remained on the man approaching. "We heard you were a great walker, but we did not expect to find you so far from home and so early, too. We are very *pleasantly* surprised."

Elizabeth tensed and sprang away just as the darker man reached for her. She dashed into the woods she had played in as a child and heard cursing behind her. Out of the corner of her eye, she saw that only one man was following and heard the other galloping away.

She leapt over a muddy inlet and flew into bramble, where the trees grew thicker. She ran faster, nimbly weaving between them, clambering over the uneven ground without faltering—she knew every undulation.

There was a path that went the long way around—if her other pursuer had taken it, she would have to hurry. He would not be able to ride his horse the entire way, but he could ride far enough and then intercept her on foot. She was heading for the stream—it was a large, deep one, a tributary to the river—and planned to throw herself in, hoping that swimming with the current would carry her away faster than they could follow through the untamed blackberry bushes along the bank. It emptied into a large but shallow pool behind Longbourn. She could climb out there. It was not a *good* plan, but she had no time to devise another. Her dress would be ruined, and the water would be very cold, but better to suffer an illness than acquiesce to anything these men intended to inflict upon her.

Loud footsteps sounded behind her and she ran faster, holding one end of her skirt in a clenched fist to prevent it from catching on anything. She ducked under a fallen tree and reached an opening. From here she would need to traverse twenty feet of clearing to the bank, where the brush would again offer some safety. There was no other way.

She plunged ahead.

That brief vacillation was her undoing. The blue-eyed man burst through the trees and into the clearing from her right side, not five feet in front of her. "Come now, Miss Elizabeth," he said, panting, though he wore a chilling little smirk. "Let us not waste any more time."

Elizabeth darted to his left, hoping it was his weaker side, but he simply spun and caught her around the waist as she passed. She kicked and arched her back and tried to swing her arms, but he quickly pinned them to her sides. She screamed with everything she had, only to find herself flat on her back with the man sitting on her stomach and the end of a flask shoved in her mouth.

"There now, Miss Elizabeth," said the cool, quiet voice of the man with the brown eyes who had joined his friend. She spluttered, but he pinched her nose and shoved her jaw up—she had no choice but to swallow if she wanted to breathe. "Take your medicine, my girl."

Elizabeth tasted something bitter in the wine and wrenched her face to the side. Some of the drink spilled down her face and neck. She gasped, trying to pull in more air while also trying to wriggle free. She drew a deep breath to scream again.

One gloved hand struck her, hard, across the cheek. She struggled more desperately and received another, harder blow. She lay still, dazed, looking up into a pair of watery blue eyes. He had a small brown freckle exactly at the outside corner of his right eye. More of the wine was forced down her throat, and she was unable to protest.

"Just a little something to help you sleep," the man said comfortingly, and she was made to drink again. She blinked up at him, not in the least tired. The left side of her head felt as though a hot poker was being held against her scalp, and she fought not to cry out.

The brown-eyed man stepped out of her vision and reappeared with a rope. "This meeting truly could not have been more fortunate," he told the man with the blue eyes who was holding her down. "The house will be late rising, but the Darcy carriage was being prepared to depart. If we hurry, we should be able to place her in the boot."

"They will discover her," said the man straddling her. She squirmed, and he leaned one hand on her shoulder, pinning her to the ground.

The brown-eyed man shook his head. "Not until they arrive in London, which is exactly what we want." He kneeled, taking Elizabeth's hands and binding them before moving to her ankles. He paused, pulled his hands away. "Easier if she can walk. Get up." He yanked her up by the rope binding her hands. She broke away to run but was easily caught.

The blue-eyed man tossed her over his shoulder, one arm tight around the back of her knees. Elizabeth bent her arms and swung at his head with her elbow. He grunted and bent over as she flung herself away from him, but he pushed her a little as she fell, and she hit the ground hard. She tried to catch her breath as the man swore. Two brown eyes stared down at her impassively.

"Are you finished?" he asked. His voice was very deep. "You will only hurt yourself more, and I would be happy to bind your feet as well."

Elizabeth shook her head. She was beginning to feel a little dizzy. She could not say whether that was from the repeated blows or what they had forced her to drink.

Desperate now, she willed herself to make one more attempt to fight—she had seen her father force a servant to purge himself when he had taken too much . . . something. Her hands were bound before her and despite the pain and the filth on her hands, she jammed her fingers to the back of her throat. She gagged, and some of the wine came back out. Her head swam.

"None of that, now," the darker man admonished her. There was a third blow and Elizabeth's body no longer obeyed her.

Cold morning air brushed her cheek before she was on her stomach again. She smelled leather and horse, felt the agony of hanging upside down, the blood pulsing in her injured face. A hand on her back held her steady as they moved, but she felt the cadence of the horse lifting her up a little and then dropping her back down, making it difficult to breathe.

In no time, the leather smell disappeared, and she was looking up at a blue, cloudless sky.

"He has left already," one man said.

"It is all right," said the other. "We can follow his path and leave her along it. It will serve the same purpose."

"But they will not be together," his partner replied.

"We have a way around that," was the response.

Elizabeth tried to say something, to call for help, but a rag was stuffed in her mouth. "Not a word," she was warned. She could not be certain which of the men had said it before she was roughly tossed into a carriage and the man with brown eyes climbed in after. The wooden floor was rough beneath her cheek. Elizabeth turned her back to him so that she was facing the bench. She pulled out the gag and began working the ropes that bound her hands. A moment later, they were out on the road and picking up speed.

They were tossed up and down as the carriage hit holes and swung from one side of the road to the other. Somewhere in the fog of her thoughts, Elizabeth knew they were traveling too fast. Even her traveling companion had taken hold of the leather strap above him and was hanging on for dear life. She could not tell how long they had been driving, but soon thought she heard the rush of the river. She was being tossed about, but she focused on her bonds. At last, the rope around her wrists loosened.

There was laughter from above her. "You will never untie those before you sleep," the man informed her. "But by all means, carry on."

Why was he so unconcerned about her working her way free? Where were they taking her?

Taking me.

A bolt of fear briefly cleared her mind.

Elizabeth managed to slip one hand out of the ropes before the carriage hit a deep rut and something hit the ceiling of the coach with an audible *thud*. A string of curses erupted as the coach veered to one side of the road and slowed. Elizabeth turned her head. The brown-eyed man was sitting on the far end of the other bench looking down, one large hand splayed over the top of his head. Carefully, she positioned her feet under her, one hand on the bench while the other reached out to grasp the cool lever of the door.

The brown-eyed man glanced up, but Elizabeth had already shoved the lever down with force and leapt. There was a moment of exaltation as she flew free of her captors, then a realization that she was not in fact flying, but falling.

Instinctively, she tried to tuck her legs in and duck her head, flipping an instant before she hit the ground. She landed hard on one side with her left arm awkwardly tucked beneath her. She flipped over on her stomach as she skidded down a small incline, her feet slipping through mud, her hands grasping wildly at stones and bushes to slow her descent. She stopped inches from a long, rocky drop into the river, her feet dangling over the edge. Elizabeth caught her breath and then scrambled back up to safety, sending bits of rock and grass over the side.

Above her, she heard the carriage being pulled to a halt—they must have traveled some way before the driver realized she had escaped.

Elizabeth's bonnet had been shoved away from her head, the ribbons pulling tight across her throat. She ripped it off clumsily and tossed it away so she could see, then scrambled through the drier dirt and blackberry bushes, ignoring the sharp thorns, and pulled herself back up toward the road. There were more bushes and a few large trees there and she hid herself among them, panting with exertion.

Elizabeth numbly tried to take stock. Her gloves were torn and bloodstained, her coat ripped and muddy. She was hurt—after such a fall she must be—but she could not feel any pain beyond a nagging twinge in her left arm. What was wrong with her?

Elizabeth picked her way up to the road and peered out.

She heard men speaking down the road, near where she had jumped. Her heart was beating so hard that each thump hurt. She was helpless here.

"She went over the side!" one called.

The deep voice, the one she thought belonged to the brown-eyed man, replied without emotion, "Never mind. It will work just as well and with less labor for us. Have a look about to be certain."

They startled as another coach, traveling more sedately, drew to a halt some distance behind them. It stopped closer to her hiding place than the first, and Elizabeth moved slowly towards it while remaining under cover. She glanced back. Her attackers had stopped their carriage in the middle of the road, and the second coach could not pass.

The driver handed off the reins to his partner before he dropped down from his seat and walked up the road with a greeting and an offer of assistance. From her angle, Elizabeth could not see inside the conveyance.

The men all moved away to talk in front of the first carriage, and Elizabeth knew she could not remain. The second carriage would leave, and her abductors would continue to conduct their search. She could not make it home on her own. She was too dizzy to walk and so very tired. This was her only chance.

Get away, her mind screamed. *Get away.*

With a great deal of effort, she forced herself to her hands and knees. She crawled shakily through the brambles to the edge of the tree line. She checked for the men—they were moving to examine the first carriage now. They were turned away from her, and she crept into the dirt of the road, concealing herself behind the second carriage, where a large boot and several trunks were fastened on the back. She pulled out the strap securing the lid of the boot and tried to pull herself up, but her foot slipped. She tried again, this time managing to lift the lid and slip inside.

Elizabeth fell atop shifting metal . . . things. Tools? Her fingertips brushed a rough blanket just beneath her. Sleep was pulling at her, her limbs growing too heavy to move, but through sheer force of will, she did not succumb until she felt the tell-tale jolt as the carriage began to move. She heard the whisper of wind through the trees, then her eyelids dropped, and all light was extinguished.

Darcy completed his story without mentioning Miss Elizabeth. He sat back tiredly.

"I see," Aunt Matlock said, appearing thoughtful. She shook her head at a footman bearing a silver tray that held a few calling cards.

He turned and exited the room. "You do not have much luck keeping friends, Nephew."

Darcy rubbed the back of his neck. "It has been an effort, Aunt. One I am not inclined to continue."

He and Fitz had waited until Lady Matlock's usual receiving hours were over to speak to his aunt. While they waited, they had canvassed Bingley's haunts in and around Mayfair.

Fortunately, it did not appear that Bingley had returned to town. Darcy had been surprised, but Netherfield had welcomed a number of guests from London who might wonder if their host departed. Or perhaps Bingley intended to pursue Miss Jane Bennet after all. He might truly be in love with her. Or, his suspicious mind warned, it might be a way to gain footing in the family and discredit Miss Elizabeth. For her sake, he hoped that Mr. Bennet would read the letter containing his fuller explanation of events and heed his warning. Warnings. Fitz dragged him back to the present.

"Darce," his cousin said reprovingly, before he took a large bite of a seed cake and washed it down with three gulps of tea. Aunt Matlock frowned at Fitz, but he met her disapproval with a wink and a wide smile. She gave him a look that was both reproachful and affectionate.

"Yes, cousin?" Darcy asked wryly.

Fitz set down his teacup and focused his attention on Darcy. "There are good men out there who want nothing from you but your company," he said seriously. "The leeches have been out since your father's death, but we will make it clear to all that you know your own mind. And Mother will speak with Henry—he is nearly as adept at putting the word out as she."

"Indeed," the countess said approvingly. "Your brother has learned from a virtuoso."

"Do not close yourself off, cousin." Fitz's gaze darted over to his mother and back to Darcy. His words dripped with mischief. "Forget the men. You will never find a good *woman* that way."

I hate you, Fitz. Darcy watched his aunt's eyes widen and her expression grow thoughtful.

"A lively young woman might be just the thing," his aunt said fondly. "As I cannot seem to succeed with my sons, perhaps I ought to assist you. *One* of you really ought to marry before Georgiana. Let me think on the matter."

Darcy leaned over to Fitz. "Angelo's," he said calmly. "Tomorrow."

Fitz's eyebrows lifted, and his answer rang with delight. "Why not today? Shall we lay a wager?"

"William, Richard," Aunt Matlock admonished them. "Really. Please try to remain focused on the matter at hand."

"I beg your pardon, Mother," Fitz said in an excellently feigned apology.

Darcy murmured his own regrets and glared briefly at his cousin before returning to the original subject of their conversation. "What will you say to your friends, Aunt?"

"Oh, the usual, my dear," she said sweetly. "Another new family trying to overreach. It is better to keep the story simple, and I am sure Miss Bingley's reputation precedes her."

He nodded, still disappointed that Bingley was so much like his sisters. "Thank you." He hesitated, thinking about his own. "I do not suppose Georgiana would welcome a visit . . ."

Aunt Matlock shook her head. "Leave her be until Christmas, my dear, as you originally planned. I will tell your sister that you asked after her."

Darcy grimaced. "Very well. If she should desire to see me before then, send a note and I shall attend her promptly."

"William," his aunt said firmly, "she is regaining her confidence. Allow her the time she needs to face you."

He schooled his features and acquiesced. As he stood and turned to the door, Fitz followed. "Where are you going?" Darcy asked.

"With you," his cousin answered glibly.

"I have not invited you to join me," Darcy pointed out. What he wanted was to be alone to mourn the loss of his sister's good opinion and the barriers to earning Miss Elizabeth's.

"Was Angelo's not an invitation then?" Fitz inquired drolly. "Is your cook serving dinner tonight or will we dine at the club after our match?"

"You know I have hardly slept, and you are trying to gain an advantage. It will not work," Darcy responded.

Fitz slapped him on the back. Hard. "I require no advantage to best you at swords," he growled.

Darcy grinned. It was not often he was able to successfully goad Fitz—most often it was the reverse. "Swords, perhaps, but not foils. Fencing takes more than strength and endurance, cousin; it requires a quick mind and an elegance of movement."

"Yes, that sounds like you," Fitz replied. "You are so light on your feet. We all know how much you enjoy the dance."

Darcy knew the match was being observed. He even heard, distantly, the other men chattering like gossiping dowagers. But when it came to fencing and shooting, he was always focused. Fitz was his most difficult opponent, shrewd and experienced, and today they were almost evenly paired.

Darcy's boast was true—between himself and his cousin, he knew he was the better fencer. He also knew that he held the advantage only because fencing was a sport. Had he ever met Fitz on a battlefield where there were no rules, their positions would be reversed. Darcy had a great deal of respect for his cousin, and he always learned something new when they crossed blades. Today was no different. Fitz had made an alteration to a carte he had always favored, nearly winning a point with it; fortunately, Darcy had registered the move with a second to spare and stepped lightly to the right.

The tip of the weapon slid past, upsetting his cousin's balance slightly, and Darcy took advantage. Fitz's eyes narrowed as he acknowledged the hit.

Darcy's mind wandered just a bit as they moved back to their positions. Why had Bingley not returned to London? Had he stayed to damage Miss Elizabeth's reputation before he abandoned her sister? He shook his head to clear it and faced Fitz.

They traded feints and parries for a time before Fitz performed a perfect thrust, turning his wrist, raising it above his head, and striking with speed. Darcy turned again at the final moment, but the hit, while not direct, was strong enough that he acknowledged it. Fitz's expression was smug and satisfied.

Darcy recalled the way Elizabeth had stood toe to toe with him, her little chin lifted bravely, using her words as he used his blade. The way her eyes had flashed with righteous anger. The confusion that had marred her features when he explained about Wickham.

Damn it, he had to stop thinking of her.

He and his cousin moved to their original positions and began again.

"I have you this time, *Little Fitzy*," Fitz jibed as he moved swiftly to his right.

The detested nickname had gotten Darcy's back up as a young man; today he knew his own worth. Fitz would always be tougher. He had attended The Royal Military College and was a decorated colonel. Still, Darcy was no soft boy. He had survived many trials since their boyhoods, including being treated by nearly all he knew as nothing more than a bank expected to offer loans on very easy terms. Even Georgiana had expected him to sign over her fortune to that blackguard with nary a protest.

Well, his sister's situation was not precisely the same—but it still hurt. He lifted his foil in salute.

At university, Darcy had done everything to distinguish himself from Wickham. He had learned to box, refined his fencing, devoted himself to his studies. It had given him an outlet for his energies—he refused to behave like Wickham, running up debts and visiting brothels. Later, after his father passed, it was a way to release his grief and anger. He was angry at his false friends, angry at a society that cared little for his happiness and everything for his purse. Mostly, he was angry that his parents had passed so early, leaving the responsibilities of their lives for him to complete.

He advanced, his anger hardening into steel.

Fitz retreated, and Miss Elizabeth's face again appeared in Darcy's vision. She had not wanted anything from him but the truth. He chased the specter away.

During that split second of hesitation, Fitz moved his blade to his left hand. A left-handed fencer had an advantage when fighting against a right-handed man, and Fitz clearly meant to throw Darcy's concentration off by changing in the middle of the challenge. It was an unfair tactic, but Darcy merely lifted one brow and switched his own blade from right to left, erasing the benefit of Fitz's gambit.

The noise of the crowd increased and at last intruded upon his notice, but Darcy was not distracted. Fitz's eyes widened before he barked out a laugh and switched back to his right hand. Darcy mirrored the movement. He had been practicing assiduously during Fitz's time on the continent, but his left hand was still a touch weaker. Not that he would ever admit it.

Fitz advanced, then Darcy, as they circled the floor. Finally, Darcy attacked, Fitz parried, and Darcy answered. As the tip of his weapon touched his cousin's breast, the voices of the gathered men burst into loud calls and scattered applause.

"Brilliant riposte," he heard Dudley say, and "I thought the colonel had him this time," from another man, one Darcy did not know. Money was exchanging hands, but Darcy ignored it all and bowed to his cousin.

Fitz returned the bow, his expression a mix of admiration, frustration, and pleasure in the exercise. "I will best you one day," he grumbled.

Darcy laughed. "I do not doubt it, cousin," he said. "But not today."

Fitz wandered off to accept his share of the congratulations for a match well-fought and the ribbing that must accompany his loss. Darcy suspected that any felicitations he received himself would be influenced by how many pounds had been made or lost on his victory. Still, he received both the thanks and the friendly oaths graciously. He could do no less.

"Bravo, Darcy!" shouted Webb. Darcy's lip curled. Webb had been a friend at university. When Darcy had finally emerged from mourning his father, Webb had been all sympathy and kind advice, but traded on their friendship to lay wagers in Darcy's name. As if this were not insult enough, Webb had fully expected him to absorb the losses.

Rather substantial ones. When he had warned the man to stop, Webb had agreed, but the friendship was permanently fractured. Webb was far less affected by that than Darcy had been.

"See now, Darcy?" Webb asked pleasantly. "I have yet to run myself aground. You ought to take more after your cousin the viscount."

Darcy forced his features into indifference. How dare the man throw the viscount in his face? Henry was a reckless fop. He asked politely but directly, "Why do you not lay a wager on yourself and step to the floor with me?"

Webb laughed. "There would be no odds on that match," he replied, and turned away.

Darcy scowled. Though he had made no sound, Fitz's eyes were upon him.

"Now you must feed me," his cousin announced, and the men around them laughed.

"I believe I was the victor," Darcy replied sardonically. "Should you not be feeding me?"

"You do not wish to eat what I can afford," Fitz responded blithely.

Darcy shook his head. "It is hours before dinner, Fitz, but let us go back to the house and try our luck."

At home, Darcy was informed that his carriage had arrived from Hertfordshire while he was out, and that his presence had been requested. Darcy thought it strange but said nothing, instead leaving Fitz to refresh himself while he walked out to the mews to speak with his valet.

"Mr. Darcy," Slipworth greeted him, as several of the footmen carried Darcy's trunks into the house. "I had to wait a time at Longbourn, as the housekeeper was not in and the family was still abed, but eventually I was able to leave your message with a manservant."

Darcy nodded. Mr. Bennet ought to have his longer letter by now as well. "And the Bingleys?"

Slipworth shook his head. "They did not approach me, sir. The servants did say Mr. Bingley spoke with Miss Jane Bennet at length before the family left Netherfield. The Bennet carriage was the last to be called."

Darcy had no doubt of that, nor how it had happened. Mrs. Bennet was not subtle. It was interesting that Bingley had approached Miss Bennet even after Miss Elizabeth had witnessed the scene in the library. Perhaps he hoped to convince Miss Bennet that her sister was mistaken.

He wondered why Slipworth had not simply spoken to him in his chambers—there was nothing urgent in his explanation—but the man did have a few oddities. He was about to thank his valet and return indoors when his coachman cleared his throat rather loudly.

"Anders," Darcy called. "Are you well?" The coachman was sitting atop the large trunk that served as the boot at the back of the carriage.

Anders opened his mouth, but closed it again, and Darcy was alarmed by the sickened expression on the man's face. He left Slipworth and strode over to Anders, who scrambled to his feet.

"Are you ill?" Darcy asked directly.

"No, sir," Anders replied, stiffening a bit at Darcy's brusqueness. He glanced back at the trunk. "It is only . . ."

Darcy waited while Anders paused and swallowed. His impatience must have shown, because Anders glanced around and said, quietly, "It is only that some of the tools in the boot require repair, sir. I think we ought to take the entire box *inside* so I can work on 'em tonight."

"The tools," Darcy repeated, staring at the man.

"Yes, sir," Anders said stoutly.

Had the man been drinking? He stepped a bit closer and sniffed but did not detect the odor of any spirits. He was relieved. Anders was the best coachman Darcy had, one of the best in all of London, he believed; he should hate to have to send him away.

"Slipworth," Darcy called, and the valet appeared at his elbow. "Help Anders carry that trunk inside. He will show you where it is to go."

"Begging your pardon, Mr. Darcy," Anders replied, swallowing anxiously, "I think you will want to see them."

He returned his attention to the coachman. "The tools," Darcy repeated. He simply wanted to be certain.

Anders nodded, his demeanor grave.

"Why would . . ." Slipworth began to say, but Darcy cut him off.

"I will meet you . . ." He paused to allow Anders to finish the statement.

Anders did. "In the old sewing room, sir."

Slipworth's cheeks flushed. It was beneath his position to be hauling trunks, but Darcy gave him a stern look, and the valet reached for one of the leather loops. Darcy walked ahead of the pair, keeping a watch for any others on his staff.

Darcy entered the sewing room, a small room down the servants' corridor from the kitchen. It was used for storage now. When Mrs. Spencer, the housekeeper, had mentioned in her clipped, stern way, how dark this room was, he had given her leave to fit up a larger, airier room with better light on the other side of the house. No one would think twice about Anders taking a trunk there, though they might wonder why the master accompanied it. Slipworth and Anders came in behind him, struggling with the trunk between them.

Darcy closed the door and rested against it.

"What is it we have hauled in here?" Slipworth asked imperiously, addressing Anders. "It feels as if you had filled the entire thing with earth."

There was a quick knock. "Darcy?" It was Fitz, speaking just above a whisper. "What the blazes are you doing in there?"

Darcy sighed. Fitz was impossible to mislead. Whatever this was, it would be unwise to keep his cousin out of it. He opened the door just wide enough to pull his cousin inside and shut the door again.

"I was trying to procure something to eat, but your cook defends her borders better than the French," Fitz said, eyeing the trunk. "I thought I heard you in the back hall. What is all the mystery?"

"We were about to be enlightened," Darcy replied, and nodded at Anders, who silently assessed Darcy and then the other two men.

"Come, Anders, let us see what you have hidden away," Darcy said, a little impatiently.

"Oh, it was not me, sir," Anders insisted, growing paler than he had been outside, no small feat for a man whose complexion was so dark. "Not me."

Darcy frowned and exchanged a troubled glance with Fitz. His cousin motioned with a tip of his head to the valet and raised an eyebrow.

He knew that Fitz was asking whether the man was reliable. Though Slipworth was rather pompous and had his oddities, he was loyal and entirely discreet. Whatever Anders had to show them, none of the men in this room would reveal it. Darcy gave his cousin a single nod, then turned his attention to Anders. The man threw back the boot's lid, the buckles on the straps hitting the wood floor with a muted thud.

Darcy stepped forward and peered into the box. The room was rather dark even in the middle of the day. He could make out a mound of brown wool and a mop of chestnut curls. His heart nearly stopped in his chest.

It was a woman.

From behind him, Fitz released a long hiss. Darcy crouched beside the trunk to brush the hair from the woman's face. For a long moment, he could not breathe. He rocked back on his heels and grabbed at the edge of the trunk to steady himself.

Inside, curled up and unmoving, was Miss Elizabeth Bennet.

Chapter Three

"Darcy! Is she . . . ?" Fitz's question faded away.

Elizabeth. His heart was ash; his eyes watered. Elizabeth was never still. She was never quiet, even when she did not speak. He reached out a hand to touch her sleeve.

Someone had done this to Elizabeth. To cause him grief? They could have had no idea how deep that grief would go. He would run mad with it.

But not yet.

First, he would see to her—he would do what he could to restore her dignity.

"Hold Miss Bennet's legs, Fitz," Darcy said numbly, sliding his hands under her arms and pulling her up so that her head rested against his chest. "We shall have to lift her out."

Fitz eyed him and moved into position, but then hesitated. "You know her?"

He nodded once.

"Are you sure we ought to remove her?" Fitz asked tentatively. His next words were disconcertingly frank. "If she is dead, you cannot keep her here."

Darcy's eyes were on Elizabeth's face. He felt nauseous. He had left Elizabeth at Netherfield. He had made his own escape and left her unprotected.

He would not cast her off now.

Despite being dressed for the weather with a sensibly warm coat and half boots, Elizabeth was pale and cold, the lips that he had admired only the night before were tinged with blue. "I will not leave her in this damned box, Fitz," he responded hoarsely. He choked on the thought that the trunk was very much like a coffin, and he felt hot and cold all at once. Good God, had she been in the boot the entire way to London? Would Bingley have gone to such lengths to hurt him and keep Elizabeth quiet?

"Help me," he growled, "or get out."

His cousin offered no more protests. He stepped to Miss Elizabeth's feet and knelt, reaching under her legs but keeping her skirt between his hands and her stockings, a sign of respect for which Darcy silently thanked him.

"Ready," Fitz said. Anders held down the trunk so it would not turn over and make noise. Slipworth nervously placed his palms under the small of Elizabeth's back, doing not much good at all.

Anders grabbed the blanket and spread it out on the floor before they set her down. Darcy noted that her pelisse was dirty and torn, but it was still buttoned up tight. He hoped it meant she had not been accosted in that way.

He tugged lightly at a bit of rope still attached to one slender wrist, and Slipworth gasped. Darcy pulled his hand away as though he had been burnt.

"She moved, sir!" the valet said urgently.

Fitz shifted from his position at Elizabeth's feet to hold two fingers against her throat. Darcy waited anxiously, but Elizabeth did not stir.

"She is alive," Fitz said at last. He looked up and met Darcy's gaze, held it. "She is alive." He lifted his hand and ran it through his hair. "Now what do we do?"

Darcy inhaled a deep, broken breath. *Alive.* "Thank God," he whispered, laying a hand on the floor to keep himself from collapsing with the relief of it. Suddenly, his mind cleared. There were things to do—there were things he *could* do.

He ran his gaze up and down Elizabeth's prone form. "Where is she injured?" he demanded. There was a red mark on one cheekbone, whether from a hand or the cold he could not say. Darcy cupped Elizabeth's chin and carefully turned her face so he could examine the other side. There he saw a more prominent mark, red, mottled and darkening to blue, that extended from just below her cheekbone up past her temple. He brushed her curls aside to see that much of the mark was hidden beneath her hair . After having ridden so far on nothing more than a horse blanket tossed over a number of metal carriage tools, she must be bruised all over, but this—he could see that she had been struck, likely more than once. His stomach churned with acid, and he fought not to allow the rage he felt rising to overtake him. Elizabeth needed him. There would be time for anger later.

"She moved when you touched her hand," Fitz reminded him.

Darcy lifted that hand, and Elizabeth grimaced. The movement was slight, nearly imperceptible, but it was there. He tried to push back the sleeve of her pelisse, but it was fitted too tightly. Given the tattered state of the rest of it, he did not hesitate to ask Anders for a knife. The coachman held his out, but before Darcy could take it, Fitz had it and was carefully cutting the sleeve at the seam.

"You are not steady enough," he murmured.

When Fitz was done, he shifted his attention to the rope while Darcy separated the wool and gently rolled up the sleeve of Elizabeth's walking dress. The glove was pushed down to her wrist and her forearm was swollen and discolored. Very carefully, he ran his hand along the bone—it appeared to be sound. He gently laid her arm down again. As he did so, he noted that the palm of her glove was bloody, and he peeled it off, then examined and removed the second one. Her hands were abraded, but not badly. Fitz finished his work and lifted the rope away before checking Elizabeth's other arm.

"None of this would account for her remaining insensible," Darcy said, addressing his cousin. "Even with the blow to her face. Is there another injury to her head?"

"I do not think so," his cousin said. He lifted one of Elizabeth's eyelids. Darcy was nearly undone to see that brown eye dull and unfocused.

Fitz scowled. "She has been drugged. Probably laudanum. It would account for the shallow breathing and her inability to wake." He leaned over and sniffed, just as Darcy himself had with Anders. "In wine, I would guess. How long a ride is it from Hertfordshire?"

Darcy forced himself to look away from Elizabeth. "Three to four hours on horseback, depending on the roads. I was home in a little more than three."

His cousin nodded. "We cannot be certain of the dose, but typically she would wake after four or five hours. She is rather slight, so we may have some time to wait." He met Darcy's gaze, and Darcy knew he was asking how they were to proceed. "Shall we call the magistrate?"

Darcy shook his head. "And say what? That Anders found her in the boot of my carriage? Fitz, she and I had a disagreement at the ball, but it would not take long to prove that I arrived here and was seen in public long before my coach arrived. It would barely touch me. Miss Elizabeth's reputation, however, would be destroyed, along with those of her sisters. And Anders would surely be accused in the matter, whether people believed he was working on orders from me or not." He motioned to his coachman. "Between the color of his skin and his father being an American, you know he would not fare well in court." He glanced at the coachman. "I do not mean to offend, Anders."

"There is no offense in the truth, sir," Anders replied stoically.

Fitz nodded. "So she remains?"

"Until we can find a way to resolve this, yes." Darcy wondered how precisely they would be able to do that. His mind began to churn with other questions, too. Had Bingley done this? Had her attackers meant to kill her? Was the threat of the sheep farm not enough to keep Miss Bingley from telling her lies?

"Sir," Slipworth said in a hushed tone, breaking into his thoughts. "If you are to keep her here, we must remove her somewhere more private."

Darcy was surprised that his fastidious valet would even consider hiding an injured woman in Darcy House, let alone participate, but he let that pass. Slipworth's loyalty would override any qualms he might have. And Slipworth was right. They *should* move her, and quickly. Less chance of detection and less painful for Elizabeth to be moved while she was still insensate.

Anders stood. "Sirs." They all gave the coachman their attention. "It is best if I do not hear any more. The fewer who know the young lady's location, the better off she shall be, I think." Darcy nodded once. Anders continued, "I am not generally in the house and therefore cannot assist more than I have without raising suspicion. I shall keep my wits about me outside. Perhaps whoever has done this will be paying you a visit?"

"No doubt with a magistrate," Fitz mumbled uncomfortably.

Darcy rubbed the back of his neck. "Or some sort of extortion scheme." He looked at Anders.

"I would be willing to contact my family, sir, should you have need of them," Anders said, steadier now.

Darcy sighed. Anders had a large family, most of whom lived in and around Lambeth—tradesmen, mostly. Military, both active and retired. A musician. An artist. Anders was the only one in service, and only because he had a love for fine horses and carriages but not the money to acquire or maintain them himself. His family had, on occasion, offered various services to Darcy House when Anders requested it. "I hate to impose, Anders," he said, "but I thank you. We may have need of help before this is through." He gave Anders a nod. "Right," he said seriously, "off you go."

"Thank you, Mr. Darcy," Anders said, the words heavy with meaning. He bent his head in an abbreviated bow and was gone.

"Where do you plan to hide her?" Fitz asked when Anders had closed the door. "This is not Pemberley. You do not have dozens of rooms in which to secret an invalid, and we dare not involve your housekeeper or a maid in such a scheme."

Notwithstanding his position as master, Darcy knew Mrs. Spencer would have his head on a pike for bringing trouble to the house. He did not fear the housekeeper, but neither could he be sure she would willingly assist them—and he would not have caring for Elizabeth made any more complicated.

"No, we shall have to see to her ourselves," Darcy said seriously. He did not miss the scandalized expression on Slipworth's face or the grim one on Fitz's. "We cannot afford to draw any attention to this house. Word cannot be allowed to get out. We cannot even call for a doctor or a surgeon."

He saw that they understood, but he had one more thing to say. "Miss Elizabeth is a gentlewoman. I admire and respect her. Whatever this is about, she is an innocent and I suspect has been injured in a base attempt to malign me. I must do what I can to keep this quiet not only for Anders and Slipworth, but for her."

"She will never be able to return home," Fitz said—rather unnecessarily, Darcy thought.

"We shall concern ourselves with that later," he replied. "For now, it is enough that she is safe." He released a heavy sigh. "We will hide her off the study. Clear the hall for me, Fitz?"

Fitz's expression was pinched, but he nodded. Darcy was sure his cousin remembered the room he meant to use. "Of course."

"Slipworth," Darcy said, "you will need to distract Mr. Pratt. Tell him I require a report on . . ." His mind was a blank.

"Yes, sir," Slipworth replied quietly. "I shall ask him to inventory the liquor, as the colonel is in residence."

Fitz sputtered a protest, but Darcy offered his valet a nod and his thanks.

Slipworth was surprised by the thanks, his eyebrows lifted nearly to his receding hairline, but he did not respond other than to ask, "Now, sir?"

Darcy and Fitz lifted Elizabeth from the floor and adjusted her in Darcy's arms. He cradled her limp form tenderly. "Now."

❦

Darcy stepped into the room with Elizabeth in his arms. The door swung closed behind him, and he waited for his eyes to adjust to the dark. The shutters on the windows were closed tightly, and he dared not open them now. Instead, he moved towards the small bed he knew was in the far corner.

He felt Fitz maneuver around him and pull the blankets back, shaking them a bit. Darcy assumed they were dusty. He had not opened this room for many years. As he slowly kneeled to lay Elizabeth down on the bed, he was surprised to see that she fit upon it, though her legs were slightly bent.

"You were tall even then," Fitz remarked.

Darcy pulled the blankets over Elizabeth's inert form and tucked them around her. Then he moved to the hearth. It was on the opposite side of the wall from the fireplace in his study.

"There are no coals here," he said, ignoring his cousin's statement. "I shall fetch them from the other room."

"You should have someone start the fire in your study first," Fitz said. "It is probable no one will notice, but if there is smoke from the chimney but no fire in your . . ."

"Yes," Darcy replied abruptly. Grateful that he had the chimneys cleaned and repaired every summer, he stood and pushed against the wall. It was heavy but swung open to reveal both his study and his stunned valet, who was standing near the desk.

Darcy glanced back to be sure the bookshelf was in place. "Slipworth," he ordered, "go find a maid to make up my fire. Have someone bring up a new basket of coal."

Slipworth blinked. "Yes, sir," he responded.

Darcy watched his normally imperturbable valet open the door to the hall and trip slightly over the threshold, nearly tumbling into the stern woman on the other side. Without changing his expression in any way, Darcy released an irritated sigh.

"Mrs. Spencer," he said flatly, and waited for the woman to speak. She did not. She allowed her eyes to roam the room and then fix upon him.

"We shall have a proper meal for you tonight, Mr. Darcy," she said at last. "Do you wish to open the dining room?"

Darcy frowned. "No, I think not." He paused. "Tell Mr. Pratt to leave the knocker down as well. Colonel Fitzwilliam and I will be engaged in a great deal of business for the next few weeks, and I will not open such a large room for the two of us. We will take our evening meals here unless I send word otherwise."

The housekeeper studied Darcy with an unwavering gaze. "Very good, sir." She stepped back and disappeared down the hall.

Darcy stood alone in the room. Twenty-four hours ago, he had been alternately dreading and anticipating the ball at Netherfield, his concerns focused almost entirely upon whether or not to solicit Miss Elizabeth Bennet's hand for a dance.

That world was gone.

Elizabeth Bennet and his cousin were hidden not ten feet behind him in a room that, to his knowledge, had not been opened since he was a boy. Charles Bingley was a scoundrel, Elizabeth was a victim, and he must determine how to save her reputation as well as his own, all while keeping his staff—Anders in particular—clear of any suspicion.

He had allowed himself to become distracted by Elizabeth, and what had it achieved? He had nearly been caught in Bingley's trap, only to fall neatly into a scandal with the potential to rock London to its core. A Darcy scion smuggling an injured, gently bred young woman into his home? Good God, Georgiana's thwarted elopement would be *nothing* to this. He stifled a groan. Five *years* it had taken to establish himself as his own man, an honorable man, and it could be gone in an instant. He did not even know why.

One of the maids entered, dragging a large basket of coal. With a hasty curtsy, she set to her work and started the fire. When she was finished, Darcy locked the door behind her. He opened a drawer where the candles were kept and removed a few, setting them atop the pile of coal. Then he pressed a spot in the back of the bookshelf, the one directly behind his head when he sat at the desk. The door released, though it remained only slightly ajar. He took up the basket of coal in one hand and pulled open the door with the other, careful not to dislodge the books as he stepped through.

Fitz was sitting about as far from Elizabeth as was possible in the little room, and Darcy clapped him on the shoulder. "She does not bite." He dropped the basket near the hearth. "Will you fetch me the water pitcher from the study?"

His cousin was there and back very quickly. Darcy asked for his handkerchief and Fitz passed it over. Darcy carefully cleaned the palms of Elizabeth's hands. The wounds were superficial, so he did not bind them.

Fitz shifted his weight from one foot to another. "It feels deucedly awkward to be alone in here with her."

"Are you afraid I will insist you marry her?" Darcy asked lightly, reaching out to clap his cousin's shoulder.

Fitz's teeth gleamed in the darkness of the room. "She is a comely little thing, and her father will be eager to dispose of her well, I think. Perhaps he has a fortune with which to persuade me?"

Darcy unconsciously gripped his cousin's arm. Hard.

"Release me, you pathetic oaf." Fitz knocked his hand away. "I am no widgeon. I saw your face when you thought she was dead, and then you nearly took my head off over it. This is no cream pot love, but if she were eligible, you would not have left her in Hertfordshire, no matter how quickly you were forced to depart. Not without at least speaking to her father." He crossed his arms over his chest.

"How do you know I am not a molly?" Darcy asked quietly. "I know there are whispers."

Fitz's sharp laugh was disbelieving. "Because I know *you*. Not only do you clearly have feelings for Miss Bennet, I saw you fall in love with Rebecca Braggs the summer after you turned sixteen."

It felt a very long time ago. "Father told me I was in no way ready to wed, and I would not approach a gentlewoman, that being the case. He took me to . . . "

His cousin grinned. "I know. Father took me, too."

"I did not like it, Fitz. Not the . . ." Darcy's face warmed. "*That* I liked very well. But in the end, it was not what I had hoped. It was business for the girl, that was all. I felt badly for her, and I admit, badly for me. I could not help but feel I was missing something important."

"You are a romantic. Always have been," Fitz replied.

Darcy did not believe that to be true. He simply had never had the *time* for women. He refused to follow Wickham's lead at university and he would not risk disease or father a child he could not claim. His father had died only weeks after he graduated from Cambridge. There had been no time to dally in London or enjoy a grand tour. He had simply thrown all of his energy into fencing, shooting, riding, caring for Georgiana, and maintaining the family interests.

He did not bother to reply, and his cousin did not press him. "No," Fitz continued, "I would be less surprised if Henry were."

"He sees a widow when he is at Matlock," Darcy replied, shaking his head. "Henry simply enjoys fooling people."

"To what end?" mused Fitz before sighing and changing the subject. "Let us return to the issue at hand. Miss Bennet."

Darcy's cheeks warmed, and he stooped to heap the coals in the fire. Fitz pushed him away and lit the fire himself.

"Well?" Fitz asked with all the subtlety of a military interrogation. "The girl has been ruined, we presume because someone noted your interest or wished you ill. What do you plan to do with her?" The coals began to glow, and Darcy wordlessly lit the candles.

"I wish to God I knew," he whispered. "I never thought anyone would discover that I . . . Miss Elizabeth herself had no idea."

Darcy saw that the latter statement surprised his cousin. He carried the candles to a small table near the bed. Elizabeth had not moved, but something caught the flickering light and glistened on her cheeks. He bent over her.

They were tears. She was weeping.

Devil take it. Why did she not simply rip his heart from his chest and toss it under a moving carriage? It could not possibly hurt more.

"Miss Elizabeth?" he murmured.

She did not move. He sat on the edge of the little bed. "We need to do something for her arm," he said. "The bone feels intact, but there is certainly an injury."

Fitz nodded. "Could be a fracture. We should splint it."

"You are a surgeon now?" Darcy asked wryly.

"I am a soldier, cousin," Fitz replied smugly. "There is no end to my talents. You have used my handkerchief already. Have you one of your sister's monstrous cloths on your person?"

Darcy disapproved of his cousin's flippant remark. "Georgiana requires a canvas for her embroidery, and she knows I will not laugh at her."

"Why must she make them so large?"

At this even Darcy had to smile. He offered the explanation his sister had given to him. "Because it offers more room for her attempts.

Why ruin ten handkerchiefs when you can ruin one?" Georgiana was a wonderful musician and a gifted linguist. She even enjoyed painting. But she had little patience for sewing and embroidery. He missed her gentle humor.

"She may as well call it a tablecloth and be done with it." Fitz pointed at the old log leaning up against the hearth and Darcy held out his hand for Anders's knife. Fitz fished it out of his pocket and turned it over in his hand. "I rather like this knife," Fitz told him, as he passed it over. "I think I will keep it. Give Anders a replacement."

"It was provided as part of the position." Darcy grumbled as he stripped four long, thin pieces from the log. "Anders will appreciate a new one." He paused. "You have earned much more from me today."

"One more," Fitz said, waving at the log, and Darcy complied. "I will have earned far more than a knife by the time this is over, cousin. But I have never required payment from you, nor you from me."

Darcy nodded, too overcome to speak. He whittled the wood down so there were no sharp edges and then cut the handkerchief into strips. He gently raised Elizabeth to remove her pelisse, and then, with Fitz's direction and aid, arranged the splint over the sleeve of her dress so the wood would not rub against her skin. She moaned softly as he tied off the final knot.

His heart leapt. "Miss Elizabeth?" he asked hopefully.

Nothing.

Fitz cleared his throat. "It will take time, Darcy. Waking from laudanum is a bit like being underwater and pushing up towards the surface—and remember we do not know how much she was given."

There were no more handkerchiefs, so Darcy removed his cravat, folding it into a rectangle, dipping it in the cold water, and applying it to the worst injury on Elizabeth's face. "So now we wait," he said glumly, sitting uncomfortably on the floor beside the bed.

There was a scuffling sound as Fitz sat down near the doorway and leaned back against the wall. "Now we wait."

※

Elizabeth heard the voices in her dreams. Deep voices, speaking in a cadence that washed over her like a soft rain. Her fingertips grazed a soft mattress and scratchy wool blankets. It was warm. She sighed and straightened her legs, relieved that she could. She opened her eyes briefly, staring up at . . . the world was dark colors all run together, so she closed them again.

Someone took her hand. "Miss Elizabeth?"

She forced her eyes open again and tried to focus on the voice. It was an effort, but she managed it. "Where . . ." she asked, but it was garbled.

"You are safe," someone informed her.

Her left arm felt heavy. She tried to move it and gasped, a flash of pain waking her. Panicked, she attempted to sit, but there were hands pushing her down.

"No," she said, determined, twisting her shoulders to break free. "Do not touch me."

The hands fell away. "You are injured, Miss Elizabeth," the voice said. It was deep and very formal. "You must remain still."

She tucked her left arm to her stomach and used her right to push herself into a seated position. Her entire body ached, but her face and her arm were particularly painful. She took a deep breath and looked up when she heard a short but disapproving huff.

Mr. Darcy's cool gaze stared back at her.

He had left Hertfordshire, had he not? What was he doing here? She glanced down at herself—she wore her walking dress, and the discomfort around her ribs alerted her that her stays were intact. Her gloves and boots were gone though, as was her pelisse.

"Do be careful," Mr. Darcy said in the grave manner she had learned to expect from him. "You will aggravate your injuries."

Fear flared inside her, and an overpowering impulse to flee. She pulled her legs up to her chest and kicked. She felt the heels of her feet connect with Mr. Darcy's hip, and she rolled to a crouched position on the floor. She knew her strike was poorly aimed and could not have hurt him, but Mr. Darcy was surprised enough by the contact to fall from the bed. He sat where he had landed, watching her. Elizabeth felt the wall at her back, and she leaned against it as she stood. Her breath came too quickly, and she attempted to regulate it.

"What did you do to me?" she hissed. "Who were those men?"

Elizabeth slid away from Mr. Darcy, but there was nowhere to go. In the candlelight she spied a tray, the remainders of a meal still upon it.

Mr. Darcy stood and approached her cautiously. "I do not know who those men were. I was hoping you might tell me." He held out a hand, palm up. "Please, I will not harm you."

She squeezed her eyes shut, trying to quell the dizziness that washed over her. For the moment, her fear overrode her pain. "Stay away," she warned him, her good arm outstretched.

But Mr. Darcy, no doubt more used to giving orders than following them, took another step in her direction.

Elizabeth lunged for the tray and grabbed the first thing her hand landed upon—a plate. She hurled it at Mr. Darcy, who ducked to the left as it flew past. Bits of food showered him as the dish crashed to the floor. She grasped at the silverware and darted away from him, holding her prize out before her as she searched for the door. Where was it? A sob built in her throat as she passed the fireplace. Was there no door here at all? Was she a prisoner? She glanced down at her hand. She was brandishing a fork.

She stepped back, her eyes on Mr. Darcy, who observed her progress but had not moved to stop her. Had he always been so tall? She wondered why he was not moving to stop her, but not soon enough. She lifted her foot to take another step and ran into something hard.

In an instant, the fork was gone and there was a hand over her mouth. She thrashed wildly and tried to scream. She freed herself enough to sink her teeth into a finger.

"Hell and damnation!" she heard from behind her, and the hand clamped over her mouth again. Her heart sped up in a kind of desperate terror. Then Mr. Darcy was there, crouching before her. He gently placed his hands on either side of her face and peered intently into her eyes. She continued to struggle, but as his steady gaze continued, Elizabeth felt both her fright and her strength ebbing away. His hands were large, but they were gentle. A thin stream of brown gravy was dripping off the end of his nose, which made him less threatening. She calmed, slowly recalling the events in the Netherfield library. He had not been to blame. He was not the man she had believed him.

She sniffled.

"Please," Mr. Darcy said urgently, "you must not alert anyone to your presence. We are trying to keep you safe while we determine what is best to be done."

Had Mr. Darcy said as much before the ball, she would not have trusted him. Now she did. Though she remained anxious, she stopped struggling. Mr. Darcy's eyes bored into her, but they were calming, somehow.

"All right, Fitz," Mr. Darcy said, and the hand lifted away. Elizabeth twisted away until both men released her. She scurried out of their reach, back towards the bed.

"This is my cousin, Colonel Fitzwilliam," Mr. Darcy explained, waving a hand at a lanky figure she could not see well. Elizabeth shifted uncomfortably.

"I apologize for hurting you, Colonel," she said, annoyed at how shaky her words sounded.

The colonel scowled at Mr. Darcy. "You said she did not bite."

"I stand corrected," Mr. Darcy said drolly. Were they laughing at her?

"I might have stabbed you with the fork," Elizabeth retorted. "Surely that would have been worse."

The colonel grunted. "The fork would have been less sharp than your teeth, Miss Bennet."

Both her ire and her apprehension rose. "Then perhaps you ought not to have detained me." She turned her attention to Mr. Darcy. "Let me go," she begged. "Please, I want to go home."

Mr. Darcy's expression softened into something like tenderness and regret, and her stomach lurched. "Miss Elizabeth," he replied somberly, shaking his head. "I am afraid that at the current moment, that is impossible."

Chapter Four

Darcy picked up a napkin from the tray and wiped his face. A soggy bit of crust fell from his hair. Elizabeth muttered a few words of apology and bent awkwardly to collect the pieces of the plate she had thrown.

"Miss Elizabeth," he said immediately, "please leave that. You are still recovering from the laudanum. You ought to rest."

Her hand hovered over the broken china but then withdrew. "Is that what I was given?" She sat warily on the end of the bed.

Fitz finally took a few steps into the room. "We believe it was, yes," he said.

Even in all the commotion, they had managed not to upset the candles, and in their light Darcy could see that Elizabeth was not well. She cradled her splinted arm in her good one, and despite the cold compress he had held to her face, the bruise had swollen a little along her cheekbone. She lifted one shoulder uncomfortably, and he was reminded that she had ridden to London on a bed of metal tools. He tried to control his frustration. She must be in considerable pain. Why could she not just have listened to him and remained abed?

"I must apologize, Mr. Darcy," she said almost as though she could sense his thoughts. "I am not myself. I cannot tell if it is still daylight or what day it is at all. I left my home for a walk, was forced into a carriage by two men I have never met, and then I awoke . . . here."

Her distress was genuine, and Darcy's irritation dissipated. Elizabeth was still under the influence of the laudanum. She was not thinking clearly. It was not her fault. Indeed, the spirit she had shown in attempting an escape was rather remarkable.

Elizabeth had Fitz's attention. "These two men, Miss Bennet. Can you describe them?"

She closed her eyes. "Yes," she said resolutely. She explained their features. Darcy did not recognize either man.

He tried to recall any new acquaintances he had made at the ball, but he had declined Miss Bingley's repeated requests to join them in the receiving line, insisting that he was a guest, not a member of the family. It was difficult enough when his Aunt Matlock pressed him into service for her annual ball, and he owed Caroline Bingley nothing in terms of her arrangements. Thank heavens he had not given in; he would not wish his presence to corroborate any gossip about a closer connection between himself and the Bingley family. His typical reluctance to engage in social niceties had served him well there, but had it made Miss Bingley desperate? Had his determination to avoid Miss Bingley led to the compromise attempt or the attack on Elizabeth?

Fitz was staring at him, and he shook his head.

"If you are well enough," Fitz said, returning his attention to Elizabeth, "perhaps you might explain how you came to be in the boot of Darcy's carriage?"

Darcy nearly protested that Elizabeth ought to rest, but Fitz was correct. The sooner they had the information the better off they would all be, including Elizabeth.

She took a deep breath. "I . . ." She stopped. "I beg your pardon?"

Fitz began to repeat his statement.

"Perhaps," Darcy interceded, "you would just tell us what happened to you this morning, Miss Elizabeth. From the beginning." He motioned to her clothing. "You say you walked out, and you are indeed attired for a walk."

"Yes," she said slowly. "I could not sleep after our . . . conversation at the ball, Mr. Darcy."

Darcy gave her an encouraging nod.

"We had arrived home quite late and my family was still upstairs. I went out for a walk after the sun rose." She shivered and sniffled but continued. "I needed to think about the things you had said. I was not attending to my whereabouts and had nearly reached the edge of my father's lands. I turned back for home but my way was blocked by two men on horseback."

"Had you seen them before?" Darcy inquired.

She shook her head. "No, but the path they were on leads from Netherfield Park to Longbourn. I presumed they had attended the ball."

"They may have," Fitz said thoughtfully. "Or they may have pretended to be invited."

"They said they wished to call upon my father," Elizabeth said tiredly. "But it was far too early to call." She worried her bottom lip. "Do you suppose they meant to take me from the house?"

Darcy exchanged a glance with Fitz, whose expression was stony. It was possible, but it would have been difficult with such a large family still inside.

"Are there windows in your room, Miss Elizabeth?" Fitz asked.

She nodded. "One large window that faces the gardens in the back of the house."

Fitz lifted one shoulder. "They may have only wished to scout the premises and watch for an opportunity to take you, but if they were in a hurry, they might try it. After a ball, I would hazard a guess that everyone was sleeping late, and the servants were less likely to be upstairs..."

"Better to be taken away from the house, then. Had I been with my sisters..." Elizabeth closed her eyes. "At least no one else was hurt."

Fitz was silent, but his steady gaze meant that Elizabeth had impressed him. Darcy understood the feeling. "Do you recall anything else?" he asked.

She shook her head. "They forced me to drink, and one of them hit me, but I do not recall much more. It is all a bit hazy," she said.

"Did they say anything else to you, anything at all?" Darcy asked.

"One said he was pleasantly surprised to see me," she replied, her eyes haunted.

Darcy ran a hand over his face. Not enough that they had dosed her with laudanum, accosted her, torn her from her family. They had taunted her, too. His thoughts turned dark as he considered how to make them answer for it. Darcy meant to speak, to comfort her, he truly did—but the words would not come. What comfort did he have to offer?

Elizabeth rubbed the heel of her hand against her forehead. "May I inquire where I am now?"

"In a hidden room off my study," Darcy informed her.

Her eyebrows lifted. "In London?" She shook her head slightly. "No, of course it is London." She sagged, the strength that had propelled her to fight for her release entirely gone. "How long have I been

. . ." Her voice trailed off, and Darcy saw the moment she realized her predicament. A deep sadness shadowed her eyes and pierced his heart.

"Miss Elizabeth," he said soothingly, "I promise to explain everything, but perhaps you ought to rest a bit more first."

She squared her shoulders and raised her chin. "I do not believe I will rest until I know the worst of it, Mr. Darcy. If you would indulge me, I promise not to interrupt."

He explained how they had discovered her. At the end of his recital, she sat for a time. "How long?" she asked.

Darcy glanced at Fitz and pulled out his watch. "I do not know when you left your home this morning, Miss Elizabeth, but you have been sleeping a rather long time. It is nearly four."

"Could we not steal back into Hertfordshire?" she pleaded. "I could act as though I had taken a fall on my walk and could not make it back on my own." She was holding back tears, he suspected. "No one need ever know."

Fitz snorted from his place across the room. "Do not be ridiculous. You would expect us to leave you outdoors after dark?"

"I could wander home."

"And what then?" Fitz asked. "What would stop the men who attacked you from doing it again and succeeding this time?"

"Fitz," Darcy said warningly.

Elizabeth's brows pinched together. "Then . . . you might send me to my Aunt and Uncle Gardiner here in town. They are not expecting me, but they would not turn me away."

"You would draw these men to their home, Miss Bennet? Do they have children?"

"*Fitz*," Darcy said again.

Elizabeth was silent, and Fitz pressed on.

"There might even be spies watching my cousin's house to alert them should you step one foot outside, so they can proclaim to the world that Darcy is a debased seducer of gentlewomen."

"Enough!" Darcy said emphatically, rising to his feet.

Elizabeth closed her eyes and said, quite steadily, "I am sorry for Mr. Darcy, Colonel, but he has family and resources enough to protect him. I am not in such a fortunate position, nor is my family, and even you must see that none of this has been my doing. You are spending your anger upon me because you do not know where else to put it, and I must say that I do not appreciate it."

Fitz leaned his head back against the wall. "My apologies, Miss Bennet," he said gruffly. "Perhaps I have been too direct."

She waved him off. "My mother often behaves in this manner, sir. You are forgiven." Elizabeth focused on Darcy. "My family," she said plaintively. "My sisters . . ."

"Will be protected," Darcy assured her. "I give you my word."

He heard Fitz strangle a protest.

Darcy's promise seemed to placate Elizabeth. "Thank you, sir. I suppose," she said with a little sigh, "that is the best that can be accomplished."

He did not like the resignation in her response.

Elizabeth's head began to droop, but she recovered enough to push herself back and settle on the bed. Darcy helped her recline without straining her splinted arm and pulled the blankets up so she would be warm enough.

"I will say," she told him softly, "that I never thought I should be tucked into my bed by you, Mr. Darcy."

A hundred fantasies of Elizabeth he had shoved aside over the past months broke free to riot before his eyes. *She is not herself*, he told himself sternly. *She does not realize . . . Behave like a gentleman.* He stepped back.

Fitz waited until Darcy was finished, but then motioned angrily to the doorway. Darcy did not appreciate the summons, but he understood it. He glowered back at his cousin but followed his lead, stopping first to add a few more coals to the fire. As Fitz passed through the opening, Darcy turned his head to look at Miss Elizabeth.

She was staring at him.

"Thank you, Mr. Darcy," she said. She appeared miserable and fatigued.

He gave her a curt nod and stepped out of the room.

Darcy had no idea how he was going to get them all out of this—but he would, and Fitz would help. Elizabeth Bennet deserved to live a long, happy life, and he was going to be certain that she did.

Fitz stood in the middle of the study, his arms folded over his chest.

"What is it, Fitz?" Darcy asked impatiently. "You had better just say it. We need to devise a plan."

"What in the blazes do you think you are doing, telling Miss Bennet that you will save her family?" Fitz snapped. "We cannot make promises we do not know we can keep. The girl's life is already in ruins. Do not make it worse."

"It sounds as though you actually care what happens to her, though you attempt to hide it," Darcy retorted. "Where was that concern when you were in her company?"

Fitz shook his head. "You may not like it, but it is unfair to allow her to develop a friendship with you, to depend upon you, when you shall have to send her away. If I am unpleasant, she will not regret having to go."

Darcy sat heavily in the chair behind his desk. That was what the end must be, he knew. They could not save Elizabeth's reputation if she remained at Darcy House, but they could not ensure her safety were she to depart. As much as he did not wish it to be true, Miss Elizabeth had been absent from her family for an entire day and would soon be missing overnight. It was unlikely her family could hide that fact. His heart ached for her.

"Before we decide what to do with Miss Bennet," his cousin continued, "we need to discover who is behind her abduction. We must not give anyone an opportunity to connect you to her."

"Fitz," Darcy asked softly, "do you believe they were going to kill her?"

"I do not know," Fitz responded plainly, "but they did not care about her seeing their faces, and they forced laudanum upon her without any apparent concern for the dose. Whatever they had planned, it was not pleasant."

Darcy's frustration mounted. "What was their aim? Who benefits if Miss Elizabeth were to disappear or was killed and I am blamed for it? It cannot be over Pemberley. Georgiana would inherit and as angry with me as she is, I doubt she desires to see me hanged."

Fitz rolled his eyes. "It might be a gambit to wed her for the estate, but she is very well protected."

Now, Darcy thought guiltily.

Fitz rubbed the back of his neck. "Bingley is the obvious choice. He cannot be pleased you refused to wed his sister." He paused, thinking. "You say he is courting Miss Bennet's elder sister. Were the Bennets mired in a scandal it would certainly limit any competition for her hand or make the father willing to acquiesce to his offer. Is there a fortune involved?"

"Mrs. Bennet informed the entire neighborhood that Miss Bennet's eldest son would inherit the estate." Darcy's disdain rang loudly in his words. He could not help it—the woman was foolish and vulgar. "Still, would not a scandal frighten Bingley away more than draw him in?"

Fitz shrugged. "Bingley would gain the estate his father wanted without having to deplete his own fortune. His alliance with the family might mitigate the damage, or he could be willing to marry her and wait for the scandal to pass."

Darcy rubbed his eyes with one hand. "*If* Mrs. Bennet is correct. Apparently, there was an entailment, but the heir presumptive has died. If Mr. Bennet was the tenant in tail, he could pursue a common recovery. As he has not, he is likely not working with an entail but a strict settlement. In any case, an estate generally does not revert to the current family in residence, though there might be a remainder man named in the original document."

Fitz stared at him blankly.

"A contingency," Darcy explained. "Another man to inherit, even if he is not from the Bennet line. Eventually, it all depends on how it was written and what the will says."

"Does Bingley know that?" Fitz asked, moving to pour himself a glass of port.

Darcy lifted his shoulders. "He should. I tried to teach him. But I find that he was often not listening."

"I cannot imagine why," Fitz said sardonically, and took a sip of his drink. "He expected you would be his brother and do his schoolwork for him. Besides, you are fastidious in your work whereas Bingley tends to flit from one thing to another."

Darcy accepted a glass of his own port from his cousin. "I believe you just told me I am prone to delivering jobations."

Fitz met his gaze and lifted his eyebrows. Darcy thought he would deliver another jibe, but instead, Fitz asked, "Perhaps Bingley's sisters? I cannot imagine they are in favor of his suit."

Darcy pondered the notion. "Miss Bingley and Mrs. Hurst were not pleased, but I cannot see them engaging in this kind of behavior. They enjoyed the connection. They are not violent. In fact, they are more averse to scandal than Bingley himself."

"Miss Bingley nearly knocked you over in a bid to force an offer," Fitz reminded him.

"That is true, but you know, I would not have expected it of her." Darcy sipped his drink. "She would have *liked* to wed me for Pemberley—but I never had the sense that I was her only target." Miss Bingley was anxious to marry a man of the first circles, but until the ball he would not have thought her desperate. Perhaps his intimacy with her brother had led her to act as she had—she certainly had a level of access to him she did not have with many other men of his station. She had seen Elizabeth as a rival, no doubt thanks to his impertinent remark about her fine eyes. Then, to have Elizabeth witness her failed attempt at compromising him . . .

"I cannot eliminate her," he said begrudgingly. "Nor can I eliminate Bingley himself, of course." He recalled Sir William Lucas's thinly veiled hints at the ball. "Though I am not certain Miss Elizabeth's sister returns his regard, he has raised expectations."

"And you are no longer there to save him from an imprudent attachment," Fitz replied with a snort. "He is justly served."

Darcy wondered whether it was rather Miss Bennet who required saving but did not think of it for long. She had a father, and Mr. Bennet had been warned. Elizabeth's predicament required his complete attention.

Fitz opened a drawer in the desk to withdraw a piece of paper. He took up a pen and handed it to Darcy. "Write them down. Miss Caroline Bingley. Mr. Charles Bingley. What think you of Hurst?"

Darcy raised his eyebrows. "I think it would be too much effort for Hurst to be involved in anything that required him to leave his port. I cannot say as much for his wife."

Fitz shrugged. "Add them. We cannot rule them out."

Darcy did so. He was by virtue of his experience a suspicious man, but Fitz was ruthless. It was a dismal business, making a list of his former friends and acquaintances who might have reason to harm him through Elizabeth. They went through his more recent business dealings, adding another name to the list and discarding several more.

"Who else have you disappointed lately?" Fitz asked.

He snorted. "Must we list them all? It will take a great deal of time."

"Limit them to people who would have heard about Bingley's little ball."

Darcy rubbed his eyes. "That leaves out Crossley and Waring. They do not know Bingley, and the last I heard they were in Liverpool, trying to find investors for a shipping concern."

"Ah. You were not interested, I take it?"

He shook his head. "If they wish to squander their principal on leaky boats and shoddy merchandise, that is their business. They should not have counted on my participation before they had spoken with me."

His cousin nodded. "You would think that after you have turned away so many petitions they would know not to assume."

Darcy shrugged. "I have not relayed these stories to anyone but you. Perhaps the others have not, either."

Fitz pinched the bridge of his nose. "You are *too* discreet, cousin. Not all men deserve it." He gestured at the paper. "Write the names down, and we shall discuss each one."

Darcy did so. He stuck a line through Crossley and Waring. "Edgerton. He does not have the stomach for this sort of intrigue. Indeed, our business has concluded rather successfully for him." Another name eliminated. Fawkner, Howard, Masterman, Seymour, Webb. All were discussed and dismissed. "Wickham."

Fitz stood abruptly and began to pace. "Now there is one who never has a feather to fly with. It is highly suspicious he came to Hertfordshire when you had been there but a month, particularly after Ramsgate. He also knows you well. If anyone was going to discover your tendre for Miss Bennet . . ."

"Really, Fitz," Darcy protested. "I do not have a tendre for Miss Elizabeth. I admire and respect her, that is true, but you must stop allowing your imagination to conjure up an attachment of that sort."

His cousin's expression was skeptical. "Do not lie to me. Worse yet, do not lie to yourself."

Darcy tipped his head back against his chair and squeezed his eyes shut. "Her situation is such that I *cannot* have a tendre for her. If I did, I should have to act upon it." He opened his eyes, determined to maintain his composure.

His cousin scratched his ear and released a weary sigh. "Have it your way." He tapped the paper. "But whether you love her or only admire her, Wickham would not much care. Leave him on the list."

"Wickham has spoken with Miss Elizabeth, told her his lies. He was not at the ball, so as far as he knows, she still believes him. He would have no reason to harm her and there is no money in it for him."

"Unless he was hired by someone else," Fitz concluded.

Darcy conceded the point and added Wickham to the list. "That leaves us with five names," he said, setting the paper down. "Presuming there are not others out there who hold a grievance against me they have not yet voiced."

Fitz tipped his head to the side and pulled a face. "Have you offended anyone else lately?" he asked.

"Other than Miss Elizabeth? No, I cannot say I have."

"How did you manage to offend Miss Bennet?" Fitz poured himself a glass of port. "Besides running afoul of the sort of men who would attack and abduct her, of course. Oddly, once she had her wits about her, she did not seem to blame you for that."

"Not yet," Darcy grumbled. "She would at least have grounds in this case."

"Therein lies a story," Fitz said. "Let me hear it."

It took Darcy nearly an hour to tell the whole of his visit with Bingley, ending with the confrontations at the ball—first with Elizabeth and then with the Bingleys. Fitz found most of the story highly amusing, and he expressed his appreciation for Elizabeth rather more warmly than Darcy liked.

"When I rode away, she was standing in the window watching me," Darcy said at the end of his recital, his chest tight and his head aching. "I wanted nothing more than to go back for her like some fool out of one of Georgie's novels." He propped his elbows on his knees and dropped his head in his hands. "How have I made such a muddle of my life?"

Fitz was quiet for a moment. "You consider this attraction a muddle?"

"Of course," Darcy responded with a groan. "I am expected to make a very different sort of match. You know that."

"To increase the family's standing. Yes, I have heard it my entire life."

"Then you see the problem." Darcy ran a hand over his eyes.

"No," Fitz replied sharply. "I cannot say that I do. My mother might once have had high expectations, but she has waited many years for Henry to marry. She is growing quite concerned that none of us mean to wed at all."

Darcy sighed. "Henry does not wish to spend his allowance on anyone's clothing but his own. He will marry when he can no longer put it off. He may ask his widow." They would all marry eventually. "I have a duty. An obligation to my parents."

"Your parents are dead. And despite my father's insistence that he is the head of the family, he is not the head of yours."

Fitz was being purposefully obtuse. "You need not remind me of my place," Darcy replied, resigned. "I am well aware of what my honor requires."

His cousin frowned, then drank deeply from his glass. "Your choice of wife is not a matter of honor, you idiot." He studied Darcy for a moment. "You still believe that those around you are governed by the same set of rules you insist upon for yourself."

"And this is wrong?" Darcy asked, incredulous.

"No," Fitz replied. He set his glass down. "Just naïve. Most men carefully consider the appearance of honor, but do not attend to a demonstration of it. Their lives are all about pleasing themselves. No wonder you are continually disappointed in your friends."

"I am not a child, Fitz," Darcy grumbled. "I understand better than you know how dark men's hearts can be."

"But you always hope for better." His cousin chuckled. "And, like a child, you *are* rather fractious when tired."

Darcy was put off by Fitz's patronizing tone, but he could not deny he was exhausted. He stood and moved to the chaise by the fire. "Wake me if Miss Elizabeth needs anything." She was just on the other side of the wall. Close, yet impossibly out of reach.

"I will." There was a pause. "You *are* an honorable man, Darcy," Fitz said quietly.

Darcy removed his shoes and reclined on the chaise. The last thing he heard before he drifted into a deep sleep was Fitz adding, "Which is why you need me."

Chapter Five

Elizabeth woke herself with sneezing. She blinked rapidly until the room came into focus. *Oh.* London. Mr. Darcy's house.

She longed to have the shutters open but suspected he and his cousin would forbid it, and she was too sore to rise from the bed herself. Her arm was the worst by far, but her face was also painful. Her ribs, hip, and leg on the right side felt bruised and stiff. There truly was not a single part of her that did not ache. She longed for a hot bath and Jane's willow bark tea, but she knew that there would be none to be had here. The men could not allow anyone to know she was hiding within their walls.

"Good morning, Miss Bennet," she heard a man say. Not Mr. Darcy. Her sluggish brain identified the voice as belonging to Colonel Fitzwilliam. He was sitting as he had before, across the room and on the floor, his back against the wall, his knees drawn up to his chest, his arms folded atop them.

"Good morning, Colonel," she replied, but did not attempt to move.

"I hope you are feeling better this morning," he replied. It was the most civil thing he had said to her.

"I am well enough." *Well enough to lay in bed and wait for something to happen*, she thought darkly. She disliked being ill and positively despised being confined. "Might we open the shutters for some light?"

As she had feared, the colonel shook his head. "I am afraid we cannot make any changes. It might be noticed from the street outside. We do not know whether the house is being watched."

She heard a hard edge to his words. "May I assume you will be making an effort to discover this?"

He did not reply, but she thought she caught a glimpse of a smile.

She placed her good hand around the splint and discovered that exerting a little pressure on it helped ease the throbbing. She tried to move her fingers and was pleased when they obeyed. She was thinking about how hungry she was and deciding whether to ask for breakfast when she noticed that the colonel was watching her intently. It made her nervous.

"Where is Mr. Darcy?" she asked. Strange that she should wish for *his* company to make her more comfortable.

"Sleeping."

"I see." Her patience was wearing rather thin. Considering her plight, she had nothing to lose by being direct. "Is there something you wish to say, then? It might better achieve your purpose than that glare."

He was not offended by her impertinence, but neither was he pleased. "Forgive me, madam," he said stiffly, but did not move his eyes.

She sighed. "It is a family trait, then?"

This was rewarded with a slight tip of his head to one side. "I beg your pardon?"

"That stare," she told him. "Your cousin is forever staring at me to catalogue my many faults. Has he sent you here to continue his work?"

The colonel buried his face in his folded arms. "Idiot. Bird-witted idiot," she heard him say to his boots, and she flinched.

His cursing should not have startled her so. She was no swooning miss, though she had little enough experience in the company of men. Her entire life, she had been surrounded by women. She had not thought she would miss that until now.

Her solace was that she had spoken with Papa before retiring. He would keep Jane and her other sisters safe from Mr. Bingley and Mr. Wickham. And Mr. Darcy had promised to help.

What had Papa thought when he realized she was gone? Elizabeth hoped he had not believed she had run away. While she was aware of his faults, her father was an intelligent man. She prayed he would connect her disappearance to her story of witnessing a damaging scene at the ball. Could he devise an explanation that people would believe?

The door opened, revealing a tall, broad figure in the doorway. Elizabeth drank in the sunlight from the study and breathed in deeply, taking in the aroma of eggs and ginger cake. Her stomach rumbled, a loud sound in the quiet room.

"Pardon me," she said, embarrassed.

"You did not eat at all yesterday," the figure said as he stepped to the bed. Mr. Darcy gazed down at her from above. "Did you even break your fast before your walk?"

"I did not," she said. She pulled herself up to a sitting position, attempting not to grimace, and leaned back against her pillow. Mr. Darcy—stern, proud, arrogant Mr. Darcy—was carrying food to her like a footman. Even given their circumstances, she had never imagined such a thing. Had the world changed so completely?

His expression was faintly disapproving as he bent to place the tray over her lap. Perhaps the world was not so different after all.

There was a blue and white ramekin filled with shirred eggs, a dainty china plate with a thick slice of ginger cake set in the middle, and a cup of black tea, still hot. "Oh, this is lovely," she said gratefully. "Thank you, Mr. Darcy." She glanced up at him as she took up the fork. "Are you and the colonel not eating?"

"I have already partaken," Mr. Darcy said. "Fitz, there is food for you in the study." The colonel shoved himself to his feet and exited the room without a word.

Mr. Darcy stepped back but hovered awkwardly.

"If you brought a chair, you could sit and keep me company." Elizabeth meant to alleviate her host's uncertainty, and he nodded. He disappeared into the study for a moment and returned with two sturdy wooden chairs. They did not appear particularly comfortable, but they were light enough to be easily moved. He dropped one near where the colonel habitually rested, then drew the other up to her bed, just far enough away that they might converse comfortably.

"I must ask you, sir," she said as she dipped her fork into the eggs, "how is it you have a secret hideaway behind your books?" She slipped a bite into her mouth.

"It was originally a storage room of sorts." Mr. Darcy leaned forward a little. "I believe there were a mountain of trunks kept here when my grandmother was alive. She loved to remake her favorite gowns as the fashions changed. Any material or lace or other embellishments that might one day be useful were packed and left here. She did not like to clutter up her dressing room."

Elizabeth laughed merrily. "So she cluttered your grandfather's study instead?"

He chuckled and shook his head. "My grandfather, I believe, was more than pleased to allow it, given how much money she saved him by reusing items rather than insisting upon new. My own mother was not raised to be so thrifty."

"Did it shock your father," she asked lightly, "to be required to supply his wife with a new wardrobe every year?"

He glanced at her askance, and she nodded encouragingly in response. It was nice to hear a little about Mr. Darcy's family. It made him less intimidating.

"He loved my mother," Mr. Darcy informed her gravely. "Whatever he was able to offer for her comfort, he was pleased to provide."

"He sounds like an excellent husband. Was it a love match, then?" Elizabeth asked, taking a small bite of the ginger cake. Her hunger was such that it was difficult not to pick it up in her hand and stuff it into her mouth, but she refrained.

There was just enough light through the closed shutters to see Mr. Darcy's pensive expression. She noticed that his eyelashes were long and very dark.

"Eventually," he said, sounding rather far away. "My father was in love first, but he managed to persuade my mother that she ought to love him in return." He paused, interlacing his long fingers. "She was the daughter of an earl. He was the son of a gentleman. My father was a wealthy man in his own right and heir to a great estate, but he was untitled."

Elizabeth finished her eggs and reached for her tea. She kept one eye on Mr. Darcy as she sipped it. He was watching her, as he always did, but this time his eyes spoke of kindness.

"Is the tea to your liking?" he asked.

"Everything is very good, Mr. Darcy," she assured him.

Mr. Darcy observed as she ate the cake in small, proper bites, savoring the sharp sweetness on her tongue. When her appetite was at last satisfied, she placed the fork down.

Mr. Darcy blinked and then continued his story. "My grandfather Matlock was not wild for the match, but neither was he averse to it. He had arranged a marriage for Lady Catherine, my aunt, to a baronet, and I have no doubt my mother wished to outdo her elder sister. It took the better part of a year before she reconciled herself to the attentions of an untitled suitor."

"She had other admirers, I imagine," Elizabeth prompted him when he fell silent once more. Now that her stomach was satisfied, she could feel how her head ached and her throat tickled. She reached for her teacup.

"A few," he admitted. "My mother once told me that it was my father's constant heart that won her. She desired a title, but in the end, she was unwilling to sacrifice her happiness to gain one."

"A wise woman," Elizabeth said, finishing her tea and wishing her own mother might be as perceptive. "Is she still with you?" All of Meryton knew that Mr. Darcy had already come into his inheritance, so she did not inquire about his father.

"Sadly, no. She died when I was a boy."

Elizabeth began to feel something like real compassion for Mr. Darcy. "I am sorry to hear it," she said sincerely.

Mr. Darcy nodded, but said nothing more. Instead, when Elizabeth had returned her cup to its saucer, he stood. "May I take that, Miss Elizabeth?"

She thanked him, and as he disappeared through the door, Elizabeth determined that she rather liked this Mr. Darcy. He was quiet but attentive. Had he shown this side of himself to her when he first arrived in Hertfordshire, she might easily have lost her heart to him. It was a shame that he had revealed himself to her only when it was too late to do anything about it. Or perhaps her current situation had simply rendered her so far beneath his notice that he felt his kindnesses could not be mistaken for anything but pity.

Darcy swept out of the darkness of the hidden room into his study and blinked in the light. He sat with Fitz as his cousin finished enough food for two active men. When at last Fitz tossed his napkin over the tray, Darcy gathered the plates and unlocked the door. Pratt was waiting with a footman, who took the tray while Pratt handed him a note.

"For the colonel, sir," he said placidly.

Darcy took the note and closed the door, locking it behind him.

"Now that you have played the servant, what is our course of action, cousin?" Fitz asked. He had resettled near the fire, his boots on the ottoman, a toothpick hanging from his mouth.

Darcy dropped the note in Fitz's lap and waited as Fitz read it. "Has your man determined whether the house is being surveilled?"

"It does not appear to be," Fitz told him with a frown. "It makes no sense." Fitz did not like things that made no sense, and his dark expression confirmed his unease.

"Have you already sent a rider back along the route?" Darcy inquired.

His cousin nodded. "He was off at dawn." Fitz consulted his watch and sat for a moment, toying with it. "I know you will not like it," he said finally, without looking up, "but I shall have to reverse my position. Despite what I said to Miss Bennet, if no one is watching the house, we should move her now."

Darcy shook his head. "No."

"She mentioned having family in town. Surely she would be more . . ."

There was no need for his cousin to complete the thought, and Darcy interrupted it. "No."

"*Darcy*," Fitz said, exasperated. "It would be better for you and for her. If whoever took her does not know she made it to London, there is little danger."

The very notion made him angry. "Little danger? Miss Bingley and Mrs. Hurst knew of Miss Elizabeth's penchant for walks. They also know that Miss Elizabeth's family resides near Cheapside, and they would have no trouble discovering the exact direction from Mrs. Bennet. If any of the Bingleys are involved in this, they would have all the information they required." He folded his arms across his chest to keep himself under good regulation. "We have not yet identified the men who accosted her. Shall we fob her off on a tradesman and his wife who cannot possibly hope to protect her? Who might be harmed themselves if they take her in?" He moved to stand between his cousin and the fire. "These were your own arguments only yesterday! We do not yet know whether there are rumors, or if there are, how far they have traveled. Where would she go should these relations decide they cannot accept her? How would we even keep a journey to that part of town private?" Anders might not draw scrutiny there, but a carriage as fine as Darcy's would certainly invite notice. And how would they even remove her from the house? Did Fitz expect her to hide in another trunk? No.

Darcy placed a hand upon the mantle and eyed his boots, polished to a high shine. "You wish me to expel her from my home when I am the reason she has been injured?" He shook his head. "It will not do, Fitz."

"We do not know that for certain, and you would not be casting her out," Fitz protested levelly. "You would be protecting both her and yourself. We could continue to investigate without the additional burden of hiding a woman in your house. If you are concerned about her safety, we could take her to my mother."

"You believe your father would sanction that? Who would I have to marry to gain his agreement?"

Fitz shook his head. "It would not come to that. He thinks well of you. He might suggest, but he would not impose. And you know that even if he did, my mother would not allow it."

Darcy shook his head. "Henry is in town. Do you really think he would pass up the opportunity to gossip? And the servants? There are three times the number at Matlock House than there are here, at the least. Can you vouch for them all?"

Fitz only shrugged.

Darcy's heart contracted. He had not seen to Georgiana's safety as he ought to have. He would not make the same mistake with Elizabeth. "Please, Fitz. Her reputation is damaged beyond repair if we cannot keep this quiet."

"Is it not already?" Fitz asked. "Do not you think her absence has been noted? That her family is afraid for her? They ought to know she is safe."

"And they will," Darcy replied. "But Mr. Bennet knows what happened at the ball. He has likely come up with some excuse for Elizabeth's absence. I dare not send a third letter in two days to Longbourn. It would raise too many questions."

"You are being purposely thick, cousin," Fitz responded. "What of her family here in town?"

"We can send someone with an anonymous note to tell them she is well. I do not know these relatives, but the uncle is brother to Mrs. Bennet. If they knew she was here, they might rush directly over no matter what I said."

Fitz was skeptical.

"Just last night you told Miss Elizabeth that her family, including the children, would be in danger if we sent her there. Was that not the truth?" Darcy was frustrated. He could not deny that they *ought* to contact her family. It was the proper thing to do, though the rules of propriety did not cover discovering an insensate woman in the boot of one's carriage. But he knew, *he knew*, that Elizabeth had been hurt because of him. To allow her to be sent away where he would be unable to protect her . . . "She has no enemies. Her father barely stirs from his estate, so it is unlikely *he* has any. We must face the truth—I am the one who gives offense wherever I go. I am the one who has drawn this disaster to her." He tapped the mantle with a closed fist and wished they could take their argument to Gentleman Jack's. He was wild to hit something.

"Your honor must tell you . . ."

Darcy shook his head. "My honor is my own. It has never gone by the book, but rather by what I know to be right. And I cannot explain it, but this is the right course."

His cousin considered that, and then changed direction. "I must ask," he said, apparently unmoved by Darcy's confession. "Is it possible that Bingley has nothing to do with it? Might there be a scorned lover?"

Darcy found himself hauling his cousin up from his seat and holding him by the lapels of his coat.

"No, I take it." Fitz's words were laconic.

"No," Darcy said angrily. "I warn you, cousin. Do not insult her again."

Fitz was unmoved. "It was a reasonable question." He met Darcy's glare, unperturbed. "You are very quick to defend the honor of a woman you cannot admit you love."

"I will see her safe," Darcy said, releasing Fitz with a little shove.

The momentum forced Fitz to sit again on the settee, but he immediately bounced back up to his feet. "Shall we ask Miss Bennet her thoughts on the matter?" Fitz was at the bookcase before Darcy could even respond, but Darcy was hard on his cousin's heels as they entered the small room.

Elizabeth was sleeping. The light from the doorway spilled over her. She had propped herself up against her pillow and the wall, her splinted arm held carefully across her stomach. The bruise on her face was blue across her cheekbone. Beneath the discolored flesh, her complexion was flushed. It was not cold in the room, but neither was it hot. Darcy shoved Fitz aside, lowered himself to one knee beside the bed, and placed the back of his hand against her forehead. Another breach in propriety.

She did not stir at his touch. Her skin was warm. "And now she is ill," he nearly spat out as though the illness itself was what affronted him. "I will not send her out in the cold. Do not suggest it again."

"You make it impossible to help you, Darcy," Fitz said heatedly, losing a bit of his composure at last.

Fitz was correct, and Darcy knew it. It did not matter. "I must do what is right. I will not be able to live with myself if I do not."

"Very well," Fitz said, more formally than his wont. "Have you considered whether or not your *sister* can live with it?"

Darcy gripped the edge of the bed. "I cannot believe you would . . ." He pushed himself suddenly to his feet but stopped. He tugged furiously at the hem of his waistcoat while he regained his self-control. "Your mother has Georgiana well in hand. Should I be disgraced in this, I have no doubt she and the earl will help my sister weather the scandal." It was not as though Georgiana desired his company.

His cousin frowned and continued to pry. "I simply want you to think this through. You have not been your usual clever self since Miss Bennet arrived." He smoothed his waistcoat back into its proper place. "You have always been so careful to avoid any hint of impropriety. Yet you would sacrifice your reputation for Miss Bennet though you know it will not save hers?"

Yes. "Miss Elizabeth interfered to save me from an entanglement to Caroline Bingley. What kind of man would I be to turn from her when she required my assistance?"

"Do not hand me that bag of moonshine, Darcy," Fitz replied, exasperated. "Of course you should assist her. It is the *manner* of that assistance that has me concerned. You will not marry her? Very well. But there is no need to throw yourself upon your sword." The fire of his cousin's temper had subsided, but he strode back out into the study.

"Where are you going?" Darcy asked, surprised.

"There are things to be done, cousin. I will return before dinner. Take care of the lady," Fitz said.

"Fitz . . . " was all Darcy managed to say before his cousin was gone.

"Blast," someone said from above her. Elizabeth opened her eyes.

"Mr. Darcy?" she asked, confused, and the man flushed a very deep red.

"Miss Elizabeth," Mr. Darcy said, shifting uncomfortably from one foot to another. "Might I have the name of your uncle here in town?"

"Are you to send for him?" she asked, pleased but weary. "His name is Edward Gardiner," she replied. "He owns several warehouses—Gardiner's Trading Company, best known for fine fabrics. He and my aunt reside in Gracechurch Street."

Elizabeth had been dreaming about bitter wine and pale blue eyes before she had been awakened, and despite the subject, she rather wished she was dreaming still. Everything ached, including her head, and she felt hot. She kicked feebly at her blanket to remove it but succeeded only in freeing one foot.

Mr. Darcy nodded, then stepped forward to gently take the corner of the covering and tuck it back around her. Of course he did. She could not even remove a blanket without him disagreeing. Then she remembered that he had recently been very good to her. She really had to stop believing that everything he did was meant to be contrary. She rubbed a cheek against her shoulder. Oh, but it was warm.

"I am hot, Mr. Darcy," she complained. "May I not remove the quilt?"

He stared at her. "You are ill, madam," he said quite formally, and she wondered what had happened to "Miss Elizabeth."

"Yes, I *am* ill," she confirmed. She could feel it, after all, and it was not as though Mr. Darcy would allow her to deny it. "I am also too warm. I should like to remove the quilt, please."

A crease appeared on Mr. Darcy's forehead. His hand reached out to the blanket but then dropped to his side. She could see he had been perplexed by her request, both wishing to comply and feeling it might harm her. Had she not felt so wretched, Elizabeth might have laughed. The imposing Mr. Darcy, undone by so simple an appeal. It was rather endearing.

Perhaps he would do better were he given something to do.

"Willow bark tea," she informed him, and was annoyed by how hoarse the words sounded. "Would you request some for me, sir? You can tell your housekeeper that you have a headache." She forced a small smile. "You need not inform her who is causing it."

He bowed and walked away. The moment he closed the door behind him, Elizabeth kicked off her blanket.

This was all so infuriating. She was never injured or ill, and to be both just when she most required her strength was unbearable. She struggled to pull herself up a bit more. Exhausted by her efforts, she glanced around the chamber. Her eyes had become accustomed to the dark, so that even with only a few candles, she could make most of it out.

The room was large enough for the bed, the chairs, and the hearth. The wall directly opposite her would accommodate a desk and bookshelf, but not much else. It was fortunate that Mr. Darcy had a warm, dry room to conveniently hide her away, but could he not have chosen one with a little sunlight? Although perhaps it would only make her headache worse.

She *was* being terribly ungrateful. Mr. Darcy was making every effort to see to her comfort. Jane would be disappointed in her.

Gooseflesh rose on her arms. With an impatient huff, Elizabeth used her foot to pull the quilt back up to her good hand, and she maneuvered it over her legs. Before Mr. Darcy returned with the tea, she was already falling asleep, shivering and burning in equal measure.

Chapter Six

Elizabeth was flying through the air and then sliding towards a cliff. In vain, she tried to gain a foothold as the edge grew ever closer . . . Her fingers dug into the earth, seeking a way to slow her descent.

Her eyes opened to see the light of day bright around the edges of the shutters. She tried to still her pounding heart and coughed. Another day gone. She was still on the little bed in the corner of the room. She struggled to sit up.

A female voice came to her in the dark. "Are you awake, Miss?"

Elizabeth froze. Slowly, she turned her head and saw an elderly woman sitting nearby. She could just see that her visitor's hair was a dark gray and her face was lined and thin. When she stood, the keys on her chatelaine jingled.

"I am Mrs. Spencer," she announced.

Mr. Darcy had not prepared her to meet the housekeeper, but he must have thought it important. Elizabeth wished he had remained to introduce them.

"I am Miss Elizabeth Bennet," she said directly, and cleared her throat. "I presume Mr. Darcy and Colonel Fitzwilliam have explained why I am here?"

Mrs. Spencer tipped her head to one side. "They did not."

"Oh." Elizabeth felt a stirring of panic. How did Mrs. Spencer know she was here if Mr. Darcy or the colonel had not told her? Why had they not told her? Was this woman not to be trusted?

"I can see you are anxious," Mrs. Spencer said flatly. "You need not be. I am loyal to the Darcys." She approached the little table next to the bed. "I brought you more willow bark tea." She carried the teapot to the fire, where she lifted a kettle out. A thin tendril of steam escaped from the spout. "I thought you might be in need of it." She completed steeping the tea and spooned a little honey into the cup.

Elizabeth took it and lifted the cup to her lips. The honey could not entirely mask the terrible taste, but she was grateful for the tea's soothing heat on her parched throat.

"Thank you, Mrs. Spencer," she said appreciatively. She glanced around the room. "Is there . . . Might I . . ."

Mrs. Spencer seemed to know what Elizabeth was asking. She glanced around and found the chamber pot, assisting Elizabeth before helping her back into bed.

"What was it," Elizabeth asked, "that gave us away?"

Mrs. Spencer shook her head and clucked disapprovingly. "Several things. Mr. Darcy was suddenly quite interested in willow bark. The man would no more know what willow bark is than he would understand how to care for an infant."

Elizabeth laughed quietly. "Is he never ill?"

"Not often, Miss. Mind you, he has been given willow bark tea before, but he would not know the name of it if asked."

Curious, Elizabeth asked, "Was that the only thing you noticed?"

"Oh, they are not nearly as smooth as they would like to believe," the housekeeper told her slyly. "They took their meals here, and Mr. Darcy even slept in his study, near the fire. The colonel asked me not to wake the master, said they were deeply involved in business matters and he needed the rest. As if he would not rest easier in his own bed." She shook her head. "When Mr. Slipworth did not object to the master sleeping in his clothes, I knew something was amiss."

Elizabeth finished her drink and handed the cup back to Mrs. Spencer. The woman stood to pour another cup.

"You should have at least one more," she commanded as she poured. "I cannot imagine you are feeling comfortable."

Elizabeth agreed.

"There now," Mrs. Spencer said, handing her the tea and patting her leg. "You just drink that down." She hesitated, one hand still resting lightly on the bed. "Miss, I mean nothing untoward, but I do hope you might assure me that you are . . . well?"

Elizabeth paused with the teacup halfway to her mouth. She understood the housekeeper's concern and was grateful for it. "Mr. Darcy and the colonel have acted with honor. As have I."

The housekeeper appeared relieved. She nodded her head once, as though her world had fallen neatly back into place. "Well, I knew that, of course," she replied, her cheeks flushing. "The master is the best man I know. It was my duty as a Christian to inquire, is all."

Elizabeth set down her teacup just as the doorway opened and Mr. Darcy stepped inside. "Mrs. Spencer," he said, sounding both astonished and frustrated. "What do you do here?"

Any uncertainty Elizabeth had witnessed in Mrs. Spencer vanished. "I am sitting with this poor creature, Mr. Darcy." She peered up at her master, her eyes narrowing.

Mr. Darcy scowled, but he did not reply. When the housekeeper raised her eyebrows without flinching, he shifted his feet. Apparently he had lost some unspoken argument. Elizabeth was pleasantly diverted.

Mrs. Spencer took in Mr. Darcy's petulant expression and cleared her throat. "You might have spared yourself and the young lady a great deal of trouble had you simply come to me, sir. I am surprised, I must say, that you did not."

Mr. Darcy sighed, a deep, unhappy sound. "I did not wish to involve anyone who did not already know. I . . ." He closed his eyes. "I have been rather at a loss since this began."

"I presume there was a falling out with Mr. Bingley," the housekeeper said, and Mr. Darcy lifted his eyebrows at the direct address. "I would not be so candid, sir, but you have brought a young woman into this house. When you did so, she became my responsibility." She paused. "Are the two events related?"

"Yes, there was a parting between Mr. Bingley and myself," Mr. Darcy replied heavily. "And I believe the reason this young lady is here has to do with it. She stood against the Bingleys on my behalf."

"And you believe yourself now bound to see to every detail of her recovery?" Mrs. Spencer asked. "Forgive me, sir, but you are no longer a ten-year-old boy and she is not a wounded bird you discovered in the park."

Mr. Darcy grimaced. "I dared Wickham to throw that rock. It was my fault."

"You made yourself ill taking care of it."

"Yes, well." Mr. Darcy chuckled uneasily. "One must always do what is right."

Elizabeth closed her eyes. It felt wrong, somehow, to observe Mr. Darcy when he was so vulnerable. She could not close her ears, though.

"Surely Miss Bennet would have been more comfortable with a woman to attend her," Mrs. Spencer said, somewhat more gently.

"Of course," Mr. Darcy said contritely. "But I could not . . ." Mr. Darcy did not finish his statement, and Elizabeth wondered what he had been about to say.

There was silence for a long moment, but then Mrs. Spencer spoke. "Now that Miss Bennet is somewhat improved, we ought to move her to a better room while the staff is on their half-day."

Elizabeth opened her eyes.

Mr. Darcy's attention fixed upon her, and his face lit up in a bright smile. Elizabeth's heart fluttered. *Such a smile!* Then she pondered Mrs. Spencer's comment. *Now that I am improved?* She lifted a hand to her cheek. Her head no longer ached, and the bruise on her face was only painful if she touched it. Even her left arm did not throb quite so much. When she gazed at it, she thought the swelling had eased rather significantly. Although she was still very tired and sore, she was indeed feeling a good deal better.

While she was thinking, Mr. Darcy had continued speaking with Mrs. Spencer. "They are all on half-day at once?"

"Yes sir," the housekeeper said dourly. "When the family is not at home, I find it useful to have most of the staff take their time on Sunday. They attend services in the morning regardless, and then most of them like to visit their families. We eat cold meals on Sunday and are at nearly full strength for the remainder of the week. Mr. Pratt and Cook will remain, of course." She cleared her throat. "It was your order that we not change our plans due to you being home earlier than expected."

Mr. Darcy nodded, glancing at Elizabeth again before returning his attention to Mrs. Spencer. "So it was. How do you propose to keep Miss Bennet's presence here private should we move her?"

"Yesterday we finished a thorough cleaning of the upper floors, sir. This week we shall be working on the first and second, including the study. If you and your guests keep to the upper floors of the house, there will be no intrusions. I will bring your meals myself, or Mr. Slipworth can come for them." Her expression was pensive. "How long will Miss Bennet be in residence?"

Mr. Darcy frowned at his housekeeper. "I am afraid I cannot answer that, Mrs. Spencer."

"I mention it only because we shall be at full staff in a fortnight, sir." Mrs. Spencer was respectful, but not intimidated. Elizabeth was impressed by her firmness.

"I will inform you when we know more." He sounded tired. "I thank you for your discretion, and I welcome your assistance."

She shook her head at him. "I may not have known *what* you were up to, Master Fitzwilliam, but I knew you were up to something. You and that cousin of yours."

He chuckled softly, and Elizabeth was struck by how happy it made her to hear it. "You always knew," he said to the older woman.

"I always *know*." Her eyes twinkled. "I shall await your orders, sir. The staff will be on their way out to services shortly." She raised an eyebrow. "I will not be away long."

"Thank you," Mr. Darcy said, and Elizabeth detected a hint of wry warmth in the sentiment.

Mrs. Spencer said nothing, merely nodded and retired from the room.

Elizabeth would never have guessed that Mr. Darcy could have such an exchange with a servant. She was pleased to watch each of her mistaken prejudices being so merrily overturned. She wished she could say as much to Jane.

Mr. Darcy turned to face her, and as he drew near, Elizabeth saw dark half-moons beneath his eyes and lines of strain on his brow. His clothing was slightly rumpled, and he had all this time been holding a basin with a small towel tossed over his arm. Why had she not noticed that before? It struck her then, something Mrs. Spencer had said.

"It is Sunday?" she asked. Her voice cracked, and she reached for her unfinished tea to hide her blush. "How have I lost track of the days?"

"You have been ill," Mr. Darcy said, his eyes boring into hers. "I was beginning to grow concerned."

Elizabeth knew instinctively that Mr. Darcy had *already* been concerned. She thought of the chamber pot hidden beneath the bed. Oh no, had he helped her with that? "Did you tend me yourself, Mr. Darcy?" she asked, feeling the heat of her blush spreading . . . everywhere. Vaguely she recalled being helped from bed and someone turning his back. But he must have removed the . . . *Oh, no.*

He observed her closely and set the basin down. "You are still unwell, Miss Elizabeth," he told her anxiously. "Here,"—he moved to aid her—"lie back against the pillows."

She had an answer to her question. Clearly, he had seen her in a dreadful state. She lifted her fingers to her hair. How wild she must appear! Her fingers trailed along the bodice of her dress. Except it was not her walking dress, but a nightgown. Had he changed her into it? She wished to pull the blanket up over her face and disappear.

He dipped the white cloth into the basin, squeezing out any excess water and placing it on her forehead. It felt cool and soothing. She allowed herself to calm.

"I admit that I have never taken on nursing anyone quite so intimately before," he told her, sounding abashed. "Even when my sister has been ill, she has her maids to attend her. My efforts usually amount to making a nuisance of myself by bothering the staff for news and reading to her when she is feeling better. I must apologize for my inept attempts at comfort."

She plucked at the nightgown. "Did you . . .?"

He drew in a deep breath and shot her a rueful look. "It was either me or my cousin." He hastened to add, "I did not remove your chemise."

That was hardly a comfort. Elizabeth's eyes widened, and she shivered. Mr. Darcy must have believed her cold, for he removed the cloth, then reached down to the foot of the bed and drew a heavier quilt over her.

She could not look at him. "You could not have asked Mrs. Spencer?" she asked mournfully.

Mr. Darcy sighed. "We did not wish to alert anyone to your presence, madam. Had I known Mrs. Spencer would discover us anyway, I would have left it to her, of course." Elizabeth peeked up at him in time to see him run a hand through his hair distractedly. "If it is of any consolation, it was dark, and I was concentrating on getting through the experience as quickly as possible."

Caught between a hysterical laugh and a sob, Elizabeth turned her face towards the wall. She was so very confused. Bad enough that both men were willing to curse with her not ten feet away, but Mr. Darcy had seen her . . .

"Miss Elizabeth," he said sympathetically. "Please, do not hide your face. You have done nothing wrong." When she reluctantly met his gaze, he pursed his lips. "It was my fault entirely, but I was far more anxious for your health than propriety. I beg your pardon for the insult to your sensibilities, but you were so ill." He had to catch his breath. "I could not trust anyone else to . . ." His words trailed off, and he rubbed a hand over his eyes.

The poor man was exhausted. Mr. Darcy had cared for her as her sister Jane might have, and without any help. Elizabeth's heart softened, and she determined she must forget her own embarrassment. What else could she do? "Mr. Darcy," she said slowly.

"Yes?" he whispered.

"I am well. Truly. You, however, look entirely done in. You should rest."

"You are not well, not yet . . ." He stopped to sit in the chair next to her. "I cannot tell you how sorry I am. It is my fault that you have been caught up in some sort of intrigue against me. In consequence, you have been hurt and fallen ill. You would never have had to suffer the indignity if not for . . ."

Elizabeth shook her head. It was not right he felt himself to blame. She was not a bird with a broken wing. A pain in her arm reminded her that it was, in fact, a rather apt comparison. "Mr. Darcy, it is not your fault I threw myself out of a moving carriage."

He blinked at her. "Pardon?"

She blinked back. "I jumped to get away. I dreamt it, but . . ." She paused. "I dreamt it, but it was not a dream—it was a memory."

Mr. Darcy leaned forward, abandoning their former conversation. "You could not have thrown yourself out of *my* carriage. Slipworth, my valet, was riding inside, and he does not match the description of either abductor."

"But how did I appear in the boot of your carriage?"

Mr. Darcy stroked his chin. "I cannot explain that."

"I always hid in trunks and cabinets when we played hide-and-go-seek," Elizabeth said fondly. "I was smaller than my sisters and took delight in fitting into spaces they could not." Mr. Darcy's gentle smile encouraged her to continue. "There was one in the attic that held some of my father's old clothes. They still smelled like him." She looked away. "It always felt safe to me."

"Are you *certain* it was not just a dream?" He sat down and his pensive expression suddenly cleared. "No, not a dream—this explains the bonnet."

"The bonnet?"

"Fitz sent a man to track your route. While you were ill, he told me that there was talk in Meryton about a rather fine bonnet being found along the carriage road just south of Meryton. Someone thought it might be yours." His eyes were grave. "It was located on the bank of the river, along the road to London. At the bottom of a twenty-foot drop."

She shook her head. "I recall leaping and sliding very close to the edge, but not how I lost my bonnet. Did I arrive without one?"

Mr. Darcy's face had paled, and she wondered whether he had contracted the same illness she suffered. He nodded. "You did."

She gasped. "My family! Do they believe I fell into the river?"

"I believe the gossip included that possibility, but your father has put the rumor to rest very neatly," Mr. Darcy assured her. "According to him, you were called to London to assist your aunt, and your youngest sister wished to go instead. In a fit of jealousy, she stole one of your favorite bonnets and threw it in the river. It must have washed up onto the bank a few miles away, he said." He paused before saying carefully, "Perhaps not everyone believes the story, but enough people know your sister to make it plausible. The more she denies it, the more they condemn her behavior."

Elizabeth did not feel sorry for Lydia. Papa had not prevaricated—her youngest sister had done that very thing last year, and Mama had taken Lydia's side.

When had they discovered her missing? If it had been a normal morning, Papa would have arisen before the rest of the family, she and Jane soon after. Mary would have been next to wake, sequestering herself with her books and not emerging until dinner. Given that Mama and her two youngest sisters had freely sampled the punch at the ball, Papa might have had several hours before Mama and the younger girls asked after her. Despite his reluctance to leave his books, her father had searched for her before when she was overdue. Surely he would have gone out to look for her again.

She suspected he would have written Uncle Gardiner at once, and together with Jane would have devised a plan to support the tale and maintain the family's reputation.

"My family," she said breathlessly. "Have you contacted them?"

Mr. Darcy nodded. "I sent a message to your uncle at his warehouse, explaining that you were safe, but that you could not return to them just yet. I did not tell them where you are or identify myself, because I was afraid to involve them until we knew more. I would expect your uncle sent a note to Longbourn, and I apologize if this is not enough."

Elizabeth was very sorry for the pain her family must feel, having to conceal their own fears for her safety in order to protect her reputation, but she was also enormously reassured. As long as her presence here was not revealed, her sisters would not be harmed. When this was over, she might even be able to return home. No, perhaps that was too much to ask. Too many questions might be asked. Suddenly, a wave of fatigue washed over her. "Clever Papa," she mumbled.

"There was even talk about a carriage leaving Longbourn that morning." Mr. Darcy groaned and covered his eyes with one hand. "Oh, I am insufferably dim!"

"Surely there can be no cause for such censure," Elizabeth told him with a quiet laugh. "It is my friend you speak of—I insist you be kind."

It was Mr. Darcy's turn to blush, and Elizabeth was charmed by his ruddy cheeks. He was so very handsome, and his steadfastness only served to make him more appealing. Despite his self-chastisement, Mr. Darcy was also quite clever, though in a different manner than her father. Abruptly, she turned her head away. She should not think about him in such a way. He had aided her when she most required it. She tucked the knowledge away. It would cheer her, one day, to remember his care for her.

"I thank you," Mr. Darcy said almost bashfully. He leaned forward. "Your father must have used the fact that *my* carriage stopped at Longbourn that morning to support his version of events, claiming it was your uncle's conveyance. It was only Anders, another coachman, and Slipworth, so I did not require them to wear their livery. With the family sleeping late, it is not surprising that no one recalls it clearly, and that is to our advantage." He tapped his fingers on his thigh in a distracted manner. "You said you were still on your father's lands when you were taken, and that you leapt from a carriage. Yet somehow you ended in mine." He shook his head, and Elizabeth heard him whisper, "A moving carriage."

High-handed, tender-hearted man. He was blaming himself for this as well. "Mr. Darcy," she said, stifling a yawn.

"Yes, Miss Elizabeth?" He opened his eyes. They were dark, expressive eyes, and she hated to see them so haunted.

"If you do not stop doing that, you will drive me to some drastic act."

"I do not understand you." His forehead creased, and she attempted not to chuckle at his befuddlement.

"You really must stop taking responsibility for the actions of other people," she scolded him firmly. "It is a little arrogant, sir, to think that you can claim fault for the decisions I have made."

"I am not arrogant," he protested. "In truth, I seem to have little pride left at all where you are concerned." Mr. Darcy shook his head grimly. When he glanced at her, though, she could see his lips twisting up.

"As it should be," she told him cheerfully. "Now, if I promise to rest, will you promise to go upstairs to your chamber and do the same? It is entirely self-serving, you know. I am afraid you will fall ill yourself and leave me to the mercy of your cousin and Mrs. Spencer."

"I shall, Miss Elizabeth," he said warmly. "Once we have you settled upstairs."

Miss Elizabeth. She enjoyed it when he said her name. She tipped her head to one side, and he held his hands up, palms out.

"Mrs. Spencer has already outwitted me today. I simply wish to be certain you sleep." He gave her a crooked grin. "Please, may I remain until then?"

She was quite tired, and he had asked politely. "Very well," she told him, and leaned back into the pillows. She said a little prayer for her quick-thinking father and was soon drifting away.

"Pleasant dreams," she heard Mr. Darcy say, but she was too far gone to reply.

It was a fortunate thing, Darcy thought with some exasperation, that most of the staff were from the house. Moving Elizabeth from the room off his study was not proceeding smoothly.

Elizabeth had insisted upon walking, rather than being carried. *Of course* she had. Infuriatingly obstinate woman! She simply would not admit that she had been ill and could not expect to have the strength to climb three flights of stairs. He watched as she took another step, pulling herself up as much with her one good arm as with her legs, then standing still and taking a breath. It was so excruciatingly slow he was certain his hair would be gray by the time they reached her new chambers.

Step, rest. Step, rest. Step . . . They were no more than halfway up the first flight. Elizabeth's head was bowed, and her breath came too quickly. Darcy glanced downstairs. He had sent his butler to the wine cellar, but how long would he be gone?

Elizabeth's hand tightened on the bannister, and she lifted her head. Darcy's impatience vanished when he saw the defeat in her expression.

"May I assist you?" he asked gently.

She offered him a smile—a pale imitation of the one he loved. "Please," she whispered.

He positioned his feet to support her weight and swept her up into his arms immediately.

As he reached the top of the second flight, his arms began to complain. As light as Elizabeth was, lighter still, Darcy thought, from her lack of appetite these past days, it was still no easy feat to carry another grown person up so many stairs.

He glanced up, spying Mrs. Spencer waiting for them on the landing. He shifted Elizabeth in his arms and then, intent on his goal, mounted the final flight, feeling his burden growing progressively heavier. He was nearly there, one foot on the landing, when his trailing foot caught the edge of the final step. Darcy lunged forward with one leg, then, still off-balance, spun around to keep them both upright. Elizabeth released a little squeal of surprise and her arms tightened around his neck as his elbow knocked into a table in the hall. He had watched, helpless, as his father's Qing Dynasty porcelain vase teetered, tipped, and plunged over the side. Only Mrs. Spencer's quick hands kept it from hitting the floor.

In the end, he found himself kneeling in the hall, still holding Elizabeth. "Are you well?" he asked quickly, hoping she had not been further injured by his clumsiness.

Miss Elizabeth had the good grace not to laugh aloud at him, but she was greatly tempted. He could tell by the way her eyes shone. Darcy swallowed, trying not to respond physically. Laughter, even at his expense, was preferable to the look in her eyes when she had reluctantly allowed him to carry her.

He set Elizabeth on her feet and stood up next to her, straightening his coat and pulling at his cuffs before leading her to the bedroom they had designated for her use.

Fitz was waiting there with his arms crossed over his chest. "What took you so long?" he asked peevishly.

Elizabeth worked valiantly to hold her laughter in, and Darcy glowered at his cousin. Fitz did not appear to notice.

"Thank you, gentlemen," Mrs. Spencer said with a pointed look at them both. "We will carry on from here."

Darcy hated leaving Elizabeth with Mrs. Spencer. He knew his housekeeper was in every way more qualified to see to Elizabeth's health and comfort. Still, it felt wrong to relinquish her to the care of another.

He rubbed the back of his neck. Every interaction with Elizabeth increased his danger. He needed to revisit the rules of propriety that so far had been disregarded. It was not wrong to leave Elizabeth to Mrs. Spencer's care, it was right. It was proper and prudent, yet it had never been so difficult to persuade himself to gentlemanly behavior.

He had been justified in his original decision to leave Netherfield after the ball, and after the events in the library, his departure from

Hertfordshire had been earlier than intended. But not even a day later, Elizabeth had been thrust back in his path. God help him, though he wished to erase the terrible ordeal Elizabeth had suffered, Darcy could not be sorry for her presence here with him.

Was it simply bad luck, or was it fate? He could not think about it too carefully, as Fitz was already hurrying him downstairs.

Fitzwilliam Darcy, master of Pemberley, did not believe in fate. He did not even believe in luck, good or bad. He believed that it was one's preparation for either opportunity or adversity that determined outcomes. But even as he continued to work through his jumbled thoughts, he had to admit that he had not been prepared for his life to be so thoroughly set on its end by Miss Elizabeth Bennet.

The morning after she had been moved to her delightful little bedchamber, Elizabeth awoke and sat up carefully. When she did not feel any dizziness, she slid her feet into a pair of silk slippers and donned the matching silk dressing gown, both of which had been left out for her. She padded across the floor cautiously—the slippers were too large, and the dressing gown too long—and sat in a beautifully embroidered wingchair near a large window. She sighed happily at the view of a rather bare garden in the back of the house and turned her face up to the late autumn sunlight. It was nothing short of glorious after having been cooped up in the dark little room off Mr. Darcy's study, no matter that she had slept much of the past several days away. She was feeling much better, despite the weakness that plagued her. The Darcy townhouse had so many stairs! There were yet two floors above this one, the top floor serving as servants' quarters, but Mrs. Spencer had locked the doors that led from the servants' stairs to the family floors. Elizabeth closed her eyes to revisit the feeling of being held safely in Mr. Darcy's arms. He had stumbled near the end, to her great amusement, but despite her initial protestations, she had been grateful for his help.

She dozed for a time in the chair. When she woke, Elizabeth opened and closed her left fist. It was painful, but improving, and she wondered whether the splint on her arm was still necessary. She should very much like to remove it. Then she walked around the room, fingering a few small porcelain figurines and examining the relief on the fireplace. "Fluted pilasters and Ionic capitals," she told the room, touching the cool, hard marble. "Very elegant." When she was finished, she stood in the middle of the room. There were no books here, not even a work basket. What was she supposed to do to pass the time? Mr. Darcy must have thought she would still be sleeping all day, but instead of being frustrated at his lack of foresight, she chuckled a little. He really was so intent on seeing her well. She would not be surprised had he purposely removed everything from the room so that she would sleep for want of any other employment. Sadly, she was not tired.

Elizabeth tiptoed over to the door. Pressing her ear to the wood, she listened for any activity, but it seemed she had been left on her own. *Excellent.*

The brass knob turned easily in her hand, so she pushed the door open just a crack and peered out into the hall. Nobody.

Perhaps she might just look at the room next door to see whether someone might have left something to read or to work on. Almost anything would do.

Elizabeth opened her door a bit wider and crept into the corridor. After several quick steps, she opened another door, and stepped inside.

It was a light and airy room, just a bit smaller than her bedchamber. There were two leather armchairs with a small round table between, settled in the center of the room upon a deep blue, patterned rug. Three of the walls were lined with mahogany bookshelves. One set of shelves displayed a collection of very colorful pottery—Spanish, perhaps—but the other two met at the corner of the space and were filled with books. Elizabeth was elated. Such a luxury of choice! The bookcases were tall rather than wide, in keeping with the proportions of the room, and there was a rolling ladder attached to the side of the bookshelf closest to the door.

After running her eyes along the shelves that she could reach, Elizabeth set two tomes on the little table and carefully pulled the ladder around the side of the shelf so she could see the books at the top. It was difficult to climb with only one good arm, but when she reached the upper shelves, she secured herself by wrapping the crook of her left arm around the rung, leaving her right hand free.

When she had found a history she wished to take back to her room, she had to consider the best way to transport it. She had only one good hand, and that would be required to steady herself on the ladder. Tossing it to the floor would make too much noise, and she did not want to damage the cover. She decided to set it on the next lower shelf, then climb down a few steps and repeat the process. She had the book in her hand and was about to move it when she heard a young female voice out in the hall, calling out to someone else. Her eyes moved instinctively to the door, which was slightly ajar.

Her mind whirled. She shoved the book back in its place and turned her head to gaze desperately around the room. The chairs, the table—there was nowhere to hide. She looked up to the top of the ladder and spied a small space between the top of the bookshelf and the ceiling. Could she fit?

"Sally!" The name was said urgently, and quite close.

In one swift move, Elizabeth had ascended the last rung of the ladder and wedged

herself into the gap. One of her slippers dangled precariously from her toes.

The voices were just outside the door now, and Elizabeth realized that the ladder was out of place. She reached out—not an easy thing to do as her good arm was positioned against the wall—and with one finger, guided the ladder back to its original position just as the two maids entered the room.

"We shouldn't be in 'ere," the first girl said anxiously. "Mrs. Spencer will toss us out."

"Oh, but the books are so lovely," her friend replied wistfully. "And I don't suppose Mr. Darcy will miss one or two, so long as I bring them back and don't hurt them. These are for the guests to read, not like the fancy books in the big library."

The *big* library? There was another library?

"You and your books, Emily," Sally scoffed. "Well, 'urry up then."

"I wish I could climb the ladder. I'm sure the best books are on the top shelves. The master's ever so tall."

It was quite dirty atop the shelves. Perhaps Emily had spent more time reading the books than dusting them. Elizabeth took in a quiet breath and immediately felt a tickle in her nose. *Oh no.*

She pinched her nose closed. *Do not sneeze. Do not sneeze.*

"Don't you dare, Emily Claybourne," she heard Sally say. "Just find something quick like that won't be missed."

A deep male voice broke into the girls' conversation. "Are you lost?"

Emily gasped loudly. "No, sir. I mean, yes, sir, Mr. Darcy."

Sally was silent. *Terrified*, Elizabeth thought. Mr. Darcy's voice had startled her as well. She could only imagine how frightened the girls were, to be caught out in such a way.

"You are not to be on these floors until the rest of the staff are returned," Mr. Darcy said, displeasure dripping from his words. "Mrs. Spencer is looking for you." Elizabeth could not help but feel a little sorry for the girls, but she was, quite literally, in no position to interfere.

Mr. Darcy would go to her chamber next to check on her, and she would not be there. What would he think? Perhaps she could use that time to remove herself from this predicament, though she feared it would be more difficult to leave her hiding place than it had been to lodge herself in it.

The maids scampered out of the room and down the hall rather quickly if the scuffling sounds were any indication.

Elizabeth felt the tickling inside her nose increase. She pinched it harder, but the sensation only grew worse. Dread knotted her stomach as she involuntarily drew in a sharp breath.

"Aaaa-choooo!" Her feet were tossed slightly upwards with the force of it. *Oh dear.*

There was a brief moment of silence as she watched one pretty slipper fall gently to the floor next to Mr. Darcy's boot. He stooped to pick it up.

"Miss Elizabeth," Mr. Darcy said in that terribly flat tone of his. She could not make out whether he was angry or laughing at her when he spoke like that. "It is safe to come down now."

She peeked over the edge of the bookshelf to see him gazing up at her. His expression was disapproving, but his eyes were suspiciously bright. Laughing, then.

Elizabeth assessed the ladder skeptically before acquiescing to necessity. "I may require some assistance..."

That did it. He laughed aloud, and she felt her cheeks flush.

"I can well imagine," he said. With one hand, he swung the ladder to her position. "However did you fit up there?" He tucked the slipper into a pocket and stepped up a few rungs.

She shrugged as well as she could in the confined space. "I am not entirely sure?"

He stepped up another rung, his eyes now level with her. She stared into them and felt a little lost.

"With your permission?" he asked, his hands hovering near her waist.

Her foolish heart fluttered wildly. Mr. Darcy had seen her in nothing more than a shift, she reminded herself; he had carried her upstairs in the dressing gown she now wore. She did not wish to think about what he had fetched and carried when she was ill. What difference did it make if he viewed her one bare foot as he helped her down the ladder? It was gentlemanly of him even to ask her permission.

She nodded, and two large hands nearly encircled her. She swallowed. It was strange to have a man touch her this way, but it was wonderful, too. Would any man create such feelings? Elizabeth did not know, but she rather doubted it. She had danced with other men, but never had the touch of their hands created a sensation such as this.

It was madness to fall in love with Mr. Darcy. She should not do it. He would be dismayed to know he had raised her expectations in such a way. He had *not*, she argued silently. She *could* have no expectations of Mr. Darcy, and therefore she *would* have none.

Mr. Darcy carefully positioned her feet, and Elizabeth felt her slipper being guided back on. "Step down, just here," he said, guiding her with one hand on her heel.

Oh, he was not wearing gloves. His fingers grazed her skin and gave her shivers. Did he feel it, too?

She stepped down according to his instructions, but inadvertently used her left arm to steady herself. All euphoria was lost in the jagged pain that traveled up her forearm. She inhaled sharply.

"Careful," Mr. Darcy murmured, and coaxed her to lean against him. "Put your trust in me," he said quietly. "I will not allow you to fall."

Elizabeth swallowed. There was a pleasant tingling up and down her spine, and she unsuccessfully attempted to ignore it.

When she was standing safely on the ladder, Mr. Darcy asked, "How did you manage to climb up here with only one good arm?"

She was looking away from him as he descended the ladder below her. "Determination," she told him, and heard him laugh softly. She wished she could see his face.

They were at the bottom, then, and Elizabeth touched the beautiful dressing gown sadly. It was very dusty.

"My apologies, Mr. Darcy." She looked up at him, embarrassed.

He smiled broadly. She was stunned, again, at how handsome it made him.

"No harm done, Miss Elizabeth," he told her, holding out his arm. "But in future, I recommend you allow me to retrieve your books."

She sighed a little, and his smile disappeared, like the sun behind a cloud.

"Are you well?" he inquired, and Elizabeth saw that he was still holding out his arm. She took it.

"I am very well," she told him. As he steered her from the room, she cried, "My books!" She blushed. "That is, *your* books."

Elizabeth watched his eyes twinkle and wondered that she had ever considered him humorless. He turned slightly to show her the volumes he had tucked under his other arm.

"You think of everything, sir," she said brightly.

"I did not think to search for you atop my bookshelves, madam," he replied drily.

"Well, I should not like to be predictable," was her pert response.

He shook his head as he opened the door to her room and stood aside for her to enter. "I would never accuse you of such."

She stepped inside, and he followed. Elizabeth marveled, not at how all restraints of propriety between them had utterly collapsed, but how at ease she felt without them. They should not have been alone; Mr. Darcy certainly should not have been in her chambers under any circumstances. As proper as Mr. Darcy had always been in Hertfordshire, she would have expected he would see her safely to her room and then immediately withdraw. Instead, he lingered. She considered herself a proper young woman—she ought to be scandalized by the liberties Mr. Darcy was taking. Yet she was not. She was instead grateful, for had they not been thrown together in this odd way, she would never really have known him. She had to remind herself of the irony. Just as she wished to learn more about him, it had become impossible that she ever should.

Though Elizabeth warned herself that this golden season of privacy could not last, she thought there was little harm in storing up pleasant memories for a time in her life when they would likely be scarce. There was no way forward other than marriage to a man she did not know or to enter service. She would not make a good governess, for she spoke only French and her playing was proficient but not exceptional. Perhaps she might be a good companion for an elderly woman.

That was her future. For now, she would give herself leave to enjoy this friendship with Mr. Darcy. Her heart sank when she thought of how much time she had wasted.

"Oh," she cried impulsively, "how I wish I had never heard your slight at the assembly!"

Mr. Darcy's complexion paled.

Good God, she heard me! Darcy thought, exceedingly shocked. He had in truth forgotten that the woman he had insulted that night was Elizabeth. She had meant nothing to him then, other than an object for his derision—it might have been any woman sitting in her place. He did recall that he and Miss Bingley had spent their first fortnight in Hertfordshire exchanging criticisms of the society near Netherfield Park, including Elizabeth. In all fairness, it was no wonder Miss Bingley had been so dismayed when he had allowed himself to notice the beauty of Elizabeth's fine eyes.

He frowned. Again, he wondered whether it was possible that Miss Bingley, seeing his admiration for Elizabeth, had somehow contrived to ruin her reputation? Was this entire debacle Miss Bingley's revenge on them both? How could she have managed it? No, he thought. It could not be her. At least, not her alone.

"Mr. Darcy," Elizabeth said contritely, breaking into his thoughts, "I must apologize for speaking out of turn . . ." She averted her eyes, and he did not like the pallor of her complexion.

"Why are you offering *me* an apology?" he exclaimed, aghast. He shut the door behind him. "I am ashamed to admit that I did indeed utter that gross falsehood, Miss Elizabeth. You must know that I . . ."

He stumbled to a halt and briefly squeezed his eyes shut. "I think very highly of you."

He opened his eyes. What he had said . . . it was not a lie, but it was certainly not the entire truth. Elizabeth did not raise her head. Gently, he added, "Miss Elizabeth, please look at me."

She lifted her chin and her eyes sought his. Darcy was reminded of their confrontation at the Netherfield ball, and his heart contracted painfully. It was a gesture she made, he realized, when she was distressed but refused to be cowed.

"I heard what you said to Mr. Bingley that night, sir," she told him. "And I did not hesitate to repeat it to others. In fact, I made a joke of it."

Without thinking, he moved closer.

Elizabeth drew in a deep breath. "I . . ." She shivered.

Worse and worse. Elizabeth was barely out of her sickbed. She might still relapse. "Please," he said, leading her to a chair. "Let us sit."

She obeyed. He took a blanket from the foot of the bed and spread it over her lap, then placed a chair across from her and sat down himself.

"I made a joke of the insult, I made a joke of *you*," Elizabeth explained in a rush. "I am ashamed of myself, Mr. Darcy," she told him before he could gather his thoughts.

He stared at her uncomprehendingly. "Why would *you* be ashamed?" Not that he relished being made sport of, but truly, it was nothing more than he deserved. Darcy knew that if a man had dared say such a thing about Georgiana, he would never have let it stand.

She made a small, exasperated sound. "Because despite all evidence decrying it just now, I *am* a lady. I ought to have comported myself better. I overheard you insult me to one person. I compounded the error by insulting you directly to all my friends!"

He chuckled.

Elizabeth frowned at him, and he enjoyed her confusion.

"Your behavior is less abhorrent than my own," he told her sincerely. "I cannot blame you for your reaction." He looked at her earnestly, but with good humor. "I expect you made a grand tale of it? The princess and the ogre?"

The corners of her mouth turned up ever so slightly. "I may have embellished a little."

"I do not doubt it," he assured her.

"I dearly love a laugh," she said, tipping her head to one side mischievously.

He drank in the sight of her. "So you have said, Miss Elizabeth." He reached out to touch her hand. "I am only too happy to forgive you if you would be kind enough to offer me the same respite."

He wanted to kiss her when she smiled, but of course he did not.

"I accept your apology," she said, a touch of triumph in her words.

"And I accept yours," he said, "though it is entirely unnecessary."

"No, no," she said with a little laugh. "That will never do. You must accept without the codicil."

"Must I?" he inquired curiously. Gads, but she was lovely. And witty.

"Indeed you must," she assured him.

And kind.

Darcy could have continued their banter for some time, but he thought again that Elizabeth ought to rest. "Then I must surrender, madam." He stood. "I shall leave you to your repose."

"And to your books, Mr. Darcy." She stood as though to walk him to the door.

He gave her a quick bow. "And to my books."

"Do not be too hard on the maids," Elizabeth said as he turned to go. "Emily only wished for something to read. I do not think that a bad thing, all in all, though it is true she should not have come to borrow a book without permission."

Elizabeth was kind to *everyone*, he thought. He was not special in that. Darcy nodded once without turning back to look at her and stepped out into the hall.

Chapter Seven

"Second carriage," Fitz murmured. He sighed. "We have to find out who was at that ball, Darcy. All week I have been tracking down those you remembered were in attendance as they returned to London, but I have little to show for it. If we had the guest list, we could simply compare it to yours."

Darcy nodded. "A simple enough task had I not severed all ties with Bingley before I left."

"You could ride back and say you have forgiven him," Fitz suggested.

"Forgiven him for attempting to tie me to his sister? Lie outright to the man?" Darcy asked, aghast.

"Pretend," Fitz corrected him.

Darcy stopped walking to stare at his cousin, incredulous. He could do many things well, but acting a part was not one of them. "Pretend," he said flatly. "Me."

Fitz grimaced. "No, you are correct. Dreadful idea. You could no more convince Bingley you have forgiven him than you could pay a woman a charming compliment."

Darcy sighed. "Thank you?"

His cousin laughed. "Still, this is something. I suppose Miss Bennet still cannot recall precisely how she came to be in your carriage?"

He shook his head. "But she recalls leaping from one. It likely happened near where her bonnet was found."

Fitz stopped just inside the door. "She leapt from one and appeared in another. She may have escaped by hiding in the boot herself—this may have nothing to do with you at all."

Darcy rubbed the back of his neck. "I have thought as much. Crawling into the boot to hide is consistent with what I know of her. But I have been trying to work it out, and I cannot think of any reason Miss Elizabeth would be targeted other than her interference at the ball. We need more information." He led Fitz to his dressing room.

Slipworth looked up from his work cleaning several combs and a brush. He stood hurriedly. "Sir?"

"Slipworth," Darcy said as Fitz found a chair and slid into it, "on your journey from Netherfield to London, did you stop anywhere other than Longbourn?"

"I could not say, Mr. Darcy," Slipworth admitted. "I slept from the moment I returned to the coach at Longbourn until we arrived in London. You decamped rather abruptly, and I had been up much of the night seeing to your packing."

Fitz frowned, but Darcy knew this was not a complaint. The valet never complained, at least, not to him. It was merely a statement of fact.

"Thank you, Slipworth," Darcy said calmly. They would need to speak with Anders next. Fitz was already up and through the doorway.

"Mr. Darcy," Slipworth called, and Darcy waited. His valet's face was flushed. "Your evening jacket has lost a button. It is not in the trunk. Nothing else is missing—I have looked everywhere and simply do not know where it could be." He frowned, clearly frustrated.

"It is all right, Slipworth," Darcy replied. A button was the least of his concerns.

But Slipworth was not placated. "It is quite an ornate one and must be specially made to match the others. I would like to send it out."

"Order whatever is needed," Darcy said hurriedly, and strode after his cousin.

"What was the man on about?" Fitz asked.

Darcy shrugged. "Lost button. Slipworth is fastidious, almost to a fault. It bothers him that he did not see it was missing before the jacket was packed."

Fitz gave him a sidelong glance. "You live in a different world than I, cousin."

They strode past the few maids who were cleaning the public rooms. It felt odd to see them—he had been in hiding nearly as much as Elizabeth since she arrived. Fitz, on the other hand, had been occupied with unraveling the mystery that surrounded them all. The men he had sent to Hertfordshire had brought back their only useful knowledge. The cold air out of doors roused Darcy a bit, and by the time they found Anders working in the carriage house, he was feeling more alert.

When they posed the question, Anders nodded. "We were forced to stop when another coach blocked the road. I had to come down off the coach to speak with them. Two men. One was very fair with pale blue eyes. He had a mark . . ." His hand hovered near the outside of his left eye.

"A freckle?" Fitz asked.

Anders nodded. "A bit larger and darker than a freckle, but yes, brown like that. The other man was not at all remarkable. Neither tall nor short. Dark blond hair, cut short. Brown eyes."

Elizabeth had described the same men when she woke from the laudanum. He exchanged a look with Fitz. "Did you recognize the carriage? The horses?" Darcy asked.

Anders shook his head. "No, sir, but I was in the neighborhood for only a few days before you departed."

Fitz laughed at that and poked Darcy with his elbow. "You were already thinking of making your escape."

Darcy sighed. "Miss Bingley's ability to speak without cessation left me determined not to be confined in a carriage with her again." It was not Caroline Bingley he had hoped to escape. "I was glad to have Newton," he said, referring to his thoroughbred. "Bingley is still building his stables."

Anders lifted an eyebrow at that but did not speak. Darcy *was* being rather generous. Bingley had allowed other men to tell him which horses to buy. Some of those men had been honest, but not all.

"Sir," Anders said slowly, "the coach was black with yellow wheels, no coat of arms and a bit battered. Likely a coach for hire." He closed his eyes, and Darcy knew he was trying to recall more details. "And one door was open—when I walked over to speak to the driver, I saw that the handle had hit the side of the coach hard enough to remove a bit of the paint. I think one of the wheels had been cracked, though they refused my help."

"Good," Fitz said smugly, "we can seek out where they might have made the repair."

"They were still rather close to Meryton, Colonel," Anders informed him. "I would have returned the coach there for repairs."

"We shall have to send someone else, Fitz," Darcy cautioned. "We cannot have the same men making repeated inquiries."

Fitz nodded. "We also need to be seen out. Anders, would you make the carriage ready?"

The coachman turned to Darcy and waited for his orders. Darcy nodded. Anders touched the brim of his hat and set to work.

Fitz watched Anders go, and shook his head. "I will never understand how you inspire such loyalty in your servants yet manage to offend nearly every person in your own circle."

"I treat each as they deserve," Darcy said gruffly. "My staff is not afraid of honest work. Regrettably, I cannot say as much for many in our circles." Fitz had no idea. His cousin's men would follow him through fire. Darcy did not inspire that kind of devotion. It was his privilege to treat his staff fairly and with compassion, but they were still servants and he could not also be their friend—some would certainly seek advantage. Acquaintances he had. He was even friendly with some men at the club. But a good friend? A confidante? Fitz was the only one he had.

"Now," Darcy said, facing his cousin. "I know I have been distracted. But how is it you did not think to ask Anders about the trip before now?"

Fitz was incredulous. "I am not a bloody magistrate at Bow Street, Darcy. How would I know to ask? We knew nothing of a stop on the road or Miss Bennet leaping out of a moving carriage. Anders and I assumed Miss Bennet was already in your boot before it left Netherfield. She said herself she was out walking near the estate." He huffed. "Point out the enemy, and I will run him through. *That* is my profession—and may I remind you I am spending my leave keeping your arse out of the fire? You owe me at least a case of your best brandy for this—I know you still have some." He crossed his arms over his chest and settled into an offended silence.

"Of course," Darcy replied with a wave of his hand. Fitz was right. He had been of no help, caught up as he was with caring for Elizabeth, and she had not recalled leaping from a carriage before today. Fitz had been working on the information they had—working on his own because Darcy could not bear to be away from Elizabeth.

Darcy's thoughts wandered back to his earlier conversation with her. She had called him her friend. Was it possible for men and women to be friends? Would it matter when she went away?

There was a snap next to his ear, and he flinched before scowling at Fitz.

"What are you doing?" he asked, drawing himself up.

Fitz lowered his hand. "Your distractions are why we are missing things. Keep your mind on our task, Darcy. I swear, I have never known you to drift away as you have since you returned from Hertfordshire." He gave Darcy a wicked grin, irritation suddenly abandoned. "Angelo's again?"

Normally, Darcy would take his cousin up on any challenge, but he was not inclined to exertion just now. Elizabeth's fever had never climbed so high that he was truly afraid for her, but after three days with little change, he had been anxious. Thankfully, the illness had run its course and Elizabeth was much improved. Although he had slept well the previous night, it had not erased the consequences of three nights spent in a chair. Between his concern for Elizabeth's health, the consequences of his behavior on her reputation, and his growing feelings for her, Darcy was wrung out. He hated to do it, but he had to admit his limits.

"Not today, Fitz," he said tiredly. "Another time."

That Fitz was shocked by his reply he had no doubt—his cousin started a little before narrowing his eyes and assessing him silently.

"The club, then?" he asked at last.

Relieved that Fitz had not demanded an explanation, Darcy nodded his head in assent.

∞

Before they could find a place to sit, Darcy was approached by a few men. *Dudley*, he thought, and . . . he searched his mind for the name of the other. *Mann, perhaps?*

Dudley began the conversation with a hearty greeting before launching into his real purpose. "Darcy, is it true you have had a falling-out with Bingley?"

He nodded once. "It is."

"How did you hear of it?" Fitz asked with all the appearance of surprise. Other than himself, no one could be less surprised than Fitz that Lady Matlock's news had already made the rounds.

"It was all my wife could talk about at dinner the other night," Dudley said with a good-natured laugh. "She insisted the two of you must have had words about Miss Bingley. I presume either she or her brother made you an offer and you declined?" he asked, clapping Darcy on the arm. "Make me my wife's hero and give me something she can use."

Despite their actions, Darcy had no desire to drag the Bingleys over the coals. Even more, he detested trading on his privacy to protect his reputation, but it was the truth, and it must be done. "Bingley did have hopes in that direction, but I could not encourage them."

Mann snorted. "I daresay Bingley was not the only one in that family with hopes. Though I must thank you, Darcy. I have made a pretty penny on your flight. I had odds on one of them making overtures once they had you out in the country. Had you waited even a few days more, I should have lost a hundred pounds."

Bile burned Darcy's throat. He rarely checked the books at the club. He was not averse to laying a bet on the outcome of a fencing match or a horse race, but never more than he could afford to lose, and never on the events of another man's life. It was a distasteful practice. He recalled that Bingley had teased him about his disinclination to wagering—Bingley, who had, once, on a whim, bet fifty pounds on the speed of a raindrop as it made its way down a windowpane.

He felt dull, even stupid. Had everyone seen Bingley's ploy coming but him?

Suddenly, he wondered whether Bingley himself had gambled on the outcome of the visit. Darcy made his excuses to the men, his cousin included, and strode into the room where the betting books were laid out. As always, it was crowded and noisy, but he flipped through the pages, seeking Bingley's name, and mentally noting each credit and debt.

At last, Darcy paged back to the most recent entries and left the books open on the table.

Dudley and Mann had drifted away, and he found Fitz conversing with two other men. "Reid," he said with a nod, greeting the man he knew. Jonathan Reid was an acquaintance from last season that he would not mind getting to know better. He was a bit older than Darcy and had inherited his family's property in Surrey a few years back.

"Darcy," Reid replied good-naturedly. "Tell me you understand cabbages. This weather is driving me to the madhouse."

"Corn and barley, lead and coal, cattle and sheep," Darcy replied with a grin. "None of your cabbages here. Potatoes, either."

Reid chuckled and motioned to a thick-set but solid man on his left. "Darcy, this is my friend, Mr. Ward. His estate is not far from your own, as it happens."

Mr. Ward waved off the introduction. "Ward, if you please. I am not one to stand on ceremony—you are practically a neighbor."

Darcy nodded and offered the same informality.

Ward's property was known to Darcy, but he had never met the family. It was a pretty piece of land in Staffordshire, not more than fifty miles from Pemberley, though no more than half its size. Ward had inherited from an elderly relative after some time in the army, he explained, and had been quite busy setting the estate back on firm footing. The three of them chatted about crops and livestock until poor Fitz's eyes glazed over.

Darcy finally took pity on his cousin, excusing himself and tipping his head to a more private corner of the room. Fitz joined him there after making his own farewells. As they settled into a pair of chairs near the fire, Darcy poured them both some port, but he did not drink it. Instead, he turned the glass in his hands and gazed into the dark liquid. Fitz took a sip from his own glass and waited.

"Bingley did not gamble on the result of my visit—at least, it is not recorded in the books," Darcy informed Fitz. "He has, however, lost a substantial amount of money over the past year and a half."

Fitz sat back in his chair. "How much?"

Darcy glanced around the room. Their corner of the room was private enough and he spoke in a hushed tone. "Between the off-book wagers I have witnessed and those in the books here? Nearly twenty thousand pounds."

His cousin paled. "Good God, Darcy." After a moment's reflection, he asked, "Has he satisfied them?"

Darcy nodded. He had wondered, too. "As far as I can tell, yes—which must have created a significant strain on his income. And he has often complained about his sister's unwillingness to be constrained by her allowance."

His cousin's expression cleared. "Miss Bingley is certainly an expense he would like to unload, then." Fitz set down his glass. "The fact that his new brother might be willing to help him recover financially would be an added advantage to the match."

"And Mrs. Bennet announced that her eldest daughter's son would inherit Longbourn," Darcy mused. "Without the need to cover Miss Bingley's expenses or to purchase an estate, Bingley would still have ample funds to expand Longbourn and make it more prosperous." He shook his head. "But surely he would verify Mrs. Bennet's claim before paying his addresses to Miss Bennet."

Fitz snorted. "Indeed. Thoroughness in his financial and personal dealings perfectly describes what we now know of his character, you are quite right."

Darcy's head ached.

It had been his belief since entering Meryton society months ago that the Bennets were fortune hunters. The Bennets, with their ties to trade and their respectable but small estate, were barely clinging to the lower rungs of the gentry. Even without an estate, the Bingleys were well-off. If their money was new, they had at least been brought up to understand and demonstrate proper manners and behavior.

Yet it was the Bingleys who had sought access to his fortune while none of the Bennets ever had.

The middle Bennet girl was less accomplished than she believed, and her younger sisters paid rather more attention to the officers than they ought, but they were all of them young. He had neither witnessed nor heard anything worse of them. To Darcy's knowledge, none of *them* had considered an elopement, as his own sister had. Mr. Bennet, who had appeared disinterested in his family, had been quick-witted and ingenious in their defense when Elizabeth disappeared. Mrs. Bennet was a loud, crass woman, but she had not, after their introduction at the assembly, sought his notice. In fact, she had gone out of her way to both avoid and insult him, which was not behavior typical of a fortune hunter.

"Darce?" Fitz asked warily. "Are you well?"

"No," Darcy replied, setting down his glass. "I am a fool."

Elizabeth pulled a cloth from the work basket Mrs. Spencer had just set down beside her. She had thought it was a handkerchief, but its size was . . . prodigious. She stared at it for a moment before looking up at the housekeeper. The older woman was wearing a affectionate expression.

"This cloth is too large for a handkerchief," Elizabeth said playfully. "May I assume it is meant to propel a ship on its way to the peninsula?"

"It is one of Miss Darcy's embroidery cloths," Mrs. Spencer informed her. "She is still learning." She chuckled. "She does not wish them to be seen, therefore she chooses a size she believes will render them unusable—but Miss Darcy makes them, so the master carries them anyway." She shook her head fondly. "I do not think she knows."

"How old is Miss Darcy?" Elizabeth asked. Mr. Darcy's actions made him sound more a father than a brother.

"Sixteen, Miss," the housekeeper replied.

More than ten years his junior, then. Mr. Darcy would make a very good father one day. Elizabeth loved her father, but Papa would more likely laugh at such an item. He would certainly never carry it on his person. Her heart warmed at this latest evidence of Mr. Darcy's kind, even sentimental heart. "Very well," Elizabeth said, rummaging through the basket. "Might you tell me whether there is anything here that is more urgent than the rest?"

"Given your indisposition, it might be easier to embroider," Mrs. Spencer observed. She stood, shaking out her skirts, and moved to one side of the room, plucking up a wooden embroidery stand and bringing it back. "I thought you might have need of this."

Elizabeth longed to be useful, but evidently, she was simply being given things to bide her time. It was a shame she could not explore the house. There had to be more surprises like the secret room in Mr. Darcy's study. Once Mrs. Spencer had stretched the fabric taut and tightened the frame, she bade farewell to Elizabeth and returned to her duties.

Elizabeth stared at the practice cloth that Mrs. Spencer had fastened in the frame. One of Miss Darcy's practice cloths. Did the woman think she required practice? After a moment, she sighed, and began to stitch. She worked for a few hours before the light grew dim. Not long after she had given up for the evening and settled near the fire, there was a scratching at the door and a quiet "Miss Elizabeth?"

Her heart leapt. Mr. Darcy had come to join her. "Enter," she called, just loud enough for him to hear.

He opened the door and came inside, followed closely by a man who was carrying a laden dinner tray.

Mr. Darcy motioned to the servant. "This is Mr. Slipworth, my valet."

Mr. Slipworth set the tray down on a little table near the settee.

"Thank you, Mr. Slipworth," Elizabeth said, and he offered her a bow.

"Would you care to dine with me?" Mr. Darcy asked. He tugged at his cuffs and then once at his cravat. Elizabeth could not fathom what was making him so uncomfortable.

"Of course," she replied pleasantly. "I would appreciate the company." She was not used to being alone so much of the day. Longbourn could be rather loud and at times feel somewhat confined, but she longed for the chatter now that there was none to be had. "Where is the colonel?"

"He decided to have dinner at the club."

"I see," she replied.

Mr. Slipworth served the meal and then retreated to the far corner of the room. It was odd to have him there, but Elizabeth supposed he was serving as a chaperone of sorts. No stranger, she thought, than anything else that had occurred in the days since the Netherfield ball. It would be a week tomorrow. A week away from her family, with no word on what was happening or whether she might ever see them again.

As though he could hear her thoughts, Mr. Darcy poured a glass of wine and passed it to her. "I am afraid Mrs. Spencer would be missed."

She lifted her shoulders.

"My cousin and I intend to make a trip to Longbourn to speak with your father," Mr. Darcy announced.

"When?" Elizabeth asked, trying not to sound envious.

"Tomorrow. Should you wish to send him a message, I will be certain to put it in his hands."

"Will you not be recognized?"

Mr. Darcy pulled a face. "Fitz will disguise me, he says."

Elizabeth watched him expectantly, but he only picked up his fork and began to eat.

She waited for a time, growing more indignant as he ignored her. "Sir," she began, and he lifted his eyes to hers. "Will you not tell me what you hope to accomplish?"

The tip of his fork rested on his plate. "To speak to your father," he said again. His brows pinched together. "Did I not say?"

She released a short, surprised laugh that had nothing to do with humor. "You did, Mr. Darcy, but what you did *not* say could fill all the volumes in your library."

"I would not wish to concern you, Miss Elizabeth," he told her seriously. "I only intended to inform you why you are unlikely to see me tomorrow."

Apparently, Mrs. Spencer was not the only one who believed her incompetent. It was as though Mr. Darcy had reached out to pat her on the head and offer her a sweet. A half-hour ago, she would have said she would miss sitting down with this man for dinner on the morrow. Now she believed a little distance might be for the best.

"Mr. Darcy," she said, disappointment making her words a little sharp, "whether you wish it or not, I am very closely concerned with the events prompting your return to Hertfordshire. Having known me only a short time, perhaps you are unaware that I wish to be informed about anything which might"—here she leaned in for emphasis—"alter the course of my life."

It was a little dark in the room despite the candles, but Elizabeth detected a faint blush on Mr. Darcy's cheeks. "Quite so, madam," he said stiffly, and set his fork down. "We wish to discover more specifically who arrived in the area from out of town before the ball."

"And you believe my *father* will know this?" she asked disbelievingly.

"He is the primary land-holder in the area and has been at Longbourn many years. He would at the least know where we ought to begin." Mr. Darcy seemed to feel this a very reasonable course of action.

Elizabeth shook her head. "Papa does not pay attention to such visitors unless it is to laugh at them. He will send you to Sir William. You may as well begin there."

Mr. Darcy coughed and lifted a napkin to his mouth. "I beg your pardon?"

"My apologies, Mr. Darcy," she said, arching an eyebrow at him. "I did not understand you to be hard of hearing."

"Surely you do not mean Sir William Lucas?" he asked dubiously.

Her irritation flared. "Why would I say it if I did not mean it?"

"But he is so . . . so . . ." Mr. Darcy glanced at her and swallowed.

"Amiable?" Elizabeth supplied, the tone of her voice a warning.

Mr. Darcy nodded, but it was clear from his expression that this was not the word he would have chosen.

"Do you think that because he began his life in trade that he is not astute? He was the mayor, Mr. Darcy. He addressed the king."

Mr. Darcy did not appear impressed. "Yes, but . . ."

"Have *you* addressed the king, sir? In any manner at all?"

"No." Mr. Darcy appeared as though he had swallowed something very sour.

She felt a small sense of vindication. "Have you been knighted, sir?"

"Of course not," he replied, exasperation sneaking into his voice.

"Then perhaps you should not look down on him for an accident of birth. Do you think him unobservant?" She lifted her eyebrows.

"No," Mr. Darcy protested. "Not precisely. I merely thought him . . ."

"Simple." That was the heart of the matter. Mr. Darcy thought himself so very clever.

Mr. Darcy lifted a shoulder. "Well, yes."

"This is why you ought to have sought my opinion from the start, Mr. Darcy," she told him seriously. "Having been at Netherfield for a few months, during which time you managed to offend nearly everyone you met, does not qualify you to judge the inhabitants of the area." Truly, many of her friends had taken up against Mr. Darcy on her behalf so perhaps she bore some of the blame, but he had given them additional reasons for affront without any assistance from her.

He sighed and sat back. "Very well, madam. Tell me of Sir William Lucas."

His unwilling resignation, as though he still could not trust that she had something of value to say, provoked her. "Sir William perhaps ought not to have sold his business with so many children to settle, and possibly he enjoyed his time at St. James a bit too much. He tells the same stories many times over until we know them by rote. But we all have faults, sir. Despite them, Sir William is one of the most honorable men I know."

Mr. Darcy's face expressed his surprise, but he was wise enough not to speak.

"Did it never occur to you that Sir William is affable for a purpose?" Elizabeth asked. "That as the former mayor he is protective of all of us in and around Meryton? That particularly with a militia quartered nearby, he wishes to know every visitor or new resident who appears in our area? How is that object best served? Does haughtiness invite confidences?"

Mr. Darcy appeared quite abashed. Good. He should be. The heat of her temper abated.

"Who was Mr. Bingley's first caller at Netherfield, Mr. Darcy?" she asked with more gentleness. "Who attempted to save your reputation among the local families by arranging that you dance with me at Lucas Lodge?" She removed her napkin from the table and shook it out with one snap of her wrist. "I refused because I did not *wish* for your reputation to be salvaged. Sir William was rather disappointed in me, I am afraid." She sniffed. "For some reason, he seems to like you."

"Your refusal did you no injury with me, Miss Elizabeth," Mr. Darcy said contritely. "I admit, I was intrigued. I do not believe I have ever been refused before."

"Did you ever think that it is because you never ask?" She prodded at the roasted beef on her plate. The scent of rosemary drifted up to her nose, but the beef was not so well cooked that it obligingly fell apart. She would have to cut it. She glanced quickly at her injured arm. How was it to be accomplished? She would not ask Mr. Darcy to cut it for her. She was upset with him.

Mr. Darcy reached for her plate, and she idly fingered her knife. He withdrew, perhaps recalling how recently she had wielded a fork. "I *have* asked," he objected. "I asked you. I also danced with Miss Bingley and Mrs. Hurst."

Elizabeth glared at him. "Were you not *required* to ask them? I am rather surprised that they did not ask you." She set her fork and knife down on her plate and sighed, deflated. "Truly, Mrs. Hurst and I have not exchanged more than ten words between us. That was unkind."

Mr. Darcy chuckled, and the tension between them ebbed away. "But rather accurate." He gestured to her plate. "May I?"

Elizabeth frowned, but had to admit that he had asked politely. She hated to have someone cut her food as if she were still in the nursery but reminded herself that she required the assistance, and she *was* hungry. Elizabeth took a deep breath and let it out slowly. By making the request aloud, Mr. Darcy had offered her a small concession. She would do the same. "Yes, thank you, Mr. Darcy," she continued calmly as he picked up her plate, "who pointed out that Mr. Bingley was expected to offer for my sister Jane?"

Mr. Darcy managed to cut her meat while still appearing deep in thought. "I did not believe it was knowingly done. To my shame, I intended to advise Bingley against a hasty alliance."

Elizabeth shook her head at him. "I might have been furious with you before . . . well, before," she admitted. "Now I can only hope Papa has not allowed Mr. Bingley to call at Longbourn."

Mr. Darcy sat back to stare at her. "Would he not? I thought . . ."

She shook her head. "When I spoke with Papa before we retired that morning, I won his agreement to keep both Mr. Bingley and Mr. Wickham from calling. He asked whether he ought to speak with Sir William, and I told him he should."

Mr. Darcy tipped his head slightly to one side. "You have lost me again, Miss Elizabeth."

His puzzlement offered her a glimpse into what he might have been like as a boy. It was rather endearing, and she laughed softly. "Mr. Darcy, you thought Sir William was inadvertently alerting you to a potential problem. Knowing Sir William as I do, I rather suspect that he was purposefully warning me."

A crease appeared at the bridge of Mr. Darcy's nose. "About what?" He resumed the task of cutting the meat on her plate into small, precise pieces.

Elizabeth shook her head. "I do not know, precisely. I presume now that he was concerned Jane might find herself engaged to Mr. Bingley without meaning to. She was enamored of him, but not yet ready to accept an offer. Jane is steady and methodical, but she is also in possession of a very soft heart. She might not feel comfortable deflecting

Mr. Bingley's pointed attentions." She frowned. "Sir William rarely says anything without intent. Unfortunately, I was too angry with you at the time to inquire."

Mr. Darcy set Elizabeth's plate before her, and she nodded her thanks. The beef smelled wonderful, but the potatoes also drew her attention. They had been formed into small balls and then fried; a white sauce was drizzled prettily over the whole. She ate one and took a moment to savor it. Next, she tasted the roasted beef. It was simple, perfectly cooked and seasoned, and she nearly groaned with the pleasure of it. Instead, she delicately touched her napkin to her mouth and said, "Meet with Sir William first, Mr. Darcy." She gazed up at him through her lashes. "And yes, I would be pleased to have you deliver a letter to my family. I will write it tonight."

He was watching her closely. Elizabeth felt a thrill at the warmth in his gaze. She even believed she detected admiration in his dark eyes but dismissed the idea almost immediately. She chided herself for the thought. With his fortune and connections, he had never been for her. It would be foolish to entertain any such thoughts as *that*.

"We shall seek Sir William out first, Miss Elizabeth," Mr. Darcy promised.

He had heard her out and was taking her advice. Elizabeth smiled. "I think you will find there was no cause to be stubborn, Mr. Darcy." She placed a piece of the meat in her mouth and savored the taste.

He grinned on the word *stubborn*. "How is the beef, Miss Elizabeth?"

Oh, dear, Elizabeth thought. Despite his wealth and connections, Mr. Darcy and she were rather well matched. She swallowed and impishly replied, "Excellent, Mr. Darcy."

Chapter Eight

Darcy rolled his shoulders back and adjusted his hat so he could see past the visor. The uniform Fitz had insisted he wear was ill-fitting and ridiculous. It was covered by a large, navy blue cape, which was neither as warm nor as comfortable as his own greatcoat. Fitz had grinned wickedly when Darcy appeared in it. Darcy had protested—it was clear to him, at least, that he was not a military man. He complained that the moment he spoke it would take mere seconds for anyone they met to determine the same.

His cousin was unrepentant. "Then do not speak."

As they approached Meryton from the south, Darcy thought that this had been the entire point—Fitz wished to keep him from speaking or drawing attention to himself in any way. He had been reluctant to allow Darcy's presence at all, but Darcy was finished with hiding at home and waiting for something to happen. Elizabeth's situation—*their* situation—was untenable. He must *do* something to bring it to a successful conclusion. If only he knew how to accomplish it without making everything worse.

Elizabeth had a great deal of faith in Sir William Lucas. He hoped she was right.

Just outside town, Fitz pulled up and Darcy joined him. "Well, cousin, I never ignore a good scouting report," Fitz informed him. "Where does this former mayor, now a knight, reside?"

Darcy led the way, skirting around Longbourn's village and heading north and east to Lucas Lodge. When they arrived and were allowed to wait in the small front hall, Darcy glanced around. He had not really observed more than the drawing rooms when he had been here before. There were few objects of any significant value, though the items on display were chosen with taste and discretion.

An elderly manservant returned to lead them inside; a maid showed them to a small room on the main hall where they were able to refresh themselves from the ride. They passed by several open rooms. Sir William and Lady Lucas had a great many children, if he recalled correctly, and yet all was neat and orderly. He was not certain why he had assumed it would be otherwise. They were escorted back to a small study closer to the front door.

Inside the room, shutters open to take advantage of the light, sat the gentleman himself. He rose to greet them, staring at Darcy for a moment before leaning into a polite bow.

"Colonels Fitzwilliam and Black," he said genially, "welcome. What business brings you to me on this fine December day?" He waved a hand at the two chairs that faced his desk.

"Thank you for seeing us, Sir William," Fitz said amiably as he sat down. Darcy followed his lead. "We have come to ask about certain men from London who attended a ball here on the twenty-sixth of November. Several of them seem to be officers who have abandoned their posts without leave."

"I see," Sir William replied, eyeing them both cheerfully. He set his hands on the desk, meaty fingers laced together, and twiddled his thumbs. Two blue eyes lit upon Darcy, and finally, Sir William spoke, but it was not in answer to Fitz's query. "You look a great deal like a young man who came among us this autumn, Colonel Black. My friend Bennet has mentioned something about the reason for his sudden departure. Have you any relation to the Darcy family?"

"I do," Darcy responded without elucidation.

The older man stood. "Excellent. I have something for Mr. Darcy, if you would be so kind as to pass it along."

"I would be pleased to do so, Sir William," he said.

Fitz shot Darcy a murderous glare, and Darcy lifted his shoulders. He knew he was not supposed to speak, but what had Fitz expected? Elizabeth knew her neighbor well. Clearly Sir William was not likely to be fooled by a change of clothing and a refusal to converse. Darcy had been in the man's home more than once over the past months, and they had seen one another only a week past. The uniform would keep the townspeople from recognizing him atop his horse, but once they could see his face, those who had been introduced would of course be able to identify him.

Sir William disappeared into a closet, and Darcy heard squeaky hinges. A safe? He wondered what Sir William could possibly have to give him.

The older man reappeared with something clutched in his fist. His expression was pensive. "I am the local magistrate, Colonel Black. Were you aware?"

Darcy shook his head. "I was not."

"Most believe that duty belongs to Bennet, but he was pleased to hand it to me when I opened Lucas Lodge some years ago."

Fitz's eyes were narrowing. Darcy could tell his cousin was growing agitated, but Elizabeth had said this man was shrewd. He listened carefully.

"It was rather fortunate on this occasion that it is no longer Bennet's duty. This incident, oh, about a week ago now, was said to involve one of his daughters, and if he still held the office, he should have been forced to recuse himself. I fear that in such a situation Mr. Bingley might have been called to serve. Although he has only leased Netherfield, he is still the master of the largest estate in the neighborhood." He tapped his closed fist lightly on the surface of his desk. "You will forgive me, but he is not the man for this job."

"Why is that?" Fitz asked. He sounded merely curious, but Darcy knew better. Fitz would decide whether they could trust the man based on his answer.

Sir William lifted an eyebrow. "I believe you know, Colonel. It is why you are here, speaking with me, when the guest list you want is at Netherfield."

Fitz stared unblinkingly. Darcy waited until Sir William continued.

"The lady's family has said she is in London, but she has always made her farewells to my daughter before she travels. It was a surprise to Charlotte to hear her friend had removed to town, and she has watched for a letter since."

The skin on the back of Darcy's neck prickled, but he would not allow any emotion to cross his face.

He was pleased when Sir William frowned. The man leaned over the desk. "Might you recognize this, Colonel Black?"

Darcy inclined forward as Sir William lifted his hand, something small and round pinched between his thumb and index finger. Metal-rimmed, with a hand-painted scene on ivory-colored porcelain.

He recognized it immediately as the missing button from his evening coat. "I might," he said slowly, reaching out to take it. Fitz leaned over to have a look. Darcy noted that there was still some thread attached and studied the ends. They were clean and even.

"You see it too, then?" Sir William asked.

"It has been cut," Darcy said, and both Fitz and Sir William nodded grimly.

"Where did you discover it?" Fitz asked, his voice unnaturally calm.

"Conveniently handed to me inside a bonnet owned by Miss Elizabeth Bennet," was the reply. Sir William held Darcy's gaze. "The man who left it had said he found it alongside, and Mr. Wickham was kind enough to imply it belonged to Mr. Darcy."

Fitz began an angry protestation, but Sir William held up his hand. "Colonel Fitzwilliam, Mr. Wickham himself has declared his disdain for Mr. Darcy, and I do not believe in coincidence. If Mr. Darcy had been struggling with Miss Elizabeth, the button would have been pulled away and the thread would be frayed, not cut." One corner of his mouth turned up slightly. "I believe I know enough of Miss Eliza to be certain she would never be accosted without mounting a vigorous defense."

Darcy recalled that Elizabeth's vigorous defense had required a leap from a moving carriage. It was remarkable she had not been more grievously hurt.

"Further," Sir William continued, "this is clearly the button of an evening jacket. When Mr. Darcy left Netherfield, he was in his riding clothes."

"You saw me leave?" Darcy asked, startled out of his stoicism.

"Miss Elizabeth Bennet was standing at the window. Not her normal position during a ball." Sir William lifted two bushy eyebrows. "I saw *Mr. Darcy* leave."

Fitz sighed, but Darcy could not bring himself to care. He abhorred disguise, and Fitz had forced this one upon him.

"Slipworth remained to pack my things," Darcy said seriously. "He was sure that all the buttons were on the jacket after he had brushed it, but it would have remained out of the trunk until the last, to be placed on top." He rubbed the back of his neck. "He secures every one of them as though they are worth a king's ransom. Whoever it was could not have pulled it off, not quickly. He would have to cut it." He was silent as he worked this over in his mind. "The Bingleys would not have chanced leaving their guests until the last family was gone, and Slipworth would have been up quite early."

Sir William nodded. "Might there have been another man in the house, someone who knew you had gone?"

Darcy shared a look with Fitz. He had wondered the same. Might someone other than the Bingleys have witnessed the failed compromise? Been a part of it? He had not seen anyone, but it had been dark enough that the Bingleys had not noticed Elizabeth until she announced herself.

A shadow fell upon Sir William's face as he asked, "Given that these items were located together . . . I should like to know, gentlemen, whether you might have seen my daughter's friend Miss Eliza Bennet in town. I know London is a big place, but certainly Mr. Darcy would have called on such an acquaintance. Perhaps he mentioned it?"

Darcy knew he should not say anything in response to the older man's inquiry. He was the magistrate, and a clever one. It might be a trick, and it was certainly a risk to answer. But Elizabeth trusted this man, in some ways even more than her own father. He had spent the past week trusting no one but Fitz, refusing to say anything about Elizabeth's plight to anyone who did not already know, and what had that achieved? After he delivered Elizabeth's note to Mr. Bennet, he suspected Sir William would be told in any case. More to the point, Elizabeth would not wish Sir William to continue to fear the worst. Although he could feel Fitz's glare boring into the side of his face, he nodded and said, "I have seen her myself, sir. She sends her regards."

Sir William's face paled as he asked, "She is well?"

Darcy coughed. "She is recovering."

Fitz stood abruptly and began to pace. His cousin would likely have his head, but Darcy could not regret watching Sir William's anguish fade.

"That was not the expectation, then?" Sir William asked flatly.

"We do not believe so, no." Darcy confirmed.

The man released a breath and gestured to the button in Darcy's hand. "So, Colonel Black," he said grimly, "who wants to see Mr. Darcy hanged for her murder?"

Darcy closed his fist around the button and thanked God that Sir William was exactly the man Elizabeth believed he was. "That," he told the older man, "is what we are here to learn."

Sir William dropped himself into the chair behind his desk. "There were a great many new faces at the ball," he said thoughtfully.

Fitz offered the description of the two men who had accosted Elizabeth.

The older man shook his head. "There was no one in the ballroom with hair as light as you have described. He sounds quite distinctive. As for the second man, there were at least half a dozen men at the ball who were not from the neighborhood and had the same sort of looks."

"Might you have noted anyone acting oddly?" Darcy asked.

Sir William leaned back and cast his eyes to the ceiling. "Mr. Bingley was restless. He left the ballroom before supper, which I found strange." He was quiet, thinking. "He poured himself a cup of punch when he returned and took up his duties as host."

"Did he speak with anyone you can recall?" Fitz inquired.

"Everyone," Sir William replied. "As host, he spoke with everyone." His bushy eyebrows pinched together.

"Perhaps we ought to think about those with whom he did *not* speak," Darcy said. "Perhaps there was someone with whom he would not wish to be connected?"

"Well," Sir William said slowly, "there was a man hovering near the musicians. He was thin, dark hair, rather large ears. A London friend of Mr. Bingley's, I presumed." He blinked. "He was not wearing dancing shoes, which is why I remarked him. I wondered why he would travel all the way to Netherfield if he was not prepared to dance."

"Was he tall?" Fitz asked.

"Medium height, I would say, though I was across the room. His hair was worn rather long. And now that I think on it, he did send a look or two in Mr. Bingley's direction, though that might mean nothing."

Darcy turned this over in his mind. "Did he wear spectacles, Sir William?"

Sir William considered it. "No."

"Do you know the man, Darcy?" Fitz asked.

"No, I do not think so." Darcy replied after he considered it for a moment. "To whom *were* you introduced, Sir William?"

This sent Sir William on a long recitation of the guests he had met and conversed with, and he always had some way to recall them—a mole, a certain style of dress, a cravat with an intricate knot, a hand that shook.

They had been speaking for some time when there was a knock on the door. Darcy rose immediately from his chair and turned his back, but before he could move to the window, he heard Mr. Bennet and his eldest daughter Miss Jane Bennet announced.

"Bennet," Sir William said warmly as he rose to greet his guests, "Miss Bennet, I thank you for arriving so quickly."

Beside him, Fitz stood to be introduced. Darcy did not move.

"Oh," a soft voice said. "Mr. Darcy. It is good to see you again."

Miss Bennet had recognized him even without seeing his face.

There was a quick laugh from behind him. "You have an excellent eye, Jane," Mr. Bennet said. "I would not have guessed it."

Darcy did turn, finally, to see Mr. Bennet's sharp eyes upon him. "Well," the man said slowly, "I would now."

Both Bennets looked to Sir William. "You said you had news," Mr. Bennet said bluntly. "I presume these gentlemen are a part of it?"

"How did you know there would be anything to tell?" Fitz asked Sir William.

The older man shrugged. "Mr. Darcy disappeared in the middle of the ball at Netherfield. Miss Eliza watched his departure from the ballroom. Then Miss Eliza disappeared, as best we can tell, eight or nine hours later. When Colonel Black appeared this morning, it seemed certain there was a connection."

"Colonel Black?" Miss Bennet asked, her forehead crinkling in confusion for a moment before her expression cleared.

"Ah," Mr. Bennet said. "Very well. Colonel Black."

Darcy grimaced and ran a hand through his hair. "Mr. Bennet, Miss Bennet," he murmured, and offered a curt bow.

Sir William motioned for them all to sit. Darcy observed Miss Bennet. Although he preferred Elizabeth's dark hair and eyes, her older sister was as beautiful as ever. Her complexion was like porcelain, her features aligned in an almost perfect symmetry. Large blue eyes were fixed upon Sir William as though awaiting some pronouncement.

Darcy was not so lost to her beauty that he did not see the fear and grief reflected in her countenance. Miss Bennet clasped her hands together in her lap, the fringe of her shawl wrapped around her fingers, and Mr. Bennet was little better, his face pale, his eyes shadowed with the pain of sleepless nights.

Sir William did not allow them to suffer long. "Eliza is safe," he said quietly.

Mr. Bennet sank limply against the back of his chair.

"My wife's brother received an anonymous note saying as much," Mr. Bennet said, closing his eyes briefly before opening them again. "But it seemed too much to hope for."

Sir William appeared surprised to hear it.

Mr. Bennet turned to Darcy. "Gardiner sent it to me, but it was not the same as your earlier missives."

"Darcy said you would recognize his hand. I copied it out before it was sent," Fitz said.

Miss Bennet's head was bowed, her lips moving silently in what could only be prayer. Darcy watched her until she looked up. "Forgive me for asking so directly," Miss Bennet asked in a clear, ringing voice, "but I wish to know what has happened to my sister."

Darcy looked over at Fitz to see whether he would explain. His cousin was also watching Miss Bennet. There was a brief, wistful expression in Fitz's eyes before it vanished like smoke up a chimney.

Fitz nodded at him. "They all recognize you. You may as well explain what we know."

Miss Bennet met Fitz's eye, and his cousin froze. When Miss Bennet broke her gaze and returned her attention to Darcy, he thought she appeared a bit dazed. Soon, though, she was watching him expectantly.

Darcy nodded at Fitz and addressed Miss Bennet and her father. "First, I have a message for you." He removed Elizabeth's note and handed it to Mr. Bennet. She had only written to assure them she was safe, but she had told Darcy that it would be enough.

Mr. Bennet read the message and handed it to Miss Bennet.

"Next, my cousin and I are trying to understand what has happened. It would be a great help were you to relate your actions on the morning Miss Elizabeth disappeared," Darcy said.

Mr. Bennet nodded. "The morning after the ball, I was awakened by your valet, who brought your first message. I learned little that was new, for Lizzy had already explained what had happened. When I noted her pelisse was gone, I waited for her to return." Miss Bennet handed the note back, and Mr. Bennet tucked it away. "When she did not, I sought her out along her usual walking paths. I found a handkerchief I knew belonged to her, but nothing else." He met Darcy's eye. "When I returned home, I found your second letter. Jane had risen by then, and I asked whether she knew where her sister had gone."

"I wished to ask the servants, but my father requested that I wait," said Miss Bennet.

"Given what had occurred at the ball and Lizzy's concerns—well, I was nearly certain this was not happenstance," Mr. Bennet said. "I rode out to Meryton on a contrived errand to see whether I might discover anything. It was there I received a summons. Sir William had a bonnet he wished me to see. It had been left in town by a man who said he found it by chance near the river—his carriage had broken its wheel nearby, and he had returned to have it repaired. He had been in a hurry to get to town and left before Sir William could speak with him. It was Mr. Wickham," he said as his expression soured, "who suggested to Sir William that it was similar to a bonnet he had seen Elizabeth wear." Mr. Bennet sighed and ran a hand through his hair. "I could not deny it. Fortunately, the most troublesome members of my family slept late and kept to their chambers most of the day. It offered us time to consider what was best to be done. Jane was of great use there." He looked at his eldest daughter, and she picked up where he had paused.

"Our housekeeper's daughter had been taken to bed with her first child," Miss Bennet said. "Lizzy might have accompanied Mrs. Hill to tend her had she thought she could be of use, but I knew Mrs. Hill would never allow it." She wound and unwound her shawl's fringe around her fingers as she spoke. "Papa was certain something dreadful had happened, and I walked to the church to ask Mr. Tompkins whether he might ride out to the river to see the scene himself. I knew we ought not send anyone connected to our family."

"Mr. Tompkins was given the living in the village six months ago," Sir William said. "Entirely trustworthy, but beyond the appointment, not believed to have a particular connection to the Bennet family."

Miss Bennet nodded. "Mr. Tompkins saw two men searching the blackberry bushes on the side of the road."

Did they believe Elizabeth was in the river, or that she had escaped? And if they believed she was alive, would they attempt to track her down or hide themselves?

"How well did your Mr. Tompkins see those men?" Fitz asked.

"Well enough," Mr. Bennet replied. "One rather average-looking man, one with very fair looks."

Sir William was surprised. Mr. Bennet must not have shared this information with him. It had been a wise decision. The fewer who knew the details, the better.

Fitz offered a description of the two men, and Miss Bennet sighed.

"The same men," she said quietly. "How did Lizzy escape?"

Darcy glanced at his cousin beseechingly. He could not bear to tell this part of the tale, and was grateful when Fitz explained it for him.

The room was silent for a time until Darcy asked Miss Bennet to continue. "While we awaited our carriage after the ball," she said, "Mr. Bingley mentioned that Lizzy was in some sort of trouble with Mr. Darcy. Mr. Bingley was very kind, very concerned, and he hoped to call at Longbourn to discuss it discreetly once his friends had departed for London." She lifted her gaze to Darcy's. "I do not know Mr. Darcy very well, but I know my sister. I told Mr. Bingley he must have misunderstood. He behaved as though I was too naïve to accept my sister's duplicity." Her jaw tightened. "It annoyed me."

"Jane's temper is something of a legend—rarely seen, but a sight to behold," Mr. Bennet said fondly. "The surest way to light the fuse is to patronize her. Between that and Lizzy's story, she had heard enough. By the time I returned from Meryton, she had already penned a note declining Mr. Bingley's visit."

Sir William smiled. Darcy glanced at Fitz. He had a smile on his face, too. A small one. But it was definitely a smile.

"I attempted to dissuade him at the ball but he would not desist," Miss Bennet said slowly. "It began to anger me. It was the first time we had disagreed, and his unwillingness to admit that my understanding of Lizzy was better than his showed me the man he is beneath the charming façade."

"He did not know you, my dear," Sir William said reassuringly.

"I am not certain he wished to," Miss Bennet replied. "I pondered it for hours before I could sleep that night, wondering whether I was being too unforgiving. But in the morning, when Papa related Lizzy's story and she did not return, I did wonder whether Mr. Bingley was involved." She swallowed and gave Darcy a remorseful look. "I might have believed you involved, sir, but Lizzy would not invent such a tale, not even about a person she disliked. And she *liked* Mr. Bingley. As did I." Her hands stopped their work. "My sister walks to find peace, to think. If only I had spoken with her before we retired, perhaps she would not have felt the need to walk out."

With a good deal of sympathy, Darcy recounted his actions, beginning with Elizabeth's response when she awoke in the secret room off his study. He did not tell them about the room but did mention how it had ended with him wearing the remains of his dinner.

As intended, this made Sir William and the Bennets laugh a little. His description of Elizabeth's spirit, more than anything else, reassured them that she was well. As well as could be expected, in any case. Darcy mentioned her illness, her recovery, and how relieved she had been to hear the story that had been devised to keep her family safe.

"She was more concerned for her sisters than herself," Fitz added.

"That is very like her," Miss Bennet replied. "There is no one more loyal to those she loves than Lizzy."

Fitz cast a quick glance at Darcy. *Except you,* his eyes said. Darcy ignored him.

"When shall we retrieve her, Mr. Darcy?" Mr. Bennet asked. "I appreciate the need for secrecy, but she cannot remain with you. We really should move her to the Gardiners' home for a time before bringing her back to Longbourn. It will give truth to the story of her visit and allow us time to find her a husband."

Darcy felt the blood drain from his face. They still did not know who had attacked Elizabeth—surely it was too soon to speak of her leaving him?

"I had thought of that, Bennet, while we waited for you to arrive," Sir William said. "For more than one reason, it would be risky to bring her home without word of a betrothal. Given that this situation remains unresolved, it would be better still to have her a married woman." He tugged at his ear. "You can tell Mrs. Bennet you sent her to the Gardiners to meet a possible suitor but did not wish to say as much in case it all came to naught. I considered my Sam, but he is perhaps too young for her, and it would be unnecessary to send Miss Eliza to London to meet him."

"Sam is a good boy, but I think we can agree that Elizabeth would be too much for him," Mr. Bennet said.

Sir William stood and motioned to the side of the room. Bennet nodded, and Sir William poured. "What think you of Andrew Long? He is in town currently."

Sir William harrumphed. "If Sam is too young, Andrew is far too old. Were he fifteen years younger, he might have a hope of keeping up with her, but now?"

Bennet snorted. "Fair enough, but our prospects are rather limited."

Fitz nudged Darcy. "Breathe, cousin," he said in a low whisper. The words rang in Darcy's ears.

Until Fitz said the word, Darcy had indeed forgotten to draw breath.

He had fought his feelings for Elizabeth. His allegiance to his family prevented it, and she might not wish it in any case. She had been warming to him, he believed, and his admiration for her had only grown deeper and steadier. Duty still insisted that Elizabeth would not suit. But his heart was overwhelming those long-held convictions.

He loved Elizabeth. Darcy blinked. Good God, he loved her. Could he bear to see her betrothed to another?

"We should have Goulding here. He is our most creative thinker," Sir William mused.

"He would put Eliot forward," Mr. Bennet responded. He glanced at Darcy and Fitz. "Goulding's nephew," he explained.

Listening to these men sorting through Elizabeth's prospects was akin to sitting atop an anthill.

Sir William considered it. "Eliot would be a decent match if it were not for..." He made a wide circle with one finger near his ear. "It still makes him a little... you know. Sometimes."

Darcy's eyes widened. They would wed her to an idiot? Clever, witty Elizabeth?

Miss Bennet interrupted the discussion. "I believe Lizzy should be involved in this conversation, Papa," she said firmly. "She may not wish to be married at all."

Though he said not a word, Darcy could not have agreed more heartily. Miss Bennet was everything good and trustworthy.

"I am afraid that time is past, Jane," Mr. Bennet said with regret. "While we have covered the truth, there will always be the potential for gossip. Even with all these gentlemen have done to protect her, Lizzy has been in Mr. Darcy's home without a chaperone for more than a week." He raised an eyebrow at Darcy. "I have not asked who cared for Lizzy while she was injured and ill as I suspect I do not wish to know, but Jane, surely you can see that she *must* marry."

"I am not the one you must convince, Papa," was Miss Bennet's serious reply. "Lizzy's reputation has not been tarnished thanks to your quick thinking. We have heard no gossip. *Must* she wed?"

Mr. Bennet shook his head. "Lizzy is a sensible girl. She will understand."

Miss Bennet was shaking her head, and Darcy quite agreed. It was not right. Mr. Bennet was a tyrant. To tie Elizabeth to any man who was not... was not... Darcy's shoulders slumped.

Who was not *him*. Mr. Bennet should not betroth Elizabeth to anyone but him.

"I suppose we could ask Gardiner," Mr. Bennet continued. "His circle is mostly tradesman, but he has connections, men with significant fortunes who would be pleased with a gently bred wife, particularly an intelligent one. Frankly, Lizzy might thrive in such a marriage."

"Or Darcy and I could enlist my mother," Fitz added, all affability. Darcy glared at his cousin, but Fitz continued to speak. "The countess knows nearly every family in the ton and has an exact knowledge of marriageable men and their situations. I am sure my mother would like her. Miss Elizabeth is a rather spirited, intelligent woman." He caught Darcy's eye and spoke directly to him. "Pretty, too, which a young woman ought to be if she possibly can."

Mr. Bennet made a sort of growling sound in his throat, and Miss Bennet released a startled laugh.

"Pardon me," she said, raising one hand to her mouth. "That is just like something Lizzy said once about . . ." she faltered. "About a man we know."

Darcy knew just the man she meant, and he felt a little twinge of pity for Miss Bennet, though he dared not display it. He faced his cousin. "Fitz," he said, "may I speak with you in private?"

Fitz appeared as though he would demur, but Darcy took his cousin by the arm and half-pulled, half-shoved him to the door.

Out in the hall, Darcy looked up and saw four or five small children of varying ages sitting on the floor above watching from the landing, their legs dangling through the railing. Behind him, Sir William gave directions to his butler. Darcy and Fitz were led to a small, empty parlor. They heard Sir William calling out to the children to return to the schoolroom and a chorus of disappointed replies. The sound was cut off as the butler shut the door.

"What the blazes are you doing?" Darcy asked his cousin curtly.

"Helping these men locate a good husband for Miss Elizabeth," Fitz replied, all pleasant innocence.

"You do not even like her!" Darcy cried. "You avoid her, you chastise her, you try to persuade me from showing her the least consideration!" Darcy stalked over to one of the windows, placing his hands on either side of the casement and gazing out upon the bleak, muddy fields beyond.

"Are you mad, Darcy?" Fitz shot back. "You are the one who said you would not consider her. I acted to protect her *and* you. I think Miss Elizabeth is perfect, you great ox!"

Darcy swung back to scowl at his cousin. He could feel himself grow hot with anger. "I beg your pardon?"

Fitz not only rolled his eyes—he rolled his entire head. "Perfect for *you*, you bird-wit!" He linked his hands together behind his head, something Darcy did himself when he felt short-tempered. "Darcy," he said slowly, and Darcy could hear the bitterness in his cousin's words, "*you* are the one who refuses to see it." He rubbed the back of his neck tiredly before waving a hand in the direction of the study. "There is an uncommonly beautiful, intelligent, spirited, loyal young woman in that room. I would very much like to know her better, but I never shall. Do you know why?"

Darcy glanced away, ashamed. Of course he knew.

"Indeed," Fitz said in response to the look of sympathy Darcy wore. "I have my allowance. Should Miss Bennet and I like one another, I could marry her—but when the children come, as they so often do, we would have nothing to give them. They would all of them become the relatively impoverished grandchildren of an earl. As the dependent second son of an earl, I can say that it is not a position I recommend." He held Darcy's gaze. "Therefore, I will not approach Miss Bennet. I will not speak with her or try to know her better. We must both of us seek other matches." Darcy had never seen Fitz so cold, so angry—not with him. Fitz ground out his next words. "That is not *your* fate.

You can afford to marry where you choose." He paused to regain his composure. When he had, he said, "I have seen how hard you work. I have never been jealous of your good fortune, Darcy. You know that."

Darcy nodded. "I do know it."

Fitz's hands curled into fists. "Then you must also understand how deeply it *galls* me to see you throw away that gift—the opportunity to seek your own happiness. And for what? You would make yourself forever miserable for connections and fortune you do not require?" He glared at Darcy. "I would plant you a facer if it would not distress Georgie."

It embarrassed Darcy to think that he had not recalled Georgiana's situation in some days. She had not written him; she was safe with their aunt and uncle. His aunt said that she was recovering. Still, Elizabeth's plight had entirely consumed him. He was not certain his sister *would* be distressed should Fitz follow through on such a threat, and he could not fault her for it.

A deep weariness washed over him, and he wondered tiredly whether Georgiana would like Elizabeth. Before last summer he could have said for certain, but now—well—he *thought* she might.

It had been a fortnight following his insult at the assembly before he admitted to himself that he admired Elizabeth. Then he had spent nearly a month hiding that admiration from its object. It was during Elizabeth's sojourn at Netherfield to care for her sister that he had first felt himself in real danger, but he suspected he had been infatuated with her long before he allowed it to be so. He had believed some time away to clear his head was in order, and he had sent for Anders, intending to leave a day or two after the ball with the other guests. Darcy had not yet mentioned anything to Bingley about leaving, but it was not a secret he had sent for his coach. He wondered whether the

Bingleys had seen his behavior more clearly than he had himself and acted out of fear their designs would come to naught.

Fitz was still talking. "Miss Elizabeth is a gentleman's daughter. She would benefit from your wide knowledge of the world, and you would benefit from her open manner. You also trust her. You require someone you can trust implicitly." Fitz frowned, but something like humor finally kindled in his eyes. "And you cannot marry me."

"I do trust her," Darcy muttered, thinking of how she had defended him from the Bingleys. He shot a scowl at his cousin. "*More* than you, in fact." In the brief moments when he had thought Elizabeth dead, his world had been torn asunder, and when he realized she was alive... He would not lose her again. Family connections be damned, wealth be damned—he could not endure the pain of seeing her bound to another.

Fitz smiled broadly. "Then you had better marry her."

He knew Fitz was congratulating himself, and he would never hear the end of it. He did not care.

Darcy simply nodded. "I have come to the same conclusion."

Once he said the words aloud, a little of the weight he had carried around the past weeks lifted from his shoulders. He could not say precisely when it had happened, but marrying Elizabeth had become his dearest wish.

His mother, despite her own decision to marry an untitled man, had expressed higher hopes for her son, and his father had strongly supported her. Darcy had thus always been taught that marriage was an obligation to improve the family's standing and not an opportunity for self-satisfaction. Yet he could not regret having Elizabeth always with him.

His parents would have been disappointed, and this gave him some pain. Yet he knew that they would have come to love Elizabeth. Perhaps begrudgingly at first. But eventually, they would have seen her worth.

He hoped Elizabeth thought somewhat better of him now than she had at the ball, or even than she had at dinner the previous evening. He gave Fitz a small, sheepish smile. "Do you think that when she realizes I have spoken with her father before her, she will throw another plate at my head?"

Fitz snorted. "I hope she does, you mutton-head. We might have cleared up this question of her reputation days ago had you just admitted I was right."

Darcy's heart filled with a kind of cautious joy. He could not help it. He walked past his cousin without a word and returned to the study.

Miss Bennet and Sir William were speaking quietly together. Mr. Bennet was penning a letter at Sir William's desk.

"Mr. Bennet, sir," Darcy said, and Sir William smiled knowingly. Mr. Bennet stopped writing and peered at Darcy over his spectacles. Fitz came in behind him and sat in a chair close to the fire.

"Yes, Mr. Darcy?" the older man asked.

Darcy felt everyone's eyes upon him. He cleared his throat. He had always expected that when he had this conversation, it would be in private. He took a deep breath and attempted to ignore the others. "I request your permission to marry Miss Elizabeth."

There was a small gasp from Miss Bennet, and Darcy was sure he heard the ghost of a laugh from Fitz. Sir William laced his hands together over his stomach, and rocked back and forth on his heels. "Capital, capital," he said warmly.

Mr. Bennet carefully wiped his pen and set it on the desk. "Well," he said thoughtfully, "that is a rather unexpected application, Mr. Darcy. May I ask why you have made it?"

To say he was surprised by Mr. Bennet's inquiry would have been too weak a word. He was shocked. Mr. Bennet's daughter—nay, all his daughters—were facing ruin. Only minutes ago he had been preparing to send her to an uncle in trade to find her a husband. Surely he was a better prospect?

Darcy frowned. He would not make a cake of himself in front of Elizabeth's family and friends. "She is in need of a husband," he said, "and her reputation is at risk due to some plan to harm me. Surely you would not refuse such an offer."

"Oh, for . . ." Fitz's irritation exploded. "Darcy is so much in love he cannot sleep at night. I beg you, Mr. Bennet, put me out of my misery and offer my bumbling cousin your consent."

Darcy knew his face was aflame, but no one mentioned it.

Mr. Bennet's unwavering gaze held Darcy's.

"I cannot say to you what I have not yet said to her, sir," Darcy explained. "But please believe that there is more than a desire to rescue Miss Elizabeth's reputation in my request."

Mr. Bennet was silent for a moment before nodding his head.

"Papa," Miss Bennet said gently but firmly, "Lizzy will never be forced into an alliance. Please do not ask it of her."

"Jane," Mr. Bennet replied gravely, "she no longer has a choice. She must marry." He stood to take her hand. "Lizzy thought better of Mr. Darcy after the ball. It will be well."

Miss Bennet worried her bottom lip, a habit she had in common with Elizabeth.

Darcy hated to see her anxiety. Miss Bennet deserved more consideration. She was Elizabeth's favorite sister, after all, and he prayed she would soon be his sister as well.

"Miss Bennet," Darcy said, "if Miss Elizabeth does not wish it, I will withdraw. It is not my intention to compel her in any way." It pained him to say it, but he could never insist that Elizabeth marry him. It would spoil everything he wished for if Elizabeth were made unhappy.

Miss Bennet's expression was one of gratitude. "Thank you, Mr. Darcy," she said simply. "If you would be so kind, tell Lizzy that I miss her."

While Mr. Bennet had already given his assent, Darcy could not but feel that Miss Bennet's approbation was more important. He bowed and turned to his cousin.

"Netherfield Park next, Fitz."

Fitz gave him an amused glance. "You will have to wait outside."

Darcy shrugged. "As you say." He offered his farewells.

His cousin stood. "Mr. Bennet. Sir William." Fitz lingered near the chair where Miss Bennet was seated. "We shall reunite you with your sister as soon as possible, Miss Bennet."

Miss Bennet said something too softly for Darcy to hear, but he suspected it was her thanks.

A short time later, Darcy stood in front of Netherfield in the cold, minding two horses and trying to focus on something other than his frozen toes. They had arrived half an hour ago, whereupon Fitz had tossed his reins at Darcy without even looking and had headed up the stairs. Just as Darcy was considering giving up his position as a stable boy to search for his cousin and a little warmth, the door opened, and Fitz stepped outside. Darcy lifted his head to complain, but someone else called Fitz's name.

Someone female.

Darcy ducked his head, but not before he caught Miss Bingley's gray eyes upon him. His heart squeezed with anxiety. He peeked up at her from beneath the brim of his hat.

Miss Bingley's gaze flicked in his direction, and Darcy held his breath. Then, with haughty, cold indifference, she turned her attention back to Fitz.

She had not recognized him.

Darcy moved to the other side of his horse. As he swung himself up into the saddle and turned his back to the house, he realized that he had given Elizabeth just such a superficial, disdainful glance at the assembly before he had roundly insulted her. Miss Bingley's slight meant little, but it taught Darcy again how arrogant he had been.

"Not so great a man without your own clothes, are you?" Fitz teased as he approached.

"Miss Bingley was never interested in me, Fitz, only my situation, and you have just seen the proof." Darcy handed Fitz's reins back to him. "Did you learn anything?"

Fitz nodded. "I am not certain Miss Bingley was an author of that scene in the library, no matter how well she fulfilled the role. She asked, just now, that I deliver her apologies to you." He mounted his horse with a practiced ease.

"She may be attempting to mitigate the consequences of her behavior," Darcy said bluntly.

"Perhaps," Fitz agreed. "But let us not hold that conversation here. It will be dark before we reach home as it is. We can speak on the way."

"Excellent," Darcy replied. He was anxious to leave Hertfordshire behind. He wanted to speak with Elizabeth.

Fitz looked smug. "In a hurry, are we?"

Darcy made no answer to his cousin. There was no need to encourage him.

As they cleared Netherfield's borders, Fitz maneuvered his mount within speaking distance and began. "I am not sure the Bingleys targeted Miss Elizabeth. Bingley himself does not seem ruthless enough."

"He maintained his position with me well enough," Darcy grumbled.

Fitz snorted. "Did Bingley try to prevent you from leaving his home before you had made his sister assurances? Has he done anything to discredit you since, to force you to the point? Did he follow you to London, start a rumor about you or Miss Elizabeth? As a fortune hunter and a schemer, he is rather a disappointment."

Darcy considered this. Bingley had clearly expected his initial plan to work and had not created contingencies if it did not. He lifted his shoulders and let them fall. "Did you learn anything new?"

Fitz nodded. "I told Bingley you sent me to speak with him about Miss Jane Bennet. He took it as a sign that you were recovering from what he termed your 'pique' with him and became quite loquacious as to his intentions with her. It is essentially as we surmised: Bingley believes Mrs. Bennet's proclamation, as a number of the families hereabouts have repeated her claim. He does seem smitten with Miss Bennet, but without the financial inducement, it is difficult to know whether he would have pursued her. In his mind, she is a wonderful solution to his current problem, a beautiful woman with the promise of an estate. He did not own to me that he had lost so much of his fortune. Whatever she said in her note declining his visit he has not taken seriously."

"He disregards it at his own peril, I think," Darcy replied, and watched his cousin's response closely.

Fitz's expression did not change. "Bingley *does* owe money, Darce. He lost a large wager early in the year to a man named Walter Howard. Bingley mentioned Howard as regards the bet, but nothing more. When I asked just now, Miss Bingley confirmed that her brother had invited Howard to the ball. She said nothing about a wager, but then, she may not know." He glanced over at Darcy. "Was there not a Howard on our list?"

"Yes, Walter Howard," Darcy replied immediately. "I did not know he and Bingley were acquainted, but Sir William's description of the man with the large ears, long hair, and without the proper attire made me think of him. It is only that he always wears spectacles, and Sir William was sure his man did not." He considered the unlikeliness of the connection. "It makes no sense. Howard clings to his honor more rigidly than any man I know."

"Including you? Remarkable," Fitz remarked.

Darcy shook his head. "He has good principles. Though I am surprised he has been betting. To my knowledge, he always eschewed it entirely." He pursed his lips. "Howard is the one who wanted me to marry his sister early last March."

His cousin was quiet for a moment. "Did he believe the babe was yours?"

"No!" Darcy exclaimed, shocked at the question. "He never made any such claim, and you know I would never . . ."

Fitz held up his hands, palms out. "You say he is a man of honor. It is just curious he would risk you knowing his secret if he did not believe you already knew."

They trotted on without speaking, guiding their mounts fluidly around a slow-moving cart. When it was well behind them on the road, Darcy addressed Fitz again. "I am sorry to say it, Fitz, but similar requests have been made of me before." The surprise on his cousin's face was clear. The anger was unexpected.

"Who?" Fitz demanded. "You did not mention this when we made the list."

Darcy sighed. "I tell you this only because of this mess I am in. You must swear to be discreet. The girls were quite young, prey to men like Wickham." Knowing as much as he did about how easily a young girl could be seduced, he ought to have been more careful of Georgiana. But they were Darcys, and Darcys did not succumb to such temptations. Until they did.

"If you had been *less* discreet, you might have received fewer insults of this sort," Fitz grumbled, but he agreed to keep Darcy's confidence.

"Fawkner and Masterman, after I inherited." Darcy felt a wave of melancholy crash over him. He knew the whispers about him not being interested in women had begun at Cambridge, and was certain he had Wickham to thank for that. "Perhaps they believed that since I had shown no inclination to marry that who my bride was would not matter, only what she brought with her. Money and connections were a part of each offer, and they were significant."

Fitz was quiet, evaluating him, but Darcy said nothing more. He was so very weary of the ton. He had loved London once. The museums, Angelo's, lectures, theatre, opera, the bookstores, his club . . . it was a place of infinite variety. Except on the marriage market, where the demands for his attention had grown more and more insistent and the women had all begun to run together.

None of them stood out in the way Elizabeth did—her unaffected beauty, her genuine concern for others, her sharp wit that was as often turned against herself as others. Darcy was nothing more than a target in London, a man who had come into his fortune young, who would not be an heir-in-waiting until he was forty. As though the death of his father was an asset. He knew without asking that Elizabeth would not see the loss of a beloved parent in such a way.

Darcy maneuvered his mount around a hardened rut in the road while his cousin returned his attention to Bingley.

"He would never own Longbourn himself, of course," Fitz said, "but he does not seem to mind." He sniffed. "If this scheme was successful, Bingley would act as trustee until his eldest son came of age, and he would then consider his promise to his father fulfilled, both through the acquisition of such a property and by marrying the daughter of a landed gentleman. He explained he would use his fortune to expand Longbourn once his heir is born, though he did not mention how that fortune has been depleted." Fitz glanced over at Darcy. "According to Bingley, he believed you and his sister were friends and would make a decent enough match of it. I supposed that to mean that her expenses would become your problem."

"Did he invite me to Netherfield with this end in mind?" Darcy inquired.

Fitz shrugged. "He did not say, but I would presume he did. He certainly did not admit that as your brother, he would have approached you for assistance remedying his financial predicament, but I suspect that he would have done that as well." Fitz frowned. "Perhaps Howard is the one who encouraged him to saddle you with her? I am sorry to say it, but Bingley might not have thought of it on his own. He is not deficient, but he does not seem much of a plotter, either."

"But why would Howard care whether I was married to Miss Bingley? And why would Bingley not lay the blame on Howard if it were true?" Darcy asked, frustrated.

"If Howard is the man you say he is, perhaps it is not," Fitz replied. "Miss Bingley would not hand over the guest list, but she did let me read it. She confirmed that a Mr. Webb and a Mr. Seymour were present. Did we not discuss them as well?"

Darcy nodded. He had not seen them either, but he realized, thinking back, that he recalled little other than Elizabeth. Her clumsy first partner, the young officer with whom she had danced the second. The Lucas boy who had asked her for the third. Darcy had asked her to dance before he realized what he was doing and was silently thrilled when she had said yes. Still, he had to wait for her next open set. He had been given Bingley's message just before he led Elizabeth to the floor.

They rode along for a time, the only sound that of the horses' hooves hitting the packed dirt of the road. Could Miss Bingley have been mistaken? Had Howard truly been at the ball? And if so, could Howard have been involved in Bingley's scheme?

Darcy kept his head down as they entered Meryton. So determined was he not to be recognized that it was only Fitz's voice, raised in falsely jovial tone, that broke into his thoughts.

"Wickham!" his cousin called merrily. "Well met!"

Chapter Nine

When Elizabeth woke, the sun was already high in the sky, and she knew that the colonel and Mr. Darcy must be nearly to Meryton. She ate breakfast, read, finished her embroidery, released the cloth to cut it into four handkerchiefs, and set to hemming them. It was more difficult without the frame, but she managed. When that was finished, she stood to pace the room.

Where were they now? Had they spoken to Sir William? What had they said? Would they see Mr. Bingley? Would they visit Longbourn? She longed to be doing something to help end their predicament in a positive way. Instead, she sewed. Would that she could sew her way to freedom.

Elizabeth sighed and admitted, if only to herself, that she would miss Mr. Darcy terribly when this nightmare was over. He would be free to return to his calm and well-ordered life, and she wanted that for him, but when their immediate situation was resolved, she would have to leave and never see him again. She placed a hand over her aching heart, determined not to regret a man she had so recently hated, though she thought very differently now. Love was a luxury she could no longer afford.

She paused. Could she really *love* Mr. Darcy? He could be terribly stubborn, and his unyielding sense of pride sometimes fueled an unbecoming arrogance. Yet he was also intelligent and funny and gentle. Handsome, particularly when he smiled. And he liked her. He must, to put up with her own stubbornness, her scolding, her teasing. He had begun to tease her back. Had he not cared for her when she was ill? She felt her cheeks warm. Perhaps it would be better not to recall. Elizabeth closed her eyes.

Yes. She could love Mr. Darcy. Perhaps she already did.

She removed another large cloth from the basket and struggled to secure it in the frame, but with one hand's movement restricted, she could not stretch the fabric tightly enough. Finally, in frustration, Elizabeth removed the splint. Her arm was tender and there was yellow and green bruising between her elbow and wrist, but it was beginning to fade around the edges. She wiggled her fingers and felt only a slight twinge. Gingerly, she worked the material into the frame. Once it was taut, she began again, focusing all her thoughts on the fine fabric and beautiful colored threads.

She worked for several hours before she wandered to the window. How much longer would she be confined to a single room? She could not bear it, even in a home as lovely as this.

Mr. Slipworth returned to remove the dishes. "I waited until Mrs. Spencer gave me permission," he said, his skin crinkling at the corner of his eyes. "She is quite fierce in your defense, Miss Elizabeth."

Elizabeth offered her thanks, and Mr. Slipworth left her to her idleness. She moved back to the window. Mr. Darcy's home was a few streets away from a large park. She knew this because her window had a small glimpse of the trees over the other buildings. The treetops were either bare or brown now, but they would be gloriously green in the spring.

What would Mr. Darcy's townhouse be like in the spring? Would it be like Longbourn, bustling with family and friends and morning calls? Mr. Darcy was so quiet a man that the thought greatly amused her. Perhaps he would not be at home to anyone. She laughed softly. More likely he would be home to those he could not avoid and gruff even with them. She could not deny that the man was proud, but the thought did not bother her as it once had. There was so much consideration and compassion—even humility—beneath that haughty façade. She would always be glad to have witnessed it.

Her ruminations were interrupted by a crash that sliced painfully through the quiet. Elizabeth started and placed a hand over her pounding heart, then stood and turned towards the front of the house. Outside, voices cried out in fear and anger. She dared not leave her room to cross the hall and look out a front-facing window, but she feared something terrible had happened.

For no better reason than needing something to do, Elizabeth moved the sewing frame back into the corner of her room and put away the workbasket and thread. She straightened the bedclothes before glancing around the room. Despite assurances that she was safe, she still feared detection, so she was continually putting things away. With no maid and no wish to demand much of Mrs. Spencer's time, she was simply dressed. Her few borrowed gowns were hanging neatly in the wardrobe. The items for her toilette that Mrs. Spencer had left for her were soon tucked away as well.

Then she waited for someone to come explain to her what had happened. Mrs. Spencer and Mr. Slipworth had been discreet and solicitous of her; perhaps they were investigating and one of them would come to her when there was more information. She opened a book but could not focus.

Muffled voices and scraping sounds still made their way up from the street, and Elizabeth could bear it no longer. She tucked the book into a drawer and opened her door just far enough to peek down the hallway. There were five rooms on this side of the hall, including her own and the library. These rooms overlooked the back garden which she found lovely even in December. Opposite them were four rooms on the front side of the house overlooking the street. The largest one, judging from the spacing of the doors, was the third from the servants' stairs. It would likely have more windows and the best view of whatever was happening.

The corridor was empty, and Elizabeth dashed across it to the largest room. It was clearly a parlor for the bedchambers on this floor. She moved directly to one of the two large windows and lifted the curtain just far enough from the window that she could see a coal wagon tipped over. A mound of the dark black fuel had spilled all the way over the coal hole and piled up against the servants' entrance. The horses had been unhitched and removed a bit from the scene. Someone held the reins and the animals appeared calm.

Elizabeth could make out a few men, servants and passersby, helping the coal men right the wagon. Two others were using wide, flat shovels to clear the coal hole so that the spilled coal could be loaded in. A long line of carriages, obstructed by the accident, snaked slowly past. Elizabeth hoped no one had been hurt.

She carefully replaced the curtain, meaning to return to her chambers, but when she opened the door just a tiny bit to check the hall, she saw the entrance to the servants' stairs open and a male figure emerge. Her heart flew into her mouth. It was not Mr. Slipworth; it was certainly not Mr. Darcy or Colonel Fitzwilliam. It was a man with a shock of very blond hair, so blond it was nearly white. A shiver ran down her spine. She had only seen hair that color once before.

She dared not move as he strode to the room closest to him, glanced around the hall, and then stepped inside. The door clicked closed behind him.

Elizabeth's mind raced. She waited for two or three minutes before the man exited the room and moved to the next on the same side of the hall, where the library and her chambers were located. He was being methodical, she thought. He would check all the rooms on that side of the hall before he moved to this one. Instinctively, she stepped into the hall, closed the door behind her, and entered the next room, intending to move closer to the servants' stairway. She waited, one hand on the knob and an ear to the door, for the sounds of someone moving in the hall and the click of a door opening and shutting. When she heard it, she peered out, then moved silently into the final room at the end of the corridor and waited again. Her hands were shaking. She pressed them together angrily. This was no time to give in to fear.

When she again heard him open a door, she waited. *Please,* she thought, *move down the hall.* She had not heard him enter the library, which should be next. What was he waiting for? She pressed her ear to the door and strained to hear him. There was a sort of huffing sound before she heard what she wanted—another click.

Elizabeth peeked through the keyhole, the brass cold against her cheek. Nothing. She peered cautiously into the hall. Empty. She paused to be certain he would stay in the room, but then realized he might already be finishing his search. She opened her door and closed it behind her. She stepped quietly towards the end of the hall, glancing over her shoulder. It was silent, but then she heard it.

A knob rattled. She whirled around, her gaze drawn directly to it.

It began to turn.

Elizabeth tore her eyes away and nearly leapt through the entrance to the servants' stairs.

She hit something—someone—hard. A bolt of pain traveled up her left forearm, but she freed her right arm and formed a fist. She swung, connecting with something soft. She heard a grunt before a strong hand grasped her wrist and she struggled wildly to free herself.

"Miss Bennet!" a man hissed. "Why are you out of your chambers?"

"Mr. Slipworth?" she whispered. The relief was exquisite, and she slumped against the wall. "I am so very sorry, sir." He released her arm, and Elizabeth pulled herself to her feet. Mr. Slipworth bent to retrieve a key that had fallen on the steps.

"I was coming to relock the door," he said, "I forgot to bring the key when—"

"One of the men who took me is here, looking through the rooms," Elizabeth said breathlessly, interrupting him. Mr. Slipworth stared at her, bemused. "Who took me from Longbourn," she added.

From the light of the candle in the stairwell, she could see the valet's expression harden.

"Our attention was diverted by . . ."

"Yes," she said in a rush. "I saw it."

Mr. Slipworth tipped his head towards the next floor. "Continue up the stairs, Miss Bennet, and find a place to hide. He may not be the only one inside." He turned the lock.

Elizabeth fled.

※

Darcy's gaze snapped to the side, and his hands balled into fists. Wickham was standing outside the cobbler's shop, uncharacteristically alone. Of all the luck! Fitz had not seen Wickham since before the miscreant had attempted to elope with Georgiana. He would never pass up this opportunity, but the timing could not be worse. Wickham would love nothing better than to spin a tale about what Darcy was doing back in Meryton posing as a colonel. Darcy dismounted but did not approach.

As he moved behind the horse's neck, Darcy had a fleeting glimpse of Wickham's face as it paled even more than it had when he and Bingley had encountered him being introduced to the Bennet women. Fitz's hand rested lightly on the hilt of his sword, and Wickham's eyes were fixed upon it.

"Darcy mentioned you had joined the militia," Fitz said pleasantly. "I am much obliged. The red coat has made locating you a simple thing."

"What do you want, Fitzwilliam?" Wickham asked bitterly.

Fitz's laugh was hearty and dangerous. "Do you not know?"

Darcy snuck a look around his horse's head. Another man in a red coat approached cautiously but made no move to intervene. He recognized him as Captain Denny, a friend of Wickham's.

Wickham must have seen his comrade, for he sneered and raised his voice. "Darcy has made certain I shall never be prosperous. What worse can you do?"

Fitz stepped forward again, and Wickham retreated, his right hand moving to the small of his back and under his coat. Darcy glanced to his right. Captain Denny was too far removed to be of use.

Darcy cursed silently. If Wickham pulled a weapon, Fitz would run the man though, and though it was unlikely Fitz would be sent to prison for defending himself, it would make a timely return to London rather difficult. He deftly stepped around his mount just in time to capture Wickham's wrist as the man withdrew a long, thin knife. "Drop the blade, or I will break your arm," he said darkly.

Wickham stilled for a moment, but then cried "Darcy!" His words were gleeful. "Back to the scene of your crime so soon?"

Darcy's hand tightened on Wickham's wrist, and he bent the man's hand inward until the knife dropped, hitting the wooden sidewalk at an angle and tumbling into the mud on the road.

Fitz gave the weapon a cursory glance where it lay on the ground. "You meant to wound me with that child's toy?" His laugh was scornful. "You never properly prepare for anything, do you?"

"I am fully prepared to explain to the good people in this town that Darcy is responsible for Miss Elizabeth's death," Wickham said calmly. "The magistrate has her bonnet and Darcy's button. Now that he has returned in disguise, I do not see how even Darcy could deny it."

Darcy twisted Wickham's arm back with one hand and placed the other on Wickham's shoulder.

Fitz fished the knife out of a puddle. He tucked it into his own belt. "You are free to do so, if you wish."

Wickham's muscles tightened under Darcy's hand. "Do you not believe me?" he asked, incredulous. He struggled, spitting the words at Fitz. "I will do it. It would be a pleasure to watch the man squirm."

Darcy tamped down the urge to strangle his father's godson. Fitz must have a plan. He was rarely without one. He caught his cousin's eye and was reassured by what he saw there.

Fitz grabbed Wickham's elbow, the one not pinned to his back, and motioned to Denny that he should follow. Darcy and Fitz hustled Wickham around the building and into the alley between them.

"For a certain price, I am sure, you would be willing to forget everything," Fitz said thoughtfully, stepping back. "How much this time, Wickham?"

"Ten thousand pounds," Wickham said. He struggled to break Darcy's grip, but his gift was in charm, not strength. "Far less than the thirty you owe me. Your sister was only too pleased with me, Darcy."

Darcy strengthened his hold on Wickham's arm, and Fitz laughed, smiling darkly in a manner that was almost feral. "You mean she would have been pleased to watch you gamble and whore your way through her fortune? I know my cousin, Wickham, and I assure you she would have been wretched. But no matter. You would never have lived to spend it." His pat on Wickham's cheek was more like a slap. "You ought to thank Darcy for not calling me home. He saved your life."

Wickham struggled to free himself, but Darcy held firm. "Good God, Darcy, stop it this instant. Is this how you tossed Miss Elizabeth into the river?"

"Interesting," Fitz mused, not at all averse to playing a part. "You claim that my cousin Darcy has murdered a gentleman's daughter, but you are willing to remain silent about it for the princely sum of ten thousand pounds?" He glanced back at Captain Denny, who was listening very closely.

"Fifteen now," Wickham shot back without looking up. He lurched forward, trying to break free.

Darcy sighed. The man never learned. With a single hard strike of his boot to the side of the man's leg, he forced Wickham to one knee.

"Fifteen," Fitz repeated slowly. He drew his sword with a theatrical flourish. "You would allow a man you say murdered an innocent girl, a gentleman's daughter no less, to flee from justice for the price of fifteen thousand pounds?"

"Yes, and the entire town will know what Darcy has done," Wickham spat. "How long before the news is carried to London? Put up your sword, Fitzwilliam. No one is impressed."

The angry huff behind Darcy told him that Wickham was wrong.

"Alas, Wickham, I fear your attempt at blackmail is doomed to failure." Fitz emphasized the word "blackmail." He sheathed his sword and continued with an air of self-importance. "Captain Denny, this morning Mr. Bennet, Miss Elizabeth's father, and Sir William Lucas, the local magistrate, have both informed me that Miss Elizabeth is, at this very moment, safe in London." He nodded once at Darcy. "Colonel Black?"

Darcy released Wickham, who struggled to his feet as Darcy stepped to the side. Without appearing to move, Fitz landed a crushing blow to Wickham's nose and then an uppercut to the chin that saw Wickham laid out on the ground. He was not unconscious, but he was temporarily incapable of coherent speech.

Without pausing, Fitz addressed Captain Denny. "I am Colonel Richard Fitzwilliam of the Light Dragoons and the younger son of the Earl of Matlock. Lieutenant George Wickham is well-known to my family. I am sorry to say he has squandered every opportunity my uncle offered, and there have been many. You, captain, are a witness to his attempts to blackmail my cousin. If he owes you money, I would not depend upon him paying the debt, and I certainly"—here Fitz winked at a gaggle of young girls who were staring admiringly at him from the pavement back near the shops—"would never expose innocent ladies to such a scoundrel."

Darcy watched Captain Denny's scowl intensify. Wickham's former friend leaned over the prone figure and helped Fitz drag Wickham to his feet.

"We ought to leave him with Colonel Forster," Darcy said flatly. He removed a length of rope from his saddlebag and securely bound Wickham's hands. "The militia is quartered a mile or so to the south."

"We could just leave him here," Fitz replied, indicating the merchants.

Darcy shook his head. "Wickham would simply steal a horse and ride off, Fitz. He is not one to stay and fight."

"I will ride with you," Captain Denny said, speaking at last. He sent a look of disgust in Wickham's direction. "I should never have agreed to introduce him to Colonel Forster. He has been nothing but trouble from the off."

Fitz's eyes lost their false merriment and darkened precipitously. "Right then." He shoved Wickham forward. "You are fortunate we wish to be on our way, Wickham. Otherwise, I might make you run behind my horse all the way to London. As it is . . ." He motioned to Darcy, who helped him secure Wickham over the horse's back and bind his ankles together. Fitz climbed on behind him, and Denny led the way.

He made a sorry sight, Wickham did, his head hanging down one side of the horse and his feet on the other, swearing and hollering the entire journey. Darcy felt a deep sense of satisfaction seeing Wickham in such a position and would have greater pleasure still in charging the man with blackmail. Fitz had set that up perfectly. No better witness than a friend of the accused. He would enjoy telling the story to Elizabeth.

Denny had ridden ahead, and Forster was awaiting them. Wickham was hauled off by a few unsmiling fellow officers, and this time, Darcy refused to wait outside.

Fitz took the lead in introducing them and explaining what had happened. Forster listened carefully.

"I am not sure what I can charge him with, truly," Forster said grimly. "It will be his word against yours. It is not as though he wrote a note."

"He was not discreet, Colonel," Fitz argued. "Captain Denny heard it all."

Forster glanced at the captain, who nodded. "Mr. Wickham is your friend. Will you give testimony against him? You will not suddenly change your mind?"

Denny shook his head.

"If it is not enough," Darcy said roughly, "speak with the merchants. Wickham has undoubtedly purchased on credit with many of them." He paused. "It is unlikely that he has a way to pay them, meaning that the regiment shall have to make it good."

Forster's jaw tightened. "I shall, Colonel Black."

There was no hesitation, no irony in Forster's use of his new name. Was the man that good at his job? Or that bad?

"You may also be hearing from some rather irate guardians," Fitz said. "I would not wish for you to be taken unawares."

Forster rubbed his forehead. "Excellent," he said sarcastically. "I have half a mind to let him fend for himself there."

Fitz grinned. "Your regiment, Colonel. I would never presume to instruct you."

"Is there is anything more you require, gentlemen?" Forster asked.

"Yes," Darcy said. "May we speak with him again?"

Forster nodded and issued a command to a man just outside the door. When Wickham was shoved into the colonel's office, he had clearly been on the wrong side of some additional blows. His lip was bleeding now as well as his nose, and a red welt was rising near his eye.

"What do you want?" he sneered. All pretense to gentlemanly behavior had vanished, leaving behind the real Wickham, the one that Darcy knew better than he wished. Fitz stepped forward, but Darcy stopped him with a glance.

"A name," Darcy said coolly.

"Darcy," Wickham said glibly. "There, may I go?"

Darcy ignored the jibe. "I want to know the whereabouts of the men who told you Miss Elizabeth Bennet was going to be killed." It made him sick to say it, but he did not allow his revulsion to show.

Forster's eyes widened and his nostrils flared, but thankfully he remained silent.

Wickham smirked. "What is it worth to you?"

Damn the arrogance of the man. Darcy remained outwardly calm. He would not allow Wickham to rattle him. "The question is," Darcy replied, "what is your life worth to you?"

Wickham rolled his eyes. "You will not kill me, Darcy."

"You will call your superior officer by his rank, Wickham," Forster barked.

Wickham frowned. "He is not . . ."

"Colonel Black," Forster told him.

"You will not kill me, *Colonel Black*," Wickham spat out.

Darcy would have laughed if the situation had not been so serious. "I need the name of the man or men who told you this."

"No man told me this," Wickham shot back. He turned to Forster. "May I go, sir?"

Forster's gaze was steady. "No."

"Wickham," Darcy said nonchalantly, "you can offer the names and earn fifty pounds, or I will accept Colonel Forster's offer to invite the father, brother, and uncle of every girl wronged by you since the militia's arrival to meet with you personally." He pretended to inspect the office. "You will, of course, require a larger room."

The sullen look Darcy received quite delighted him.

"Money first," came the demand.

"I do not carry that amount of coin on my person," Darcy replied without losing his composure. "Nor would I release it to you before verifying your information. But I will sign an avowal to be kept in your colonel's possession."

Wickham relented, though his words were resentful. "I was not told," he growled. "An acquaintance of mine from London came to Meryton for the ball. I invited him to cards, and he put me off rather rudely. I made it *my* business to discover his. Tobias is his name. Tobias Henderson."

"And what did you discover?" Darcy asked when it appeared Wickham would not continue.

"His job was to watch you." Wickham replied indifferently. "He had a partner. I wanted in, but they did not wish my help. Not my sort of thing, Toby said. I did not see why watching you would be so difficult."

"Who hired him?" Darcy asked insistently.

Wickham shrugged. "Someone with cash to spare and a grudge against you, I suppose. Netherfield was likely filled with men who fit the bill."

"What does Henderson look like?" Fitz inquired.

"He blends in," Wickham said with a shrug. "Dark blond hair, brown eyes, entirely unremarkable."

"Scars? Birthmarks?"

"He has a tattoo of an English rose." Wickham grinned. "On his arse."

Darcy stifled the instinct to goad Wickham by asking how he knew the location of such a mark, instead simply gesturing to Forster's desk. Colonel Forster nodded, and Darcy picked up a pen. He held it over the inkpot. "Where can we find Mr. Henderson?"

There was no response. Darcy set the pen down.

"Without a location, we cannot find your friend. If we cannot find him and determine whether he is the man we seek, you will not receive your payment."

Wickham sniffed and dabbed at his nose with a bloodied handkerchief. "He can usually be found at The White Bear in Piccadilly," he said, refusing to meet Darcy's eye.

Darcy was pleased to hear it. He had been halfway convinced this would require a trip somewhere far more unsavory, like Seven Dials, where he knew Wickham had once spent some time. He wrote the note with a flourish and handed it to Forster for safekeeping. The colonel read it, and the infinitesimal lift of one eyebrow led Darcy to believe that the man approved.

"I thank you for your assistance, Colonel Forster," Darcy said by way of farewell. Forster nodded, a stoic expression still writ upon his countenance. The man was animated enough in mixed company, but his professional demeanor was impressive. Darcy was ashamed that though he had dined with the officers more than once, he had not previously bothered to take note of the colonel. Had he been so assured of his own superiority that he did not even bother to observe the people around him? Elizabeth had been right to chastise him. Fitz was right, too. He *was* a mutton-head.

Wickham was ushered outside again, and Forster waved a hand at Darcy's uniform. "I presume there is a reason this man is in military dress, Colonel Fitzwilliam?"

"There is, Colonel Forster," Fitz replied. "A good one."

"I presume he does not intend to spy on Boney?"

Fitz shook his head.

"Good," Forster replied stonily. "I would fear for us all."

When they were at last on their horses and heading for London again, Fitz shot a disappointed look at Darcy.

"What?" he asked.

"I cannot believe you gave that cretin more money, Darce," Fitz complained. "I would have enjoyed taking it out of his hide instead."

Darcy released a soft laugh. "When Wickham reads my avowal, he will see that the money must first be applied to his debts in Meryton. He will never see a farthing."

"Debts you would have felt obligated to pay in any case. Well, I feel a good deal better now." Fitz pushed his mount to a quicker pace. "Let us get you back to your beloved so you can stun her with your proposal."

"What do you mean, *stun* her?" Darcy asked as his cousin widened the distance between them. Elizabeth might not want to marry him, but she must have *some* inkling . . . "Fitz?" His cousin was gone.

"Smug, infernal . . ." Darcy grumbled, and urged his horse on.

As she raced up the stairs, Elizabeth heard a set of tinkling bells being pulled three times, very distinctly. She hoped that it was Mr. Slipworth summoning aid. As she reached the servants' floor at the top of the house, all was quiet below. There were more doors along the corridor here, but one was smaller than the others. It was stuck. She threw her entire body against it, squeezing through when it gave way a little, and shoved it closed behind her.

There was another set of stairs inside, only half as long as a normal flight, the treads smaller and narrower. Elizabeth's head ached. Her breaths were short and shallow. She stepped up carefully but with haste and found herself in a dark room the length of the entire townhouse. The ceiling was low, and there were no windows. It was an attic of sorts. At the far end, she could make out a chimney in the center of the wall. As she carefully picked her way closer, she saw that the hearth was surrounded by wooden boxes stacked three high and three across on each side. Several dozen trunks were stacked haphazardly throughout the room.

Where to hide? There was no obvious place. The wooden boxes were too small and appeared to be stuffed with files. Elizabeth tugged at the lid of the trunk closest to her. Locked. She dragged herself to the next one and shook the latch. Locked. She tried a third. Locked.

Downstairs she thought she heard a man shouting.

"Who locks trunks in an attic?" she asked as her fear and frustration grew. Sixth trunk. Locked. Seventh trunk. Locked. Perhaps she could hide behind them?

Finally, on the eighth try, when her distress had nearly consumed her, she tugged on a trunk and the lid lifted. Elizabeth stepped inside and curled up, pulling the lid shut.

Inside, it was dark and quiet. Her legs were cramped, and the clothes were musty, though there was a faint odor of citrus. Elizabeth tried to slow her breathing. She focused on the pleasant scent and the rhythm of her breaths. Her heart was beating so hard that the sound of it filled her ears, making it impossible to hear whether anyone was entering the room. Elizabeth touched the wooden lid only inches from her face and tried to recall happier times, when hiding in trunks was a game, one at which she excelled. As she imagined playing with her sisters, her breathing slowed, and her heart calmed.

Thump. Thump. Thump.

She held a hand over her chest, but it was not her heart making the sound. Someone was ascending the stairs.

"Miss Elizabeth?" called a voice she recalled, low and menacing. "I know you are hiding somewhere."

Elizabeth clapped her hand over her mouth and shivered.

The floorboards creaked, and she swallowed, closing her eyes tightly. The footsteps stopped. Then there was another step. Another pause.

"We saw the broken bushes. We saw the bits of cloth you left in the brambles," the male voice sang. "And Darcy's coachman is very distinctive."

Elizabeth remained still—she dared not move. She took a tiny breath.

"I heard someone tell you to run up the stairs," the man continued, and she heard him shake another trunk. "We are not paid until you are . . ." He sounded amused. "Well, best not to discuss that, I suppose."

Another movement and this one was close—Elizabeth heard the tapping of a foot and a deep sigh of irritation. It was a heavy tapping. Probably a boot. "Miss Elizabeth," he crooned.

Something was dropped to the floor near her, and she flinched. Another trunk, probably.

"I need that money," he said harshly, apparently to himself this time. "Where the devil is she?"

Elizabeth knew that if he continued much longer, she would be discovered. She would not, she told herself sternly, go quietly.

The lid shook.

This was it. Elizabeth raised her knees as far as she was able and prepared to kick.

There was a bit more shaking before one end of her trunk was lifted, then dropped. Her head snapped back but was cushioned by the fabrics that half-filled the box. A string of curses was uttered near her ear.

The lid did not open.

There was more noise drifting up from the lower floors, and the movements stopped. She let herself relax just a bit when suddenly the trunk tumbled on its side.

Heavy footsteps headed away from her now, and there was a pounding sound as the person left the attic in haste. Whoever it was must have given her trunk a sound shove. Thankfully, her right arm was beneath her. She had been too shocked to make a sound, but now she pushed against the lid. It held fast.

She tried to quell the panic that threatened to overtake her. The lock was broken, she told herself firmly, and a good thing it was. The man searching the attic might have found her otherwise. Her shivering increased, and she covered herself with the clothing as best she could so that she would warm. She took deep, regular breaths, forced herself to regain her composure, and considered her predicament. Mr. Slipworth knew she had hidden upstairs. When it was safe, he would come find her. She would simply have to wait.

Darcy and Fitz rode hard towards London until the light faded and they were required to slow their progress. The days were short in December, and it was getting much colder, too. They were likely in for another frigid January.

To get his mind off the cold, Darcy tried to compose his proposal, ideally in a manner that would not insult his intended. *You have already done that*, he reminded himself wryly, and he would not wish to traverse that path again.

It had made him ill to know that Elizabeth had heard his insulting words. In his arrogance, he had become truly blind to the characters of those around him. He had been surprised to discover both Sir William and Colonel Forster were keenly observant men, because he had not expected them to be. He had been fortunate that for whatever reason, Sir William had decided he liked Darcy. Colonel Forster, though, had not been impressed with him. Darcy had also been astonished by Mr. Bennet's hesitation to give his consent when he asked for Elizabeth's hand. Not only was Elizabeth's reputation in peril, but the reputation of all her sisters was at stake. Marry she must, Mr. Bennet had agreed, but he had not been certain Darcy was the best choice of groom.

Darcy was tired of being humbled. No one liked it, and he less than most. He did not intend to propose in such a way that Elizabeth would hesitate as her father had. His battered sense of self-worth could not bend that far. If she refused him, it would break. He was certain of it.

"Rider," Richard called, and motioned ahead.

Darcy nodded and moved his mount to one side of the road. They were not so far from London now. There would be more travelers, even after dark, so he was not unsettled to see a figure riding in their direction.

Not until he began to feel that the figure was familiar.

He recognized the lines of the horse first, then the unique white blaze with five points that stretched from the mare's forehead to her nose. The horse was Duchess, the fastest mount in his stable. And if Duchess was being ridden after dark, it had to be Anders on her back. Fear made him shiver as though he was riding through a snowstorm.

Darcy commanded his own mount into a gallop, closing the gap between them. "Anders," he said breathlessly as he pulled alongside his coachman. "What has happened?"

Fitz came to a halt behind him. "Darcy, what in the blazes . . ." He fell silent when he saw Anders.

"The house has been breached, Mr. Darcy," Anders explained, his breath escaping in frozen puffs of air. "We caught two men. Mr. Slipworth sent Miss Elizabeth upstairs to hide, but he cannot find her, sir. He sent me to intercept you both."

Darcy was flying down the road almost before Anders had finished speaking. The bitter air bit at his cheeks and made his eyes tear. He had left her alone in that house. Fitz was right, he should have stayed. Damn it all, would he never learn?

It was only when he was forced to slow his mount as he entered town that Darcy remembered: Elizabeth was very good at hiding. She had said hide-and-go-seek was a favorite game in the Bennet household, and she had quite effectively wedged herself atop the bookshelves in the upstairs library to avoid detection by the maids. He took a deep breath and released it slowly. Elizabeth would not have allowed herself to be removed from the house without making a great deal of fuss. He refused to consider a scenario where she had been unable to protest.

She was still in the house. He repeated it like a prayer. *Elizabeth is still in the house.* But where? Where would she hide?

When he arrived home, Anders and Fitz were still somewhere behind him. He tossed the reins to a stable boy and went inside directly.

Slipworth was waiting for him by the back door nearest the mews. "There are two men being held in the cellar," he told Darcy. "We captured the first one on the guest floor. The other managed to evade us at first. Anders saw him leaving. He followed the man to Piccadilly, and a good thing too—he was very good at blending into the crowd. Anders had him brought back here before leaving to find you."

"Who is watching them?"

"Anders's cousins," Slipworth informed him. "They helped apprehend him. Strapping fellows."

Darcy had hired these particular cousins before. They were former sailors, and he knew them to be honest and efficient. He would have liked to employ them permanently, but they did not wish to belong to any great house. They made themselves available because Anders was family and he had asked it of them. Darcy could only be grateful.

"Walk with me," Darcy ordered Slipworth, and the valet fell in step. They climbed to Darcy's chambers. The instant the door closed behind them, Darcy asked, "Where were you when you met Miss Elizabeth?"

"We were on the servants' staircase, sir, nearest her room. She fled up the stairs. I have completely searched the floor above and all the servants' rooms. The staff is still downstairs, so we have time if you would like to start over."

Where would Elizabeth hide? She had mentioned hiding in trunks as a girl.

"Slipworth," Darcy asked, "have you searched the attic?"

Slipworth's face paled. "No, sir," he said, closing his eyes. "It did not even occur to me. There is naught up there but locked trunks, and the door is so difficult to open."

Darcy knew a frightened Elizabeth would be able to push her way inside, but had she? With an assurance he did not feel, he said, "Ask my cousin to wait here for me."

Slipworth lit a lamp for Darcy, who made quick time up the servants' stairs. He located the door to the attic, shoving it open with a shoulder and stooping to enter. He was careful as he walked up the steps, for he could fit only half his foot upon each tread. When he reached the top, he could not stand straight—the ceiling was at most six feet from the floor and perhaps a little less. He held the lamp up high, the flames throwing eerie shadows along the floor and walls. He gazed at the wooden boxes lining the back wall, and then at the trunks, which were strewn about.

"Miss Elizabeth?" he called, keeping his voice low. "Are you here?"

There was no answer, and he was just about to raise his voice and try again when he heard something.

"AHH-SHOOOO!"

He tipped his head to one side.

"AHH-SHOOOO!"

The stifled sound was coming from inside a trunk, one lying on its side up against the wall and separate from the others. Darcy strode over to it.

"Elizabeth?" he asked from only an inch away.

"Mr. Darcy?" came the muffled question, then a sniffle and a plaintive explanation. "The lock is stuck."

The release of tension was exquisite; Darcy had to quash a powerful desire to laugh. Instead, he brought the light close to examine the lock. The brass was sound, but the trunk was old. He gave it a little tug just in case, but it held fast.

"I will have you out of there shortly," he assured her. "Please await my word. I should not like you to be injured."

Darcy removed the knife he kept in his boot when he traveled and, after a few minutes, was able to separate the top half of the lock from the splintering wood. He slid the blade back into place.

Elizabeth rolled out of the box and onto the open lid. She sat up, the sleeve from one of his old shirts draped over her face.

"I did not say it was safe," Darcy chided her gently, plucking the shirt from her head and tossing it aside. "You must learn to be more patient."

She wrapped her arms around her waist. "I have been in this box for *hours*, Mr. Darcy," she said stoutly. Darcy wondered if anyone else would notice the slight trembling of her bottom lip. "I have been patient long enough."

They looked at one another without speaking before Elizabeth abruptly threw herself at him without warning and wound her arms around his neck. Darcy felt her body shaking with soft sobs, and he knelt there, holding her as she explained what had happened. He pulled her close and whispered words of comfort, his cheek resting against the top of her head.

He had nearly lost her again.

His staff had detained the men downstairs. They would all be receiving a generous bonus this quarter. He told her as much, and felt her fear give way to relief.

Eventually Elizabeth regained control of herself and he stood, gently lifting her to her feet. He held her left arm gently and frowned. "You removed your splint?"

She stepped cautiously from the lid and onto the floor with a sniff and a glare. "Yes." Her eyes narrowed, and she touched his sleeve. "What are you wearing?"

It was so different a meeting than the last time he had removed her from a trunk that he was quite overwhelmed. He laughed a little and shook his head. What a very odd thing to think. What a very odd thing to experience!

Had Elizabeth been brought to Darcy House only just more than a week ago? He hardly recognized himself, and she was the reason. Darcy pulled back so he could see her face. He swallowed, he blinked, he stared. "Elizabeth," he said, his voice resonant with emotion. With fear. With longing.

With love.

"I ardently admire and love you," he blurted out.

Elizabeth's dark eyes met his, warm and happy. The elegant proposal he had composed on the ride back from Hertfordshire slipped completely away.

"Please," he spluttered, "would you . . . will you marry me?"

So much for a romantic proposal. Never mind. He would have botched it anyway.

Elizabeth gazed up at him, suddenly distressed. "But my situation—my *reputation*, Mr. Darcy, your sister . . ." She blinked back tears. "I thought . . . You *cannot* marry me."

The disappointment stung, but it took Darcy less than the beat of his heart to realize that Elizabeth had not said she did not *wish* to marry him. She had said he ought not marry her. She was trying to protect him. No, not only him, but Georgiana too, even at the cost of her own feelings. The elation that followed his epiphany was nearly overwhelming, and he could not help but smile at her. Never had he been more certain that Elizabeth was meant to be his wife.

"Your father and your friends have kept your reputation safe, Elizabeth, but even had they not . . ." Darcy paused to be sure it was the truth. It was. "Even then, I should have found a way to ask for your hand." Elizabeth was silent as she considered his offer, and Darcy was in agony as he awaited her response. Fitz had been right—she had been very surprised to receive his proposal. "After all, I cannot always rely upon your sneeze as a signal that you require rescuing," he teased her. He boldly cupped her cheek with his hand and rejoiced when she leaned into his palm. "As your husband, I will know where you are at all times."

She glared at him, her spirit returning. "*Will* you?"

Darcy nodded solemnly. "Given the events of the past week, I think it would be for the best." He gazed at her with all the love he felt. "I do not think my heart could stand it otherwise." He tucked an errant curl behind her ear. "I love you, Elizabeth. The only question is—do you love me in return?"

She stared up at him with dark eyes full of longing. "We shall have to ask my father," she said.

"Is that a yes?" he asked, hope surging through him.

"If you are certain it will not harm you or your sister," she said earnestly, "then yes." Her eyes sought his. "My answer is yes." Elizabeth placed her good hand over his where it still cupped her cheek. "I am not quite sure when it happened," she said tenderly, "but I do. I love you, too."

Darcy impetuously bent to capture her mouth, but Elizabeth held her hand up, palm out. "Perhaps we should continue this conversation elsewhere?" Her hand was shaking.

Darcy brushed his lips against her forehead, then grabbed the lamp, holding it out so that Elizabeth could walk before him and still see where she was going.

"By the way," he said as he stooped to keep from hitting his head on the low doorframe, one hand on the small of Elizabeth's back, "I have *already* spoken with your father, and he has given me his approval to marry you. Sir William knows, too. Oh, and Fitz and Miss Bennet as well."

"I beg your pardon?" Elizabeth exclaimed indignantly.

"Shh," Darcy replied with a grin. "Perhaps we should continue this conversation elsewhere."

Chapter Ten

"I would like you to tell me that I am the best cousin that has ever been or is ever likely to be," Colonel Fitzwilliam announced as he joined them in the hall near Elizabeth's chambers.

"I am certain you would," Mr. Darcy replied drily. "Is there some reason to believe you deserve it?"

Elizabeth laughed quietly. A kind of giddiness had overtaken her. "Please forgive me," she said. She reached to take Mr. Darcy's hand in her own. She marveled at her boldness, at how large his hand was, at how tenderly it held hers.

Even in the flickering light provided by the lamp, Elizabeth saw the colonel's features soften briefly before he realized he was being observed. *Too late, colonel,* she thought, her heart warming to him at once.

"First, because my men should arrive shortly and take care of the men in the cellar. By morning, they should be ready to talk."

"And the second?" Mr. Darcy inquired.

"Last week, while you two were . . . well, I am not sure you were doing anything at all, to tell the truth," the colonel said drolly, stepping into Elizabeth's room behind them and closing the door. "Miss Elizabeth has an excuse, but I hope you realize that I was quite busy while you were playing nursemaid, Darcy."

Mr. Darcy muttered something under his breath.

The colonel snorted. "Last week, among the *many* heroic efforts I ventured on your behalf, I spoke to my mother."

"Come, now," Mr. Darcy scoffed. "Your mother might be a bit overbearing, but I hardly think facing her requires heroic effort."

"Do you want this or not?" the colonel asked, holding up a piece of paper.

Mr. Darcy frowned, took the paper, and held it close to the light. "This is a common license!" he exclaimed. "When did I sign this?"

Elizabeth stepped closer to see for herself. "That is right, Mrs. Spencer called you Master Fitzwilliam," she said. "Like the colonel."

Mr. Darcy colored, but nodded. "I know it is rather unwieldy. I would prefer you call me William."

She touched a finger to his signature. "It is strong and elegant. It suits you."

"Thank you," the colonel replied, and Mr. Darcy made a warning sound very much like a growl.

"*However*," Elizabeth said cheerfully, ignoring the colonel, "I should be pleased to call you William if that is the name you prefer." She returned her attention to the document. Her head lifted suddenly. "When did *Papa* sign this?"

The colonel addressed Mr. Darcy. "You signed this when you were so dead on your feet from caring for Miss Elizabeth that you could barely see straight."

Elizabeth blushed. Mr. Darcy had driven himself to great lengths to care for her. He would be a wonderful husband. She silently pledged to be an excellent wife.

"Your father signed it today," the colonel told Elizabeth. He shrugged. "Not that it mattered. Neither of you *had* to sign. I just thought it might keep Lady Catherine away."

"Who?" Elizabeth asked.

Both men groaned. "Our aunt," Mr. Darcy explained. "She is . . ." he paused. "She can be rather . . ."

Elizabeth waited expectantly.

"She has lately been insisting that Darcy marry our cousin Anne," the colonel said at last. "And by insisting, I mean demanding. Neither Darcy nor Anne is amenable."

"Nearly five years, Fitz," Mr. Darcy said and rubbed the back of his neck. "It is hardly new, though her memory of my cradle betrothal to Anne was miraculously and conveniently restored the day after my father's funeral."

"Oh," Elizabeth said, laying her hand upon Mr. Darcy's arm. "Then I am very sorry for your aunt, but I shall not give you up."

"I would not allow it in any case," Mr. Darcy murmured. "You have said yes. I shall never let you go now."

"That sounds rather ominous, Mr. Darcy," Elizabeth said playfully.

"Be that as it may, Elizabeth," he said, bringing her good hand to his mouth for a brief kiss, "it is the truth."

"For me as well," she replied truthfully. Her spirits soared as Mr. Darcy's face lit up brighter than the lamp. "I suppose I should be pleased. I am, after all, receiving the better part of this bargain." Mr. Darcy shook his head and squeezed her hand.

"I doubt that, Miss Elizabeth," the colonel said gallantly, though Elizabeth could see they had made him uncomfortable. He cleared his throat. "I do have news."

"News?" Mr. Darcy asked.

The colonel nodded. "I had a note awaiting me here. I am instructed to escort Miss Elizabeth to my mother's home tonight."

"May I ask why?" Elizabeth asked, glancing at Mr. Darcy when she realized he had asked the same question.

"Because she would like to have you wed from her house," the colonel replied. "We should perhaps also invite your relations from town."

"What?" Elizabeth asked, her voice growing faint. She had only agreed to be wed scant moments before. Was there to be no time at all to grow used to the idea? She pressed her eyelids shut. Foolish girl. Of course not. She had been living in Mr. Darcy's home for more than a week, unchaperoned. Hiding that fact was essential. She must be practical.

Colonel Fitzwilliam was not distressed by her lack of enthusiasm. "My mother is adept at managing gossip, Miss Elizabeth. She plans to use your father's explanation—that you were called away to stay with your relations—to have a laugh at Darcy's well-known dislike of gossip. Apparently, that is the story Darcy told Mr. Bennet to circulate. The *truth* is"—and here the colonel winked—"Darcy has been quietly courting you since just after Michaelmas when he arrived in Meryton. Neither of you wished for the society wedding my mother has been longing to plan. She has been arguing with him over the matter for some weeks. To placate her, you have now both agreed to be wed from her house." He snorted as he reread the missive. "According to her, it is the least you and my unfeeling cousin can do."

"The groom's family does not plan or host weddings," Elizabeth reminded him. "Why would your mother have such expectations?"

Mr. Darcy chuckled. "I am afraid that part of the story is true. Henry, Fitz, Anne, and I have all proven rather resistant to matrimony. My sister Georgiana will not come out for another year or two. My aunt is growing rather desperate. Her friends know this."

Elizabeth tried not to feel overwhelmed. She considered the story and the plan. "Her very influential friends? Who will happily spread this story?"

Both men nodded.

"When, precisely, is the wedding to take place?" Elizabeth asked, bracing herself for the answer.

"Mother says, 'The sooner the better,'" the colonel said. He turned his attention to Mr. Darcy. "She wishes Miss Elizabeth to have some family around her so it appears this was planned. Mother would have preferred tomorrow." He handed the letter to Mr. Darcy. "However, the day after will do." He grinned at Elizabeth. "Perhaps she is afraid you will change your mind."

Elizabeth felt a little numb. She watched Mr. Darcy as he read the note. He smiled just a little at the end, and then handed it to Elizabeth.

She opened it to read the message. It was as the colonel had explained, but the warmth of the closing reassured her. *Tell William I anticipate his marriage with great joy.* Certainly his aunt would support them, even if only for Mr. Darcy's sake.

Elizabeth held the note out, and the colonel tucked it away.

"You did not mention your mother's involvement before now," Mr. Darcy grumbled at his cousin.

"There was no need to mention it before today," Colonel Fitzwilliam replied calmly, and Mr. Darcy gave him what Elizabeth thought was a grudging nod.

"What does your father say?" Mr. Darcy asked.

Colonel Fitzwilliam shrugged. "You know he trusts Mother's instincts."

Something occurred to Elizabeth. "Miss Bingley mentioned that you have an uncle who is an earl. Is that the man of whom you speak?"

Mr. Darcy nodded. "The earldom itself is a young one, and Fitz's father is certainly not of the same ilk as Lady Catherine, but I cannot say how well he will accept . . ." His voice trailed away, and Elizabeth knew he did not wish to offend her.

"How well he will accept your choice of a wife?" she finished for him.

"Elizabeth, I have no qualms about my choice," Mr. Darcy told her firmly.

"I do not doubt that." Elizabeth tried to exude confidence though she was uncharacteristically anxious. She was entitled, she thought. Today she had spent hours locked in a trunk, only to be released and offered a proposal of marriage, followed immediately by wedding plans. It was enough to topple even her own vaunted composure. Add to the mixture the acceptance of a countess but the disapprobation of an earl, and Elizabeth was in some danger of running mad.

She touched two fingers to her temple to rub away the ache. "It is important, however, to account for those in your family who may not understand your marriage to a girl without exalted connections or any fortune to speak of."

She felt Mr. Darcy touch her hand. He was so close she could feel his warmth. "Are you well?" he asked.

Elizabeth took a deep breath and nodded.

"My father does expect those things in a marriage, Miss Elizabeth," the colonel told her bluntly. "However, he also believes there must be mutual admiration and respect between a man and the woman he takes to wife. He may resist Darcy's decision initially, but I do not believe he will be obstinate." He glanced around the room. "It does not appear that you will have an issue with your packing."

Elizabeth's heart sank. "I cannot arrive at the home of an earl after dark and with little more than the gown I am wearing."

"It is not as though you would arrive uninvited, Elizabeth," Mr. Darcy said, the timbre of his voice low and soothing. "We shall make sure you have all you require." He knelt and gazed up into her face. "The earl's home is better guarded than my own. After what has happened here today, I would prefer to have you safely away until this is completely resolved."

"Will you remain there as well?" Elizabeth asked, hating to sound so unsure but hoping Mr. Darcy would not return to his own home without her.

"If you wish," he told her, sounding quite pleased by the request.

Elizabeth took a deep breath. "My aunt Gardiner keeps several of my best gowns here in town with her, for I have no need of them at home. Now that you have those men in your custody, perhaps we might travel to Gracechurch Street to collect them." The dresses were an excuse, though she did want them. More importantly, she longed to speak with her aunt. *And issue an invitation to my wedding.* It felt entirely unreal.

"If you wish," Mr. Darcy said again.

"I should also like to have my father and eldest sister with me when we wed," Elizabeth told Mr. Darcy. "Jane should stand up with me. It has been our intention for many years."

Mr. Darcy shifted his weight from one foot to another. "Will you be able to invite them without your mother?" He was clearly embarrassed, but Elizabeth, though irritated, had to admit it was a concern. Mama was incapable of subtlety. She would quite likely spoil all the countess's well-laid plans in one ill-conceived cry of delight. "I planned to write Papa and have him escort Jane to town, but I shall speak of it with my aunt." She pressed her hands together. "Shall we go, gentlemen?"

"I will tell Slipworth that we are ready," Colonel Fitzwilliam informed them. "Mrs. Spencer has the staff at table and will keep them there until we are gone. Anders is waiting for us." He stepped out of the room.

Elizabeth moved to the wardrobe to collect her repaired pelisse. It was pretty, she thought as she draped it over her arm, a dark brown wool with light blue and yellow flowers embroidered along the lapels and cuffs. Pretty, but certainly not the pelisse she would have chosen for introductions to her betrothed's family. She closed her eyes. She wished fervently for just a bit more time to prepare. First impressions were important, even if they were not always lasting. When she opened her eyes again, she found Mr. Darcy was watching her with some concern.

"Elizabeth," he said, his voice pitched low, "if you do not wish this, you need only say."

She could have kissed him for offering her a choice, but truly, she did not mind meeting his relations, and she was quite happy to leave off hiding. Most of all, she *wanted* to marry Mr. Darcy. Her regard had been growing steadily from the moment he had deigned to explain himself to her in a dark hallway at Netherfield Park and managed to extract her from an uncomfortable confrontation. She had learned to respect him then. When he treated her with such kindness even after she had attacked him with his own china, she had begun to admire him. And somewhere between falling ill and finding herself atop a library bookshelf, she had fallen in love with this enigmatic, infuriating, stubborn, endearing man.

Elizabeth had always anticipated being courted, but their situation would not allow it. Did it matter, in the end? She loved him. She would be brave. "William," she asked earnestly, "do you believe that marrying the day after tomorrow would be for the best?"

His expression grew inexpressibly tender when she used his Christian name. Elizabeth felt a little thrill pass through her. She would be certain to use his name whenever possible. "I do. As your husband, I shall be able to truly protect you. No more hiding. I should marry you this instant were it possible." He turned her hand over in his own and kissed her palm. Elizabeth felt a shock that traveled all the way up her arm.

Evidently Mr. Darcy knew just how to persuade her.

Elizabeth swallowed, but her throat was suddenly dry. Now she regretted leaving the attic so precipitously—she longed for more kisses like the one he had bestowed upon her. Surely as her husband, he would kiss her more often. Elizabeth blinked and gazed up into his dear face. Oh, but he was handsome.

Perhaps he could court her after they were wed.

Elizabeth shook herself a bit and laughed at the thought. "I cannot believe I am to be married. It is as though the week we have all just survived has lasted years. I feel quite an old woman now."

"You?" Mr. Darcy asked with an incredulous laugh of his own. "I believe I saw a gray hair in the glass this morning. I hope our marriage shall be a great deal less eventful."

Elizabeth knew that once she stepped foot outside of Darcy House, her life would be forever changed. She intended to sweep out to the carriage with the kind of aplomb she imagined Mrs. Darcy should display. "Shall we, gentlemen?"

Mr. Darcy shook his head. "Please wait, madam." He gathered the pieces of her splint that she had left at the foot of the bed.

Elizabeth sighed and held out her arm. "You do know how to spoil a moment, Mr. Darcy."

⁂

"Wait here," Darcy instructed Anders. "We shall not be long."

Anders tipped his hat, and Darcy escorted Elizabeth up the steps where she knocked on the door, Fitz following behind.

The night was rather dark, but Darcy could see enough to know the home was located in an affluent part of Gracechurch Street. Whatever her uncle's business concerns might be, he had clearly been successful.

Elizabeth pulled the bell confidently. "Good evening, Mr. Paulson," she said to the man who stood framed in the doorway. "I am come to see my aunt and uncle."

"Miss Elizabeth!" he cried before regaining his composure. "Of course, do come inside. I apologize. I was not told you were expected." He opened the door wide so that they could all step inside.

Elizabeth handed Mr. Paulson her things but offered no response to his comment. "I hope we have not interrupted dinner?"

"Elizabeth?" A man perhaps ten years older than Darcy stood down the hall, his expression a muddle of relief and anger. "Come inside, my dear." He glanced at Fitz and then Darcy, but his voice remained steady. "And you are welcome too, sirs."

Darcy nodded. Mr. Gardiner's reserve indicated that the servants had not been told Elizabeth was missing. Like her father and sister, the Gardiners had protected her reputation at the cost of their own peace of mind.

They had not been in Mr. Gardiner's study long enough for Elizabeth to explain their presence when the door opened and a slender, extremely well-dressed woman several years older than Darcy slipped inside. Without uttering a single word, she enfolded Elizabeth in a tight embrace, and Darcy had the fleeting thought that they appeared more like sisters than aunt and niece.

"Oh, my dearest girl," the woman cried with relief. "Thank God you are safe."

"I thank both God and these gentlemen, Aunt Gardiner," he heard Elizabeth say. She stepped away from her aunt and made the introductions.

Mr. Gardiner was entirely different from his sisters. His dress was fashionable without ostentation, and his entire demeanor displayed a keen intelligence. "Do your parents know you are well, Elizabeth?" he asked gruffly.

"They do, sir. My cousin and I were with Mr. Bennet and Miss Bennet earlier today," Darcy replied. "You will no doubt receive a letter tomorrow."

"Yes," Mrs. Gardiner said weakly. "Jane will write."

Elizabeth took her aunt's hand. "I am so very sorry for worrying you and uncle."

Darcy wanted to declare that it was hardly her fault, but Mr. Gardiner was impatient for an explanation.

"Ladies," Mr. Gardiner said, gesturing to the chairs, "normally I would ask to speak with the gentlemen privately, but these are not ordinary times."

"No sir," Darcy agreed. "They are not."

They took turns telling the story as they knew it. Elizabeth began, and then he and Fitz told their parts in equal measure, including the afternoon's frightening events and the countess's invitation, which produced a small gasp from Mrs. Gardiner.

"Elizabeth, you are to marry Mr. Darcy?"

His lovely betrothed beamed as she confirmed the news. Mrs. Gardiner offered her best wishes for them both and hurried Elizabeth upstairs to pack her belongings.

"Oh, Elizabeth!" Aunt Gardiner cried, her relief and happiness apparent in the way the words tumbled from her. "I have been so distressed for you. But now you are to marry—and to a Darcy of Pemberley! I knew of his parents, for I spent much of my childhood in Lambton within five miles of that great estate."

"So near?" Elizabeth inquired with interest. "Have you acquaintances there? Will you and my uncle visit us?"

"You could hardly keep me away," Aunt Gardiner said with a laugh and took Elizabeth's hand. "Oh, Lizzy. Mr. Darcy seems to be a fine man. Only tell me that this is a marriage of mutual respect and affection, and I shall be entirely well."

Elizabeth squeezed her aunt's hand. "If you had posed this question before the ball at Netherfield, aunt, my answer would be quite different. I have mistaken Mr. Darcy for weeks, but once I knew the truth, I could not help but love him."

Aunt Gardiner touched her left arm. The splint was hidden beneath her sleeve, but her aunt possessed sharp eyes. "What happened here?"

"I was injured before I arrived at Mr. Darcy's home," Elizabeth explained. She frowned. "He has been a rather determined nurse."

Aunt Gardiner laughed softly. "A good match for you, then," she teased. "He is a bit stately, but his care for you is evident. Do you respect him as well as love him, my dear? For I know you, more than most, require both."

"He is not perfect," Elizabeth admitted. "But neither am I. He is everything good, and I do not believe I have ever met a better man. He *is* stately and stiff at times, but he is also clever and strong and kind."

Aunt Gardiner sighed happily. "I never thought to see you besotted, Lizzy. It is enough for me. We must pack your trunk."

"It will not require a great deal of time, Aunt," Elizabeth said. "I have only a few gowns here, and Jane's would not suit." Her sister was several inches taller and her figure more fully formed.

Her aunt waved a hand in the air. "But mine will, at least until your handsome Mr. Darcy sends you to the modiste for your own."

Elizabeth shook her head vigorously. "Oh no, Aunt Gardiner, I could not!"

Aunt Gardiner crossed her arms over her chest. "And why is that? You and I are nearly of a size. Do you think my dresses are not good enough for a countess? Your uncle's fabrics grace all the shops in Mayfair as well as Cheapside."

"You know very well that is not my complaint, Aunt," Elizabeth said with a fond shake of her head. "I could not rob you of your gowns when you might have need of them!"

Aunt Gardiner lifted an eyebrow. "Do not be ridiculous, Lizzy. One thing I have in abundance is gowns made up of your uncle's best fabrics. I am a walking advertisement, he says, and therefore must always look smart." Her eyes shone. "My husband is not a romantic, but he has his own ways of spoiling me. Besides, you are only borrowing them, and you have nothing to wear on your wedding day. Oh!" she cried enthusiastically. "I have just the thing."

Elizabeth's eyes teared as she watched her normally composed aunt dart to her wardrobe and, with a flourish, remove the most stunning dress Elizabeth had ever seen.

It was made of ivory silk with a lace overlay for the skirt. The lace was embroidered with a tiny geometric pattern in the same color as the satin. The gown was complemented by a long robe of evening primrose crape that fastened below her breast. Large, colorful flowers were embroidered along the hem. She reached out to touch it. "Oh, Aunt," she said quietly. "Would not uncle be offended were I to wear this when it is so obviously a special gift from him?"

Aunt Gardiner huffed. "If only it were, dear. This was meant to impress a potential investor and so it did. The fact that your uncle loved seeing me in it does not mean that he had any other inclination. He might even have complained about the cost were he not a little afraid of my response."

Elizabeth laughed in disbelief. "He would not. He adores you, Aunt Gardiner."

"Oh, well, I suppose that is true," her aunt replied slyly. "I might like him a little as well." She rang for her maid. "But you will take the dress and no excuses. I will not send you to be wed to a Darcy of Pemberley in a morning dress, and your uncle will be delighted that it is being worn for such an auspicious occasion. He does like to get his penny's worth."

<hr />

Darcy watched Mrs. Gardiner and Elizabeth remove from the study, their heads bent together as they whispered to one another. It pleased him to observe how much the Gardiners cared for her.

He was duly impressed by the behavior of Elizabeth's family. The story to which they had been subjected was fantastical, yet there had been no outraged protests, no interruptions, no weeping or calls for salts. Although she had finally given way to tears today after a week of nearly constant strain, he saw hints of Elizabeth's practiced composure in that of her relations.

Mr. Gardiner had questions. Many of them. After he had been satisfied as to the men's treatment of Elizabeth, he finally asked, "What reason would these men have to trespass upon your home? I cannot fathom what they might hope to gain."

"I am afraid we are not certain either," Darcy admitted. "Elizabeth heard the man say that they recognized Anders, so they knew it was my carriage that had stopped. They did not follow us to town immediately, however."

"Waiting for additional instructions, perhaps," Mr. Gardiner replied.

"At first, they were waiting for some sign that Miss Elizabeth was not in the river. When she was not, I suspect they worked out that she was in my home," Darcy said. "But there would have been no sign of her. We concealed her presence even from most of the staff. Evidently, they could wait no longer."

"They tipped the coal wagon as a diversion and stole inside," Fitz mused.

Mr. Gardiner's brows pinched together. "Do you think they created the diversion or simply took advantage of an accident?"

Darcy shook his head. "Does it matter? All it would require was a glance in the mews to realize two horses were gone, but they would not have known how long we would be gone. When they spied the wagon, they took their opportunity."

"But why?" Mr. Gardiner asked, returning to his initial query. "This is all rather poorly planned. It is not as though they could carry Elizabeth away without being noticed."

"They did just that at Longbourn," Fitz reminded them.

Darcy felt his stomach turn to ice at the words, but he and Fitz felt the same—whoever had been hounding him and threatening Elizabeth had been biding their time and waiting for their chance. He hated to think it, but had they been better organized, better prepared, he and Fitz may never have had a chance to get their feet under them. "We dismissed Howard when we discussed him, but Bingley says he owes the man money and Miss Bingley says he was invited to the ball. I also believe that Wickham knows more than he told us."

"By the by," Mr. Gardiner asked curiously, "how did Mr. Wickham recognize Mr. Darcy's button? Or was that another prevarication on his part?"

Darcy shrugged. "They originally belonged to my grandfather. My father used them on his own jackets. Wickham would have seen them any number of times over the years."

"You are not bothered that one was taken?" Elizabeth's uncle asked.

"They are not sentimental items, Mr. Gardiner," Darcy informed him. "They are only buttons."

Fitz sat back in his chair. "We know the substance of Wickham's grievance. Perhaps we should hear the details of your quarrel with Howard, Darce. There must be some reason for all of this and if he is the man, he could easily hire others to do the job."

Darcy nodded. "It was about nine months ago, I think. Before my annual visit to Rosings." He turned to Mr. Gardiner.

"Howard approached me at the club, and he asked that I attend him the following day. When I did, he was not prepared to take no for an answer."

Mr. Gardiner frowned. "I do not understand."

Darcy grimaced. "He had a younger sister who needed to be married rather quickly."

"Ah," Mr. Gardiner replied, and settled into his chair. "Proceed."

Fitz grinned at the nonchalant command, and Darcy frowned at him. "I politely declined."

"Exact words, Darcy?" Fitz prompted.

He thought back to the conversation which had shocked him so completely. "I believe I said something like, 'I am sorry for your predicament, but your sister is your concern. I have my own to consider and no inclination to marry at present.'" He frowned. "Howard would not relent, and eventually, I said that there were certain expectations for any Mrs. Darcy that his sister obviously could not meet."

Mr. Gardiner tipped his head slightly to one side.

Fitz winced. "*That* is what you said?"

Darcy nodded.

"And I presume," Fitz continued, "that was just the way you said it?"

"Why?" Darcy asked, confused. "What have I said that was untrue?"

"Sometimes," Mr. Gardiner responded drily, "*how* you say a thing is just as important as what you say." He shared a glance with Fitz. "However, in this case, you may have failed on both counts. Insulting both Mr. Howard and his sister might not have been the wisest course."

"Precisely," Fitz concurred.

"It was the truth," Darcy insisted. Fitz and Mr. Gardiner were being obtuse, the pair of them. It had been an affront, and Howard had not been put off by his initial refusal. Darcy did not see any profit in disguise. Was he to make a fool of them both by pretending he was amenable to such a request? That he would welcome a connection to Howard no matter how it was obtained? Howard was a man of honor—he should have understood Darcy's refusal and not pressed him. Indeed, the question ought never have been asked. No, the situation had required clarity, and he had provided it.

It had been a terrible interview, Howard sitting behind a large mahogany desk in an overly decorated study, Darcy seated before it. Darcy had refused, and then, as he was leaving, he had tried to be compassionate, saying something about them both having sisters for whom they stood guardian . . .

"Oh." He lifted his face to meet Fitz's curious gaze. "Oh, good God. Ramsgate . . ."

"What are you saying, Darcy?" Fitz asked sharply.

"I did not mention Ramsgate, I am certain of that, but his sister and mine were part of a group of girls who are preparing together for their come-outs. Miss Howard might easily have known of Georgiana's travel plans." He rubbed the back of his head. "Mrs. Younge's loyalty was easily purchased, and Wickham was in Ramsgate before he appeared in Meryton. We believed Ramsgate was *Wickham's* plan, but when has he ever planned anything? He seeks opportunity, but he does not create it." He dropped his head into his hands. "It is too great a coincidence."

Fitz's voice was cold. "You believe Mrs. Younge and Wickham were in Howard's employ."

"I believe it is possible. Mrs. Younge attended those gatherings, so she would know of Miss Howard. And as it appears she already knew Wickham, she might easily have introduced him to Howard. Wretched woman."

Fitz crossed his arms over his chest. "Then it is revenge. A sister for a sister?"

Darcy had not thought of it in quite so stark a manner, but it made a twisted sort of sense. He nodded. "Yet to ruin Georgiana over a perceived slight—I cannot reconcile that with the man I believed him to be."

"Whatever has happened, Lizzy has been caught up in it." Mr. Gardiner's stare was not cold, but it was steady. "I do not wish to pry, Mr. Darcy, but as it has placed my niece in danger, I must know what happened in Ramsgate. Did Mr. Wickham plan to ruin your sister?"

There was a knock at the door, but it opened without pause. "Do excuse us, Mr. Gardiner," his wife said. "Elizabeth and I are ready to depart. Might you continue your conversation on the way?"

Darcy noted Elizabeth had changed her clothing and done something with her hair that was quite becoming. With chagrin, he realized that in their rush to leave Darcy House, she had not been able to exchange the damaged gown she had been wearing all day for another. He had made quick work of discarding the uniform Fitz had provided, but Mrs. Spencer was not available to help Elizabeth. His intended always appeared lovely to him, but of course she would not feel confident arriving at Matlock House in a wrinkled gown and a repaired pelisse. Yet she had uttered no protest, only asked to travel here first.

"Ah," Mr. Gardiner said approvingly. "The sarsenet. It does make up rather well, does it not, Lizzy?"

"Are you fishing for compliments, Uncle?" Elizabeth asked pertly.

"It is the only fishing I *can* do in London," Mr. Gardiner replied with good humor. He moved towards the door. "Gentlemen, I believe we have been given our marching orders."

Chapter Eleven

By the time Mr. Darcy's carriage arrived in St. James's Square, its occupants had been informed both of what had passed in Mr. Gardiner's study and of Mr. Wickham's actions in Ramsgate.

Their party was shown into a small drawing room brilliantly lit with candles. Elizabeth saw three figures—an older couple who must be the earl and countess, and a girl who appeared to be about the age of her younger sisters.

"Georgiana," Mr. Darcy breathed. He seemed to shake himself. "Forgive me. Aunt, Uncle, Georgiana, may I introduce Mr. and Mrs. Gardiner? Mr. and Mrs. Gardiner, the Earl and Countess of Matlock and my sister, Miss Darcy." He turned to Elizabeth and held out his hand. She took it, and he gently guided her to his side. "This is my betrothed, Miss Elizabeth Bennet of Longbourn."

The countess stepped forward to take Elizabeth by her hands. She was rather tall and stout.

"My dear girl," the countess said warmly, "We have been expecting you. I am so happy that one of my boys is finally settling down." She sent an icy glare in Colonel Fitzwilliam's direction before examining Elizabeth. "Oh! You *are* a pretty little thing."

The earl, barely taller than his wife and so thin as to appear nearly gaunt, simply nodded a welcome.

Mr. Darcy spoke a word in his sister's ear. She paled, but he took her hand and squeezed it gently before stepping away. He and the colonel moved to another part of the room to speak with the earl while Mr. Gardiner and the ladies made polite conversation. It was not long before the Gardiners had been assured that Elizabeth would be well taken care of and took their leave.

"We shall return for your wedding," Aunt Gardiner whispered to her. "We would not miss it." She briefly glanced across the room at Miss Darcy, who had wandered to a settee near the fire. "Do see if you can cheer that poor child up. She appears positively miserable."

Elizabeth kissed her aunt's cheek. "I will. Thank you for everything." She would say more were she not in a crowded room where anyone might overhear, but her Aunt Gardiner, as always, understood. She touched Elizabeth's cheek affectionately, then took her husband's arm, and was gone.

Mr. Darcy startled at their departure, and Elizabeth met his gaze. He appeared abashed that he had not farewelled them, but in fairness, his attention had been commanded by his family.

"It is a pleasure to meet you, Miss Darcy," Elizabeth said after following the countess to the settee. The men remained standing, speaking in hushed tones on the other side of the small room. "I do hope you are resigned to having a sister. I have four more at home and shall miss them when I marry your brother."

This produced only a tiny smile, but it seemed a genuine one. "I *am* resigned, thank you."

Elizabeth could not help but laugh a little. "Oh, I think we shall get along very well, you and I." She raised her voice. "Together we shall tease your brother to distraction."

"As if you do not manage that already," Mr. Darcy replied with an affected sniff. "Do not recruit my sister to your devious cause." Elizabeth pretended to be affronted. She lifted her eyebrows at him. He did the same and returned to his conversation.

Miss Darcy's eyes widened a bit at the break with propriety, but after a glance at the countess, soon calmed herself. Elizabeth realized that being in company was an effort for the girl, but Miss Darcy seemed resolved to be successful.

She was still wondering how to ease Miss Darcy's way when the girl spoke.

"My brother says that you know about last summer," Miss Darcy said, the volume of her words nearly inaudible. "He was so disappointed in me. I have been so very upset and angry with myself that I have not really been able to face him, not even to apologize."

It was Elizabeth's turn to exchange a look with the countess, who gave her a small but encouraging smile. "I cannot speak to his emotions before he was known to me," Elizabeth told the younger girl. "Only that when your brother told me what had happened, his anger was not for you."

"No?" Miss Darcy asked. It was easy to hear the hope in her question.

"He was very angry at the scoundrel who so abused you, Miss Darcy. And although he did not say as much, I could see he was angry with himself for not protecting you." As Elizabeth spoke the words aloud, many of Mr. Darcy's unconventional actions this past week suddenly made sense to her.

"But he *did*. He warned me about Mr. Wickham." Miss Darcy's expression was both surprised and morose. "But I would not listen."

Elizabeth shook her head. Jane had advised her that things might not be as she believed. "I was cautioned, too, and ignored it. Your brother set me right." She did not mention the insult the lieutenant had uttered about Miss Darcy.

"William never makes mistakes," the girl said, biting her lower lip.

"Oh," Elizabeth said, surprised that anyone could see Mr. Darcy as flawless, "I am afraid that he does. Your brother is a good man, but he is as human as the rest of us." She glanced over at the others in the room, who were still caught up in their discussion, and gave Miss Darcy a mischievous grin. "Let me tell you a story."

The countess sat up very straight, turning her head slightly towards Elizabeth in anticipation.

She focused on her future sister. "Your esteemed elder brother came into Meryton like a tall black cloud."

Miss Darcy blinked. "A tall black cloud?"

Elizabeth met the eyes of the countess, who nodded. "Yes. A very tall, black cloud. Does he own a single coat in another color?" Georgiana's eyes darted first to her brother and then back to Elizabeth. "The first time I saw him was at a dance, where he flatly refused to stand up with me. It was a terrible performance on his part."

"Oh, William," the countess chided, though the object of her scold had his back to her.

At the same time, Georgiana addressed Elizabeth. "He refused to dance with you? But then . . ."

"That is only because he did not yet know me," Elizabeth explained playfully. "For soon he was asking me to dance, and *I* was refusing to stand up with *him*." She felt Mr. Darcy's presence behind her. "I believe I refused him twice before relenting."

The earl laughed, a short, barking sort of sound. "Serves you right, Darcy. You always have been far too stiff outside the family circle."

"I have my reasons, Uncle," Mr. Darcy protested. "Though I admit in this case, I was mistaken." He looked down into Elizabeth's upturned face and lifted an eyebrow. "I think."

Elizabeth pretended to be affronted, and Colonel Fitzwilliam snorted. "A fine concession, Darcy," he cried.

"You see, Miss Darcy?" Elizabeth said pertly. "Even your brother admits that he makes mistakes." He joined them on the settee. "Large ones." She smiled innocently. "Potentially calamitous."

Mr. Darcy huffed, but Miss Darcy giggled, and his petulance immediately transformed into a surprised pleasure.

"Georgiana," the countess said, "It is growing rather late, dear. We shall have time to speak in the morning."

Miss Darcy rose obediently and curtsied to Elizabeth. "Shall I see you at breakfast, Miss Elizabeth?"

Elizabeth nodded. "Indeed you shall."

The girl stood and addressed Mr. Darcy. "Good night, brother. I am glad you are here."

Mr. Darcy swallowed, and his eyes were suspiciously shiny in the candlelight. He reached for Miss Darcy's hand and held it for a moment. "Good night, sister. Pleasant dreams."

As the door shut behind her, Elizabeth felt flush with success. It lasted nearly half a minute until the earl declared, "I want the entire, unvarnished story. Who wants to begin?"

Darcy rubbed a hand over his eyes. It was very late. They had been through this story so many times this day he was beginning to forget that it was meant to be a secret. Beside him on the settee, Elizabeth's head drooped before jerking up again. He was no less exhausted after being in the saddle for a good part of the day and having had precious little rest since. He would not have minded a hot meal, but it would have to wait until the morning.

He stood and helped Elizabeth to rise. "Come, my dear. It is time to retire."

Aunt Matlock stood. "I shall see Elizabeth to her room, William."

Darcy handed a sleepy Elizabeth off to his aunt. "Sleep well, love," he murmured.

"I feel I shall awake and discover all this has been a dream," Elizabeth murmured.

His aunt chuckled.

"I feel the same," Darcy said, "but I suppose the morning will come soon enough and then we will know for certain." He exchanged one last look with his betrothed and then watched the women exit the room before sitting again near the fire.

"You know, Darcy," his uncle said nearly the instant the door closed behind them, "you are giving up a great deal to wed that young lady."

He met Fitz's sympathetic gaze. It was difficult hearing his own pompous arguments against attaching himself to Elizabeth coming from someone else. Now that he had decided to wed, it exasperated him to hear anyone question it. He felt again how much he owed Fitz for making him see reason. "I am giving up nothing that matters, uncle, and am gaining a great deal."

Uncle Matlock sighed. "Fortune and connections are not insignificant things, my boy."

"That is true," Darcy admitted. Fitz held up the decanter of port, but Darcy shook his head. He was too tired for wine. "However, the crux of it is this: I love her. She loves me." He shook his head. "Fortune I have. Connections I have. What I do not have is Elizabeth." He stared at the earl, willing him to understand. "And I need her, uncle. If I do not marry Elizabeth Bennet, I shall not marry at all."

His uncle drank deeply from his glass and set it down. "Your aunt would hang me by my heels were that to happen."

Fitz coughed at the word *heels*.

The earl glared at Fitz before he again spoke to Darcy. "Very well, nephew. As long as you know what you are about."

Darcy knew his uncle was sincere. Disappointed, but sincere. It was better than he had hoped, to be honest. "I am," he replied.

"Tell him we will support him, father," Fitz insisted. "We are family, after all."

"Well, of course we shall support the boy," Uncle Matlock snapped. "Darcy is his own man. He might have done far better, but we all know he might also have done worse." He took another drink. Thoughtfully, he said, "She is at least a gentleman's daughter and a pretty, genteel sort of girl. She is also quick-witted enough to keep him interested. No mean feat, that. Henry will like her," he grumbled. "And Georgiana already seems taken with her." A sly, almost wicked smile suddenly stretched across his face. "Hmm. Perhaps there is some consolation in this after all. What do you think, boys?"

Both Darcy and Fitz were silent, not understanding the earl's change of attitude.

The earl clapped his hands together. "I shall be able to tell Catherine the news!" he cried. "I am so excessively tired of hearing her go on about infant betrothals that I could spit. Anne, poor girl, has never been really well. We all know she does not wish to marry at all, let alone our proud, aloof fellow there—and the cold in Derbyshire would finish her off entirely."

"I feel I should be insulted both on my behalf and Derbyshire's," Darcy replied drolly, "but as I care for Anne, I will not take umbrage." He stood. "I should be the one to tell Lady Catherine, but I admit, Uncle, I would be pleased to have you undertake it."

His uncle quickly swallowed the rest of his wine. "I do believe I shall write her immediately! Where is my pen?"

Darcy shared a laugh with his cousin before saying, "Do not send it express, if you please. I hope to be wed before she charges up to London to berate me." He tugged at the hem of his waistcoat. "I have a note to write, but then I am for bed. I am done in. I may have played a soldier today, but I am not used to being in the saddle for so many hours."

Fitz grinned. "You become used to it. Of course, you are too tall and heavy for a Light Dragoon."

"The fit of the uniform told me as much," Darcy replied. "It is just as well that my talents lie elsewhere."

His cousin shook his head. "As much as it pains me to admit it, Darce, you did well today. But do not take to the boards just yet—your acting requires improvement."

Darcy finished his message and dropped the sealed note on his uncle's desk with a few quick instructions. His uncle agreed with a nod and waved him off, already dipping his pen into a bottle of ink. It had been an extraordinary day. Darcy dragged himself to bed, where his fatigue overtook him at once.

Elizabeth woke to a bright sunny morning. She sat up abruptly, recalling that she needed to send a letter to Papa if she wished to have Jane with her for her wedding. Her feet touched the cold floor, but she disregarded it. The day must be far gone already! What time did the post go out? Was she already too late? She rang for the maid and wrote a hasty note before dressing for the morning in one of her aunt's gowns. Her hair was quickly put up in a becoming but simple style, and then she nearly bolted from the room.

No one was in the hall and she hurried downstairs, clutching her letter. She was guided to the breakfast room by one of the earl's tall, austere footmen.

She stepped inside to find the men sipping coffee. Miss Darcy's plate was still full, and the countess was not present. Elizabeth hoped that meant she had not slept so long as to be rude.

The men stood when she entered. "Good morning, gentlemen," she greeted them. "Mr. Darcy, might I have a word?"

"Of course," he said, and stepped around the table. He was only a foot from her when he stopped, close enough that the scent of his cologne wafted over to her. She took a deep breath. "How may I be of service?"

"I have slept so long I am concerned Papa will not receive my letter in time to come to town," she said, fretting. "I do not like to ask, but might you be willing to send this express?"

"Even an express would not arrive in time for your father and sister to reach town today," he told her in a low voice.

"Oh," Elizabeth replied, and looked at the floor. Her disappointment was acute.

Mr. Darcy placed two fingers under her chin and gently lifted her face up until her eyes met his. "Which is why I sent word express last night. The rider was to stay at the inn in Meryton and deliver the note as soon as it was light."

Elizabeth smiled brightly at her betrothed. "Mama does not rise before nine. Papa is normally downstairs by seven."

"As I thought," he replied drily.

"Well," she said. She blinked back her tears and regained her high spirits, gazing up at him impishly. "You are quite high-handed, Mr. Darcy, taking it upon yourself to write my father." It was impossible to sound as though she disapproved.

"A simple 'thank you' would suffice, my dear." He did not return her smile, but there was a gleam in his eye. "He will be my family as well after tomorrow. I thought this once my presumption might be forgiven."

He had done all he could to be certain her father and sister would be able to attend their wedding. That was more than enough. But when he called her "my dear," in his deep, gruff voice, her knees nearly gave way. Elizabeth knew she could not embrace Mr. Darcy in the breakfast room. It would only embarrass them both. She settled instead for a gentle "Thank you, dearest." The endearment felt a little strange on her tongue, and she glanced away, unaccountably shy. That was a new feeling, too—she was never shy. Mr. Darcy did not seem to mind, only offered her his arm, and led her to the table.

"May I?" he inquired, eyeing her plate, and Elizabeth nodded. She would normally have accompanied him to the sidebar to point out her favorites, but she would eat anything he brought without complaint this morning.

When he set a plate before her filled with all the foods she favored, she gazed at him curiously. He did smile this time.

"We spent several days together at Netherfield," he reminded her. "I could not help but notice that you had certain favorites."

"You are a constant source of surprises, sir," Elizabeth said honestly, and noted that the other men at the table were smiling into their coffee cups. "Thank you again."

"It is my pleasure," Mr. Darcy replied, and returned to his coffee.

Elizabeth turned to Miss Darcy. The girl's large brown eyes were wide, and she had barely touched her food.

"Now, Miss Darcy," Elizabeth declared, feeling excessively light and cheerful, "what are your plans for the day?"

Darcy watched the happy conversation between Elizabeth and his sister with increasing pleasure. He would have enjoyed taking Elizabeth and Georgiana to Gunter's or Hatchard's or even to stroll along Bond Street. It would have given him great delight to show off the two women most important to him. Yet until he unraveled Howard's plan—for he was increasingly sure the man behind it all must be Howard—it would not be safe for any of them, particularly Elizabeth.

His uncle dismissed the footmen as the men stood to walk out. Fitz was headed back to Darcy House to lead the interrogation. Darcy expected to accompany him, but when they moved into the hall, Fitz shook his head.

"My men have been with them all night, so they should be ready to talk," he said seriously. "Your presence is not required."

"Should I ask what your men have been doing?" Darcy inquired.

Fitz shook his head. "Not allowing them to eat or sleep or relieve themselves is my guess. I do not guide this part of the process."

Darcy rubbed the back of his neck. He did not like this.

"Darcy," Fitz said slowly, "Elizabeth has been the target thus far, but you cannot deny that if Howard has an opportunity to hurt you as well, he would take it. And you are not practiced in interrogation as I am. I would prefer you remain here."

Darcy's frustration and anger exploded into flames, but a sudden thought doused them. "You mean that my presence would make the interrogation more difficult."

"I will not deny it."

Fitz knew him too well—his cousin was not forbidding him from leading the interrogation. Instead, he was appealing to Darcy's logic and reason. *Damn it all.* "Then I will not accompany you." The words were nearly bitten in half as they left his mouth.

"Thank you." Fitz rubbed the back of his head. "I know it is difficult, but I believe it is for the best. Let us get you married, and then you can help us finish the rest of it."

"Fitz," Darcy said quietly.

"Yes?" Fitz asked.

"You may have the two lackeys. But Howard is mine."

"Darce . . ."

"I will not kill him, Fitz," Darcy assured his cousin. "But neither will I allow him to escape his actions without consequence."

Fitz sighed. "I will not stop you, Darcy, but understand that I will also be with you. You will not face him alone."

It was a warning as much as a promise. Fitz would not allow him to go too far. It was a comfort, he supposed. "Send word immediately if there is anything I can do."

"I will, I promise you." Fitz turned on his heel and was gone.

Darcy returned to the breakfast room, where Georgiana was finally standing, preparing to meet her music master. After they had both bid the girl a good morning, Elizabeth wandered over to him and sat herself by his side. "William," she said thoughtfully, "you said that Mr. Howard had a sister whom he wished you to marry."

He nodded. "She was in need of a husband."

Elizabeth frowned. "Where is she now?"

"I must admit I do not know." He was unsure why Elizabeth had asked. "I suspect she is in the country. Howard has a second estate in Cumbria."

"In the carriage, you said he sent Mr. Wickham after your sister first." Elizabeth tipped her head to one side. "As though he had lost his sister to a rake and he perhaps wanted you to lose yours."

Darcy nodded. It made sense if revenge was Howard's purpose. "Fitz made the same connection. If we are correct that Howard is at the center of everything that has happened—and I grow increasingly convinced that we are—why did his approach change? Wickham is many things, but I have never seen him become violent with a woman. He prefers to charm them into willing acquiescence."

"Which is perhaps the reason the men who . . ." Elizabeth clasped her hands in her lap. "Which is perhaps why different men were sent to abduct me." She closed her eyes tightly, thinking. "Mr. Wickham did try to charm me, but then he removed to London and missed the ball." She blushed and cast a rueful look at him as she admitted, "I thought at first you perhaps had something to do with that."

"Which is why you brought him up during our dance." Darcy sighed. "I was concerned he intended to do you harm, Elizabeth. Yet if you had not followed me into the hall to insist on an explanation, I am afraid I might have left Netherfield without saying anything useful at all."

"You were protecting your sister," Elizabeth reassured him. "I do think it was a mistake, but I understand it. I have four sisters of my own."

He rubbed a fist along his jaw and silently cursed Howard. "If Wickham was meant to charm you, why send other men? It is the *why* that concerns me, Elizabeth. The man I knew had a strict sense of honor. I was certain Howard would be above any such behavior."

Elizabeth laid her hand over one of his, and Darcy marveled at that small, strong appendage. Her figure was slight, but it was easy to forget that when her spirit was so imposing. She stood and turned to face him. "Perhaps something changed?"

"What has changed?" asked the countess, who had entered the room so quietly that neither he nor Miss Elizabeth had been aware of her presence.

"Howard's methods," Darcy explained as he stood to greet his aunt. "With Georgiana, there was no physical attack."

"Perhaps he thought Georgiana, being so young, would be easier to persuade," the countess offered. "Or perhaps he was made angry when Miss Howard's ruination became known."

"What?" Darcy asked, shocked. "There are rumors? Who started them? How could I have been unaware?"

The countess raised her eyebrows. "I do not know, William. They have been in circulation for some time."

Elizabeth leaned forward. "Pray, pardon me for asking, Lady Matlock, but is the source of the rumors something you *could* discover? It might be important."

"Why?" the countess asked.

Darcy groaned. "Because Howard may believe that I am to blame."

Elizabeth barely had time to register Mr. Darcy's statement when the door was flung open and a fashionably dressed man entered the room, the butler trailing helplessly behind him. She had teased Miss Darcy about her brother's penchant for black clothing, but she preferred his sober appearance to the dandy who appeared before them now. He was handsome in a way the colonel was not, but his auburn hair was the same color and fashionably disarranged. He was arrayed in a bright blue coat, a waistcoat adorned in wide horizontal stripes of blue and gold, and a gleaming white shirt. He wore buff-colored trousers cut long with a slit over the shoe. There were no buckles on those shoes; rather, they were fastened with silk bows.

The countess was affectionately exasperated with the man. "Henry, when did you arrive home? You have not yet met Miss Bennet, your cousin's betrothed."

Henry. It must be Colonel Fitzwilliam's elder brother.

Mr. Darcy sighed. His exasperation was not as fond as his aunt's. "Miss Bennet," he said formally, "may I introduce my most troublesome cousin, the Viscount Milton?"

"Your best-dressed cousin, you mean. Miss Bennet," the viscount bowed so deeply Elizabeth suspected he was mocking her. "Your servant."

"It is a pleasure to meet you, sir," she replied, casting an uncertain glance at Mr. Darcy. That worthy gentleman was frowning.

"I arrived late last night, Mama," the gentleman said as he took a seat next to her. "Or rather, early this morning. Father was in raptures over some letter he was sending off to Kent."

The countess shook her head fondly. "I should have known he would write Catherine."

Viscount Milton shrugged. "I hope you do not mind, Miss Bennet, but I have come to take Darcy away for a time."

"Of course," Elizabeth replied hesitantly.

The viscount nearly bounded over to Mr. Darcy to take him by the arm. He was immediately shaken off. "Come, Darcy," the viscount reprimanded. "Father told me all. No one will believe for an instant that you have married willingly if you do not show your face at the club with me and offer a toast to your lovely bride!"

"You really are the most insufferable peacock, Henry," Mr. Darcy responded, crossing his arms over his chest.

Elizabeth bit her tongue. It was all she could do to keep from laughing at the pair of them. She could imagine them as boys together, the elder always goading the younger. She wondered whether the colonel had sided with Mr. Darcy or with his own brother. The viscount had likely taken them both on without a single qualm.

The viscount elbowed Darcy in the ribs. "You must write your name and wedding date in the books, Darcy! Fortunes will be made and lost today!" He exited the room in a flurry of arm waving, a call for his hat traveling back to them from the hall.

Elizabeth was still forming the question when Mr. Darcy shook his head. "I am not going, Elizabeth. I would prefer to spend the day with you."

"Oh, pish-posh," his aunt protested. "You shall have her all to yourself after tomorrow. Elizabeth and I have yet to discuss the wedding breakfast. It will be a small gathering as so many of our friends are not yet in town. Still, we must make what we can of it."

"Aunt," Mr. Darcy said warningly. "Fitz was not sure it would be safe."

"Pair of old ladies, the two of you," the viscount scoffed as he returned, doffing his hat, tossing a greatcoat at Mr. Darcy, and reaching back to take a walking stick from the aged butler. "I receive threats on my life every day."

Mr. Darcy folded the coat over his arm. "You deserve them."

"True," his cousin agreed amiably. He gave the head of his stick a twist and lifted it from the wood by a few inches.

Mr. Darcy rolled his eyes. "Which is why you carry a blade hidden in your walking stick."

"You ought to have one made, Darcy, now you shall have a pretty wife to protect," the viscount advised, smiling at Elizabeth. "You are not half bad with a foil, and it is always wise to be prepared." He slid the weapon back into place. His dark eyes twinkled. "Also, I have been in three duels this week."

"Really, Henry," said the countess with a sigh. "He has done nothing of the sort, Miss Bennet. You must excuse my son. He really does exaggerate dreadfully."

Mr. Darcy's mouth was slightly agape. "Please tell me that you are indeed exaggerating, Henry," he said.

"Of course I am!" exclaimed the viscount. "It is really only three in the past month. And do not fret, Mama. They were none of them over you."

Elizabeth was just close enough to hear the viscount as he whispered, "Not this month, anyway."

Mr. Darcy was about to refuse. She could see it in his inflexible posture and wrinkled brow. Although she wished to deny it, the viscount had a point. If the men at his club were to see that her betrothed was a happy man rather than one who hid from view, it might make the early days a little easier to bear for them both.

She stepped forward. "Might I borrow my intended for a moment, my lord?" she asked politely.

He offered her another sweeping bow, and she could not help but answer it with a small but impatient huff before taking Mr. Darcy's arm and stepping away.

"Elizabeth," he said firmly, "if you would prefer I remain, I shall. I have no desire to visit the club with Henry."

She worried her bottom lip before replying, "As long as you are safe, William, I believe you should go."

His confusion was endearing. "You do?"

"As long as you believe your cousin will keep you safe," she repeated.

"Yes."

"I do not require Henry to protect me," he grumbled.

Elizabeth searched Mr. Darcy's face. He was clenching his jaw. "Would you normally have done as your cousin recommends, had our courtship transpired in a more traditional way?"

Mr. Darcy considered her question before answering. "I do not know, to be truthful. It is more in Henry's style than my own, but I might have been more easily persuaded had I not lately been required to remove you from quite so many trunks."

She touched his arm. "I am in your uncle's house, the same house that protects your sister."

"And turned Howard's notice from Georgiana to you." He took her hand and traced the palm of it with the pad of his thumb.

"None of that, William," Elizabeth told him sternly. "It was not your fault. I will say it again and again until you agree—you are responsible only for your own actions."

He gave her a sly look. "Actually, once we are married, I am legally responsible for your actions."

"Are you?" Elizabeth placed a finger on her chin. "All of the mischief and none of the punishment. I think I shall enjoy being married."

"Minx," he said. "I would kiss you now, you know, were the room not so full."

Elizabeth's cheeks warmed. "Go out with your cousin. I promise I will not leave the house today."

"Very well. If you insist."

She felt him squeeze her hand before he raised it to bestow a kiss. He had given her one after all. "I do. You might even try to enjoy yourself a little."

"Well done, Miss Bennet!" cried the viscount, who had sidled over to listen. He pointed at her, ignoring her surprise and Mr. Darcy's scowl at his rudeness. "You may call me Henry!"

Chapter Twelve

"I doubt she shall return the compliment and allow you to call her Elizabeth," Darcy muttered. "What possessed you to point at her like that?"

Henry played the servant and held out Darcy's hat. "Put it on, you chucklehead."

Darcy grabbed the hat from his cousin's hand and set it on his head as they stepped out of doors. The air was biting. "You call me a chucklehead when you are going on about duels in front of your mother and my betrothed?"

Henry grinned. "Do you believe I jest?" He held up three fingers. "And it *was* this week. But this week is also a part of the month, so I have not spoken false."

They climbed into Henry's carriage and Darcy settled against the squabs. "I do not believe you. I have seen you shoot. You would be in the ground by now."

Henry laughed. "Most of the time they do not even show. Pity. I do like a good battle in the morning. It strengthens the blood."

"Provided you do not lose too much of it." Darcy retorted. The man refused to take anything seriously. It was provoking.

"You really are too somber, Darcy," Henry replied, his spirits not at all dampened. He reached across the coach and flipped up the end of Darcy's cravat. "Loosen up your small clothes, cousin. There is a point to all this, you know."

"So you tell me," Darcy replied sullenly, reaching up to repair the damage.

Henry shook his head, but his expression was warm. "You need to be seen going about your usual business. You and Richard were at Angelo's a week ago, but you have not been in public since."

"We were at the club on Monday," Darcy argued.

"For how long? A quarter of an hour?" Henry scoffed. "Today we will let everyone know you have been busy arranging your wedding. And that your bride is a woman you met a few months ago on your sojourn to . . ." Henry paused. "Where was it again?"

Darcy rubbed his eyes with one hand. "Hertfordshire."

"Yes. I had forgotten. Well, Bingley catapulted Miss Bingley at you . . ."

Darcy's glare made Henry stop for a moment, but then he smiled wickedly and continued. "Richard told me about that. What a pity I have no talent with a pencil or brush, but I shall cherish the image forever," he tapped his temple with a finger, "in here." He turned to observe the scene out his window before continuing. "Have you sent word to Gunderson?" Darcy was silent, and Henry leaned forward. "It would help our story a great deal if you acted as though you had. Shall we stop there first?"

"We may as well," Darcy replied, trying to ignore the warmth flushing his cheeks. "He ought to have the papers drawn up by now. Some information is missing, of course."

"What is this?" Henry inquired gaily. He always knew how to find the weaknesses in Darcy's armor. "I thought you only made the offer yesterday?"

"I have wished to make Elizabeth an offer somewhat longer than that. It was a bit of . . ." Darcy rubbed his eyes with one hand. The night Miss Bingley had paraded about the drawing room at Netherfield with Elizabeth, he had a very vivid dream. In the morning, he had indulged himself by sending off a note to Gunderson to draw up a marriage contract, though he had not specified the woman nor her financial particulars. He had felt incredibly foolish about it afterward and, though he had authorized payment for Gunderson's work, had not corresponded with the man since.

Darcy wanted to leap from the carriage and walk to Gunderson's office when he saw Henry's brightened visage. It seemed impossible, but Henry was even more self-satisfied than when they had left Matlock House.

"Oh . . ." he drawled and arched one eyebrow. "A tangible bit of fantasy? *You*?" Henry's eyes narrowed as his lips curled upward. "Envisioning the delectable Miss Bennet in less than gentlemanly ways and feeling rather guilty about it, eh? Must be noble even in your dreams? Excellent. The follies of men do so divert me."

"Henry," Darcy warned. "Cease your prattling. I am not above striking you for such an offense against Elizabeth, and I am not a boy of twelve any longer."

Henry's sharp eyes assessed Darcy, and at last, the viscount spoke sense. "I am not certain the offense was mine, but no, you are not a boy. In fact, my brother thinks you have brokered a match that will at last make a man out of you."

An angry rebuttal was on Darcy's tongue, but Henry held up his hands in a signal of surrender. "He did not use those words, and I mean that in the best sense, Darcy. You know I respect Richard's opinion."

"If you respect him so much, why do you insist on calling him Richard?" Darcy inquired, trying to regain his equanimity. "You know he hates it."

"Only because it reminds him that he was once 'Dickie.' It makes him feel like a nine-year-old boy." Henry shook his head. "Richard has hundreds of men following his every command. It is good for him not to have things all his own way. You know that as well as I."

"I value his opinion," Darcy objected, but relented. "Though I do not always agree."

"I value his opinion as well," Henry agreed. "Almost as much as I respect yours."

The unexpected compliment flustered Darcy, and by the time he had recovered, Henry's earnest expression had disappeared. Instead, he was hanging out of his window to give the driver their new direction.

<hr />

After the men left for their club, Elizabeth listened to the countess explain her plans for the wedding feast. It would indeed be rather small by London standards, she supposed, but not much smaller than the one she would have had in Meryton. When asked, she explained that as long as the Gardiners, Papa, and Jane were present, she would be satisfied. The countess might invite whomever she chose to the meal, and Elizabeth would be pleased to accommodate her.

The countess had been everything welcoming. While Elizabeth suspected that the earl had spoken of his disapprobation to Mr. Darcy once she had retired, the older man had been polite enough to her. She was exceedingly grateful to all the Matlocks for their acceptance. She knew it was evidence of their high regard for Mr. Darcy.

"Thursdays are my day at home," the countess said, consulting a delicate gold watch with pearls circling the face. "I do expect a few ladies to make a visit. Will you sit with me?"

Elizabeth touched the splint on her arm. "I should . . ."

"Remove it." The countess nodded. "Yes, if you can bear it, I believe that would be wise."

"I shall return shortly, my lady," Elizabeth replied, and rose to depart.

"Aunt Matlock will do," the countess said.

Elizabeth waited for the countess to complete her sentence. "I beg your pardon, my lady," she asked respectfully. "You will do what?"

The countess laughed, and Elizabeth covered her face with one hand. "Oh." She peeked out at the countess between her fingers. "And of course, you may call me Elizabeth, if you wish."

"Where is that vaunted wit of yours, my dear?" the countess asked, amused.

A strangled sort of chuckle escaped and Elizabeth was a little startled by the harshness of the sound. "I do apologize. I flatter myself that I have courage to face most trials, my lady . . ." She paused and shook her head. "Aunt Matlock. However, I have been sorely tested of late. Somehow, finding myself not only betrothed but that my intended is the nephew of an earl, then being invited to marry from the house of said earl . . . it is somewhat overwhelming, I must confess."

"It may be an earl's house, Elizabeth," Aunt Matlock said, "but it is the countess who runs it. Remember that when William takes you to Pemberley." She again looked at the time. "You have a moment to collect yourself, but hurry back. I have written the ladies, and they are coming expressly to meet you."

Elizabeth ignored her sudden anxiety and went up to her chamber. She shook her head to think of what Mr. Darcy would say when he saw she had once again removed the splint, but even he would tread carefully around his aunt. Truly, her arm was a good deal better. She did not believe the injury was as severe as it had first appeared. She refreshed herself and asked the maid to do her hair in a slightly more complex style. The dress she wore had long sleeves, so she did not change.

"Your timing is impeccable," the countess said as Elizabeth reentered the drawing room. "Lady Montagu and Mrs. Egerton are certain to be announced any moment."

"Is there anything I should know about them, Aunt Matlock?" Elizabeth inquired. If there was one thing she had learned at her mother's knee, it was to know all she could about visitors before they arrived.

Aunt Matlock closed her fan and tapped her lip with it. "Lady Montagu wears a great many feathers and will need to blow them from her face at least twice during the call. You must not let on that she has done any such thing. She will ask about Darcy. If you tell her you are humbled and flattered by his choice, she will think you sensible and leave you be. If not, she will ask pointed questions until you scream. Do try to refrain, dear."

Elizabeth supposed she could display herself in such a way. She would tease Mr. Darcy about it later. That would make this a great deal more palatable.

"Mrs. Egerton," Aunt Matlock continued, "will wish to know if you have been to Gunter's. She will then quiz you about your favorite flavor of ice. If you tell her you prefer the parmesan, she will feel an instant kinship. If you choose lemon, she will consider you pedestrian."

"I might be pedestrian," Elizabeth replied, "but if we are hoping to glean information from her, I suppose I must defer to her tastes."

"It might be for the best, my dear. But feel free to express yourself in your own witty manner."

So she was to be herself while pretending to be someone entirely different. She felt a well of sympathy for Mr. Darcy. His own natural humor was buried under such pretense. No wonder he had been so miserable when he arrived in Meryton. Not only had Mr. Wickham betrayed him in a scurrilous fashion, but he could not express his own honest condemnation of the man if he wished to spare his young sister the criticism of the ton. It must be exhausting.

An essential part of being William's wife would be sharing his burdens, allowing him to set down his mask. William tended to his sister, that much was clear. He took on the burden of raising and protecting Miss Darcy as well as everyone dependent upon Pemberley and Darcy House in London. But who tended to him?

I will. The courage she had been lacking in the countess's presence traveled up from her toes and stiffened her spine. This was her purpose. She would care for *her* Mr. Darcy, beginning with this visit in his aunt's drawing room. She drew in a deep breath, straightened her posture, and lifted her chin.

"Well done, Elizabeth," Aunt Matlock said approvingly. The countess nodded at her silent butler, who had arrived with two cards on a silver tray. "Lady Montagu and Mrs. Egerton have arrived."

As the butler exited the room, Elizabeth folded her hands in her lap.

"Are you ready, my dear?"

"I am ready, Aunt Matlock." Elizabeth said with a nod.

Two ladies were ushered into the room. The first was tall, about Aunt Matlock's height, though she was also very stout. She wore a lovely velvet hat bedecked with three long, white ostrich feathers. The second woman was not quite as tall, though she was still taller than Elizabeth. Elizabeth thought she must not eat a great deal, for she was very thin. Her light hair tended toward a carroty color. Her hat was plainer, and her smile revealed very yellow teeth.

Elizabeth allowed none of this to show in her expression, merely curtsied when she was introduced and made a few polite remarks to each lady as they all sat down for a chat. Elizabeth allowed the countess to lead the way, and for several minutes, she needed only to listen to the older women chat about people she did not know.

At last, Mrs. Egerton turned to her. "Have you been to Gunter's, Miss Bennet?" she asked genially.

"Not on this visit, I am afraid," Elizabeth admitted. "However, my elder sister and I do enjoy it."

Mrs. Egerton was eager, but Elizabeth detected no malice in her. "Do you have a favorite flavor, Miss Bennet?"

"I do not believe so," Elizabeth said. It was true. What she loved most about Gunter's was trying something new each time they visited. Jane always selected lavender. "I have tried the parmesan and asparagus as well as the artichoke. I sampled the jasmine last summer and greatly enjoyed it."

Mrs. Egerton did not listen closely enough to realize that Elizabeth had not said she enjoyed the parmesan. "I am at Gunter's nearly every day," she said with a wave of one hand, and rattled away happily without much additional prompting. Elizabeth wondered how she could be so thin, eating at Gunter's every day, but then, perhaps that was why Mrs. Egerton's teeth were in such a state. Mrs. Egerton carried on, and Elizabeth nodded attentively.

During a brief lull, there was a puffing sound. Elizabeth followed Mrs. Egerton's gaze to see Lady Montagu blowing a long feather from her face. She looked longer than she ought, and Lady Montagu asked, with a sharp edge to her voice, "May I ask what distracts you, Miss Bennet?"

Elizabeth was startled but did not allow it to show. "Oh, do forgive me, Lady Montagu. I am simply astonished by the grandeur of your feathers."

Aunt Matlock pulled a face, but quickly smoothed her features. Elizabeth did her best to keep all teasing from her tone as Lady Montagu peered at her to gauge whether or not she was being trifled with.

"I love feathers," Lady Montagu said regally, "but after a time, they do droop."

If she had chosen feathers of a lesser length the problem might be solved, but perhaps Lady Montagu enjoyed the spectacle.

Elizabeth thought her best option was to simply plow ahead and pray that Lady Montagu did not take offense. "They are beautiful," Elizabeth mused aloud. "Peacock feathers might drape less if that is what you would prefer. They are elegant and so very colorful. I am too small to pull them off creditably myself, of course," she explained, "but . . . if I might be allowed an opinion, my lady, they would complement both your figure and the blue in your eyes." It was the truth, even if solving Lady Montagu's feather problem was not her primary purpose.

Lady Montagu considered it for so long that Elizabeth hoped she had not made an enemy. Aunt Matlock's expression signaled that she hoped the same. At last, a smile crossed Lady Montagu's face. "They would indeed. How clever of you to notice."

It was hardly clever, but Elizabeth played along. "They are elegant and require an elegant lady to display them well."

"Yes, and they are not so common as the ostrich," Lady Montagu agreed. She returned her attention to Aunt Matlock. "I like the girl, Lucy." She spoke as though Elizabeth were not sitting three feet away. "She is pretty, and she has excellent taste."

Elizabeth nearly sighed in relief. She had dug herself out of that hole rather well, she congratulated herself. Now she must avoid falling into another.

Aunt Matlock clearly felt the same and moved to change the subject. "Have you heard how Elizabeth and William met?"

Her two friends leaned in towards her. "It really is the most romantic tale. Elizabeth, should you like to tell it? You must not leave out the insult, dearest. It is the best part."

Elizabeth tried to demur, but the request had more the flavor of a command. The women refused to accept her modesty. They were quite insistent upon knowing how their dear Mr. Darcy had fallen for a young woman "like her." That they did not consider their attitude an insult offered Elizabeth another glimpse into the world Mr. Darcy had been a part of since his birth.

Perhaps it *would* be better to tell the story all in one piece instead of waiting for these visitors to interrogate her. She would have more control over the story being told, and hopefully she would only need to tell it once. The gossip would weave it into something unrecognizable, but she could not control that. Her contemplation was interrupted.

"You must admit, my dear Miss Bennet," Lady Montagu said pleasantly, "that our Mr. Darcy did find you in a rather unusual way."

"Not so very unusual, Lady Montagu," replied Elizabeth, "for he was simply visiting an acquaintance at a neighboring estate."

"Well," Mrs. Egerton responded, "it is certainly a more interesting story than Miss Howard's ruination."

"Really?" Elizabeth asked, playing the innocent. "I was not in town when the story was circulating. Who was the source of this tale?"

"Does it matter?" Mrs. Egerton tittered.

"Oh, I believe it does," Elizabeth replied warmly.

"I must agree," the countess said. "Mr. Howard has long been known as an honorable man. He has not been run out of London as a result of the rumors, but his position cannot be comfortable. Lady Kendricks rescinded his invitation to dine not a fortnight ago; I cannot believe it is the only one. I would hope the source is a creditable one."

Lady Montagu turned to Aunt Matlock. "Who knows how these things ever begin?" She paused, thinking. "I do not know the source, but I heard it first from Mrs. Doughty at Broughton House."

Elizabeth did not notice that more calling cards had been brought in and that Aunt Matlock had selected a few until three other women entered the room and she was introduced to Lady Fleur, Lady Annabella, and Mrs. Darlington.

"We are speaking of poor Mr. Howard," Mrs. Egerton informed the new arrivals gleefully. "Is it not a pity about his sister? Such a grand fortune, and instead of waiting for her presentation and a respectable suitor, she has destroyed the reputation that was so important to her brother."

"Oh," said Lady Annabella. "It *is* rather shocking. I had it from Mrs. Doughty's daughter Emma, you know, who heard it from a school friend. Miss Howard had returned to town just at Michaelmas to prepare for the season. The rumors began, and within a month, she was sent away." She sighed, and Elizabeth detected some sincerity before Lady Anabella abruptly changed the subject. "But that is old news! It is not Miss Howard who interests us today," she declared. "I hope we are in time to hear how Miss Bennet has brought Mr. Darcy to the point at last."

"Your boys are so very stubborn," Mrs. Darlington teased Aunt Matlock, "that it *is* something of a minor miracle."

Lady Fleur laughed loudly. All the women turned to stare at her ladyship. "I declare," Lady Fleur said amiably, "are we not all thinking the same thing? Is it not amusing that Mr. Darcy would be captured at last by a country maid?" She nodded at Elizabeth. "I have no female relations for whom to take offense. I believe I shall quite enjoy watching that very solemn man act the besotted fool, as Lady Matlock paints him."

There were titters all around. Elizabeth decided she *might* like Lady Fleur. But she would wait to know all the ladies better before calling any of them friends. She had learned her lesson with Mr. Darcy.

Aunt Matlock waited until everyone was settled before asking Elizabeth to begin.

Elizabeth took a moment to meet each woman's eye before she began to speak, telling the story as she had before. "The first time I ever saw Mr. Darcy was at a dance where he flatly refused to stand up with me."

The women gasped, and Aunt Matlock sent a smile in Elizabeth's direction.

"Indeed," Elizabeth said sternly. "Can you imagine? The cheek of the man!" She warmed to her story, and the ladies made a satisfyingly rapt audience. She repeated the tale she had told Miss Darcy, adding a few details here and there for dramatic effect. They tittered when she told them of her refusal to dance with him at Lucas Lodge.

"As well you should!" declared Mrs. Egerton.

They waggled their brows when she suggested that their courtship had taken flight when she arrived at Netherfield to care for her sister.

"He simply could not deny it any longer," Lady Montagu declared triumphantly as the other women nodded sagely and nibbled at the cakes that had somehow appeared before them. "What sort of feathers did Miss Bingley and Mrs. Hurst wear?"

"Ostrich," Elizabeth said. Lady Montagu seemed inordinately pleased to hear it, for she lifted her eyebrows knowingly and pulled her head in like a turtle.

Unlike the description she had given her friends in Meryton, Elizabeth did not paint Mr. Darcy as an ogre. Rather, he was a man caught between two worlds, who had ultimately decided to act with his heart.

Elizabeth knew William would not appreciate being cast in the role of a romantic hero, bravely denying his family's expectations by falling madly in love with a genteel but penniless woman and fleeing to London in the middle of the night to prevent being bound to another. He would, after all, be teased by the men in his circle for the characterization she had created while she would be lauded as the fortunate woman who had turned his head. But there was little else to be done. Mr. Darcy disliked scenes, and while there would always be jealous women of Miss Bingley's ilk to contend with, they would be less likely to confront her directly if the women in the room today were charmed. Elizabeth knew that one thing she could do, when required, was charm. And if a situation ever called for it, it was this one. She would simply have to explain her reasons and endure her betrothed's grumbling.

By the time Aunt Matlock's visiting hour had passed, Elizabeth was both invigorated and exhausted. The ladies had all remained long beyond the usual visit and were chatting excitedly among themselves as they stood to leave.

"I will see our guests out, Elizabeth," Aunt Matlock said aloud, and then whispered near Elizabeth's ear, "You have woven a brilliant tale, my dear. I believe you have made quite a conquest."

"Conquest?" Elizabeth asked, but Aunt Matlock had walked out with her friends. Elizabeth sighed. She had barely escaped disaster with Lady Montagu and had not learned anything about Miss Howard or the rumors.

***

"There is only one thing left, Mr. Darcy," Gunderson said as he organized the sheafs of paper on his desk. "You neglected to send me the young lady's name and her particulars so that I might include it in the contract. And of course, her father or nearest male relation shall have to sign it before the wedding."

"My cousin is a highly prized commodity on the marriage market, Mr. Gunderson," Henry said with a false air of solemnity. "To prevent undue speculation and unwanted attention should his note fall into the wrong hands, he chose to inform you of his betrothed's name in person rather than commit it to the post."

Gunderson nodded as though this explanation was entirely reasonable. Henry's lips lifted on one side, a signal that he was about to invent some unbelievable farce of a tale. As Darcy was sure it would be about Elizabeth and himself, he cut Henry off.

"Miss Elizabeth Bennet," he informed his man. The attorney bent his head to write Elizabeth's name and that of her father into the contract. Henry shook his head sadly.

"You are a terrible bore, Darcy," he said with a dramatic sigh.

Darcy did not reply. When their business was finished, he gathered up the relevant papers and led Henry back out to the carriage.

"Now," Henry said, clasping his hands together as Darcy put the contracts into a leather portfolio and stored them in a box secured under his seat. "I allowed you to take precedence with the solicitor."

"Because he is paid by me and would not take orders from you," Darcy replied.

Henry ignored him. "When we arrive at the club, you must follow *my* lead."

"Why is that?" Darcy inquired. Despite himself, he truly wished to know.

"Because, you dunderhead," Henry said, waggling his eyebrows, "nobody likes you there. But they love me."

Darcy laughed aloud. "You are right, though I cannot fathom why. You cheat at cards and chess, you propose outlandish wagers, encourage others to stake their fortunes while you risk nothing, and apparently challenge every third man you meet to a duel."

"Variety is the very spice of life, that gives it all its flavor," Henry replied insouciantly.

"Do not quote poetry at me," Darcy responded.

"I wager you half a crown that you do not know the poem that line is from." Henry leaned forward.

"The poem is Cowper's 'The Task,'" Darcy said and held out his hand.

Henry swatted Darcy's hand away. "I do not actually carry coin on my person."

"Yes, I know. You wager funds you never intend to pay. Henry . . ." Darcy sighed. "Henry, one day you will come across a man who will not take your flippant manner well. I do not wish to see you harmed. Have you thought at all what that might do to your parents? To Fitz, who has no desire to be the viscount?"

His cousin studied him carefully, and Darcy wondered if his words had made any difference.

"Darcy," Henry began, but paused. His expression was unusually somber. "There are things you do not know."

"Very well. Enlighten me."

Henry glanced away to view the street outside the carriage window. When his eyes returned to Darcy's, he smiled as brightly as ever. "I cheat at the duels, too."

The club was nearly full when they arrived. Darcy could hear the gambling crowd on the first floor, their shouts and laughter wafting down the stairwell. Henry headed straight for the steps, and Darcy, with an inward grimace, followed.

"The books, Darcy," Henry murmured and shoved the most recent one in his direction.

"Darcy!" a young man called from the back of the room, the high pitch of his voice cutting through the din. "What are you signing, man?"

Henry cleared his throat, ceremoniously pulled at his cravat to make certain it was straight, and announced, "My cousin is to be wed tomorrow, and I have at last convinced him to settle your bets!"

Darcy took up the pen and opened the book. He could not prevent his small, contented smile as he wrote in clear strokes: "Mr. F. Darcy married to Miss E. Bennet, December 6, 1811." *St. Nicholas's day and the day of my marriage.*

The room fell deathly silent for a second while he wrote. When he set the pen down and stepped away, there was nearly a brawl as the rest of the men shoved their way to read the page. Darcy saw Mann paying something to another gentleman with a scowl. Good. He hoped Mann had lost more than the hundred pounds he earned wagering on Darcy's trip to Hertfordshire. Someone called, "Who is Miss E. Bennet, Darcy?"

Henry stepped up. "She is the daughter of a gentleman who does not care for London, and when you meet her, you will all be rushing out to the country to seek a wife just like her."

Darcy took a deep breath. Henry had handled that deftly. Now it was his turn. He motioned to one of the servants and requested several bottles of wine. The man rushed off and returned with glasses and assistance. Darcy noted that the wine was a rather more expensive vintage than the typical drink the club served, but he did not protest. "Serve everyone who wishes a glass," he instructed the men, loud enough to be heard around the room. "For we are to toast both my enchanting betrothed and my removal from the marriage mart! For those of you who wagered against me—you are justly served. Raise a glass anyway."

The crowd laughed uproariously. Most had already imbibed despite the early hour, and the noise brought other men streaming downstairs to see what was occurring. Henry nodded at the servants, and one young man dashed back to the kitchens to replenish their supply.

When everyone had a glass in hand, Darcy raised his own. "Gentlemen," he said. "Tomorrow I wed. May you all find such felicity in marriage as I anticipate."

"*Did* you anticipate?" one man called out, as though he knew the answer. Several others guffawed.

"Darcy anticipate his vows? You clearly do not know my cousin," Henry responded with a wink. "Never a man so prudish. Why do you think he wanted to marry his betrothed within three months of meeting her? He would not bed her before he wed her!"

Darcy felt the heat of his blush not only in his cheeks but his entire face. This seemed to confirm Henry's declaration, for there was more laughter and many nodding heads.

"I never thought I would see the day, Darcy!" a man cried from the center of the crowd. It was Dudley, who was also happily accepting money from a scowling Mann.

"There are other considerations as well," Henry said in a theatrical conversation with the men at the front of the crowd.

Darcy did his best to remain stoic. His ridiculous cousin was greatly enjoying himself, but Darcy could not reprimand him here.

Henry leaned in as though revealing a great secret, though he spoke loudly enough for much of the room to hear. "You know how our aunt in Kent will respond. Darcy is hoping to spare his bride and himself an angry scene."

There were more men genuinely commiserating now. Even Mann was nodding his head. Apparently, Lady Catherine de Bourgh was not the only obstinate relation in England.

Darcy pushed away the joking insults that followed Henry's comments and allowed himself to think of Elizabeth. Her eyes. Her plump lips. He again raised his glass. "*Omnia vincit amor*!" *Love conquers all*, indeed. It had certainly conquered him. Darcy drank deeply, and the men followed suit. He was forced to submit to a great deal of back-slapping, some rather ribald jests, and numerous complaints about lost wagers.

"Beware, gentlemen!" Henry cried, "For the best among us has fallen. Who will be next?"

There were groans and some remonstration. While Henry was chuckling with the crowd, Darcy felt the hair on the back of his neck rise. He gazed around the room, searching for the source, and found it near the back wall, a thin figure with large ears and spectacles who was given a wide berth by the other members of the club. No one had offered him a glass of wine, nor did it appear he had sought one. No one spoke with him or called his name. A pair of hazel eyes stared at Darcy with an anger so intense it was unsettling. He stiffened.

Howard.

Darcy's own anger flared and propelled him forward. Before he could take a third step, however, Henry was in front of him.

"Do not alter the plan, Darcy," he murmured. "You need evidence to act. Allow Richard to do his job."

Before Darcy could reply, Henry had waded back into the throng of men and Howard was gone.

Chapter Thirteen

Elizabeth was not reading the book in her hand when Colonel Fitzwilliam returned. She and Aunt Matlock were sitting in a smaller parlor, one more suited to family parties than the drawing room they had inhabited earlier. She glanced up and set her book aside, watching the colonel's expression tighten as he realized the men had gone.

"Where is Darcy?" he asked after he had greeted them both.

There were voices in the hall. "That must be them now," Aunt Matlock said.

The colonel leveled an irate glare at Mr. Darcy, but he only shook his head slightly in response.

Aunt Matlock sighed. "Let us hear it then, Richard."

Elizabeth met Mr. Darcy's gaze with a questioning look, not knowing to whom his aunt referred. Mr. Darcy inclined his head towards the colonel.

The colonel said nothing, only lifted his eyebrows. He and Mr. Darcy then appeared to have an entire conversation between them.

There were arched eyebrows, a slight shrug, a frown—but no words. Perhaps this was why her betrothed was such a quiet man. He had no need to speak. The idea was amusing, but whatever it was that they were conveying to one another was not. They were both irritated. So was Aunt Matlock who finally asked, with some impatience, "Well?"

"You were right to tell me not to return home with you, Fitz," Mr. Darcy said. "But Henry was also right to drag me to the club."

The viscount—Henry—smirked at both men and removed a small silver item from his pocket to admire. A toothpick case, from the looks of it.

"What happened?" the colonel asked.

"Fitz," Mr. Darcy murmured, "not here."

"Why not here?" Elizabeth inquired. "We are to be wed, sir. I should be included in important matters." She nearly bit her tongue. She had not meant to chastise him in front of others. Strangely, he appeared more charmed than annoyed.

Henry laughed. Oh, it was strange to think of a viscount by his Christian name.

"And this is why I shall never wed," Henry declared, waving a hand between Mr. Darcy and herself.

"You do not mean that," Aunt Matlock reproved.

"Oh, but I do," was Henry's firm reply.

"Mr. Darcy," Elizabeth addressed him firmly, before the conversation spun entirely out of control, "I wish to know your thoughts. What is it that you have to say?"

Her intended shook his head and addressed both her and the colonel. "The club was crowded. Henry had me write the date of our marriage in the betting books, and I offered a toast to my lovely bride." He glanced at the colonel. "Then I saw Howard."

Elizabeth sat heavily. "I do not know which of those statements to examine first," she told him.

The colonel's expression hardened. "Howard was there?"

Mr. Darcy nodded. "Henry kept me from engaging with him, but his reaction to my toast was . . . he was incensed."

"Henry was right to stop you, Darcy," the colonel said roughly. "Of course, you ought not have been there at all."

Henry was nonplussed. "We know more now than we did before. Howard's reaction is telling."

Colonel Fitzwilliam shook his head. "I could have told you as much without the risk."

"He needed to be seen celebrating his marriage, brother," Henry replied calmly. "Now, tell us what you learned."

The colonel rubbed a hand across his face. "The fair man's name is James Baker. He did eventually confess that Howard hired him and Henderson."

"To do what, precisely?" Aunt Matlock asked before Elizabeth could form the words.

"To punish Darcy," the colonel said evasively. "He said Howard did not much care how."

Mr. Darcy's eyes darkened. "What of Elizabeth?"

The colonel's eyes met Elizabeth's, his gaze sympathetic and reluctant.

"Go on, son," the countess said. "We should know."

He cleared his throat before saying, "I shall not repeat his exact words. In short, Miss Elizabeth spoiled the compromise. When it appeared that Darcy had gone. . ."

When the colonel faltered, Henry finished the thought. "They thought to make it look as though Darcy was fleeing something worse than Miss Bingley's hand."

Elizabeth felt ill.

The colonel nodded. "They were directed to connect the two of you in some sordid manner. Howard left the details to them, we think." He frowned. "We have had them both arrested for trespass and burglary. They were persistent because they have not yet been paid. Unfortunately that also means there is no bank draft, no convenient letter of instruction written in his hand, nothing but the word of a man no one will believe over Howard."

"What of Henderson?" Mr. Darcy asked.

The colonel crossed his arms across his chest. "Baker is definitely the weaker of the two. Henderson believes he cannot even be identified. With his coloring and the mark near his eye, Baker has no such illusions."

They were speaking in circles, their anger making them frustrated with the lack of progress. "Pardon me, gentlemen," Elizabeth said quietly.

"My apologies, Elizabeth," Mr. Darcy said at once. "I have not even greeted you properly." He approached her to take her hands and frowned. "Where is your splint?"

Elizabeth sighed. "Upstairs. We had visitors."

"She has not held anything heavier than a conversation," Aunt Matlock told Mr. Darcy. He did not say anything to his aunt, but Elizabeth was certain he would have something to say to her. Mr. Darcy never seemed to relinquish any topic that even slightly concerned him.

Elizabeth returned to the matter at hand. "I believe we are at an impasse until we learn *why* Mr. Howard is so angry with you. Is it that he blames you for the rumors? It cannot only be your refusal to wed his sister when you have never met her."

"May I suggest a course of action?" Aunt Matlock asked.

"Of course," Mr. Darcy said, and all three men turned to listen.

"William, marry Elizabeth tomorrow," Aunt Matlock said. "Allow the rest of us to work on your behalf." She held out her hand, and Mr. Darcy stepped forward to take it.

Henry and the colonel nodded their assent. She was used to the colonel's stern looks and Henry appeared composed, though she thought his smile perhaps a little too bright.

Without warning, the door was tossed open to reveal the earl. "Why are all the doors in my house shut today?"

"Whimsy," Henry said, as the colonel slid behind his father to check the hall and close the door behind him.

"William, take Elizabeth up to the music room and ask Georgiana to play for you," Aunt Matlock instructed. Mr. Darcy appeared uneasy, but he nodded and offered Elizabeth his arm.

"Here now," the earl exclaimed, taking them all in before glancing over his shoulder at the closed door. "What are you plotting, my dear?"

Aunt Matlock waved them off, and Mr. Darcy placed his hand over Elizabeth's. "Shall we?" he asked, and Elizabeth leaned against him briefly before they began to walk.

As they exited the room, she heard the earl ask, "Howard, eh?"

∞

Darcy tried to shake the sense of foreboding he had carried since seeing Howard at the club. Elizabeth had leaned against him in the drawing room, and though they were both very properly attired, the warmth of her body against his felt like a promise.

In spite of Henry's pronouncement at the club, Darcy was no prude. He was, however, a careful man, one who was hours away from reaping the rewards of his restraint. The closer the time came, the more difficult it was to remain a gentleman, but he would do so for Elizabeth's sake.

She glanced up at him shyly, and Darcy could not help but respond with a smile.

"What are you thinking?" she asked.

"I am thinking of you," he replied, surprised at how easily the admission came. "I am thinking of being married to you." He admired the faint tint of her blush and the way she tipped her head away bashfully. He enjoyed her pert rejoinders and teasing wit, but her sudden modesty at moments such as this further endeared her to him. It was a sort of vulnerability that was for him alone, and he leaned down, brushing his lips softly against hers. His heart raced when their lips met, and he lingered just a moment before slowly pulling away. Elizabeth's eyes were closed.

"Mmm," she said dreamily. "Is it terribly wrong of me to be happy we will be wed in haste? I would not wish to wait for the two or three months my mother would certainly insist upon."

"Elizabeth, no man who loves his intended wishes to wait," Darcy informed her and laughed quietly. "It is why so many women are already expecting on their wedding day."

Her mouth dropped open a bit, and he wanted to kiss her again. He did not. The two of them were standing in the hall, and they had already managed to escape discovery once. The way his luck was running of late, he would not risk it.

Elizabeth's face was very red, and he chuckled again. "You did insist on knowing my thoughts. Perhaps I should refrain from telling you everything."

She laughed at herself. "I may be shocked occasionally, William, but I would rather know. I have a tendency to think the worst if I do not."

"Yes," he told her fondly. "I am aware. Fortunately, I am practiced at saying things I should not." His gaze fell upon her arm, and he frowned. "Let us retrieve your splint."

"Can we not send a maid for that?" she asked. "I do not think your aunt would appreciate you entering my chambers."

He sighed. "We will be wed in less than a day, Elizabeth."

"Precisely," she said, her eyes alight with mischief. "We will not be wed until tomorrow."

Darcy badly wanted to kiss her again. Not just her mouth, but the creamy skin of her neck and her shoulder and . . . Yes. Perhaps Elizabeth was correct.

"Very well," he said, and reached for the pull. When a young maid arrived, he gave her orders and she hurried away.

They were close to the music room now. Georgiana was playing something by Haydn on the pianoforte. It was in a major key, a relief from the ponderous, melancholy music she had been playing since the summer.

"Oh, that is lovely," Elizabeth whispered.

"Your playing is lovely, too," he told her truthfully.

Elizabeth lifted her eyebrows.

"What is it?" he asked, befuddled. Had he not just given her a compliment?

"Either you believe I am requesting that you flatter me," she replied jauntily, "or you are too much in love to see the truth." Her mien grew thoughtful. "Oh." Her breath came a little faster, and when she met his gaze, Darcy felt his heart skip a beat. "I prefer the latter."

Elizabeth glanced away, and he watched as she lost herself in the music, closing her eyes and swaying a little, her small hands clasped together near her chest as she listened. They stood together in the doorway, nearly touching. His breathing quickened to match the pace of his heart. Her mouth was so close—he could bend down and . . .

The music stopped. "Brother, Miss Bennet, do come in," Georgiana called.

Elizabeth left him behind as she approached his sister, and Darcy was grateful for the moment to regain his composure.

"Oh, Miss Darcy," Elizabeth said enthusiastically, "how well you play."

His sister beamed with pleasure, but did not respond. She was still learning to accept such accolades, and not all of them had been genuine.

"I play," Elizabeth continued gently, "but I am afraid I do not practice as diligently as I should."

"But my brother says you play delightfully," Georgiana said, before her cheeks flushed a deep pink. "He wrote me in a letter."

So Georgiana *had* read his letters.

Elizabeth laughed. "I think you will agree that *delightfully* is not the same as *well*." She turned to offer him an impish grin.

Georgiana looked amused. "I never thought of that. Still, you cannot play ill if William enjoys it."

"I will remind him of that the next time I learn a new piece." Elizabeth laid a hand lightly on Georgiana's arm. "May I request a great favor?"

"Of course," Georgiana said.

Elizabeth took a deep breath. "Will you call me Elizabeth?"

His sister smiled widely, and Darcy's heart swelled with love for the two most important women in his life. "I would like that, Elizabeth," his sister answered. "Please, call me Georgiana."

Elizabeth patted Georgiana's hand. "Now, I believe you ought to keep playing. Consider it our wedding gift, for I have rarely heard such an accomplished pianist."

The girl nodded. "My gift shall have to be music," she said slyly, casting a glance at Darcy. "For my brother knows I cannot sew."

"Excellent!" Elizabeth exclaimed. "For if you were to do everything as well as you play this instrument, I should be quite frightened of you."

Georgiana giggled. That was twice in two days. After being deprived of his sister's laughter for months, Darcy thought he would never tire of hearing it.

As his sister returned to the piano and began the Haydn piece from the beginning, he held his hand out for Elizabeth. "Thank you, my dear."

Her dark curls bounced when she shook her head. "Georgiana is a dear girl, William. You need not thank me."

But he knew better. Darcy would be grateful to his betrothed forever, and not only for this.

After Georgiana finished the song, she came out from behind the piano and interrupted their tête-à-tête. She sat, placed her hands in her lap, and laced her fingers together. She lifted her head and tried to speak several times before changing her mind.

"Georgiana," Elizabeth teased, "will you not speak?"

Given such permission, Georgiana blurted, "I would like to attend the wedding tomorrow. May I, brother?"

Elizabeth tipped her head to one side, bemused.

Did his sister think he would refuse? "Of course, Georgiana," Darcy told her. "Although you must promise to remain with Aunt Matlock throughout."

"Oh, thank you, William!" Georgiana launched herself at her brother, surprising him and knocking him back into the settee.

"My dear sister," he said, standing up and pulling her to her feet. "I would not have had you travel from Pemberley, but as the church is near and Aunt Matlock will be there as chaperone, I see no reason to deny you."

"I was afraid that you could not trust me." Georgiana bowed her head. "I know I have disappointed you."

He nearly denied it, but that would do neither of them any good. "I will not deny that you did, dearest," Darcy said. "But I also disappointed you. I was not there when you needed me. It is my job to protect you, and I left you vulnerable."

"No," Georgiana protested. "You warned me. I made myself vulnerable." Her expression was wistful. "It is only that I thought Amelia was so grown up. When George appeared in Ramsgate and . . . *pretended* to be in love with me, I thought that it would be a romantic adventure like hers."

Elizabeth's brows pinched together. "Amelia who, Georgiana?"

Darcy knew his sister's friends and their families. He took in a sharp breath. "Amelia Howard, was it?" He felt Elizabeth stiffen. "I had not thought she was in town at all this year."

Georgiana nodded. "She told all of us she would marry well and we should have to call her 'Lady.'" She worried her bottom lip. "I suppose she may well be wed by now." She studied the floor. "Amelia traveled north early in March, and Aunt Matlock has kept me under lock and key since the summer, so I do not know."

Elizabeth met his gaze and Darcy nodded.

"Georgiana," she said calmly, "Amelia Howard has not married. She had been sent away by her brother."

"But why?" cried Georgiana, and then her eyes opened wide in shock. "Oh . . . He . . . and they . . . did *not* marry. I should have told someone! But she only said they were meeting in the park . . ." She hid her face in her hands. "Oh no."

"You were not the only girl who knew about Amelia, Georgiana," Elizabeth reassured her. "None of them said a word, either. And this was before your visit to Ramsgate. I am sure you have learnt better now."

Georgiana nodded her head vigorously but made no sound.

"Did any of the girls know *whom* she was seeing?" Darcy asked, trying to keep his voice as level as Elizabeth's.

"No," Georgiana said. "Amelia and I were not intimate friends, but no. I do not think so."

Elizabeth patted her arm approvingly, and Georgiana stood. "I think I shall remove to my chambers if you do not mind."

"Of course," Darcy told her, his eyes following her to the door.

The maid arrived as Georgiana exited, and Darcy took the pieces of Elizabeth's splint from her. The girl bobbed a curtsy and hurried away. "Elizabeth," he said sternly, "let me see your arm."

Elizabeth pulled a face, and he shook his head. "Pouting will not help you."

"I am not pouting," she said naughtily. "This is pouting." She pushed her lower lip out just slightly and gazed up at him with sadness in her eyes. An image of Elizabeth as a small girl flashed before him. Good God, what if they had a daughter like her? He would be entirely helpless in the face of this . . . face.

"You are going to be the death of me, Elizabeth Bennet." She helped hold the strips of wood while Darcy bound her arm. He tied the final knot quite efficiently and gently pulled her sleeve down over his work. "But I will likely enjoy every moment of my demise."

Uncle and Aunt Gardiner arrived quite early the next morning. Before they could alight from the carriage, Jane was handed out, and Elizabeth would have run to her sister had Mr. Darcy not reminded her of the ice. Instead, she began to bounce on her toes. She held out her arms, and Jane collapsed into them as Mr. Darcy greeted her and stepped away to meet her other relations.

"Oh, Lizzy," Jane whispered. "I feared I should never see you again."

For Jane, such a sentence was tantamount to an oration. Elizabeth embraced her sister and teasingly whispered in her ear, "You may not weep, Jane, for it is my wedding day. It would be bad luck."

It worked. Jane straightened, and the tears did not fall. "I cannot believe it. You are happy! You were so angry with Mr. Darcy. Whatever has happened?"

Elizabeth smiled as she welcomed her aunt and uncle. "Papa?"

Her father was nearly hidden behind the others, but he stepped forward to place a kiss on her brow. "My dear girl," he said softly. "It is good to see you." He pulled away to search her face. "So very good."

She leaned in and embraced him. "I love you too, Papa. Please, everyone," she called, "please come inside."

When they arrived in the drawing room, they found Aunt Matlock and Georgiana waiting.

"William," said his aunt, "You have some preparations to make, do you not?"

Georgiana did not speak, but she was nearly glowing.

Mr. Darcy nodded. "I shall see you at the church," he told Elizabeth. "Mr. Bennet, sir, I believe there are still papers to be signed."

Papa nodded and joined her betrothed. Mr. Darcy's smile was dazzling, and Elizabeth had to catch her breath. He bowed to everyone else, and the two men departed.

Jane turned to stare at her. "I do not believe I have ever seen him smile, Lizzy."

"And such a smile," Aunt Gardiner said with a laugh. "Were I not a happily married woman . . ."

"I am suddenly feeling rather de trop," said Uncle Gardiner merrily.

The earl arrived a moment later. "Mr. Gardiner," he announced after the introductions, "if you will follow me, we shall leave the ladies to their business, whatever that might be."

"Please do," Aunt Matlock said, waving them off with the back of her hand. "We have much to accomplish, and you will only be in the way."

Georgiana did manage a small laugh at this. Elizabeth was encouraged.

"Georgiana," she said, "I know you have only just now been formally introduced to my aunt and sister, but I believe you will all get along splendidly. I do have a special request for you."

"Anything, Elizabeth," the girl assured her. "It is your wedding day."

"You will be an excellent sister, Georgiana," Elizabeth proclaimed, then nodded at Aunt Gardiner and Jane. "Do not allow them to put feathers in my hair. No feathers!"

The women laughed, including Aunt Matlock. Georgiana watched them all for a moment before breaking into a gentle laugh herself.

"Very well, Elizabeth," she replied. "I shall be your protector."

"Come, my dears," Aunt Matlock said, holding out her hand. "It is time."

Later, when the all the ladies but Jane had removed downstairs, Elizabeth gazed at herself as she stood before the glass. She heard a quiet sigh behind her.

"Oh, Lizzy," Jane said, her eyes glossy with unshed tears. "You are beautiful."

Elizabeth turned one way and then the other, admiring how the silk made the lace overlay appear to shine in the light. "It is Aunt Gardiner's gown, but I am so grateful to have it. It is quite the loveliest thing I have ever worn." She turned to her sister.

"Jane," she said quietly. "Will you not tell me what happened at home after I left?"

Her sister's expression was pained. "I believe you know most of it, do you not? Papa invented a story. Mama was annoyed with you for leaving so abruptly when she had a list of purchases for you to make in town. Lydia was angry that she was being blamed for your bonnet, but perhaps it was a good lesson for her. Her reputation for honesty has not been a good one, and she is seeing the consequences. Kitty and Mary believed Papa and are carrying on as always."

"And Mr. Bingley?" Elizabeth asked quietly. "I am so very sorry, Jane. I did not know what he was, or I would never have encouraged you."

Jane blinked. "Mr. Bingley?" She shook her head and took Elizabeth's hand. "While we were waiting for our carriage at end of the ball, he said things about you I did not like. And after what Papa told me . . . Well, I have not thought about Mr. Bingley since. Oh Lizzy," she said with a sigh. "No. All my thoughts were for you."

Elizabeth squeezed her sister's hand and released it. "Had you truly been in love with him, you would have desired his presence to aid you through such a trial. You would have missed him." She did not how she would have survived had Jane been the one who vanished.

Jane tipped her head to one side. "You must be correct."

Elizabeth lifted her nose in the air. "I very often am, you know."

"Is this truly what you wish to discuss on the day of your wedding?" Jane gave Elizabeth a mischievous look.

"No," Elizabeth agreed. "So long as you are uninjured, let us speak of other things."

"Such as the way your betrothed smiles at you?" Jane's own smile was radiant. "I was so frightened for you, Lizzy, when all along you have been falling in love."

"Well," Elizabeth replied, "it did not happen precisely like that. First I . . ."

"Threw his own dish at him. Yes, I know," Jane teased.

"He told you that?" Elizabeth was surprised, but Jane nodded. "I was so confused. I woke up in a dark room, and he was there. I did not think, I just . . . reacted. But he was so kind about it, Jane. It quite unarmed me."

"And then you fell in love," Jane added, almost singing the words.

Elizabeth glanced away and nodded. "And then I fell in love." She twirled before the glass, taking pleasure in the way the skirt and lace moved together. "Did the colonel tell you how I held them off with a fork?"

Jane burst into an astonished laugh. "No, he neglected to relay that part of the story."

"Well," Elizabeth conceded, "It did not hold Colonel Fitzwilliam off for long."

"He *is* a colonel, Lizzy," Jane admonished her gaily.

Elizabeth sighed. "I do not know what to expect from him. He has been very distant. Until Mr. Darcy asked me to marry him, that is. He is amiable enough now."

"He was quite the gentleman when we met him at Lucas Lodge," Jane said. "Perhaps the problem was you."

Elizabeth laughed. "Oh, Jane, how I have missed you!"

Jane threw her arms around Elizabeth. "I have missed you, too, Lizzy." She stepped back and smoothed her hands along Elizabeth's skirt, and frowned. "Oh dear. I have wrinkled you."

"I do not care," Elizabeth proclaimed, just as her Aunt Gardiner entered the room.

"I shall see you downstairs," Jane whispered in her ear as she hurried away.

"Aunt?" Elizabeth asked, surprised at Jane's sudden exit. "Is something amiss?"

"Not at all, my dear," Aunt Gardiner replied. "I simply thought you might wish to discuss what happens after the wedding."

Elizabeth blushed, but teased her aunt anyway. "We gather for a meal in an earl's grand home?"

"Elizabeth," her aunt said. Her exasperation was good-natured, but it *was* exasperation. She reached out to touch Elizabeth's dress. "I knew this would be perfect on you." She motioned to two chairs set near the fire. "Shall we sit?"

When they were settled, Aunt Gardiner began. "What do you know about marital relations, Lizzy?"

She caught her bottom lip between her teeth before admitting, "Only what I have read in the books Papa did not want me to see."

Her aunt rolled her eyes and sighed. "Elizabeth Bennet."

"In my defense, aunt, he did not lock the case." Elizabeth tried to appear innocent.

"Which you took as permission?" her aunt inquired.

Elizabeth barely met her aunt's eye. "Yes?"

"Never mind," Aunt Gardiner said, resigned. "It will make our little talk easier. You know that there will be some pain, the first time?"

Elizabeth nodded.

"And you are aware of the mechanics of the act?"

"Yes, although I presume it will be different in practice."

Aunt Gardiner smiled. "Your husband will show you." She perched on the edge of the chair. "Now, when the time comes, you may think it is impossible for his part to fit into yours. Do not be anxious. Your body was made to accommodate his." She reached forward to pat Elizabeth on the hand. "Mr. Darcy appears to be very much in love, Lizzy, and for men, the physical part of your relationship is an essential part of how you show him your love."

"Is it only men? Is it wrong for me to anticipate that part of our marriage?" Elizabeth asked, embarrassed.

"Of course not! When two people love one another, the marriage bed can be wonderful for both," Aunt Gardiner fell quiet. "I think the best advice I can give you," she said at last, "is to be patient with yourself and with him. And that when you two are alone in bed—Lizzy, that is *not* the time to tease him. You often use humor when you are overwhelmed for good or ill, but if you tease or laugh at the wrong time, even if your laughter comes from anxiety, you may hurt his feelings."

Elizabeth was dismayed. "Would it really? I would never wish to do that."

Her aunt nodded. "That is not to say that humor has no part in your . . . activities. But you are marrying very quickly. Until you know one another better, allow him to take the lead."

This was not something Elizabeth would ever have considered. Aunt Gardiner had likely saved her from a dreadful mistake. "I am so grateful, Aunt," Elizabeth said warmly. "I will certainly follow your advice."

They stood, and Aunt Gardiner kissed Elizabeth's cheek. "You will make Mr. Darcy a wonderful wife, Lizzy," she said affectionately.

There was a knock, and Jane appeared in the doorway. "The countess says that the carriages have arrived."

Elizabeth's excitement soared. It was time.

Darcy tugged at the hem of his glove as he waited near the altar of St. George's. The building was drafty, and he hoped Elizabeth had dressed warmly. At least the ceremony would not take above half an hour.

Aunt Matlock had enjoyed using her status as a countess to persuade the church to make room for her nephew's nuptials. As the largest church in Mayfair, St. George's was also responsible for the most marriages—over a thousand a year. It was a busy place—there were three other weddings scheduled this morning. The vicar would not dally.

A young couple had just finished signing the register and departed with their families. Almost the moment they stepped out the side door, he and Fitz were joined before the altar by Miss Bennet. Mr. Gardiner and the earl stood to hand the other women in their party up the step and into the pews. Henry was not inside, but then, he was not reliable. It would not surprise Darcy at all were Henry to miss the ceremony altogether and only appear for the breakfast afterward.

Henry might not be here, but activity near the back of the church told him that Elizabeth was. Darcy stood a little taller. From the corner of his eye, he saw Miss Bennet offer him a tender smile. Fitz shuffled his feet noisily, but all of Darcy's attention was now focused on the spot where his bride stood with her father.

Darcy remembered how beautiful Elizabeth had been at the Netherfield ball, the last time he had seen her so formally attired. He had known that night that he would have to leave Hertfordshire if he did not plan to offer for her, for his heart was in danger. But now his heart was safe in her keeping.

Elizabeth was attired in a beautiful gown, but all he could think of was how well she appeared in it and how this evening he would be allowed to see her out of it. He stared as she approached, unmoving until there was a small nudge at his back. Fitz was standing beside him.

"Church, Darcy," his cousin hissed in his ear. "You are in a church."

He blinked. Right.

Mr. Bennet smirked, but Elizabeth returned Darcy's look with a bashful one of her own that did not help him to focus upon the ceremony.

As expected, they proceeded without delay. By the end, he barely recalled the words other than a few scattered phrases. Elizabeth, promising to love, cherish, and obey him, the last to which she would undoubtedly append "when he is correct." Sliding his grandmother's ring on her finger and repeating, "With this ring I thee wed, with my body I thee worship, and with all my worldly goods I thee endow: In the Name of the Father, and of the Son, and of the Holy Ghost. Amen." He remembered kneeling, but the next phrase that really made its way into his consciousness was "let every one of you in particular so love his wife, even as himself." He had sent up a little prayer of his own that he would deserve her love in the same way, for if Elizabeth respected him, loved him, he would truly be a wealthy man.

Then they were at the register and he signed his name. He was pleased to see that his hand was steady and his signature clear.

As Elizabeth signed herself as a Bennet for the last time, Darcy heard the heavy footsteps of someone in great haste drawing closer. As his wife completed her task and her sister picked up the pen, Darcy turned to see Fitz stepping forward to position himself between the intruder and the women.

Their surprise guest ought not to have been much of a surprise at all. Darcy glowered at his uncle, who grumbled something under his breath and had the good grace to look abashed. The man could not have waited another day to goad his sister?

For it was Lady Catherine de Bourgh stalking to the altar of St. George's with the speed of Arion.

And Henry, blast him, was right behind her.

Chapter Fourteen

Elizabeth watched Jane sign the parish register before she moved to peek around her new husband. The intruder was a tall, thin, elderly woman whose clothing was very well made, though somewhat behind current fashions. She clutched a mahogany walking stick with a silver head. A rather tall hat was perched precariously atop her head, slipping to one side as she strode purposefully up to the altar.

The earl had extricated himself from the knot of well-wishers who awaited the happy couple and was approaching the woman from one side while the viscount trailed her. One the other side, William and the colonel had stepped between her and the intruder. The woman was surrounded.

Elizabeth blinked as the stranger reached the vicar and stated, firmly and loudly, "I declare an impediment to this disgraceful spectacle!"

Elizabeth should have been mortified to have her wedding disrupted in such a way. Instead, she was forced to stifle a laugh at the aristocratic woman whose tall hat seemed to protrude from one ear.

"A spectacle it is," Henry said loudly, "but you should not be so harsh upon yourself, Aunt Catherine. You are, at the least, well-dressed."

Oh! It must be William's Aunt Catherine—Lady Catherine, the woman who wanted him to marry her daughter Anne. The older woman whirled to glare at Henry but was not distracted by him for long.

The vicar eyed Lady Catherine warily. "The time to declare impediments has passed, madam."

"I am Lady Catherine de Bourgh, and I shall be heard," the woman stated boldly, striking the stone floor with the stick to emphasize her words.

The vicar sighed.

Lady Catherine gazed down her nose at the shorter cleric. "This man"—she pointed at William with one long, slender finger—"is engaged to *my* daughter! Now what have you to say?"

"Only that he is now *married* to mine," Papa replied, and for once, he did not sound as though he was teasing. Elizabeth was quite proud of him.

Jane took Elizabeth's arm. "Who *is* that woman?" she whispered.

"I believe she is Mr. Darcy's aunt," Elizabeth responded.

"They are *related*?" Jane asked, incredulous.

"Who is this person, Henry?" Lady Catherine inquired disdainfully as she looked Papa up and down.

Jane lifted a hand to her mouth. "Oh. I see the resemblance now."

"*Jane*," Elizabeth whispered, trying desperately not to laugh.

"Only the father of the bride, Aunt Catherine," Henry replied merrily. "He clearly knows she is old enough to wed. Therefore, the impediment of the bride's age has been satisfied." He glanced over at William. "Is there a Bennet in the Darcy bloodline?"

"Do not be ridiculous!" declared her ladyship.

"Then they could not be sister and brother." Henry stroked his chin. "I presume you do not intend to claim impotence as an impediment?"

Elizabeth's cheeks warmed.

"*Henry,*" William growled, but the viscount only grinned.

"I was not addressing *you*, boy," Lady Catherine said icily, then turned to the earl. "Henry, how could you allow this to happen?"

"Darcy was never going to marry Anne," the earl told his sister. "Neither he nor Anne wish it. What would you have me do?"

"Lady Catherine," the vicar said in the tired tone of a man well used to complaining relatives, "if *wishing* Mr. Darcy would marry your daughter rather than Mr. Bennet's is your only impediment, I am afraid it will not stand. If you have a contract, you must seek your remedy in the courts. I cannot help you." He addressed William. "If you would kindly take your party home, sir, I have another couple waiting to say their vows."

"This is not to be borne!" Lady Catherine exclaimed, waving her fist in the air. It would not have been so concerning had it not been the fist clutching her stick. The vicar stumbled back, and William and the Fitzwilliam men surged forward to interrupt Lady Catherine's tirade. Jane hurried to Papa's side, but Elizabeth remained still, hoping to avoid the woman's notice.

Elizabeth was so entirely engrossed in the scene before her that the deep voice in her ear made her tremble with shock. "I should not be surprised he has jilted even his own cousin. It should have been my sister here today, not you." The man's breath was hot in her ear. "You may tell him he will hear from me." Her heart raced wildly as she took a step away to view the man who was speaking to her. A deep chill overtook her as she stared at him. He looked familiar . . .

"Who are you?" she asked weakly, thinking she ought to raise her voice but feeling entirely unequal to it. She was only just able to turn her head to look at him.

A pair of hazel eyes glared at her, through her, but he did not answer. He just gave her a small, sickly smile and walked away towards a side entrance, placing a hat on his head. There was a sudden splash of light from the street as the door opened, and then he was gone.

"Elizabeth?" She swiveled back to view William's concerned expression. "You are as cold as ice, dearest," he said with some surprise as he took her hand and chafed it between his own. "Lady Catherine blusters, but she has no power to challenge our marriage."

Elizabeth shivered, and her husband placed an arm around her.

"Come, let us return to Matlock House."

"Elizabeth," Georgiana said, embracing her. "I am so happy for you." She pulled back, still holding one of Elizabeth's hands. "Why was Mr. Howard here? Did you invite him, brother?"

William's grip tightened. "Howard? Where?"

Elizabeth blinked. "He was the man," she said, barely above a whisper. "The man I saw in the ballroom at Netherfield."

<hr />

"He dared!" Darcy roared. His cousins had placed themselves strategically between him and the door. "I will hear from him? He will hear from *me*!"

The moment the final guests had departed Matlock House, his cousins had waylaid him, dragging him into the library while the rest of the family removed to the music room. The mask he had worn for Elizabeth's sake had slipped away once they were sequestered.

"No," Fitz said calmly. There were lines of strain around his eyes. "He will not."

"For once, the estimable colonel is correct," added Henry, and Fitz struck his brother's arm with the back of his hand. "Howard would be pleased to have you chasing him through London like a madman."

Darcy ran both hands through his hair. "He approached my wife not a quarter of an hour after we spoke our vows." He took a step towards the door, but his cousins closed ranks and would not allow him to pass. Frustrated, he cried, "I cannot, I *will* not allow this to go unanswered."

"We are not suggesting that you should," Fitz replied. "Only that you do not fall prey to his provocation. Kindly recall that you do not believe in duels. Use your talent for strategy instead."

"It does not help to have Fitzwilliams who are constantly interfering in my life," Darcy complained, though he was no longer shouting. "I asked your father not to send his letter to Aunt Catherine express. And you ushered her right in, Henry."

Henry smirked. "She did not arrive in time to disrupt the actual ceremony, did she?"

"No thanks to you," Darcy shot back.

"You think not?" Henry asked challengingly.

Fitz eyed his brother. "Please tell me you did not, Henry."

Henry shrugged and examined his fingernails. "It fits our story perfectly. Darcy and the radiant if rather unconventional Miss Elizabeth were forced to marry quickly and quietly to avoid Lady Catherine's wrath. With the assistance of the countess, you were hoping to present Lady Catherine with a fait accompli and thus prevent a breach in the family. You were *forced* to rush—you barely finished the ceremony as it was." He grinned. "And Aunt Catherine was so obliging as to play the outraged mother. Given that, what is an express or two between cousins?"

"I do not need your help managing rumors," Darcy said, his annoyance plainly evident. "The fracas my aunt kicked up was the only reason Howard was able to speak with Elizabeth. My God, man, what if he had meant to harm her?"

What he would not do to have Howard in front of him now! Elizabeth was the bravest woman he knew, but no one could withstand these repeated attempts to injure without consequence. She was as afraid as she had been when he found her hiding in the attic, and on their wedding day! He could run the man through and not feel an ounce of regret.

No, it would not stand.

He turned to Fitz. "And you, going to your mother . . ." He stopped. Truly, that had worked out rather well. "Never mind," he said gruffly when Fitz raised his eyebrows. "In fact, I thank *you*."

"Darcy, you addlepate," Henry said, "why are you spending your wedding day closeted with us when you ought to be closeted with Elizabeth?"

His temper could stretch no farther, and he stepped to Henry with every intention of flattening the man. Henry just grinned.

Fitz restrained him, placing two hands on his chest. "Darcy, you need to release your anger, or you will not be able to help your wife. She needs you to be your usual steady self."

Darcy stared at Fitz. Blast it all. Elizabeth's health and happiness were the only things that would have any influence on him today, and Fitz knew it. He made his way over to a window and leaned against the sash. The glass panes were cold, and he stood there for a few moments, allowing them to cool his temper.

"Angelo's," he said at last, though it was far less than the man deserved. "I will meet Howard there."

"To what end, Darce?" Fitz asked quietly.

Darcy's grip on the window frame tightened. "It will not go unanswered, even if sport is the only way to do it."

"Well," Henry crooned, ignoring Fitz's scowl and rubbing his hands together, "I do enjoy a wager."

On the evening of her wedding, Elizabeth stared into the glass, chastising herself for so thoroughly losing her composure over Mr. Howard's words. It had upset her husband terribly. He had hidden it well until the final guests had departed, but she had noted it. His Fitzwilliam cousins must have as well, for they had pulled him into the library shortly after. He had emerged from their meeting more himself, for which she could only be grateful.

Mr. Howard had only spoken a few poisonous words to Elizabeth. He had not even touched her, not really. If only she could have raised her voice, she would have had assistance in an instant. She was unhappy she had allowed herself to be frightened into uselessness.

Elizabeth dismissed her maid and drew her brush through her long hair. Jane, considerate as ever, had brought to London the few items she knew were of sentimental significance to Elizabeth. The brush and comb set matched the one Jane had received from their parents on her own come-out. It had been the only thing that had marked the event, for Meryton's society was not particularly grand. But being gifted something valuable, something beautiful that was just like Jane's—the distinction had been deeply felt. As she awaited William, this physical reminder of her family and her life at Longbourn grounded her. Calmed her.

She was determined to be the wife William required, and although her name had changed today, she must be the brave Elizabeth Bennet her family knew. That was the woman with whom her husband had fallen in love. Her courage *would* rise with every attempt to intimidate her. In the past fortnight she had been used, accosted, even abused in the most wretched manner. But she was not broken. In fact, the end result of it all was that she was married to a man she loved. A man who ardently admired and loved her.

The door to her chamber opened, and she spied her husband's figure in the reflection of the glass.

"Elizabeth?"

Her smile was genuine. "Good evening, Mr. Darcy," she said.

"Good evening, Mrs. Darcy," he replied softly.

William entered, approaching her and placing his hands on her shoulders. She exalted in the contact and tipped her face upwards to view his. "I have been waiting for you."

His expression clouded over. "Are you quite sure, love? After everything that happened today, I would not blame you if you wished to wait."

She stood and turned to face him. His hands fell to his sides as he awaited her answer.

Elizabeth took his hands in her own and placed them on her hips. *Be bold, Elizabeth Bennet Darcy. You must begin as you intend to go on.*

William's hands curled around her, and his thumbs stroked her skin through her nightgown. He pulled her closer.

Elizabeth's legs weakened. "I do not desire to wait," she said softly, placing the palms of her hands on his chest. Her fingertips grazed bare skin beneath his banyan, and curious, she slid her hands inside.

Her husband's breath was ragged. "What is it that you *do* desire, Mrs. Darcy?" he inquired. Without breaking the gaze they shared, he reached to snuff out the candle.

Elizabeth stayed his hand. "I wish to see you."

William's hands wound themselves into her hair. He bent forward and kissed her hard on the mouth. Elizabeth groaned with pleasure and attempted to mimic his actions. Her arms snaked up to his shoulders and around his neck.

"What do you *desire*, Mrs. Darcy?" he asked again, his lips so close to her own they might share the same breath. He lingered there, waiting for her answer. "Tell me," he whispered.

Her aunt was right. This was no time to tease. In truth, she could barely form a coherent thought.

"You, Mr. Darcy," she murmured, as she lost herself to his touch. "Only and forever, you."

∞

Darcy awoke to the singular pleasure of Elizabeth in his bed. In all those nights at Netherfield, he had dreamed of her. When she had come to Darcy House, he had dreamed of her. Now he was almost afraid to wake her for fear that this was a dream, too.

She was curled up on one side, her long, thick hair tossed out behind her.

For a time, he simply watched her sleep, tracing the curve of her cheeks and her neck with his gaze. She shifted, and the blanket fell from one bare shoulder. Darcy leaned over to kiss her there and pull the covering back over her.

He had nearly denied himself this happiness, and to what end? His uncle, though disappointed, had not been unduly bothered by his announcement, and his aunt was simply relieved that one of them had finally decided to wed. Georgiana was well on her way to loving Elizabeth as a sister. Fitz admired her. Even Henry liked her, though for that Darcy thought he might need to apologize to Elizabeth.

Lady Catherine had been angry, but that was to be expected. With the marriage supported by the rest of the family, she had given way. Reluctantly and not without vociferous complaint, but she had followed the Matlocks to their London home without additional commotion. The only thing more important to her than gaining him as a son was the family credit. Though she would never admit it, she had been embarrassed by her outburst at St. George's. He felt more for Georgiana, who would be required to share the house with Lady Catherine, than he did for the older women's well-earned mortification.

Darcy brushed a few stray strands of hair from Elizabeth's forehead. She stirred but did not wake. At last he gave way to temptation, dipping to capture her plump red lips with his own. Her eyelids fluttered open, and she offered him a sleepy smile so content he pulled her into his arms as he had the night before.

"Are you well this morning, Elizabeth?" he asked, propping himself up against the headboard and easily settling her between his legs, her back against his chest. She sighed, and he kissed the top of her head while adjusting the blankets around them both.

He would be able to wake up every morning of his life in this way if he chose. When Elizabeth turned her head and rested her cheek against his chest, the luxury of it nearly overwhelmed him.

"I am well. A little sore but very happy," she replied, her breath cooling his skin and making it tingle. "And you?"

He chuckled. "A little sore but very happy, too."

"William," she said quietly.

"Yes, love?"

He contemplated her little nose as it crinkled and felt a powerful need to kiss those three small lines. He closed his eyes instead, to focus on her words. She would be angry if he did not.

"What will you do to Mr. Howard?" she asked.

Darcy had not anticipated that particular question at this moment. Elizabeth must be more distressed than she let on to ask it. He took a deep breath. He stroked the length of her right arm with his fingers. "I have not challenged him, if that is your concern, love. Not in any dangerous way. I have no doubt I can best Howard with both the pistol and the sword, but when men are angry, they are not always wise." He did not mention that they were also less inclined to follow the rules. "I would not purposefully do anything that would leave you vulnerable. I have responsibilities—to you, to Georgiana, to Pemberley—that do not allow me to take such risks."

He felt something wet on his arm, and realized it was a tear. "Elizabeth?" he asked, alarmed. "What is it?"

She shook her head. "It is nothing, only . . . thank you, William. After all we have suffered to reach this place—I could not bear it were Mr. Howard to succeed in harming you."

Darcy sighed. "He will not. But we will cross swords at Angelo's."

Elizabeth frowned. "The foils will have buttons?"

He was a bit surprised she knew the parts of a foil, but he should not have been. She possessed a strange but extensive menagerie of facts. Darcy nodded before he realized she could not see it. "Of course," he assured her.

"And the colonel will be there, so you are not alone?" she pressed.

"Yes. Henry too, for whatever good that might do me."

Elizabeth touched her top lip with the tip of her tongue, and Darcy's own mouth went dry.

"I am probably wrong," she ventured to say, "after all, you know him far better than I. But there is something almost . . . dangerous about Henry."

"Dangerously foolish, perhaps," Darcy said wryly. "Idle. I believe we all apprehend as much."

She shook her head slowly. "Dangerous as in a man who plays a role so you do not see what is underneath. Sir William plays a role as you know, although he is not dangerous." She tipped her head to one side. "Well, I suppose he is, in his own way. But your cousin is something more."

Darcy considered the notion. "I think I would prefer that we not discuss Henry or Sir William while in our bed, dearest."

Elizabeth snorted, her pensive expression disappearing. "Very well." She laid one small hand over his wrist. "You will be careful when you meet Mr. Howard at Angelo's."

He hated her distress but was proud of her strength. She did not wish him to go but supported his need to protect her. "I will be careful."

Very slowly, she turned to face him, folding her legs beneath her and sitting back on her heels. Her dark eyes bored into his. "What we did last night . . ." she began but paused.

Ah, here was a more promising subject. "Yes?" he prompted.

She blushed but did not look away. Instead, she took his hand in hers. "It made me feel so close to you."

"Perhaps that is why it is called the 'marriage bed,'" he said quietly, rubbing his thumb lightly over her fingers.

"Perhaps," she concurred, leaning forward unsteadily to place a kiss on his chest. The faint scent of jasmine mingling with citrus set him aflame.

He held in the groan he wished to release. Instead, he asked hopefully, "Perhaps we might try again?"

"Perhaps . . ." She smiled. "Perhaps yes."

He pulled her to him gently, then rolled them over, pushing himself up on his forearms so as not to rest his weight on her. He kissed her left eyelid tenderly, then the right. "I did vow to worship you with my body," he whispered.

Her breath hitched as he began to trail soft kisses down her neck. "So you did," she whispered back, "And that is one vow I shall always wish to obey."

∞

One day. One blissful day of solitude was all they had been afforded. Elizabeth knew that Mr. Howard must be dealt with, and of course she would not miss farewelling Jane. Still, she selfishly desired that she and William had been able to carve out a week, even two, before leaving their chambers.

The physical expression of love that they shared was not at all like it had been described in Papa's books. Well, maybe a little, but the mechanical act was the very least of it. None of those authors had ever explained how it could make the woman feel! The man, too, if William's extraordinarily good mood was any indication. He had even hummed a tune as he left their chambers for his dressing room.

It was nearly the end of visiting hours before the Darcy carriage came to a stop in front of the Gardiners' home. William handed her down the steps himself. When she reached the ground, he placed her hand on his arm rather than release it.

They were led into the parlor, and Elizabeth had the supreme pleasure of hearing them announced as "Mr. and Mrs. Darcy." She stepped into the room with her husband and froze.

Sitting next to Jane was Miss Bingley, and in a chair facing her, Mr. Bingley, who, though he rose as they entered, appeared none too pleased to see them.

Aunt Gardiner rose, too. "Oh, Lizzy, Mr. Darcy," she said warmly, though her gaze suggested relief. "Jane has just been relating your happy news."

"Indeed," Mr. Bingley said flatly, "Our congratulations, Darcy, Mrs. Darcy."

"Thank you, Mr. Bingley," William said, but the words were cold.

"I thank you for your visit, Miss Bingley, Mr. Bingley," Jane said, clearly dismissing them.

Elizabeth noted that Jane's color was high, and that her eyes flashed with an anger quickly subdued. Elizabeth's gaze moved to Miss Bingley, who was watching her brother with something like trepidation. How curious.

"Your uncle will be here any moment, Mr. and Mrs. Darcy. He planned to leave work early so that he could greet you," Aunt Gardiner explained.

Mr. Bingley held out a hand to help his sister up. "I thank you for your hospitality, Mrs. Gardiner." He turned to Jane. "May I call again tomorrow, Miss Bennet?"

Jane stood and brushed out her skirt. "No, Mr. Bingley," she replied, her expression resolute. "You and I see so differently on this afternoon's subject that we shall never be able to agree. I thank you for the compliment of your attentions, but I do not wish for them to continue."

Mr. Bingley opened his mouth to respond, but William spoke first. "You have your answer, Mr. Bingley," he said firmly. "Do not importune my sister further."

The man Elizabeth had once found so amiable, so ready to please, scowled. "Very well," he said sharply, and removed himself from the room.

Mr. Bingley did not wait for his sister, who took advantage of the opportunity to say, in a very low tone, "I must apologize, Mr. Darcy—for all of it. My brother forced me to it." She glanced at the hall, then whispered quickly, "I did think you and I might suit, but I should never throw myself at any man were it left to me. I have no need to do so." There was an earnestness in her expression that made Elizabeth believe her. "I do not know what has come over Charles."

"Miss Bingley," William replied seriously, "your brother has been gambling. I recommend you seek another trustee to safeguard your fortune. Perhaps Mr. Hurst might be of assistance."

Caroline Bingley paled, but was not overcome. She nodded once in a quick, tight motion, and hurried out to the hall. Nobody spoke until they heard the front door close.

"Oh, Jane!" cried Elizabeth, rushing across the room and reaching for her sister's hands. "How brave you were!"

"I never expected him to seek me out, so I did not inform anyone that he should not be announced," Jane explained, nearly falling back into her seat.

"Oh, Lizzy," Mrs. Gardiner said, touching one hand to her forehead and sitting in the nearest chair. "He somehow managed to be both charming and terribly intrusive. I thought we might never be rid of him."

Jane pressed Elizabeth's hands. "Indeed. He was so different. He frightened me a little."

"May I get you something, Mrs. Gardiner? Miss Bennet?" William inquired with real concern. He glanced around the room and motioned to a decanter. "A glass of wine?"

Both women smiled at him and shook their heads. "No, sir," said Aunt Gardiner with a little laugh, "your timely interference was all we required. I sent for Edward, but he can be difficult to locate at times."

"Where is Papa?" Elizabeth asked. He rarely left the study even here, but surely he would have come had he known Mr. Bingley had arrived.

"With Longbourn's solicitor," Aunt Gardiner informed her. "He has been gone several hours and should return shortly."

"Whatever did Mr. Bingley want?" Elizabeth asked, sitting next to Jane and taking her hand.

"He seemed to believe Mama's claim that my first son would inherit Longbourn," Jane replied. "I told him that was not the case, but he behaved as though he knew better. How can a man be so assured of his information and yet be so entirely mistaken?"

William stood where Elizabeth had left him, shuffled his feet a bit, and finally clasped his hands behind his back.

"Hello?" Uncle Gardiner called from somewhere near the front of the house.

"Late again, Edward," Aunt Gardiner said with a sigh and stood to fetch him.

William watched her go and then moved to a chair to address Jane. "Mr. Bingley followed you to London, then?"

Jane shook her head. "It is possible he had other business."

William pulled a face, and Elizabeth gently shook her head at him. "I did not prevaricate when I spoke to Miss Bingley, Miss Bennet," he said.

"You have claimed me as your sister. You had better call me Jane." There was a twinkle in Jane's eye.

"My sister Georgiana calls me William," William offered.

Jane nodded, pleased.

"How serious are Mr. Bingley's debts?" Elizabeth asked.

William grimaced. "He has paid most of them, but he has squandered a significant portion of his fortune."

"Then he was interested in me because he wanted Longbourn," Jane said quietly.

"Precisely," William said. "I ought to have waited to speak with your father about Bingley myself, rather than racing away to London like a scalded cat. If I had, none of this would have happened."

"Including this," Elizabeth replied, holding up the hand that bore his ring. "It is not your fault," she assured him, "I told Papa what he needed to know, and Mama is well aware Jane is not an heiress. She simply refuses to accept it."

"Much like Mr. Bingley," Jane said quietly.

William lifted his eyebrows at Jane's statement. Elizabeth smiled. He would grow used to Jane's intelligence as well as her humor, which she only used in company where she felt safe.

"Grandfather Bennet was not fond of women," Elizabeth explained to her husband. "He tied the estate up in such a way that it could never be inherited by one."

"Then who *is* the heir now that Mr. Collins has passed?" Aunt Gardiner asked, turning to the door as Elizabeth's father stepped inside.

"The attorneys have been searching all the branches of the Bennet tree since they first heard about Mr. Collins. Thomas does not yet know," Uncle Gardiner informed them, before he realized Papa was in the room.

Her father moved a smaller chair to their group, placed it, and sat. "Well now," he said drily. "As it turns out, we do. I simply did not wish to say before we exhausted all other possibilities."

They all waited as Papa stood silently. Finally, Jane could wait no longer. "Papa!" she remonstrated. "It is unkind of you to sport with us."

Papa stood and held out his hand to Uncle Gardiner. "Congratulations, Edward. My father must have seen something of greatness in you, for if our line failed, he named you as Longbourn's heir."

Chapter Fifteen

"Edward," Aunt Gardiner said numbly. "Eddie will be the heir one day."

Uncle Gardiner was no less stupefied than his wife. "The man barely knew me, Thomas. I was still at school when you married my sister."

"Yet you were already winning prizes in mathematics. Oh, my father likely thought it would never come to pass," Papa said, appearing quite pleased with the surprise he had sprung on them all. "After all, when the will was written, I was only thirty and about to wed. We all assumed there would be an heir. If not, Mr. Collins the elder was in excellent health—and his son was a young boy and seemed stout enough. It was entirely unexpected that the estate should fall to the remainder man. Still, I believe he made a wise choice. I even told him so at the time."

"You knew?" Uncle Gardiner asked. "You knew all along?"

Papa shrugged. "There was no need to mention it until we were certain that no long-lost Bennet relations would appear to take your place. It would have been cruel to raise your hopes in such a way."

Elizabeth was vastly pleased with this turn of events. Longbourn would stay in the family, even if it was not the Bennet family. Uncle Gardiner would be a much better financial caretaker than her father. He did not know very much about running an estate, however.

"Edward," Papa said, his thoughts clearly mirroring hers, "now you really *must* make time to visit."

"You are all welcome to Pemberley as well, including the children. We are engaged in a variety of new techniques . . ." Before he had completed the sentence, William stopped speaking. He straightened in his chair, his cheeks flushing red. "Of course, I shall leave it to my wife to offer the invitation."

Elizabeth squelched her laughter. "You usurp my duties already, Mr. Darcy?"

To her great delight, he offered her a sheepish little grin. "I have been on my own a long time, Elizabeth. Occasionally, you may be required to remind me."

"Well," Elizabeth addressed the room, "I think it a fine idea." She gazed lovingly at her husband. She did laugh a little then. "So fine an idea that I invited my aunt and uncle when we were here last."

Her husband shook his head self-consciously. "That is a great relief," he replied, and accepted the good-natured teasing of the others in the room.

Where had all his formality gone? Elizabeth knew then that he trusted the people in this room. She loved them, therefore he had decided to love them, too. It would be more difficult for him to offer the same to the rest of her family, but she suddenly had no doubt that he would be a gentleman for them as well. She smiled brightly at him.

He placed his hand over hers, much as he had when they entered the house.

"We would be pleased to have you stay for dinner," Aunt Gardiner was saying. Elizabeth hoped no one else had noted her distraction.

"I thank you, Aunt," she said. "However, cook will be upset with me were we to dine out tonight. She has already begun her preparations. Later in the week, perhaps?"

She was not watching her husband's face, but Aunt Gardiner's kindly visage shone with approbation. "That would be lovely, dear. Shall we say Thursday evening?"

Elizabeth glanced up at William. He was gazing down at her with a look she recalled from their chambers. It was time to make their farewells.

"Until Thursday, then," she said.

"Perhaps you might arrive early on Thursday, Lizzy, so we can have a proper visit," Jane said.

Elizabeth gasped happily. "Jane, will you remain in town?"

"Oh," her sister replied, a little red staining her cheeks. "I have quite forgotten to say. Aunt has asked that I remain through the festive season, as Uncle Gardiner will not be able to leave his business this year."

"It is time for him to hire a manager," Aunt Gardiner said firmly. "Particularly in the face of Thomas's news. Is not that right, Mr. Gardiner?"

Uncle Gardiner shook his head and looked sheepish. "Yes, my dear. I believe you are correct. In fact . . . " He tipped his head towards the door. "I really should get back."

Aunt Gardiner stood and placed her hands on her hips. "Mr. Darcy, Mrs. Darcy," she said sweetly, "we look forward to seeing you next week. Mr. Gardiner, may I speak with you, please?"

Mr. Gardiner made his farewells and held out his arm for his wife.

Papa came over to kiss Elizabeth on the forehead as the Gardiners exited. "I believe Edward will be hiring a manager within the week."

Jane and Elizabeth laughed.

"I am very proud of you, daughter," Papa said, taking Elizabeth's hands. "I am for Longbourn tomorrow as planned. Will we see you there before you depart for Pemberley?"

"Elizabeth and I will remain for part of the season," William said. They had not spoken of these plans, and Elizabeth felt her indignation begin to flare. Then he added, quite naturally, "I wish to show Elizabeth off, and I know she would enjoy visiting the museums and attending the theater. But when she decides she is ready to leave, we will certainly arrange a visit." He placed a large hand on the small of her back.

She wished to reprimand her husband for making such a decision without even consulting her, but my goodness, he was so very thoughtful that to rebuke him would make her feel churlish. He was correct—she would indeed enjoy visiting the museums, and she loved the theater. Perhaps he might even escort her to a concert or the Opera House. She had never attended an opera. Once this mess with Mr. Howard was resolved, they would have a wonderful time. She squared her shoulders, ignoring the apprehensive glance her husband sent her in response.

All she did, in the end, was take her father's hand. "We shall certainly make a visit, Papa. Mama would be disappointed if she were unable to pose us in the drawing room and invite all the neighbors to visit."

William coughed, a sure sign, Elizabeth thought, that he was masking some discomfort at the notion. That would be punishment enough.

In no time at all, she had farewelled her father and Jane, and was happily ensconced in the carriage with William.

He reached across her to pull down the shades, then draped one arm around her shoulders. "You are an impertinent minx," he told her.

She tipped her head to one side. "You do not appear to be distressed by it," she responded.

He kissed her. No warning, no slow approach, just his lips on hers. "Oh," she whispered when they broke apart. "What did I do to deserve that?"

William's expression crumbled. "My apologies, Elizabeth," he said, stuttering slightly. "I should not have . . ."

"Do not you dare apologize," Elizabeth said laughingly. "I quite enjoyed it. You startled me, is all."

She was relieved to see the tension in his face disappear. He cradled her hand in his own large, gentle one.

"I kissed you because"—he stopped to place his lips against her thumb, and the sensation made her shiver—"you made excuses to your aunt."

He pressed her index finger to his lips, and she drew in a quick, shallow breath. "You made excuses," he continued, "because you wished to be alone with me."

"Yes," she concurred in a shaky voice. "I did. I do."

"Then our wishes are in accordance," he said, placing a kiss on her middle finger.

"Mmm," was all Elizabeth could muster. How could something so simple addle her so completely?

He caressed her ring finger, and Elizabeth wondered if her complexion would ever recover. She placed her free hand against her burning cheek. "I am merely pleased," he whispered, placing a final kiss on her little finger, then lifting the palm of her hand to his lips, "that you feel the same."

An image of her husband when he removed his banyan flooded her mind and sent her heart racing. It took some time for Elizabeth to recover enough to answer him. "You must not do that again until we are in our rooms, William," she warned him as she attempted to regulate her breathing. "It has made me feel..." Her eyes drifted closed as he brought his mouth to her wrist.

"Yes?" he asked, sounding just as breathless.

"I do not know how to describe it." She could not, even when her mind was working correctly.

William dropped a final, feathery kiss on her temple. "It is desire, dearest. And love."

"Love," she said with a sigh, taking his arm and leaning against him. "And we almost never knew."

After a hurried entrance and a playfully indecorous dash upstairs, the newly married Darcys did not emerge from their chambers until dinner, when, truly fearing the displeasure of Cook, they removed to their private sitting room. Mrs. Spencer sent word the next morning that the full staff would return soon. She would have them prepare the formal dining room unless Mrs. Darcy did not wish it. It was a sad reminder that within the week their relative privacy would come to an end.

After dinner on Sunday, Darcy gathered their empty dishes and placed them on a tray. Elizabeth was reclining on the chaise, feet tucked beneath her, winding a lock of hair around one finger and staring into the fire. In her other hand was a copy of *Twelfth Night*.

He took the tray into their sitting room and left it for Slipworth, who was still acting as their maid, before returning and sitting beside his wife, pulling her legs over his lap and caressing her feet. He adored saying it. His *wife*.

"Where are your slippers?" he asked. The woman was forever leaving her feet bare.

Elizabeth smiled at him. "Next to the bed."

He stood to collect them.

As he returned to slip them on her feet, she asked quietly, "Will it always be like this?"

"I am not certain what you mean," he replied.

She closed the book. "Will we always be like this, together as though the world outside no longer matters?"

He stroked her cheek with the back of his hand. "Truthfully, I doubt it. We have a great many responsibilities, particularly at Pemberley. But such moments as these will be the sweeter for it."

"I am greatly looking forward to Pemberley," Elizabeth said. "I am all anticipation to see where you spent your youth. But that is not what I meant," she told him uncertainly. "I suppose I wish to know—this feeling between us . . ."

"Yes?" he prompted when it did not appear as though she would continue.

"Promise me that this is how you will always think of us," she said, placing her small hand over his heart, "just as we are today. As deeply in love as we are at this moment."

"An easy promise to make," he told her. "I shall." He watched as her nose wrinkled.

"No matter how often I vex or tease you?" She peered up into his face.

She truly had no idea. "I enjoy it when you vex and tease me."

"William . . ." she chastised him.

He recalled from his brief acquaintance with her family that her parents neither truly respected nor valued the other. "Yes, Elizabeth Darcy," he said quietly. "But you fail to understand that this is only the beginning. Our love will continue to grow, even through adversity. It will never be less than it is now—though I cannot fathom how it is possible to love you more than I do at this moment, I do expect our love to grow even greater and more profound as we live our lives together."

Elizabeth embraced him, and Darcy held her close, relieved to have stumbled upon what she needed to hear. He had spoken from his heart, never an easy thing to do, but perhaps with Elizabeth—perhaps it was what she needed. Darcy jumped when he felt her mouth on his, but when she stiffened at his surprise and began to pull away, he would not allow it. He pulled her onto his lap and kissed her deeply, allowing her to draw what reassurance she could from him.

"I love you, William," she murmured.

The best way to cheer Elizabeth when she was nervous or unsure was to annoy her. He was good at that. "I know."

She pulled away slightly to scowl at him, and he laughed. How could he not? She was very much like an angry kitten when she pulled such a face. Of course, her claws could be just as sharp. "I love you, too, Elizabeth."

Elizabeth leaned her head against his shoulder and played with a ribbon on the cuff of her dressing gown. "When must you fight Mr. Howard?"

"We will meet tomorrow, but I am not really fighting him, love," Darcy reassured her. "It is only a match. He knows I do not duel, and until recent events, I would have said he felt the same. A public set-down is the best I can do under the circumstances, and he has never been more than an average fencer. There will be money and insults exchanged, I am sure, but no blood will be spilt."

Wrapping the end of the ribbon around her finger, Elizabeth said, "His anger is incomprehensible."

"It is."

"Your cousins will make sure he does not try to injure you?"

"He may try, my dear, but he will not succeed," he said confidently. "I am very good with a foil and his men are in either in Newgate or back in Meryton awaiting court martial."

She took his hand and Darcy's heart swelled to see her concern for him. "Still, it is better that you will have family with you."

He nodded. "Yes."

Elizabeth leaned her head against his shoulder. "Have you and the colonel always been close?" she asked. "Jane and I have always been the best of friends, though I am sure I tried even her patience when we were young." She smiled wanly. "Perhaps even now."

Sated by a few days of excellent food and loving his wife, Darcy was in a contemplative mood. "Fitz and I played together as boys, but Matlock is too far from Pemberley for us to spend a great deal of time together. When I was eleven, my mother fell ill and died here in London. The Fitzwilliams came, but they spent their time with my father and sister."

"Even Henry and Fitz?" Elizabeth asked.

Darcy smirked. "Although he both looks and behaves like a child, Henry is nearly twelve years my senior. He was already an adult." Elizabeth waited as he gathered his thoughts. "I was at an age where one both wishes to weep and does not wish to appear weak. I do not think Fitz knew what to make of me."

"Oh, William." Elizabeth was all sympathy.

He bestowed a kiss on the back of her hand. "I was deeply unhappy, and I missed my father. Georgiana was just a babe and was kept in the nursery. Fitz was hiding. Father spent all day with my uncle and Henry and worked late into the evening here in his study. I realize now how terribly he must have been struggling, but at the time, I felt abandoned."

Elizabeth made a small sound of commiseration.

"Finally, I remembered the room. One night, I dragged some bedding down here and made myself a pallet near the fire before my father arrived." He closed his eyes, remembering. "I thought at least I could be closer to Papa without bothering him. The very first night, Fitz found me. He was thirteen then, already at school. I thought he would tease me, but instead, he sat near the fire. All night." Darcy rubbed the back of his neck. "He never said a word. We neither of us slept. He just sat there, next to me, all night."

Elizabeth quietly embraced him.

"I thought we had been quiet enough to escape detection," Darcy said, holding her. "But when we returned the following evening, there was a little bed in the corner. Fitz and I slept there until his family went home, and for perhaps six months, I returned each night while my father worked, and woke up each morning in my room upstairs." He kissed the top of Elizabeth's head. "I joined Fitz at school about a year later, and the boys bullied me because I was so unhappy. I missed my mother. I missed my father. But Fitz was there. It was better," he said stoically, "because I knew I could count on at least one person. Fitz was that person for me."

"And he still is," Elizabeth added.

Darcy nodded. "He still is."

Elizabeth was silent for a time. Finally, she said, "I feel a great deal better knowing he will accompany you tomorrow." She pulled back slightly to meet his gaze. "Even so, I wish that women could attend. I prefer to know what is happening to being left at home in anxiety."

Darcy shook the gloom away and glanced at the copy of *Twelfth Night* she had discarded. "Oh no," he told her firmly. "There will be no disguising yourself as a man so that you may attend, Elizabeth."

Elizabeth blinked at him, bemused. So that had *not* been on her mind. Her eyes followed his to the book, and as her countenance lit up, he groaned. Would he never learn to stop guessing at her thoughts? Now he had given her ideas.

"Do not be concerned," she told him teasingly, standing carefully and reaching out to the chair where he had neatly folded his trousers. She shook them out and held them up. "I do not believe these will fit."

Fit? There was nearly enough material there for a walking dress. He chuckled. "You might start a new fashion."

"It would certainly be warmer in the winter," she replied, and fell silent. She folded his trousers as well as Slipworth ever had and replaced them on the chair. Then she took his face in her hands and bent down for a kiss.

∞

Elizabeth lay awake long into the night, listening to her husband's soft snores. He had given her much to think on. He was a private man by circumstance as much as by preference, and sharing such a story with her was an indication of his deep and abiding trust. She took the protection of that trust more seriously than anything she had in her entire life.

Could merely telling her about his life be enough, though? Should she not do more to help him shoulder his burdens? To alleviate the problem that faced him, that faced them both? He had assured her that he was unconcerned about seeing Mr. Howard, but Elizabeth could not help but think there must be a better way to resolve everything. William had said that he had been used to thinking of Mr. Howard as a man of principle. There had to be a *reason* Mr. Howard was behaving in this vile manner.

Because she could not rest, she began to review everything they had learned about the man. It kept her awake several hours more, her brain refusing to quiet, but eventually, she could not keep her eyes open any longer. She slept deeply for a few hours and was awakened by sounds in the hallway. She sat up, stretched, and then, something occurred to her. Lady Montagu had mentioned Emma Doughty's schoolfriend as being a purveyor of gossip about Miss Howard. Georgiana was no longer at school, but she did have friends.

There *was* a link between the Darcys and the Howards, more than William knowing Mr. Howard—the girls. Girls who had been together frequently in London a year ago. They had been together as late as March, at least, learning everything they would need to enter the ton. And gossip—learning it and using it—was undoubtedly one of those lessons. It was certainly worth speaking to Georgiana one more time.

Elizabeth turned to tell her husband, but looking about the room, she realized that William was not there.

There was a note on the bed table, and she opened it eagerly. "Elizabeth," it said, "I will be home as soon as I may. Take the carriage to the Matlocks or the Gardiners if you do not wish to remain here on your own. I have left orders to have it ready for you." He had signed it, "All my love, William."

He had left her the carriage. How long had he been gone? Panic shot through her, and she nearly leapt from the bed. She rang for the maid and rushed to prepare herself for the day.

A maid entered. "Emily!" cried Elizabeth, recognizing the girl who had entered the library in search of something to read.

The girl took a step back. "I'm sorry, Mrs. Darcy. The other girls were already busy, so Mrs. Spencer sent me up. I have been trained as a lady's maid."

Elizabeth scolded herself. She had arrived with William after the wedding breakfast, and both Mr. Slipworth and Mrs. Spencer had behaved as though they were meeting her for the first time. No doubt she was the subject of speculation among the few servants in the house, but she should not have known Emily's name.

"Yes, Mrs. Spencer mentioned you might assist me for a few days," Elizabeth said calmly. "I am in a bit of a hurry just now. Might you help me become presentable?"

"Of course, Mrs. Darcy," Emily said, and set to it. Less than half an hour later, Elizabeth was more than presentable. Her hair was done up in a simple but elegant style suitable for morning calls, and Emily had selected one of her aunt's gowns, ivory trimmed with a deep green velvet. There was a matching hat and gloves, and Emily stared at the contents of the wardrobe briefly before withdrawing a Pomona pelisse that, while not as elegant as the silk robe of her wedding gown, complemented the dress perfectly. She would be a credit to her husband, dressed so smartly. She would have to consider Emily for the position of lady's maid when she had a moment to turn her mind to it.

There was no time for that now. She thanked Emily, sure the girl did not know what to make of her eccentric mistress, and rushed down the stairs.

"Mr. Pratt," she addressed the butler, "please call the carriage. I wish to visit Matlock House."

"Very good, madam," Mr. Pratt said. He opened the door for her and stepped out after her to speak with the coachman.

Elizabeth noticed that two large men with dark skin were riding atop the carriage with Anders, one in the front and one on the back. They were huge, with broad shoulders and bulging biceps, making Anders appear tiny in comparison. She herself might have been a Lilliputian. She gave each a smile and a nod before she was handed into the conveyance and they began to move over the cobblestone streets.

The journey to Matlock House was a short one—a quarter of an hour at most. When a footman from the earl's staff handed her out, Elizabeth turned to Anders.

"Please wait for me, Anders," she instructed the man, "I shall not be long." Anders tipped his hat, but his cousins had already climbed down from the carriage and escorted her into the house itself.

The butler welcomed her in his staid manner. "I am afraid the countess had an engagement this morning," he said. "You are welcome to wait, of course, but it may be some time before she returns."

"Truthfully," Elizabeth replied, "I was hoping to speak with Miss Darcy."

"She is engaged at present, Mrs. Darcy," the man said.

She did not have time to wait. "Is Colonel Fitzwilliam here, perhaps?" He was Georgiana's other guardian. He would help.

"Oh, I *am* sorry, Mrs. Darcy," he told her. "The only member of the family at home to callers this morning is Viscount Milton."

Before she could reply, Henry emerged into the hall. "Elizabeth!" he cried, removing a napkin from his collar. "I thought that was your voice. Have you left my dull, dour cousin already? Shall we take his carriage and abscond to warmer climes?"

Elizabeth lifted her eyebrows and treated him to an icy stare. She would not allow him to goad her. "I am here on business, Henry," she told him. "Will you hear me out, or shall I travel to Angelo's and speak with your brother?"

He eyed her closely. "Why would you not simply speak to your husband?"

"Because he was already out of the house when I woke. Now he is about to face Mr. Howard, and I do not want him distracted."

Henry was quiet for a moment before he motioned to the room he had just exited. "And you believe arriving at Angelo's in his carriage would not distract?"

Elizabeth just stared at him.

He tipped his head in the direction of the room from which he had emerged. "Come in."

Before she sat, Elizabeth asked, "I was hoping to speak to Georgiana."

"She is upstairs in a music lesson," Henry said slowly. "I was going to ride over to Angelo's myself. The bout is set for later this morning, but I thought to lay a wager on William. Have you ever seen him fence?"

"Will you call for her?" Elizabeth asked, ignoring Henry's question. "It is important."

Henry stood slowly and sent a maid in search of Georgiana. They sat together silently as they awaited her arrival.

"Elizabeth," her new sister said, rushing into the room and taking her by the hands. "It is wonderful to see you. I am in a lesson just now . . ."

"My apologies, Georgiana," Elizabeth said. "I have a question for you, and I am afraid it cannot wait."

Georgiana sat down on the settee with Elizabeth. "Very well. What is it?"

Henry sat in the chair opposite and gave her an expectant look.

"When we spoke about Amelia Howard," she began, "you told your brother and I that you were not intimate friends with her."

"That is true," Georgiana said. Henry straightened suddenly, his eyes fixed on Elizabeth's face.

"Did she have one?" Elizabeth inquired. "An intimate friend, I mean."

Georgiana's brow wrinkled. "Well, I have not seen any of them since the summer," she answered softly. "But last March, before Miss Howard removed from town, Miss Harriet Dixon was her very good friend."

"Miss Harriet Dixon," Elizabeth repeated. "You are sure?"

Georgiana nodded.

Elizabeth reached over and gave Georgiana's hand a squeeze. "Thank you. I will not keep you from your lesson any longer. Please apologize to the master on my behalf."

The girl nodded and stood. She seemed puzzled, but she did not ask any questions, simply made her way out of the room.

Elizabeth turned to Henry, who gave her a knowing look.

"I will take care of it, cousin," he told her, and for once, he sounded serious.

"Do you know Mr. Dixon?" she asked, surprised.

"I know everyone," Henry replied with a shrug. "I really ought to have considered this myself, but we none of us think too much about girls not yet out, do we?"

Elizabeth shrugged. "I have four sisters."

Henry nodded, though he appeared preoccupied. "Will you wait here for Darcy?"

"No," she said. "I will return home and await him there. Please give your parents and the colonel my regards when you see them." She worried her bottom lip before asking, "Will you tell me what you find?"

"I will," Henry said and offered her his arm. After an initial hesitation, Elizabeth took it. He gathered his outerwear as he walked her back to the carriage.

"Mr. Anders," she called warmly, casting a glance behind her as Henry prepared to hand her back into the carriage, "I was in a hurry before, but now that my errand is complete, would you please introduce me to your cousins?" As Anders drew nearer to comply, she added, "I am told that you have all done me a great service."

"We are all Anders, Mrs. Darcy," the coachman replied with a grin. He nodded first at the man whose facial features were much like his own. The man had a scar over his right eye and close-cut hair. "This is Mr. Josiah Anders."

Elizabeth smiled. "Thank you for your help, Mr. Anders," she said sincerely. The man nodded once.

Anders then motioned to the second man, who bore only a passing resemblance to his two relations. He had lighter skin, longer hair, and an earring in one ear. "And this is Mr. Isaac Anders."

"I thank you as well, Mr. Anders," Elizabeth said warmly, and he gave her a smile and a nod. She glanced at them both. "I feel a great deal safer with all of you accompanying me."

"You are welcome, Mrs. Darcy," Mr. Josiah Anders answered gravely.

Henry handed Elizabeth in and closed the carriage door. Henry was already mounting his horse and heading in the opposite direction.

Well, she had accomplished what she could. Soon she was back home. Acknowledging the weariness of her restless night, Elizabeth dragged herself up to her chambers to await William.

Henry might be the right man for this job after all. She certainly hoped so.

Chapter Sixteen

Over his cousin's protests, Darcy had dragged Fitz to Aunt Matlock's favorite jeweler—Rundell, Bridge, and Rundell's—to commission a wedding gift for Elizabeth. He had the sketches ready, but the goldsmith had a few questions. Fitz paced about the shop, earning himself some wary glances from the clerks.

"Sit down, Fitz, before they ask you to leave." He leaned over the sketch to point out a detail in the design. It was to be a necklace that could be converted to two bracelets or a brooch, similar to one his mother had once owned and had been left to Georgiana. The goldsmith redrew a part of the clasp on his sketch and explained why his alteration would be stronger. Darcy agreed. They settled on a price and a date when the piece would be completed and delivered.

Fitz grabbed his arm and nearly dragged him from the shop. "Your mind should not be on your wife just now, Darcy," he insisted. "You do not want to lose this match."

"My mind is always on my wife, Fitz," Darcy replied. "But there is room for the match as well." This was not hyperbole. Even as he pored over the drawing with the goldsmith, his mind had been at work on how to work this meeting to his advantage.

"You are turning my stomach, Darcy." Fitz was exasperated. "Three days married, and you are no longer your own man."

It was true, to an extent. Had he been a bachelor, Darcy would not have issued a summons to Howard. Darcy did not believe in duels, and he knew this *was* a duel in a sense, though it would end without bloodshed. There was a kind of performance that would be required of him today that he detested. But Howard was a danger to Elizabeth, and that Darcy would not, could not, abide.

"Why are you so agitated?" he asked Fitz. "You have been in real battle."

"I wish you had listened to me. This is not a good idea." Fitz replied. "This *is* a real battle, though it is for reputation rather than land."

"It is not only reputation at stake, Fitz," Darcy said seriously. "I would not meet him for that alone. I have told you before that I mean to impress upon Mr. Howard, very clearly, what awaits him should he ever make another attempt to harm me or mine."

Fitz ran a hand through his hair, something he never did. "A shot across the bow is risky, Darcy."

"You know what he said to Elizabeth. He was ready to call me out, Fitz," Darcy reminded his cousin, "and *his* summons would not have been to Angelo's. By issuing my challenge first, I seized control and set the terms."

"And Howard will not like it," Fitz replied. "I do not know what he hopes to gain from this, but the man is unstable and therefore *dangerous*. You follow the rules but if Howard feels himself at a disadvantage, he will not."

Darcy knew this, and yet remained undeterred. He had observed Howard fence at Angelo's on several occasions. Darcy's skill was superior. Howard was angry, and while it might make him behave rashly, it was unlikely to improve his form.

Howard had inserted himself into *Darcy's* life. For his supposed crime of refusing to marry Howard's sister, both Georgiana and Elizabeth had been targeted for attack. If Howard believed he had started any rumors, he was entirely wrong. When he had soundly beaten Howard, any complaints or accusations from the man would be written off as bitterness over the loss. Without more evidence, there was not more Darcy could do to stop Howard, but he could frighten him into leaving them be—perhaps even into leaving London. It was not enough, but he would ensure it was done, and done well.

Despite the fact that Fitz had delivered the note only yesterday, there was a crowd spilling out the door at Angelo's. He wondered whether he had Howard to thank for that or Henry.

Fitz cursed under his breath. "I had hoped for an audience, not a mob," he muttered. "Move aside, you maggot-pies!"

Several men turned around at Fitz's curse, and Darcy heard his name being whispered. The crowd parted to allow them through. "Not unlike the Red Sea," he said to Fitz, who snorted.

His cousin assessed the crowd. "Well, Moses, it appears you are about to become a participant in the largest spectacle of the year. Every man here has likely laid a wager."

"I would hope the odds are running in my favor," Darcy grumbled, then raised his voice. It was time to begin playing to the crowd. He and Fitz had not been the victims of Henry's skills all these years without learning a few things themselves. "Mr. Howard has made unreasonable demands upon me, and I mean to have him apologize. You should lay wager or two, Fitz. It might make your fortune."

"Already have, Darce," Fitz replied flippantly. "Why do you think I was so concerned about your focus?"

Darcy laughed at that. This was an absurd little performance. "How much?" he asked.

"Five hundred pounds," Fitz declared.

That was a tremendous sum for Fitz. Well, here was an opportunity to gift his cousin something, which was unreasonably difficult to do. Darcy was not the only proud, stubborn man in the family, but Fitz would never complain about taking money earned on bets. "That is quite a sum," Darcy declared. "Add another five hundred on my behalf. Should I lose, I will cover the entire amount."

That set the tongues afire. Darcy rarely gambled, and never so large a sum. Fitz gave him a sidelong glance but nodded and stepped back to accept a flurry of wagers.

He had the crowd of men paying attention. Now he must deal with Howard as though the man was nothing more than an insignificant irritant. He wanted those in attendance to understand that he was through with all unreasonable demands.

Howard had already arrived and, foil in hand, was taking angry swipes at an imaginary opponent. Darcy observed him coolly. Howard was slender and his footwork was quick, but his use of the foil had always been slow, flawed. That was when he was composed, and Howard's emotions were certainly not in check today.

Men stood near the walls on either side of the long room. At each end of the floor stood a rack of foils, but Darcy had brought his own. He removed his coat and exchanged it for his weapon. Howard sneered and stepped forward.

"Admit you have wronged me, Darcy," Howard hollered above the noise of the spectators.

Darcy frowned. Clearly Howard had his own performance planned. "*I* asked for this meeting, Mr. Howard. I believe we both know that *you* are the one who owes the apology. Will you not offer it?"

Howard sneered. "I have no apologies to make."

"Then," Darcy said, lifting his foil, "en garde."

Howard did not mirror his movement. "I cannot trust a man like you to admit my hits. Fawkner will score."

Darcy dropped his arm and rolled his eyes. "Very well. Colonel Fitzwilliam will also score." Fitz pushed through the crowd and stepped forward.

Howard's stare through his spectacles was murderous. "He has wagered on you."

Darcy shrugged. "As Fawkner had wagered on you. If you are seeking a disinterested party, you are in the wrong place." There was some hooting among the men, and Howard's face reddened. "Are we through with these petty games?"

A muscle in Howard's cheek twitched. "Very well. To three points?"

Darcy nodded.

The men moved into their positions, and each lifted his foil. The spectators quieted. Darcy's focus narrowed until Howard was all he saw.

They began.

Howard stepped to the right. One, two . . . he lunged.

Darcy parried with a flick of his wrist. The noise was back, increasing in pitch and drowning out the clink of metal on metal. It did not matter, for Darcy heard none of it. He simply watched Howard retreat and begin to circle in a demi-volte.

Howard advanced, then retreated quickly, attempting to lure Darcy into a lunge of his own. Darcy simply waited and watched, moving defensively, awaiting the right moment. Howard made a pass on the outside. Again, Darcy parried.

As Howard's arm and foil were thrown out to the side, Darcy advanced, turned his wrist in carte, and with a quick strike, fixed his point to Howard's right breast. The eruption of sound registered in Darcy's mind, though it was not loud enough to pull his attention away from his adversary.

"A hit for Darcy," called Fitz.

Fawkner glanced at Howard but nodded his agreement. It was not as though they could disagree.

Howard stepped back and away from Darcy's foil. "Again," he demanded.

"That is the way a match typically proceeds," Darcy said drily. Howard scowled at the catcalls Darcy's rejoinder produced.

Darcy had never doubted he would emerge the victor, but Howard was presenting even less of a test than he had expected. He was wild and undisciplined, which did not fit the man Darcy had once known. A younger sister's ruin could account for Howard's change in behavior, but this sort of sober madness was inexplicable and, as Fitz had warned, dangerous. Had Georgiana not been saved, Darcy would have been distraught, but he did not believe he would have allowed it to undo him.

Howard came at him with no grace and little strategy, his attempt to thrust under Darcy's wrist easily parried. The man retreated, and Darcy had ample time to analyze each vulnerable area. His opponent must have understood what Darcy was doing, for he launched into a series of advances so quick that Darcy retreated, parried, retreated, parried, and at last found himself with no additional room to step back. He lifted his foil to block a high strike, then, anticipating a finishing thrust, stepped nimbly to one side. There no longer being a body before him to stop the momentum, Howard flew past Darcy, the tip of his foil touching only the wall. The weapon's blade bent as Howard's forward motion sent him to one knee. He straightened and whirled to face his opponent, but the foil was not raised quickly enough.

From his superior height, Darcy reached out to tap Howard's chest with the tip of his foil.

"A hit!" Fitz cried.

Howard began to rise. As he straightened, he jabbed his foot out straight before him.

Darcy felt the impact of Howard's heel against the kneecap of his planted leg, and then a fiery pain exploding as the leg snapped back. He released his foil and dropped to the ground, instinctively wrapping his hands around his knee and drawing it to his chest.

"If you cannot finish the match," Howard said with a smirk, "you have forfeited."

"Those are the rules," Fawkner insisted, stepping to Howard's side.

"Those are *not* the rules, you ivory-tuners," Fitz growled. "You are not allowed to kick at your opponent like an unruly child. You must instead face Darcy's second." He shoved Howard back amidst a growing cacophony of hoots and hisses. "That would be me."

The pain in Darcy's knee subsided but did not vanish. He sat slowly. As he glanced around the room, he realized that Howard had already been defeated. The man had been rather isolated at the club, but now he had even lost those who had been sympathetic.

"Fitz," Darcy said, a sort of eerie calm suffusing him. "Leave him to me."

His cousin turned. "Are you able to continue?"

"Of course," Darcy replied. "Howard's kick is only a little better than his foil."

Fitz held out a hand to haul Darcy to his feet. Darcy tested his leg. It pained him, but it was sound. Fitz's eyes bored into his, and Darcy offered his cousin the faintest of nods.

"I will continue," Darcy said solemnly. He turned to stare at Howard. "And I will win, even with only one good leg." There was a rolling murmur of approval from the spectators.

"Hit for Darcy," shouted Fitz with a smug, satisfied air.

Fawkner glanced around the room. He did not look at Howard this time before he nodded.

Howard had damaged his blade in the fall. He returned to the far end of the room to exchange it as Darcy limped back to his position. Howard returned and held up his blade but did not leave it there for long, settling quickly back into the match.

Darcy parried another thrust, and for a moment he and Howard were stationary, pressed up close together, their blades crossed. Darcy's eyes watched Howard's foil as it was retracted and saw the sharp tip.

Howard was not using a practice blade.

Darcy's temper finally flared beyond control. No one had noted the exchange, and he berated himself for not checking the weapon when Howard first brought it onto the floor. He advanced steadily in a straight line, thrust and parry, thrust and parry, until Howard could retreat no farther. The man burst forward, delivering a thrust in tierce, but it was a desperate attempt to regain a foothold. Darcy parried with the edge of his foil, forced Howard's wrist upward, and seized the hilt of Howard's foil, twisting it away.

"Disarm!" someone shouted.

Darcy leaned in close to speak in Howard's ear. "You would approach my wife, frighten her half to death, on our wedding day? *I* was there—but you approached *her*." The raucous crowd had gone silent, and his words rang clear around the room. "Now you bring an unbated blade to cut me down?" He lifted Howard's foil and tossed his own aside.

Darcy lifted the foil, the pain in his knee forgotten. "It might have done you some good had you known what to do with it." He stepped forward, weapon before him, as Howard shrank back.

"You should have married my sister instead of that country chit," Howard snarled as he retreated. He stopped near the wall and tossed his arms out. "Kill me if you will. At least I know you will hang for it."

Darcy held the sharp tip of Howard's weapon above his heart and let it linger there. "It is your own foil, Howard. Most men would call this self-defense." He toyed with the blade, eyeing the precise location where it might enter Howard's heart and end this game once and for all. For a long, long moment, Darcy remained as he was, the tip of the sharp foil lightly caressing Howard's shirt. Howard's bravado waned. Darcy smiled.

Howard should be afraid. He should be as afraid as Elizabeth had been.

Darcy stared into the panicked eyes of his adversary, enjoying the way the man's complexion was now devoid of color. A bead of perspiration gathered on Howard's forehead and ran into his eye, making him blink. But Howard was in no danger from Darcy. Honor was a ruthless taskmaster. It would not allow him to kill an unarmed man. No matter if that man wished Darcy dead. No matter if had he made the attempt. Darcy scowled. "I am not going to kill you, Howard."

Howard sagged a little in relief. But Darcy leaned in with just a bit more pressure and raised his voice. They wanted a spectacle? Devil take them, they could have one. "Though every man here knows I would be justified in running you through, I will spare you." He paused. "But you must apologize."

Howard held up a shaking hand. "I apologize for the insult to your wife, Darcy." He said grimly. "And to your sister."

"Are you truly such a fool as to provoke a man into killing you?" came a voice from behind Fitz. "An honest man whom you have attacked since the summer merely because he refused to wed your ruined sister? By the by," he added drolly, "it was Lord Bartholomew Denham who did the deed." Henry stepped out onto the floor.

Howard's eyes narrowed. "That is a lie."

Henry smiled and slowly shook his head. "I am afraid that it is not."

Miss Howard's fate had been spoken of for months, but not the disagreement between Darcy and Howard and not the identity of her lover. There was surprise in the hum of voices that followed the revelation.

Of course it was Henry, publishing Darcy's private business far and wide. He wondered where his cousin had learned that Denham was Miss Howard's lover. His mind was in turmoil, but eventually, he realized that he still had Howard pinned to the wall. Slowly, Darcy lowered the blade and Howard slid to the floor.

"Apologize properly," Darcy said coolly.

Howard closed his eyes and spoke loudly enough for the gathered men to hear. "I apologize, Darcy." The tension in the room eased significantly.

"You have had your fun, and you have your gossip," Henry said, waving his arms towards the back of the hall. "Settle your business elsewhere. Everyone—out."

The spectators filed from the room exchanging a great deal of conversation. Fitz snatched the foil from Darcy's hand. "You nearly placed your head in a noose, Darce," he mumbled, his complexion ashen. "Do not ever do that to me again."

"He did no such thing, Richard," Henry said cheerfully. "I never knew you had such theatrical flair, Darcy. I quite approve. Shall we move to a more private room?"

With a single look at an attendant, Henry procured them a room in the back of the building. Fitz yanked Howard up from the floor and shoved the man into the room as Darcy and Henry followed.

Howard seethed, crossing his arms over his chest. Fawkner had slunk out with the others, leaving him entirely alone.

"You are fortunate my wife does not wish to see me in prison," Darcy told Howard. "Another man might easily have ended your life."

"Your wife," Henry said thoughtfully, "is the reason I was late."

Henry had seen Elizabeth this morning? Darcy's eyes shot over to his eldest cousin. "Is she well?"

"Quite," Henry said admiringly. "She dashed into the house some hours ago to ask Georgiana whether Miss Howard had an intimate friend. Apparently, you two had an enlightening conversation with Georgiana some days back, and Elizabeth, you see, had the notion that Howard did not ask you to marry his sister on a whim."

"A *whim*!" Howard bellowed. "Would I have gone to such lengths on a whim?"

"After your actions today," Fitz replied, stepping up until he was nose to nose with an irate Howard, "I would have to say you are thick enough to do just that."

"Your cousin deflowered my sister," Howard hissed, "and *refused* to marry her. Her honor and mine demand recompense."

"Are you mad?" Darcy cried, exasperation and rage coloring his words. "I have never even met your sister! I certainly did *not* bed her."

"You will burn for it, Darcy," Howard insisted.

"Quiet, you," Fitz said, shoving the man away.

"Stubborn, eh?" Henry asked laconically. "I rather thought you might be." He reached into his coat, removed a letter, and held it just beyond Howard's reach. "Recognize the seal?" He unfolded the page. "What about the script?"

Howard's eyes widened and then fixed on Henry's. "That is Amelia's hand. What have you done?"

Henry placed a hand against his chest. "And *I* am called melodramatic. I have done nothing to you or your sister. More to the point, neither has my cousin." He handed Howard the letter. "Your sister lied to you. She told you that Darcy was the man who seduced her."

Howard pointed a finger at Darcy. "He mocked me for it, but never did he deny it!"

"I did *not* mock you, and had you actually accused me, I most certainly would have denied it," Darcy declared. "You did not. You only pressed me to wed her."

Howard's mouth hung open, and he stared at Darcy, unblinking. "Who would press a man to wed his ruined sister were he not the scoundrel who had done it?"

Darcy rolled his eyes. He was rather tired of this particular conversation, but he could not reveal the men without identifying the girls. "I had the same reaction. You were the third."

He was met by an incredulous stare. "If it was not you," Howard asked angrily, "then who?"

"I believe I have already identified the man," Henry said. He glanced at Darcy, then Fitz, then Howard. "Why does no one ever believe me?"

"My sister said it was Darcy," Howard said doggedly, but for the first time, a note of doubt sounded in his voice.

"Well," Henry drawled, drawing it all out and clearly enjoying himself. "Miss Howard may not have told *you* the truth, but she did write everything that was in her heart to her dear friend, Miss Harriet

Dixon." He shook out the page and began to read aloud. "Dearest Harriet," he announced in a girlish tone.

Darcy ran both hands through his hair and laced his fingers together behind his head, his strength at last beginning to ebb away. "Henry," he said with a groan, "I beg you, tell us how this ends."

Henry sighed. "You spoil my fun, Darcy, but in light of your heroic turn this morning, I will humor you." He addressed Howard directly. "In this letter, Amelia tells Harriet that she lied to you about Darcy and now does not know how to take it back. Apparently, my cousin Miss Darcy made it known to all her friends that her brother would only marry if he selected his own wife. Miss Howard was quite sure he would never allow his hand to be forced." He smiled sweetly at Darcy. "You are a legend, Darcy."

Darcy glowered at his eldest cousin.

"Stop it, Henry," Fitz warned.

Henry sighed. "Very well." He handed the letter to Howard. "I have made a copy.

You will see that your sister . . ."

Howard's eyes traced the lines. He glanced up and blinked. "She thought Darcy's reputation would keep me from pursuing the matter? That I would not bother to speak to Darcy because he had declared so forcefully that he would never be coerced?" He groped behind him for a chair and finding one, sat heavily, still clutching the letter.

"Her ignorance of how men operate is shocking indeed. Sadly—and this is the greater offense—your sister thought nothing of destroying Darcy's reputation as she awaited her lover to rescue her. She must have at least understood that you would not be able to insist that the son of a duke do the honorable thing and wed her." Henry shook his head. "We do these girls an injustice, confusing ignorance for innocence."

Darcy watched Howard's arrogant righteousness and fury draining away as he read the rest of his sister's missive. When Howard had finished and glanced up, Henry continued delivering his oration. "Miss Harriet's father called her to his study. There, she was closely questioned by her pater and ultimately ordered to produce this letter. She admitted to us both that your sister was meeting the third son of the Duke of Denham. Several times a week, at the end. In various parks, and . . . other locations." He pointed to the letter. "There, third line from the bottom."

Darcy and Fitz grimaced. Lord Bartholomew was young, handsome, rich, well-connected, and a scoundrel through and through. Howard was incensed.

"Lord Bartholomew?" Howard cried. "Blast that girl! She *swore* it was Darcy, and I believed her." He covered his eyes with one hand, still clutching the letter in his other. "I believed her."

Darcy watched Howard warily. Georgiana had told him the truth. She had come so very close to ruin, but when he arrived in Ramsgate, she had acknowledged everything to him at once. *There but for the grace of God,* he thought.

"What about the rumors?" Howard asked uncertainly. "Darcy promised his discretion, and yet it was all over the ton! We had handled it. The babe was provided for and placed with our distant cousins. Amelia was preparing for the season. She would never have had the match she might once have had, but she could have had a good life. No one else knew!"

Henry reached down and flicked his index finger against Howard's ear. "You really are a stupid man, Howard. I have handed you a letter. It was only the most explicit of three sent to Miss Harriet Dixon, who is not yet out. Do you know who *is* out? Harriet's elder sister Penelope, who Miss Harriet says *reads her post*. In both deed and word, your *sister* is the source of her own downfall."

Chapter Seventeen

"I cannot believe it." Howard's mouth slackened, and his posture slumped. His face gradually turned a sickly shade of green. "I cannot..."

Howard stared at his feet. Suddenly his head shot up and turned to the right, searching the room for something. When he lunged to grab a pitcher sitting on a small table in the far corner of the room, the other men turned away but were unable to escape the sounds of the man retching. When he was finished, Howard staggered back to the chair and wiped his mouth with a handkerchief, his complexion waxy.

"You say you accepted my challenge today to satisfy your honor," Darcy said flatly. "How is any of this honorable?"

Howard was silent for several minutes. When he lifted his head, his color was a little better, but his eyes were bloodshot, and his cheeks were wet.

"I thought it was." Howard blinked. "I was furious when you refused to marry Amelia," he said quietly. "A man I had always thought to be of sterling character, I now believed was nothing more than a vile seducer. Our sisters were preparing for their first season together. I thought that must have been how you met. It felt like such a violation."

Darcy crossed his arms over his chest. "Go on."

"I made a few inquiries and discovered your sister was traveling to Ramsgate. It is no secret you have loathed George Wickham since we were all at university. I hired him. Sent him after her. Paid him to seduce her. To elope. You had ruined my sister, and so I would ruin yours. Involve you in the same sort of trouble I was suffering. But you arrived just before Wickham could carry her away."

Fitz took a step towards Howard, but Henry held out a hand to stop him.

"Tell me everything," Darcy said grimly. "From the beginning."

Howard did not look up. "In February, your friend Bingley made a ridiculous wager on a pair of horses any idiot could see were not well-matched. I intended to collect my winnings and frighten him into better behavior before eventually returning his losses." He paused. "It was a large sum, and better to lose it to me than someone who would encourage him to continue until his fortune was spent. Before I could follow through with my plan, the situation with my sister was revealed to me, and I was distracted."

"Did you tell Bingley to invite me to Hertfordshire?" Darcy inquired.

"Yes." The word rang hollow. "I told him I would forgive a part of the debt if he would. He was happy to do it, had intended to in any case, he said. Wanted you and his sister to spend time together." Howard glanced up. "I offered to forgive the entire sum if he was successful in compromising you and his sister, but I suspect he would have done it even without the inducement. He desperately wanted the connection and probably wished to have access to your pockets."

Howard stared blankly at the wall behind Darcy. "Your sister was safe with the countess. I thought perhaps a compromise by Miss Bingley *might* satisfy me—fulfill my duty to a wronged sister. If you would not marry Amelia, you would at least be forced to marry a woman I knew you could not abide."

"How would you know that?" Darcy asked.

Howard peered up at Darcy. "You have always decreed that you would never be compromised into matrimony. And you detest social climbers. To forever be attached to one through no choice of your own would eat away at your soul, or so I hoped. I would make you sorry you had not offered for Amelia instead." He shook his head. "But Bingley kept delaying. He was interested in some local girl and was not focused on my request. I wrote before the ball and insisted he follow through." He rubbed his palms against his shirt. "I did not expect him to set up the compromise during the ball, with so many people in the house. Bingley wanted witnesses to force your hand, but I thought the timing an unnecessary risk. We did not require many witnesses, only a few of the right sort. My concern was borne out when Miss Elizabeth Bennet witnessed the attempt and spoiled the whole."

"You were at Netherfield?" Fitz asked abruptly.

"You witnessed the attempt?" Darcy asked at the same time.

Howard simply nodded. "Yes. I was hidden in the library. It was quite dark." He sighed. "When you removed yourself from the room, I insisted that Bingley go after you, force you to comply," he said quietly. "I was not in control of myself, and he shoved me away when I came too close. My spectacles fell to the floor, where I stepped on them. I had a second pair at the inn, but not on my person." He looked away. "I somehow made my way back to the ballroom and awaited Bingley there. Despite your anger, I was certain he could persuade you. He was your friend, and men like us do not have many of those. Miss Bingley was in your embrace when Bingley entered the room. I did not believe you could escape your duty, despite your bluster." Howard ran a hand through his hair. "I waited in vain. He was to make an announcement of your engagement to Miss Bingley at supper, but he never did."

"Because I was already gone," Darcy added, and Howard nodded.

"Even if I could not see you clearly," Howard said, "I wanted you to see me, to know that *I* had been the one to ruin your life the way you had ruined Amelia's. The way you had ruined mine."

Darcy towered over him. "And yet I had done nothing of the sort."

Howard closed his eyes. "I did not know that. I believed my sister."

"Your sister has much to account for," Henry said, his voice even but somehow dangerous. Just as Elizabeth had said.

"Amelia was foolish and naïve, but she did not expect me to act as I have," Howard replied hollowly. "I am the one to blame for how far this has gone."

"You are," Darcy agreed. "What happened after I left Netherfield?"

Howard coughed. "After supper, I cornered Bingley, and he told me you had left the house, on your way to London, he presumed. I tried to insist he follow you in the morning to press matters, but Bingley would not. He had guests to tend to, he said, and he still had hopes for Miss Bennet. Said I had already destroyed his friendship with you and that Miss Elizabeth's knowledge of his actions might cause him to lose Miss Bennet's hand were he not close by to thwart Miss Elizabeth. He was determined to have the eldest Bennet girl—he told me if he wed her, he would not require me to forgive his debt. I threatened him with Baker and Henderson should he reveal my connection to him and left at dawn."

"Not before giving your men instructions," Fitz prompted.

"I was out of my mind with rage. Darcy had evaded me *again*." Howard ran a hand through his hair. "Bingley still owed me three thousand pounds. I told Henderson to punish Miss Elizabeth for interfering and you for escaping. I did not care how, though I offered to pay them a thousand pounds each if the two of you were found together or connected in some nefarious way. I left the details to them, but I wanted the world to know you were not the honorable man you seemed."

Darcy was shocked into silence. It was an extraordinary amount of money to have set out. No wonder the men had been willing to enter his home in search of Elizabeth. He was perversely grateful that Howard had wanted them found together—otherwise, Elizabeth might have been killed and left in Hertfordshire. His fists clenched and he had to turn away to regain his composure.

"What was Wickham's role in this?" There was a great deal of anger in Fitz's question.

Howard frowned. "I had handled the first part of my sister's problem without detection. After the birth, we brought Amelia back to town to prepare for her season as we had always planned, so there would be no talk."

Henry retrieved the letter. "This was written over the summer. When did your sister return to town?"

"Not long before the rumors began, around Michaelmas. I sent Wickham to Hertfordshire to see what he could discover about Darcy and to help us plan the compromise with Miss Bingley. The rumors began after he left. When the stories grew salacious, I sent Amelia to the country and prepared to follow Bingley myself. Wickham had failed in Ramsgate with his gentler approach. I would not allow that to happen again. I hired Henderson and Baker in the same seedy tavern in London that Wickham frequents. They spoke well enough to pass for gentlemen, like Wickham, but they had less . . ."

"Finesse?" Henry asked blandly.

Darcy squeezed his eyelids shut, his back still turned to Howard. "What was Wickham to do?" he asked stonily.

"Wickham wrote that you were charmed by Miss Elizabeth," Howard explained. "He wanted to be paid to seduce her."

Darcy spun around to glare at Howard, but the man would not look at him.

"He was displeased when I rejected the notion." Howard took hold of a dry pen and tapped it nervously against the desk. "Amelia was in a delicate state. Her disgrace was drawing room fodder. And then . . ." His voice broke. "And then I received an express from Amelia's companion. At one of the inns where they stopped to change horses, my sister had attempted to throw herself into the river."

There was nothing to be said to that. Darcy's fists unclenched.

"The staff kept Amelia sedated until they could get her home." He wrapped his hands around his head and leaned forward, his elbows on the desk. "Oh, how I wanted revenge. Seducing a woman to whom Darcy likely had no intention of making an offer was nowhere near enough. Even the compromise now seemed too little, but it was not until Miss Elizabeth Bennet helped Darcy slip through my fingers again that I took Henderson and Baker off their leashes."

Darcy might have felt more pity, knowing that Georgiana had been so close to succumbing and that Miss Howard had given in to her despair, but what Elizabeth had suffered snuffed it out. Miss Howard's actions were not his fault, and they were certainly not Elizabeth's.

Howard was speaking again. "Henderson was inside Netherfield during the ball, but I sent Wickham to London. I did not want him in the way. Baker waited at the inn for orders."

"Did one of your men take the button from my coat?" Darcy inquired.

Howard nodded. "Henderson is very good at avoiding notice. It was nothing for him. His idea, in fact. Not the button, exactly, but something that could be identified as yours. He found all your other valuables already secured."

Darcy blinked. It was a lucky thing he had not remained in those chambers overnight.

"When Miss Elizabeth Bennet interfered at Netherfield and you escaped again, I was furious." Howard gazed mournfully at the letter in his hand. "I regretted sending Wickham away after all, for her reputation was unblemished and her neighbors would believe her."

"A completely innocent woman who did nothing but tell the truth," Darcy said, placing his palms on the desk and leaning over it until he was inches from Howard's face. The man blinked owlishly.

"All I knew was that you had singled her out at the ball and that she had put her reputation on the line for you in the library," Howard said. "She helped you escape, perhaps hoping to become the next Mrs. Darcy. But if Mrs. Darcy was not my sister, it was certainly not going to be anyone you might care for or who might care for you."

Howard's breath was foul, and Darcy leaned back. "Did your men mean to kill my wife the morning after the ball?" he asked bluntly.

Howard rubbed a hand over his eyes. "I cannot say. They meant to watch the house and hoped to take her away from it. Baker would not be able to stay in the area long—his looks are too distinctive. But Henderson could. They were prepared for a few days' watch. But then Miss Elizabeth took a walk." He sighed unhappily. "I thought at last chance was falling in my favor."

"They carried laudanum on them?" Fitz inquired.

Howard shrugged. "Baker has a habit. Keeps a flask on him. I suppose they used that."

"But Elizabeth escaped," Darcy said, his voice hard but his pride evident.

Howard nodded. "So they said. Henderson and Baker had trouble with the coach. They took Miss Elizabeth's bonnet and your button back to Meryton. Wickham apparently returned to town before the ball was even over and was on the lookout. He offered to identify the evidence, for a price. They paid him. Well," Howard amended, "they were reimbursed, so I paid him."

"And my home?" Darcy had to use every drop of self-restraint he possessed to ask the question.

"Your men traveled to London and set up watch on the house?" Henry inquired.

Howard nodded. "They came to me in London and explained what had happened. Henderson and some of his friends watched Darcy's house to discover whether Miss Bennet might be there. But they saw nothing, and Baker was getting nervous. Badly wanted to get out of London. I refused to pay them until the two of you had been punished. I did not order them into your house, but they wanted to be paid, and I suppose they did not know where else to look."

"You could not even give the order!" Fitz cried in disgust. "You hired the men. You knew what they were. You knew how they would interpret 'punishment.' Yet because you did not specifically tell them to kill Miss Elizabeth or my cousin, you believed your conscience was clear?"

Howard squeezed his eyes shut. "I did. And I was wrong."

"You were a coward," Darcy said flatly.

"You *are* a coward," Fitz added.

The man's breathing quickened, but he grasped the arms of his chair and nodded. "So it appears, yes. Nothing came of it in the end, thank God."

"Do not forgive yourself so easily, Howard," Darcy said coldly. "I shall not."

Henry folded his arms across his chest. "Darcy," he said coolly, "once Mr. Howard leaves here, what would you like done with him?"

"I have a few ideas," Fitz muttered.

"There is no need, gentlemen," Howard said firmly, pushing himself up. He swayed a little before steadying himself and addressing Darcy. "I fully intended to wound you today, Darcy. I wanted you hurt. I wanted you humiliated. It was the best I could hope for now that all my plans had been laid to ruin. You showed up early at Ramsgate, Miss Bennet appeared from nowhere at Netherfield, and Henderson and Baker failed to compromise either of you. You were married, happily by the look of things. The foil was all I had left to me, and you did not wait for my challenge." He sighed tiredly. "What man of honor refuses to duel? It is illegal in word, but not in practice."

"It is a *ridiculous* practice," Darcy replied impatiently. "How is it honorable to settle an argument by trying to kill one another? I have too many people who depend on me to give way to anything so wholly reckless."

"How did you learn it was me?" Howard asked quietly. "Did Bingley tell you? Wickham?"

"Henderson and Baker were captured by Darcy's staff when they broke into his home to finish the job you set them," Fitz informed Howard. "They told us you hired them."

Howard paled so thoroughly that Darcy thought he might faint. He rather hoped the man would.

"They are both in Newgate now," Henry informed them. "My brother saw to that." He flashed a grin at Fitz. "And they were so very anxious about leaving town that I asked around. You will be thrilled to learn that there is more." He waited, but no one said anything. "Well, this is disappointing. Will no one ask?"

Darcy pinched the bridge of his nose. "What did you learn, Henry?"

"Well, Darcy," Henry said, rubbing his hands together, "It turns out that Mr. Howard hired two men with a colorful history of criminal actions. They had been doing rather well for themselves until they crippled the Earl of Wright's butler in an aborted attempt to pilfer the dowager countess's jewels. He is a friend of my father's, you know, and was very pleased to hear that these men were in prison." Henry examined his fingernails. "I believe we can all guess how they will end."

Howard's expression was tortured as he met Darcy's gaze. "I know it is not enough, but my deepest apologies are yours. My honor, as tattered as it may be, demands that I make amends." He closed his eyes briefly before opening them to address Darcy. "There is no future here for my sister or me, now."

"I should think not." Henry's voice was suddenly very cold. "You must not remain within a thousand miles of my family, Mr. Howard, or I shall tell the earl who it was that gave these criminals the clothes of gentlemen and money enough to leave London. I believe his wrath would be considerable."

Howard held up a hand. "There is no need to threaten me with the earl. I know what I have done. None of you..." He swallowed. "None of you could possibly detest me as much as I detest myself."

"Entirely untrue," Fitz replied.

Darcy said nothing. He just stared at Howard with all the anger that was still in his heart—and waited.

"As much as I deserved to have you run me through, Darcy, I am grateful you stayed your hand." Howard swallowed. "I still have a sister to protect. I have failed in that once—I cannot fail again. Please, allow me to truly apologize." Howard met Darcy's eyes, and Darcy saw a broken man. He hoped it was sincere repentance, if for no other reason than it would offer Elizabeth some comfort.

"I have some small holdings in Upper Canada," Howard continued, after a moment. "I shall secure passage to Nova Scotia for my sister and myself as soon as I am able to purchase a berth, and when the St. Lawrence thaws in the spring, we shall travel there. If I promise you that we shall never return to England, never attempt to contact you or your family in any way—will this satisfy?"

"You have more than one estate," Darcy replied. "How can I believe you will never return to England?"

"I suppose . . . I could sell them. There is no entail." Howard's color was not improving. "It will be a difficult thing to sell our family home. It is a large property and not many could afford it. I admit it would be difficult for other reasons as well." He was silent for a time. "What if I were to leave it to my cousins in trust for Amelia's child?" he asked at last. "At least the boy is of Howard blood, and my cousins are excellent people. They would be good stewards of the property." He glanced up at Darcy. "It would allow us to sail sooner."

Darcy considered the notion, thinking of the pain he would endure were he required to sign Pemberley over to someone else. After a moment, he nodded. "I insist on seeing the signed contract when it is available. The transfer must be immediate and irrevocable."

"And you will sign a contract detailing a substantial financial penalty to my cousin or his wife should you ever return to England," Henry added stonily. "Let us say thirty thousand pounds?"

Howard nodded. "I have no intention of returning, so such a contract would be no imposition."

"Understand this, Mr. Howard," Fitz added levelly. "It will not only be a financial penalty you will incur should you dare to go back on your word."

Darcy thought such insistence unnecessary. Howard had been laboring under a mistaken premise that had now been rectified. But he had no desire to meet with Howard ever again, and understood his cousins' need to be excruciatingly clear. Howard's actions had been despicable, and they were protecting their family.

Howard did not flinch. "It will take time to prepare the papers," he said. "If you can bear my presence in London, Mr. Darcy, I would have it all completed before we depart. I shall not enter society at all, not that I would be welcomed—you shall only see me by appointment, in order to conclude our business."

"Hardly enough," Fitz said. "You will still be a rich man."

Howard grimaced. "I will need money to begin again abroad," he said quietly. "But I shall never again be a truly wealthy man."

Fitz scoffed, but Darcy understood. It would take a great deal for Howard to restore his own self-worth—he had gone against every principle by which he had previously governed his life. He would have to find his way again, something which might take the rest of his life, and with no guarantee of success. Still, it was right that Howard, having transgressed every proper feeling and behavior, now cede the field. Fitz and Henry had made certain the men who had harmed Elizabeth were in prison and would be tried on other charges, relieving her from the necessity of appearing in court.

This terrible Gordian knot had at last been severed.

Darcy and Howard had both lost their parents young, inherited early, and had younger sisters in their charge. But Darcy had used the precepts of honor to guide his behavior when things went awry. Howard had twisted honor until it was unrecognizable, using it to excuse each reprehensible action.

If Howard removed himself and his sister from England, Elizabeth would have nothing to fear. That had been his purpose in this, after all. As he pondered the matter, Darcy realized that Elizabeth's good opinion was now more important to him than any code of behavior. She believed in forgiveness. Once he was assured that she was safe, it was right to offer it. But it was difficult.

"That will do for now," Darcy said firmly. He was weary to the bone. He needed to go home to his wife. "Mr. Howard, you might have responded to your sister's plight in a dozen ways that would not have harmed anyone else. You chose to make yourself a criminal, to introduce violence into our lives." He stared at Howard as though he could bore a hole through him. "Were it not for our sisters and my wife, I would see you tried and hanged for it."

"You are fortunate to be dealing with Darcy in this," Fitz growled. "Your sister is responsible for her own part here. I would not take her sensibilities into account."

His cousins were still staring at Howard with their arms folded across their chests. Darcy thought he had never seen them looking so alike.

"We will finish here and see you back at home, Darcy," Henry said quietly.

"Tomorrow, Henry." He nodded at Fitz. "Elizabeth and I will call tomorrow." He turned his back and walked away.

Elizabeth felt something tickling her nose and swatted at it. She curled up on her side, but the sensation returned. Slowly, she opened her eyes.

William was touching her nose with the ends of her own hair.

"I had visions of my wife awaiting my return, ready to throw herself in my arms," he teased. "Alas, she had slept the day away, not at all concerned for my welfare."

Before he could finish, Elizabeth threw her arms around him and nearly knocked him off the bed. "Are you well?"

Her husband smiled smugly, quite satisfied with himself. "Ah, this is the welcome I was hoping to receive." He bent forward to brush his lips over hers. "I am well. Howard did not follow the rules, but I won the day."

Elizabeth was so relieved she nearly wept. "Well done, Mr. Darcy."

"Now," he said firmly, pulling away, "I hear that you had a rather busy morning."

She gasped. "Did Henry find Harriet? Was she able to tell him anything? He was supposed to send word!"

Darcy held out a folded message. "I believe the maid was waiting for you to wake."

Elizabeth sighed. "What a time to fall asleep!"

"In response to your questions," Darcy said fondly, "Henry did find Harriet and she was able to tell him a good deal. He arrived at Angelo's fashionably late and as dramatically as usual."

Elizabeth laughed softly. She was pleased Henry had arrived before the match had concluded.

"How did you even think of it?" he asked, stroking her cheek with a thumb.

"I was up until all hours turning it over in my mind," Elizabeth told him. "Mr. Howard could not be the man you claimed him to be and yet act the way he had. Not without a reason. His sister had been disgraced. I thought that his actions must have to do with that, and I considered what my youngest sister might do in such a situation. When I woke, it occurred to me that Miss Howard might have boasted of her tryst, and if so, her friend could be worked on." She embraced her husband again. "I am so happy you are home!"

"I have married a very clever woman," he mused, staring deeply into her eyes. "It speaks well of me."

Elizabeth beamed at him as he took her in his arms. "I agree on both counts."

"I missed you," he murmured in her ear.

"Then you must stay here with me the rest of the day," she proclaimed. Elizabeth was almost afraid to ask, but she did. "What will happen with Mr. Howard? Will he keep his distance?"

William reached out to stroke her cheek. "Indeed, he will. Henry was quite convincing. Howard has admitted to being in the wrong. His sister claimed that I was her seducer."

Elizabeth opened her mouth to speak but was so angry she merely shut it again.

William smiled a little at her. "He will settle his affairs and leave England permanently. I believe Fitz is greatly anticipating escorting him to the docks."

She frowned. "What of Miss Howard?"

He shrugged. "She will accompany him to their properties in Upper Canada."

"And . . ." she peered up at him. "The babe is safe?"

William nodded. "The boy will be raised by distant relations, and Howard is leaving the family estate to him."

Elizabeth sighed. "That is good. I must say that I shall be greatly pleased to see them go." She placed her hand on William's chest. "It was very wrong of Miss Howard to lie, particularly about you. But she is so young. Perhaps in a new place, she can begin again."

Her husband pulled her close. "You are quite possibly the most generous-hearted person I have ever met, Elizabeth."

"No," she told him quite sternly. "Forgive me, but had Mr. Howard harmed you . . ." She shook her head. It made her ill to think of it. "And Henry and Colonel Fitzwilliam would help me accomplish it." She did not know what "it" might be, but it would be terrible. She was sure of it.

William gazed at her with something like adoration. He kissed her forehead. "Thank you, my dear."

Elizabeth bustled about the sitting room, picking up their books, her shawl, and a ledger William had sent Mr. Slipworth to find.

Her husband had not escaped his confrontation unscathed after all. His knee had swollen overnight—she could not persuade him to explain how he had been injured—and she was fussing over him every bit as much as he had over her.

She had been anxious for Jane's health at Netherfield, of course, but seeing her strong, active husband hobbling about their chambers in pain was almost more than Elizabeth could bear. She had taken command immediately, ordering willow bark tea and steeping it over the fire in their room, arranging for ice to be brought up every few hours to prevent the swelling from growing worse, and above all, trying to force him to remain in bed or on the chaise to elevate his leg. She had asked Slipworth for William's walking stick. Thus far her husband had refused to use it.

He grumbled, but Elizabeth suspected that he rather enjoyed being coddled.

She was clearing away their mess in the sitting room because Henry and the colonel were coming to call, and Elizabeth was adamant that her husband would not be using the stairs. Not today, and likely not tomorrow, either. She had Mr. Slipworth assist William to the chaise in their sitting room, where she placed a pillow under his leg and made certain he was comfortable while he observed her fussing with an affectionate smile. He drew the line when she approached him with a blanket for his legs.

"Take that away. I am not an invalid," he said stoutly.

"Very well," Elizabeth said with authority. "We shall save it for after your cousins depart." She folded it and put it back in their bedchamber. "There," she said as she returned, finally content with their arrangements. "Are you *certain* your cousins wish me to attend?"

"Henry insisted," her husband told her. "He has something to tell us, his note said, but it also said that you are cleverer than I and that if *I* wished to skip the gathering, I might."

She laughed. "He is an odd one, our Henry."

"But clever," Henry remarked as he and the colonel entered the room without announcing themselves.

"Very clever," Elizabeth agreed, approaching to kiss him on the cheek. She could not be certain, but she thought his expression warmed a bit.

"Colonel, please come in," she said kindly.

"No kiss for me?" the colonel teased.

"If you wish one, of course," she replied and proceeded to place one on his cheek as well.

"That is enough kissing," William called from the chaise. "She is only supposed to kiss me."

"Yes, dear," Elizabeth replied while rolling her eyes so his cousins could see. "He has become quite a bear with his bad leg."

"Not too bad, I hope, Darce?" the colonel asked as he took a chair across from William.

"Nothing a few days will not mend," William replied.

Tea and cakes were brought up as the Darcys had not yet broken their fast. Elizabeth poured while the Fitzwilliam men eyed the cakes.

"Honey cakes!" exclaimed the colonel. He grinned. "These are my favorites."

"Elizabeth asked me yesterday," William informed him. "I told her it was seed cake, but she did not believe me. She discovered the truth from Mrs. Spencer."

"I do not see *my* favorites here," Henry announced, one hand suspended above the platter.

"Only because no one seems to know them," Elizabeth apologized. "If you tell me, then I shall have something prepared for you when next you come."

Henry grinned. "Parmesan ice. Can you make that here?"

"You have been speaking to your mother," Elizabeth replied with a laugh and shake of her head. She set several seed cakes on a plate for William and placed them on a table next to him. "How is she?"

"Flush with success," Henry said. "She has her eyes set on Fitz now."

The colonel rolled his eyes.

"Now, gentlemen," Elizabeth said once everyone had their tea and cake. "I believe Henry had something he wished to say?"

Henry was at that moment devouring one of Cook's wonderful ginger spice cakes. Elizabeth took note.

He swallowed some tea as they waited. "I thought it was time you all know something." He placed his plate to the side. "I was not in jest when I told Mama I would never marry."

Elizabeth frowned. She had not been sure what Henry wished to announce, but this surprised her.

"I will say no more than that much of what I do is in service to my country. Yesterday, I used my skills to act in service to my family, and it struck me that I have been terribly remiss. I mean to make my decisions very clear, for your sake, Richard, and for the earldom."

The colonel's brows pinched together. "What do you mean, Henry? Of course you will marry, and I should hope it would be soon. You are nearly forty, brother."

Henry ran a hand over his face. "I will not marry. I cannot bring a wife into the life I lead."

Elizabeth felt William take her hand, and she exchanged a glance with him. His expression was somber.

"Henry," the colonel insisted, "you must sire an heir. It is your line that will continue the earldom."

Henry shook his head slowly. "No, Richard. That is why we are here. I am informing you that should you outlive me, a distinct possibility once you leave the army, *you* will be the heir. And *you* will sire the next generation of earls."

When the colonel froze so completely that he did not even blink, Elizabeth wished desperately there was wine in their sitting room. She spooned a good deal of honey into a cup of tea and pressed it into his hands.

"Darcy," Henry said, ignoring his brother's shock, "I intend to sign over a portion of my savings and allowance to my brother. Father can teach him politics, but you are the best of us all at managing an estate. Will you help?"

"But what will you do for funds, Henry?" the colonel asked, and waved weakly at his brother's expensive clothing. "Surely you cannot live on less."

Henry shrugged. "I have a second, rather generous allowance from the government, brother, and I am an excellent gambler. I have made quite a tidy fortune since university." He took a sip of his tea. "No, I have done very well with my money, Richard, and have ways to earn more. I would much rather you leave the army and find yourself a wife like Elizabeth." His sigh was wistful. "I will never be able to make Mother happy that way—but you can."

"Does the earl know of your work?" Elizabeth asked. She felt she could be direct with Henry. "I presume the countess does not."

Henry took up his plate again and dropped another spice cake onto it. "He knows enough to wish for ignorance. Mama must never know."

William had been very quiet. "Henry, how much will Fitz have when you are through?"

Fitz stammered a protest, but it was ignored.

"Not a great fortune, but enough to allow him to wed." Henry addressed his brother. "Several years ago, Father finally cleared the debt our grandfather left on the estate and has been putting away the extra for Richard. He and I will place the principal in the funds. The interest will generate a little more than one thousand a year in addition to your current allowance."

Elizabeth placed a hand over her heart. "Not a great deal?" she laughed. "My father has only two thousand to support a wife and five daughters."

"Four," William reminded her.

She smiled at her husband and waited for the colonel to say something. Even if Henry were to change his mind at some point, William's closest friend would be safe from the war. Her heart swelled with happiness for them both.

Still, the colonel did not speak.

"I will be pleased to assist you, Fitz," William said, breaking the silence.

"And I can provide a connection to the best fabrics in the country at excellent rates," Elizabeth assured him cheerfully. "Somewhere there is a woman who would marry you for that alone!"

"Perhaps Henry might purchase from your uncle as well," William told her dryly. "His costumes would not then pinch his purse."

"Costumes, you say?" Henry asked, his eyes dancing merrily. "In other words, I dare to wear more than three colors in a year?"

"You have more than three colors on that cravat," William replied.

Henry only laughed.

The colonel shook his head. "I cannot understand this," he said, ignoring the banter between the others in the room. "Are you quite certain, Henry?" He appeared almost pained. "I would not have you relinquish anything you will later regret."

Henry clapped him on the back. "Of course you would not! That is how I know it is the right thing to do." With that, he stood and made an exaggerated bow to Elizabeth. She rose to offer him an equally exaggerated curtsy. "Well," he said. "I am off!"

It was several minutes before the colonel stood up with a huff. "I quite forgot that I rode here in my brother's carriage. I must hurry, or he will leave me behind. Darcy, Elizabeth."

As he reached the hall, he stopped and turned. "The next time you visit your Aunt and Uncle Gardiner, may I be one of the party?"

Elizabeth nodded slowly, glancing at William. But the colonel had one more favor to request.

"Elizabeth," he asked, "would you mind terribly calling me Fitz? It seems I may not be a colonel much longer."

Chapter Eighteen

"When shall we depart for Pemberley, Elizabeth?" Darcy was nearly begging. "Please say it will be soon."

Elizabeth drew her gloves off one finger at a time, in a maddeningly slow pretense of thoughtfulness. "Well, I do not know, William. Is being my escort in London so unbearable?"

"I know you jest," he replied, handing his coat and hat off to a footman. "You cannot have missed that... *spectacle* this evening."

Elizabeth did not smile, but she pressed her lips together which meant she wished to. Minx. "I do not believe I witnessed any *spectacle*, Mr. Darcy. Whatever can you mean?"

Darcy removed his own gloves in two quick tugs and handed those over as well. "You are well aware that every person known to us at the theater this evening—and many entirely unknown to us—approached us for conversation or to be introduced. It is that wretched article!"

"Articles," she corrected him. He groaned.

Two of the London papers had made mention of his triumph over Howard at Angelo's. Both writers extolled a Mr. D. of Derbyshire who, even when set upon by a most dishonorable opponent, remained noble in all his actions and had emerged victorious. Elizabeth had read it aloud at breakfast, relishing his discomfort at being so singled out. It was even more florid than the story she had admitted telling in the countess's drawing room. Now Darcy had the approval and attention of both the women *and* the men of the ton.

It was excruciating.

The tale might have been sold by any man who had attended the bout between Howard and himself but given the timing of the publication—weeks after the fact and just at the beginning of the season—he suspected Henry. Darcy asked Fitz, but his cousin pled ignorance. The man was too caught up in his courtship of Miss Bennet even to tease Darcy about his sudden renown.

Elizabeth had teased him, but she was proud of him, too. *Her* approbation was worth having. But the theater had been . . .

This time Elizabeth did smile. "You are the most popular man in London at the moment. Enjoy it."

"*Enjoy* it, you say?" Darcy asked, bewildered. He had been unable to escape. Even the Duke of Devonshire had stopped briefly to exchange a few words. "Do you know me at all?"

Elizabeth laughed quietly and led the way upstairs to their chambers. When they were ready for bed and had dismissed the servants, she embraced him. Darcy sighed, but put his arms around her and held her close. The tension ebbed away, as it always did when they touched. "We missed half of the first act," he grumbled.

She shook her head at him. "It was Shakespeare. You told me yourself you have seen the play twice before and you have read it at least a dozen times." She gazed at him sympathetically. "This will pass, my dear. But let us try to make the best of it. It would appear ill-mannered to flee town just now." She held him tightly and raised herself on her toes to bestow a kiss. "You met several men tonight whose conversation interested you, and I met several of their wives upon whom I should like to call. Let us explore these new connections and discover who among them might be friends in time."

Darcy stiffened. "I have not had the best of luck with friends, Elizabeth."

Elizabeth's hands moved in circles over his lower back, and he bent to kiss her forehead.

"That is because you did not have me before," she assured him. "Together we shall find our circle. And you know, a number of good friends come with me—consider them my dowry of sorts."

He sighed deeply.

"What were the most common demands of these so-called friends upon you?" Elizabeth asked.

"You know what they were," Darcy answered. "Marriage."

"And money?"

He nodded. "Nearly always money, in one form or another."

"Well, as you are newly and happily wed, any requests for your hand must be at an end."

"I would hope so." Although there might be other inquiries from amorous widows and the like, hopefully they would cease when it was clear how much he loved his wife.

Elizabeth continued. "And as for money, you may again use me as a ready excuse. For you now have a new wife for whom to provide—and she did not bring a fortune with her. You have far less disposable income as a result."

He grunted, not wanting to confess that his mood was improving. "The good Lord knows *that* is true. Her gowns alone . . ."

Elizabeth laughed and pulled back, slapping lightly at his arm. "Here I am, attempting to cheer you, and you turn on me. Badly done, sir. You pay less for gowns than anyone in the ton." She smiled coyly. "Just for that, Mr. Darcy, tomorrow we shall attend the opera."

Darcy tipped his head back. "Elizabeth, no."

She wrapped her arms around his waist and gazed up at him. When he lowered his head, he saw her eyes, sparkling with joy and hope. "I have never been to the Opera House," she said.

He grimaced. She knew he could deny her nothing when she looked at him that way. "Very well. But you shall have to do something for me in return."

"Gladly," she replied, and straightened as though he might be dispatching her on a mission. "What might that be?"

Darcy lowered his head to Elizabeth's and captured her lips with his own. He pulled her close, waiting for her hands to tangle themselves in his hair and slide to the back of his neck. When they did, he swung her up into his arms and carried her to bed.

"This," he said.

"Oh," Elizabeth said languidly and reached up to stroke the side of his face with her hand. "It would be my pleasure, William."

He smiled. It would indeed.

Darcy signed the contract in his usual tight, controlled hand. He carefully handed the document back to Gunderson, who sanded the page.

"I believe that is the last of it unless you wish me to prepare a lease," the solicitor said, reaching for a ribbon to tie the packet of papers together.

"No," Darcy replied, feeling some relief that the purchase had been completed and trepidation over how best to approach the next step. "Not at the present time."

"Darcy!" came a booming voice from the doorway. "What do you do here?"

Darcy stood, surprised but unwilling to show it. "Uncle," he said. "I am completing some business with Mr. Gunderson." He knew that Lord Matlock used several solicitors, though he had not known Gunderson was one of them.

"Typical Darcy answer," Henry said, as he moved around his father and into the room. He was wearing a green coat, rather a brighter shade than typical for a man's garment. "Always so literal. Will you not tell us the *substance* of your business?"

"I beg your pardon?" Darcy asked, somewhat taken aback. "Since when do I share my financial dealings with you?"

"Boys," the earl said sternly.

Gunderson had disappeared, no doubt a skill honed to avoid the scene of quarreling family members. Darcy knew if he called, his solicitor would return, but for now, he had what he required. He gathered the neatly tied stack of documents.

"What have you there?" the earl asked quietly. "Might it be the deed to Stodley Abbey near Rotherham?"

Darcy cocked his head to one side. "It might."

"My solicitor has been viewing suitable properties for several months, and this is the closest one to Matlock. We would like to purchase it from you," the earl said. "I intend to sign it over to Richard as a wedding gift."

"There is no need, Uncle," Darcy said politely. "It is already in my cousin's name."

"I told you, father," Henry said seriously, though his eyes displayed a wicked sort of mirth. "He intends to show us up."

"It is a small estate and has been sitting unoccupied for some time, but I agree that its location is ideal," Darcy replied. "I made rather a bargain of it."

Henry studied him for a moment. "Ah, you mean to keep Elizabeth and Miss Bennet close," he said, wagging a finger at Darcy. "You are a wiser man than I thought, cousin."

"I will do what I must to see to my wife's happiness," Darcy told his cousin smugly.

"William," the earl added somberly before Henry could respond, "I am Richard's father. He will not accept such a gift from you, but he will from me. Matlock has done very well these past few years, and the Earl of Wright wished to show his gratitude to Richard for his part in discovering those ruffians. Even had Henry not declared his intentions, I would have asked Richard not to return to the peninsula."

The earl was not a man of many words, but he loved his sons—both of them. And he was correct. Fitz would accept such a gift from his father without protest.

"Very well," Darcy agreed. "But I have already purchased the property. It would be a waste of time to undo it." He handed the contract to his uncle. "Simply pay your solicitor to change my name to yours and offer it to my cousin."

"Why, thank you," Henry began to say, but Darcy cut him off.

"My more deserving cousin," he said bluntly.

All three men laughed softly.

"I will pay you for the purchase, Darcy," the earl said firmly. "It is my duty as his father and my privilege as well."

Darcy shook his head. "Half, then. A wedding gift from us all. Use the remaining funds to improve the property."

The earl narrowed his eyes. "Very well."

He had no doubt that his uncle would foist something upon him in recompense, but for now, Darcy was satisfied. "I thank you, uncle."

"On that note, gentlemen, I am off," Henry said jovially. He slapped Darcy on the back and gave his father a formal bow.

"Here now," the earl asked, eyeing his son. "You promised your mother she would see you for dinner."

"And so she shall," Henry said. "But just now, I have somewhere to be."

Darcy walked out with them and waited as the earl climbed into his carriage. "Henry," he said when the earl was out of hearing, "I have wanted to ask you something since you made your announcement, but I could not run after you, and you have been avoiding me since."

"Yes, with your injury, it was the perfect time to explain myself," Henry said, gazing down the street. "You and those great long legs of yours would have overtaken me with ease."

"Henry," Darcy said, briefly grasping his cousin's arm. "What about your widow? Did you not wish to wed her?"

Henry glanced at Darcy, his expression devoid of its normal animation. "She would not have me."

"Oh," Darcy said, his heart aching for his cousin. "I am very sorry."

"Quite a sensible decision, really," his cousin replied, lifting one hand as he watched the street. "I had to give her a faint sketch of my business. It was only fair. But she has been made a widow once, she says. Does not want to do it again."

"You might find other work," Darcy suggested. "You could settle down. Fitz has his property, and we both know he would be quite happy to remain a country gentleman. Surely . . ."

Henry interrupted him. "Darcy," he said, shaking his head, "I am making a sacrifice, that much is true. But it does not follow that I am unhappy. I am good at what I do. I make a difference. I keep my country safe." He met Darcy's gaze at last. "It is enough."

Almost as if by magic, a small black carriage appeared before them. Henry climbed in and offered Darcy a half-wave through the window. Darcy saw him check the foil in his walking stick. Then the equipage turned the corner and was lost from sight.

"Will you be needing tea, Mrs. Darcy?" Mrs. Spencer asked.

Elizabeth shook her head, and the housekeeper slipped away. William's reassuring touch on the small of her back steadied her as their visitors entered.

The Howards were dressed in traveling clothes, flanked by Fitz and Henry. Elizabeth nodded at the introduction and turned her attention to Miss Howard. The girl was about Lydia's age but shared none of Lydia's robust good health. She was slender and pale. Several limp curls framed her face. Elizabeth noted the dark shadows beneath her eyes and the trembling of her hands. "Will you sit?" she asked.

"I thank you, Mrs. Darcy," Mr. Howard said. "But we will not take much of your time. I thought it was important, before we sail, that we offer our apologies in person. I have made them to your husband, and he has been good enough to accept them, but I have not made them to you. I was badly mistaken in your husband's character and badly mistaken in my own, but you have my sincerest regrets and apologies. Please know that you have nothing to fear from me."

"Nothing *further* to fear," she replied, rather surprised with herself for the strength she now felt. She stared directly at the man who had frightened her so badly. "You lost all sense of decency when you took it upon yourself to seek revenge, Mr. Howard. I understand the need to protect a sister. I do not understand seeking to harm another in the process."

Mr. Howard nodded once.

"My forgiveness is yours, sir, so long as you do not break your promise to my husband and my cousins. Stay in Upper Canada. Live a good life there. But do not return."

Mr. Howard bowed and turned to his sister.

"Mrs. Darcy, I . . ." Miss Howard began, twisting her hands before her. "My brother has told me everything he has done, and he has taken it all upon himself, but it is not true. If I had not . . ." She swallowed and took a deep breath. "Lord Bartholomew met me one day in the park. He was handsome and charming and attentive, but when we were about to make our farewells, he spoke so my companion would not hear him. He asked me to meet him alone the next day. I demurred, but he teased me. He said I was too good a little miss to leave my governess." Miss Howard closed her eyes. "She was not my governess, but my companion!"

"Amelia," Mr. Howard said, his voice low.

The girl continued. "Instead of resting the next day, I went back to the park to show him I was not a child. Because I had my own establishment, it was an easy thing. I found it . . . exciting. He said when I came out, we could finally be together in public, but he also said if we had the chance, he would marry me straight away. It was romantic." She stopped to take a deep breath. "We met each time in the park before . . ." She looked up, her eyes glossy with unshed tears. "You know where it all led." She paused before looking resolutely at Elizabeth, then William. "Mr. and Mrs. Darcy, I was, I am so ashamed."

Elizabeth was concerned the girl would faint, she was so drained of color, but Mr. Howard wrapped an arm around his sister's waist and said something in her ear.

Miss Howard squared her shoulders. "When my brother learned of my condition, he demanded a name. I refused, but he would not relent. I panicked. I had sent a note to Bartholomew. It was discreet, but he could not have mistaken the message. He did not come, and I was so very afraid. I knew if my brother challenged him, Bartholomew would kill him." Her little hands clenched into fists. "I was so . . . confused. If I could not trust Bartholomew, I did not think I could trust any man. I did not wish to marry at all, yet I still held out hope that Bartholomew would come to me." She paused to twist her fingers together. "Georgiana had told us all that Mr. Darcy would never marry against his will. I made certain my brother knew that not only did I not wish to marry but that Mr. Darcy would never be compelled. I never thought my brother would. . ." She stared steadily at Elizabeth and shook her head. "But it was a lie. It was wrong. And I have hurt *everyone*." Her trembling increased, and tears streaked her cheeks. "I apologize, Mr. and Mrs. Darcy. So very deeply. I am grateful that you will allow us to begin again somewhere else. It is quite . . . it is *extraordinarily* gracious of you."

"Indeed," her brother murmured, his eyes downcast.

Elizabeth was angry with the girl for slandering William's good name. But beyond that offense and being foolish enough to be taken in by a scoundrel, her faults were nothing in light of her brother's. "Miss Howard," Elizabeth said. "What you set in motion might easily have ended in tragedy. I hope you realize that."

Miss Howard nodded slowly.

"You have made a number of terrible errors," Elizabeth continued. "But you are yet young. Your brother is much older and made many grievous errors of his own. If I can forgive him, I can forgive you. I do forgive you." She glanced up at Darcy, who nodded so slightly she doubted anyone else noticed. "Mr. Darcy forgives you as well. But you must never tell such a lie again."

Miss Howard's expression was grateful, almost reverential. "Oh, Mrs. Darcy, I *never* shall. I promise you that."

"Then may I say fair voyage, Miss Howard," Elizabeth said sincerely. She caught Fitz's eye and lifted her eyebrows, indicating her dismissal of his charges. He nodded and stepped to William, whispering something in his ear.

"Fair voyage," William said, his voice strained. "I am not so gracious as my wife, I am afraid, but I shall follow her example and offer my forgiveness to you both. Howard," he said, and it was as close to menacing as Elizabeth had ever seen her husband, "you understand, I am sure, how difficult this is."

Mr. Howard bowed, Miss Howard curtsied, and they left in the company of the Fitzwilliams.

As the door closed, she exhaled. "What a relief to have that done," she said. "What did your cousin have to say?"

William's expression was grim, his voice pinched. "Wickham was court-martialed and found guilty, but he was given the choice of prison or the peninsula. His ship left at the beginning of the week."

Elizabeth sniffed. "Good riddance," she began to say but found herself suddenly clasped to William's chest. "William?" she asked, her voice muffled.

"I could not have done it, Elizabeth," he told her hoarsely. "I wanted to toss the pair of them from the house and wish them to the devil." He held her tight. "Thank you, love, for being my conscience and my strength."

Eventually, she pulled away far enough to meet his gaze. "It is not really for them we have offered our forgiveness, William," she told him honestly. "I am not certain what Mr. Howard has done *is* forgivable. We forgave them for you and for me. Now that we have, I feel free of it. Do you not feel it too?"

William smiled wanly at her. "Perhaps when their ship has left the dock, I shall feel that it is all truly over and you are safe. Will you help me wait?"

"Come," Elizabeth said, and took his hand. "Come sit with me until your cousins return with the news that the Howards are gone."

"And what shall we do with the time?" he asked. He was making a valiant attempt to banish his resentment, and she admired him for it. He cleared his throat. "Will you require me to sew anything? I must warn you that I have a dreadful time threading a needle."

"We might discuss how very pleased your aunt has been to have Jane as a daughter," Elizabeth mused. "Or how well Fitz has taken to being a husband."

Darcy felt himself beginning to relax. "I thought the man would lose every button on his coat at the wedding, his chest was puffed out so far."

Elizabeth laughed a little. "It was very good of him to wait for the Howards to depart before taking Jane north. I know they are both anxious to see the estate." She paused when Mr. Pratt announced his presence with a sniff.

"Mrs. Darcy, the viscount has left a note for you." The butler walked over to hand it to her. "He asked that I see it to your hands personally."

"Thank you, Mr. Pratt," Elizabeth replied and took the note. She unfolded it and read it silently before asking, "Mr. Darcy, why is the earl giving me a house in Hertfordshire?"

Her husband's mouth fell open in surprise, and then he chuckled. "Because he knew if he gave it to you, I would not protest. He is as wily as his wife and sons. Where is it located?"

"In Ware, not so very far from Longbourn."

He took the note and read it. "I suppose it will serve as a place to stay when we are in the area, and for your mother should she ever require it. Eventually, it could be a property for our second son."

"Second son?" Elizabeth asked, amused. "Should we not have one first?"

"There is no hurry," William said, taking her hand. "I would be very pleased to have you to myself for a time."

Elizabeth considered being alone with her husband. It sounded marvelous.

"What are you thinking, my dear?" William asked. "Are you unhappy with my uncle?"

She laughed. "Yes, I am terribly unhappy that your uncle has given me a home. The audacity!" She pulled William down to the chaise with her. "No, I was simply wondering where you shall take me next."

William's eyes narrowed. "We have been to the Opera House, madam, all the museums, the menagerie..."

"And yet you have not answered my question," Elizabeth declared playfully. "Where shall we visit next?"

"I am sure I do not know," Darcy said playfully. "We have already been to concerts and plays and dinners and even three balls."

"Even after forcing you to endure *three balls*," Elizabeth said teasingly, "there is somewhere else I should like to visit."

William groaned but took her hand. "I am yours to command, my love."

Elizabeth smiled widely. "That is good to hear, William. For I should like to travel to Longbourn."

His face lit up like the fireworks at Vauxhall Gardens, where he had taken her only last week. "Does that mean . . ."

"It means that after Longbourn, I shall be ready to go home, William," Elizabeth informed him sweetly. "To Pemberley."

―∞―

Elizabeth held her hand up in the window of the carriage. She waited until she could no longer see Mama waving her best lace handkerchief in farewell before lowering her hand and leaning back into the squabs.

"You were extraordinarily kind to my family, William," she said tenderly. "I know they can be trying, but I do love them all."

"I know you do," William replied with a crooked smile. "I will do all I can to be prepared to face the onslaught of Bennets and Gardiners when they visit us in August."

Elizabeth worried her bottom lip. "I confess I am feeling equal parts delight and trepidation."

"The weather should be excellent," William assured her. "The children will have more than enough time outside to run off their exuberance."

"I think you know whose exuberance concerns me, and it is not anyone with the name of Gardiner." Elizabeth gave him a look askance.

"It will be well, Elizabeth. We are all family." He took her hand. "Now, I have only this morning received letters from both our Fitzwilliam cousins. Would you care to hear Henry's first?"

"Oh, yes," she said, lifting her eyebrows. "Henry always has the best news. I often do not know whether your aunt is his source, or whether he is hers."

"I suspect the gossip flows in both directions," her husband said wryly. "Who do you suppose his latest rumor concerns?"

She stared at William for a moment, thinking. "I am afraid I do not know. Most of our acquaintance has removed from town."

"No?" he asked. "Very well." He paused. "Mr. Bingley is married."

Her mouth fell open. "To *whom*?" she asked, incredulous.

"Miss Matilda Johnson, as was."

Elizabeth tipped her head to one side. "I do not believe I know her," she said.

William laughed. "No one does. According to Henry, she is the daughter of a moderately successful tradesman who decided she wished to wed him."

She scoffed. "And Mr. Bingley had no say in the matter?"

"Not after he was caught alone with her in his arms." William cleared his throat. "I am told that she has four rather large brothers who were not best pleased."

Elizabeth gasped. "Oh, please do tell me they were in the library during a ball."

William laughed softly. "I do not know in which room they were found, but it happened at a country assembly. The gossip is that she threw herself at him and declared her undying love. Bingley was quite unhappy. Alas, *he* has no sheep farm to make his enthusiastic bride rethink her choice."

"What?" Elizabeth asked, bemused.

He shook his head. "Never you mind."

"Well," she said, shaking her head, "my goodness. What have you to tell me next?"

"Henry also thanked me for hiring Anders's cousins so that he could meet them. According to him, they are now often in his employ and are enjoying themselves immensely."

She shook her head. "I am pleased to hear it, but I meant the letter from Fitz."

"Ah," he replied. "This is less entertaining, but I hope you will like it nearly as well. Fitz and your sister have settled into their new home and are ready for company. Would you care to visit for a few days next month?" he inquired, his eyes alight with mischief. "I believe my cousin is troubled that he cannot simply order the crops to grow in neat rows and that the weeds are not afraid of him."

"That is enough from you, Mr. Darcy," Elizabeth said with mock exasperation. "I should love to see Jane, but I believe Fitz has adapted very well from the life of a colonel to that of a landed gentleman."

William nodded. "That is because Fitz has always been a gentleman in the ways that truly matter."

Elizabeth put her arms around his waist. "Just as you have always been principled in every way that matters."

"Thank you, my dear," her husband murmured.

She had embarrassed him. Elizabeth sighed. "I have thought on it a good deal, you know."

"What is that?" William asked, holding her a little closer.

"A gentleman's honor."

"Really?" he asked, a bit of surprise in the question. "And what have you determined?"

"When I arrived in London," she began to say but stopped when William's arms stiffened. "Are you well?"

"Must we speak of that day, Elizabeth?"

She heard William's pain and tightened her hold on his hand before lacing her fingers through his. "You did not act as a gentleman of honor would, my dear."

"I beg your pardon?" he asked abruptly.

She laughed lightly. "You know you did not, dearest, but this is not a rebuke."

He relaxed somewhat at her reassurance. "You are telling me I am not honorable. Am I meant to take that as praise?"

"Allow me to finish, please."

William complied.

"A gentleman's honor required that you assist me. That you send for a physician, send for my father or uncle, do what was needed to see me safe and then see me gone. It requires that all the proprieties are followed to the letter because that is what it takes to satisfy one's honor. But in the end, it would have been *your* safety that was assured and *your* reputation that was protected—not mine."

Now there was guilt. "Perhaps, but I ought to have included Mrs. Spencer from the first."

"You did not know how she would respond," Elizabeth replied gently.

William shook his head. "You give me too much credit, Elizabeth. It was unconsciously done. It took your father and Sir William thinking up a dozen possible matches for you before I could admit that I loved you. I was rather blind to it all."

Elizabeth smiled impishly. "Well, of course you were," she said cheerfully. "You do not care for disorder, and there is nothing so disorderly as falling in love."

"And I did fall, as you say. Long before I realized it." He turned to her. "Did *you* know that I was in love with you?"

She had felt her own love but had not been sure of his. "Well, of course," she said airily. "After all, you *did* clear away my chamber pot."

William barked out a laugh. "I would make a horrible servant. I had no idea what to do with it."

Elizabeth hummed happily. He was focused on her now and not last autumn. "Perhaps our London staff deserves a raise."

"Already done, my dear," William replied.

Elizabeth gazed directly into his eyes and returned to her point. "You are not *merely* an honorable gentleman, William. You are a great deal more." She lifted a hand to his cheek. "You acted, always, in what you believed to be my best interests, even when they were not your own. That is true honor, not the ridiculous kind that expects men to fight duels over trifles."

"I suppose," he said, glancing out the window at the late spring sunshine before returning his gaze to her. "But thinking on it now, I may have kept you close because I could not bear to let you go. I *wanted* you bound to me. I wanted a way to marry you without denying my parents' expectations. *That* was not honorable."

Elizabeth looked up into her husband's face. He had done that, it was true. But William had also acted to preserve her reputation and thus her ability to choose. He might tell himself he would have bound her to him, but Elizabeth never doubted that had she wished it, William would have let her go. She could have declined his proposal. She laughed at herself. She could have, but she never would.

"For most men, honor is a very shallow thing," Elizabeth said, reaching up to touch his cheek. "I far prefer love."

William's eyes met hers with a gaze so intense that she began to tremble.

"As do I," he said, and gathered her into his arms.

The End

Want to hear more from Henry Fitzwilliam?

Download "A Gentleman's Justice" (Henry's FREE short story) here: https://BookHip.com/RLGMHHT

Excerpt from "A Gentleman's Justice"

The ballroom was ablaze with the light of hundreds of candles. The tiny flames were augmented by the reflection of artfully placed mirrors and the crystal prisms of five enormous chandeliers. Even so, the corner of the room where Viscount Milton stood was draped in shadow.

The musicians had just completed *Lady of the Lake* and after a short pause to allow the dancers to rest, were now beginning to play *La Deliberation*.

The viscount sighed. It was all becoming tedious. He had been kept quite busy with the American war being added to the one against the French, but it was always the same thing. Quiet messages being passed, a word in the ear of the right man, playing the fop at the gambling tables to pick up the warnings issued by highly placed men in their cups.

He enjoyed his work but hoped he would be sent out of London soon. A short visit to his brother Richard's estate to see his new nephew would not go amiss. Even a trip to Pemberley would be welcomed. Darcy had married a very pretty, very clever woman and through her influence, become reasonably sociable.

Richard was not missing the army—his life was more active than it had ever been. The first year of his marriage, he had written how he depended on the frame-breaking croppers to make any profit on the wool he sold—without their work to smooth woolen fabrics for use, there was little market for it. He had therefore engaged himself in wage negotiations on their behalf with the mill owners, in addition to learning how to grow crops—the poor harvest had not done him in, but it was not encouraging. However, a year on, he and his family seemed to be thriving. The workers and the mill owners credited him with helping avoid the violence engulfing other parts of Yorkshire, and his crops seemed to be growing better this year than last.

Richard had always enjoyed a challenge.

So did the viscount, and yet currently there was little to be found. He sipped the last of his wine from a glass with a twisted stem, his expert gaze sweeping over the dancers who had just reached the point in the steps where they were all moving at once. It was a crush, again. The air was hot and stale, again.

A footman stopped to take his empty glass and provide him with a full one. The new glass had a small note folded tightly and shoved beneath the base. With a practiced flip of his wrist, it was secreted in his sleeve before the man moved away to serve the other guests.

His duty complete, the viscount took another sip of wine before setting the glass aside. He stepped forward into the light before strolling languidly in the opposite direction of the footman. As he reached the doorway leading into the hall, however, a rough laugh stilled his step.

The owner of that laugh had been sent abroad a year past when he had embarrassed his father one too many times. He ought to be away still.

"Henry Fitzwilliam!" cried an older man with liberal streaks of gray in his red beard. Henry smiled. It was Lewis Dixon.

Dixon gave Henry a sharp bow. "How good it is to see you!"

"You as well, Dixon." Dixon's cousin had two daughters who had been instrumental in unraveling a plot against Darcy in the autumn of '11. Henry had not seen Lewis Dixon since.

Dixon leaned in to say, "As you can see, Lord Bartholomew has returned from the continent. He has convinced his father that he has reformed."

"Indeed," Henry drawled, cautiously turning towards Lord Bartholomew. The rogue's skin was tanner and his belly a little softer than it had been a year past. "And has he?"

Dixon snorted. "He has not."

Henry nodded thoughtfully as Dixon slapped him on the arm and returned to the festivities. Town had suddenly become more interesting.

Want to read "A Gentleman's Justice" in its entirety? Get your copy here:

https://BookHip.com/RLGMHHT

For all Melanie Rachel Bonus Content: https://www.melanierachelauthor.com/bonus-content

Or scan the QR code:

An Unexpected Inheritance
A *Pride and Prejudice* Vagary (excerpt)

https://mybook.to/AUI

August 1811

"Is this it?" Darcy asked, pulling up to study a narrow path heading away from the little market town of Meryton.

"It astonishes me," replied Fitzwilliam, "that you never once lost your way in Spain or Portugal but cannot seem to navigate good English roads."

"Yes," Darcy said drily, "there is nothing like being shot at to sharpen one's directional senses."

Fitzwilliam ignored him. "The blacksmith said that there were two paths. Netherfield to the east, Longbourn to the west. This must be it."

"Very well," Darcy replied, still rather dubious. He gazed through the trees at an opening wide enough for two horses to ride abreast. He guided his mount along the path, and they rode silently for a time. Not far along, the path opened onto a proper road, and Darcy shot Fitzwilliam a dirty look. "We turned off too soon."

Fitzwilliam grinned. "As long as we arrive in good time, does it matter?"

Darcy plucked a twig from his hat and let it fall to the ground. "It does not matter to you. You are short enough to ride through an entire forest untouched."

"That you are the size of a giant is not my fault."

Fitzwilliam was short only in comparison to him, and Darcy knew it. Fitzwilliam might be the elder, but Darcy was the taller by four inches, a constant source of irritation for his cousin.

They meandered through the village that surrounded the estate and up through the gates to the manor, where they handed off their horses to a groom. An older gentleman was waiting for them in the portico.

"Welcome to Longbourn, Colonel, Lieutenant Colonel," he said.

"Lieutenant General Bennet, sir," Darcy said by way of greeting. Fitzwilliam snapped off a salute, and Darcy looked at him askance.

Bennet returned the salute with less sharpness and a good deal of humour. "Now that we have the ranks out of the way," Lieutenant General Bennet remarked, his eyes twinkling, "call me Bennet. I am no longer in command of thousands of soldiers but a dozen or so stubbornly independent farmers of barley and corn."

"It suits you, sir," Darcy replied.

"And you are hoping it will suit you?" Bennet responded with a smile. "Come in, boys, come in." He slapped each of them once on the back before he led them into the house.

The general appeared healthier than he had after being wounded and suffering through the infection that followed. He was stouter, and all traces of the limp that had finally persuaded the man to relinquish his command appeared to have vanished. He walked them back to his study, a decent-sized room lined with bookshelves that fairly groaned with the weight of the tomes they held. Darcy smiled. "A pleasant room, Bennet."

Bennet laughed, as did Fitzwilliam. "I think you might be content all your life if you could but spend it with your nose in a book," Fitzwilliam said.

They had returned to Hatchards more than once before removing from town.

"I have a taste for books myself," Bennet replied, "but on an estate, there is always more to be done. I am pleased you arrived for the harvest. There is much to learn in observing it." He lifted a decanter in question, and they both nodded. "This inheritance was something of a surprise, your letter said?"

"I do not believe I have ever seen anyone more shocked. It was a full quarter of an hour before I could persuade him to speak of it," Fitzwilliam said.

Darcy's face grew hot. It had not been a quarter of an hour, but his inability to speak had certainly made Fitzwilliam anxious.

"I have inherited Pemberley, the family's country estate," Darcy confirmed. "And a townhouse in London."

Fitzwilliam nodded. "We toured the townhouse with the solicitor. Very fine."

"There are a number of repairs to be made, however," Darcy added. "My great-uncle had remained in the country for his health the past few years. The work should be largely completed by the time we return near Christmas."

"When you wrote, I sent out some inquiries about Pemberley." Bennet motioned for them to sit and handed them each a glass of port. "Nearly three times the size of Longbourn, and I expect four or five times the income. You shall have your work cut out for you. But then, I presume that is why you have brought your cousin home?"

Darcy nodded. "One of many reasons. I could not do it without him." He accepted a glass from Bennet.

"He could, as he is well aware," Fitzwilliam mumbled, embarrassed. "He is the clever one with books and accounts. I am here because he needs me to talk to women on his behalf."

Darcy sighed and addressed Bennet. "Obviously, I regret my decision already."

Fitzwilliam grinned, clearly pleased to have irritated him at last.

Darcy was tall, physically strong, and an excellent man on the field of battle. Fitzwilliam had often told him so, usually begrudgingly.

The problem was that it was the fashion to be slender, and his size intimidated women. A gentleman did not wish to appear as though he had to labour for his livelihood. It was all nonsense, but the women of his aunt Matlock's acquaintance were not used to men who looked like him. He tried to be gentle, but his manners were those of a soldier. Along with everything else, that would have to change now, he supposed. He might not wish to dance in London, but he would be in company with women nonetheless. Beginning with the general's daughters.

Bennet was watching him quietly, but Darcy was fully aware that the man's mind was always active.

"Perhaps you ought to practice with my girls," he remarked. "They are used to the manners of men like us and not easily frightened." Bennet's slow smile made Darcy uneasy. "As a gentleman, you know, you shall have to learn to dance."

How had the man guessed precisely what he was thinking? "I know how to dance," he said uneasily.

Fitzwilliam burst out laughing. "Is that what you call it?"

"I had a master in to teach the girls, and they are each of them beautiful dancers now. I wish Fanny could see them." He gestured at the room. "She would have loved being the mistress of an estate. Clucking over her chicks, dressing them in fine clothes." He cleared his throat and produced a handkerchief to swipe at his eyes.

The two younger men were silent out of respect for Bennet's departed wife. Darcy had thought Mrs. Bennet a bit flighty and at times a little crass, but he could hardly blame her, given that she lived all her married life among soldiers. More to the point, she had a good heart. She had treated the men under her husband's command as sons and brothers, nursing them when they were ill or injured. She set a bountiful table for the officers and had likely sent more food out for the enlisted men. With her three eldest daughters trailing behind, she had delivered baskets of food to the needy. The general's wife had always been busy. It was on one of her missions of mercy that she had contracted influenza and died shortly after the general's own recovery.

The mourning had been difficult for them all. Mrs. Bennet had been universally beloved.

"Elizabeth would be a suitable partner for you, Darcy," Bennet said abruptly, shoving the handkerchief back in his pocket. "Her feet are as quick as her tongue, and she will not be cowed by you." Bennet lifted one craggy eyebrow at Fitzwilliam. "And neither Jane nor Elizabeth will put up with any of your foolish games."

"Games?" Fitzwilliam cried, placing one hand over his heart. "My dear Bennet, I do not have the pleasure of understanding you."

Bennet tipped his head slightly to one side. "Do you not?"

In all his life, Darcy had never seen his cousin blush. It was worth everything to witness it now.

The older man sighed. "Five daughters." He shook his head ruefully. "Would that they had come out into a society where men still feared me."

There was a soft knock. "Come," Bennet called.

Darcy blinked as a young woman entered. Great God, she was stunning. Eyes the colour of mahogany, dark curls touched with gold framing her face, a light and pleasing figure tall enough that he would not appear an ogre in comparison. She was looking at her father and not at him, thank heavens. It would be a disaster to be caught ogling the general's . . . Bennet's daughter. He glanced away and spied Fitzwilliam wearing a lopsided grin.

Damnation. Fitzwilliam had noticed. He would never hear the end of it now.

"We shall join you in the drawing room, my dear," Bennet said, rising from his chair. "Come, gentlemen," he said as the woman curtseyed and left them. "It is time for you to meet my daughters."

Transforming Mr. Darcy
A Magical Pride and Prejudice Novella (excerpt)

If you like audiobooks, make sure to check out *Transforming Mr. Darcy* as narrated by Elizabeth Grace!

Ebook, paperback, and audiobook: **https://mybook.to/fttmd**

Elizabeth Bennet gazed at her sister Jane with a wistful sort of envy. She was not envious because Jane was kind and intelligent as well as uncommonly beautiful. No, Elizabeth had benefitted from her sister's generous nature too often to bemoan her own shortcomings in comparison to Jane's.

It was her sister's fairy godmother that Elizabeth coveted. If it were a sin to do so, she could only pray that she would be forgiven, for it could not be helped. She had tried.

Priscilla Roseheart hovered near Jane as Sir William conducted introductions between the Bennet ladies and the Netherfield party. Elizabeth's eyes strayed to Priscilla more than once. Jane's fairy godmother was a vision, ethereal in a luminous white gown trimmed in shimmery pink ribbons, golden tresses flowing over her shoulders, translucent wings barely seeming to move as they held her aloft. She even held a delicate silver wand in her hand.

Netherfield's newest tenant, Mr. Bingley, was a perfect match for her perfect sister—Elizabeth could see it in Priscilla's beatific smile.

Jane was not paying any attention at all to her fairy godmother. There was no need. Priscilla neither wished for nor required any management on Jane's part.

Mr. Bingley requested Jane's hand for the second set of the evening. The rest of the Netherfield party made their various excuses and dispersed about the assembly hall like so much morning mist.

Her mother immediately began to complain about their behaviour to Mary and Kitty. Mr. Darcy, Mr. Bingley's bachelor friend, took the brunt of Mamma's ire. An unmarried man of property must of course dance with all her daughters. It was unforgivably rude not to.

Lydia skipped away, saying glibly that she was perfectly content to dance with any of the men or boys from Meryton. Kitty trailed after her, and Mary wandered off to find a chair near a lit candle but away from notice, where she might read.

Elizabeth watched Mr. Darcy attempt to melt into the crowd. He was tall enough that he could never truly disappear. He was rather handsome, but alas, he seemed to believe himself above them all. Given the cut and material of his clothing, she supposed he was correct. Well, if he judged them all solely by wealth and status, it was nothing to her.

He had just turned back in her direction when she felt a sharp prod between her shoulder blades and was forced to step awkwardly forward to maintain her balance. Across the room, Miss Bingley tittered.

"Well!" Mildread Driftwort sputtered. She punctuated each following question with a stab of her sturdy pewter wand. "Did you ever see such proud creatures? And what have they to be so very vain about? There is not a single fairy among *them*, is there?"

Did men even have fairy godmothers? Papa had not, though he could see theirs. Was Mildread simply appalled by the way Mrs. Hurst and Miss Bingley were observing everyone in the room like creatures at the Royal Menagerie? If that were the case, Elizabeth could hardly blame her for it. Still . . .

"Mildread," Elizabeth whispered as she tipped her head down. "You know they cannot see you. I cannot answer your questions, or I shall be carted off to Bedlam." Or Mamma would. That was all she needed, Mamma angrily defending Elizabeth's strange behaviours with a cursory wave and an explanation of the Bennet magic. So few families still had fairy godmothers that her tales were often passed off by their neighbours as harmless lies meant to puff herself up. Mr. Bingley and his party, however, were strangers. There was no telling how they might respond.

Sadly, Mildread was ignoring her. Instead of quieting, she had created a small windstorm with her spotted wings. They lifted her in the air, beating hard and fast in some fantastical combination of hummingbird and rooster. She landed directly before Elizabeth, who raised a hand to her hair to keep it in place.

"I believe I shall do something," Mildread announced.

Elizabeth opened her fan with a snap of her wrist and held it up to hide her mouth. "Do not, I beg of you. Their poor behaviour will have its own consequences." She faltered, attempting to dredge up additional platitudes, but came up dry. Why? She could devise dozens when the need was not so urgent!

To her surprise, Mildread's annoyance subsided. "Very well, if you insist," the fairy said, eyeing her intently.

Elizabeth's relief was sweet. "I do," she replied, just before she was asked to dance. She attempted not to fret about Mildread all through the first set, and by the second, she had mostly regained her equanimity. When, due to a lack of men in attendance, she sat during the fourth, she turned her head to see Mr. Bingley approaching Mr. Darcy. The latter had already danced with the women in his party and had been slowly circling the room between dances ever since in an obvious attempt to avoid additional partners.

She heard Mr. Bingley take Mr. Darcy to task for his unsocial behaviour and smiled as she turned away. She had no desire to hear the other man's response.

Elizabeth's ears pricked when she heard Jane's name, but she was determined not to eavesdrop—Mildread disliked the habit and had made certain Elizabeth never heard anything to her advantage. Unfortunately, this left her unprepared for what came next.

Mildread's yowl of displeasure nearly deafened her. It was so loud, so shrill, that Elizabeth was certain everyone must have heard it. But though Priscilla blinked and then sighed with a serene, sweet sort of disappointment and Jane's expression tightened briefly, the other Bennets were either too far away or too much engaged with their company to notice. Elizabeth had already lifted a hand halfway to her ear before recalling where she was and allowing it to drop.

"Abominable man!" Mildread cried. She turned to Elizabeth, hands on her hips, evaluating her from head to toe. "Your dress is exquisite and your hair a dream. I have entirely outdone myself. Your beauty may not be the same as your sister's, but you are far more than tolerable even on your worst day!" Her eyes flashed and narrowed as the words were nearly thrown from her mouth in Mr. Darcy's direction. "Goosecap, saucebox, ungentlemanly oaf! What is he about, telling his Banbury tales?"

Elizabeth sighed. She never need eavesdrop when Mildread was around. She began to speak, only to be cut off.

"He would swallow his spleen if he knew what was good for him."

Mildread always had been rather hot-tempered, but Elizabeth had never heard the fairy curse—at least, she had not heard Mildread use quite so many curses all strung together. Yet as unnerving as the fairy's language had been, Elizabeth knew what followed would be much worse. For at the end of it all, Mildread raised one steel-coloured brow and fell silent.

Acknowledgments

Acknowledgments

As anyone who writes and publishes knows—you don't get to the finish line on your own. I thank all my readers, reviewers, and supporters, those who pointed out errors and inconsistencies in the drafts as well as the experts who offered their knowledge in many areas. This book is better and stronger than it would have been without your assistance.

A heartfelt thanks to Sarah Maskim, my excellent brainstorming partner and intrepid beta, who is always looking for a place to insert a joke and laughs at my repeated attempts to "just write something short." The writing would not be half as much fun without her.

As always, many thanks to my editor at Lopt&Cropt, Sarah Pesce, who offered great insights on the theme and development of this story and who keeps the copy clean. The beautiful cover art was courtesy of Midnight Muse.

Finally, I thank my husband, who gives up many hours he might otherwise spend in my excellent company and only occasionally asks me how many more books I have to write before we can afford a vacation cabin. I'm working as fast as I can, honey.

About The Author

Melanie Rachel first read Jane Austen's novels as a girl at summer camp and will always associate them with starry skies and reading by flashlight. She was born and raised in Southern California but has also lived in Pennsylvania, New Jersey, and Washington. She currently makes her home in Arizona where she resides with her husband and their incredibly bossy Jack Russell Terrier.

Want updates on special giveaways and new books? Sign up for Melanie's newsletter at https://www.melanierachelauthor.com/newsletter and all her bonus content at https://www.melanierachelauthor.com/bonus-content. You can also find Melanie at www.melanierachelauthor.com or on Facebook and Instagram at *melanierachelbooks*.

Other Books by the Author

An Accidental Holiday

An Accidental Scandal

An Unexpected Inheritance

A Gentleman's Honor

Transforming Mr. Darcy

I Never Knew Myself

Drawing Mr. Darcy (duology)

Headstrong (trilogy)

Courage Requires

Courage Rises

Printed in Great Britain
by Amazon